Zm

Malory hadn't wanted to attend the cocktail reception at Warrior's Peak. A fanciful name for a spooky old place, she thought. At another time she'd have been thrilled at the opportunity to see the inside of the great old house so high on the ridge.

The pleasure of your company is desired
for cocktails and conversation
Eight P.M., September 4
Warrior's Peak
You are the key. The lock awaits.

Now how weird was that? Malory asked herself, and gritted her teeth as the car shimmied in a sudden gust of wind. The way her luck was going, it was probably a scam for some pyramid scheme. The road forked, and the bend on the right streamed through enormous stone pillars. Malory slowed, gawked at the life-sized warriors standing on each pillar. Perhaps it was the storm, the night, her own jittery mood, but they looked more human than stone, with hair flying around their fierce faces, their hands gripped on the hilt of swords. In the shimmer of lightning, she could almost see muscles rippling in the arms, over the broad, bare chests.

She inched the car closer. Gargoyles hunched along the walls, crawled over the eaves. Gargoyles do not come to life, she assured herself, repeating the words over and over in her head as she rolled the window down a cautious half-inch. "Welcome to Warrior's Peak." His voice boomed over the rain . . .

Turn the page for a complete list of titles by Nora Roberts and J.D. Robb from The Berkley Publishing Group . . .

Titles by Nora Roberts

HOT ICE
SACRED SINS
BRAZEN VIRTUE
SWEET REVENGE
PUBLIC SECRETS
GENUINE LIES
CARNAL INNOCENCE
DIVINE EVIL
HONEST ILLUSIONS
PRIVATE SCANDALS
HIDDEN RICHES

TRUE BETRAYALS
MONTANA SKY
SANCTUARY
HOMEPORT
THE REEF
RIVER'S END
CAROLINA MOON
THE VILLA
MIDNIGHT BAYOU
THREE FATES
BIRTHRIGHT

Anthologies

FROM THE HEART
A LITTLE MAGIC

The Once Upon Series
(with Jill Gregory, Ruth Ryan Langan, and Marianne Willman)

ONCE UPON A CASTLE
ONCE UPON A STAR
ONCE UPON A DREAM
ONCE UPON A ROSE
ONCE UPON A KISS
ONCE UPON A MIDNIGHT

Series
Three Sisters Island Trilogy

DANCE UPON THE AIR
HEAVEN AND EARTH
FACE THE FIRE

The Gallaghers of Ardmore Trilogy

JEWELS OF THE SUN
TEARS OF THE MOON
HEART OF THE SEA

The Born In Trilogy

BORN IN FIRE
BORN IN ICE
BORN IN SHAME

The Chesapeake Bay Saga

SEA SWEPT
RISING TIDES
INNER HARBOR
CHESAPEAKE BLUE

The Dream Trilogy

DARING TO DREAM
HOLDING THE DREAM
FINDING THE DREAM

Titles written as J. D. Robb

NAKED IN DEATH
GLORY IN DEATH
IMMORTAL IN DEATH
RAPTURE IN DEATH
CEREMONY IN DEATH
VENGEANCE IN DEATH
HOLIDAY IN DEATH
CONSPIRACY IN DEATH
LOYALTY IN DEATH
WITNESS IN DEATH
JUDGMENT IN DEATH
BETRAYAL IN DEATH
SEDUCTION IN DEATH
REUNION IN DEATH
PURITY IN DEATH
PORTRAIT IN DEATH
IMITATION IN DEATH

Anthologies

SILENT NIGHT
(with Susan Plunkett, Dee Holmes, and Claire Cross)

OUT OF THIS WORLD
(with Laurell K. Hamilton, Susan Krinard, and Maggie Shayne)

Key of Light

NORA ROBERTS

DOUBLEDAY LARGE PRINT HOME LIBRARY EDITION

JOVE BOOKS, NEW YORK

This Large Print Edition, prepared especially for Doubleday Large Print Home Library, contains the complete, unabridged text of the original Publisher's Edition.

KEY OF LIGHT

A Jove Book / published by arrangement with the author
Copyright © 2003 by Nora Roberts

Excerpt from *Key of Knowledge* copyright © 2003 by Nora Roberts
Cover design by Rich Hasselberger

For information address: The Berkley Publishing Group,
a division of Penguin Group (USA) Inc.,
375 Hudson Street, New York, New York 10014.

ISBN: 0-7394-3791-7

A JOVE BOOK®
Jove Books are published by The Berkley Publishing Group,
a division of Penguin Group (USA) Inc.,
375 Hudson Street, New York, New York 10014.

JOVE and the "J" design
are trademarks belonging to Penguin Group (USA) Inc.

PRINTED IN THE UNITED STATES OF AMERICA

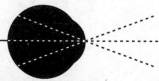

This Large Print Book carries the
Seal of Approval of N.A.V.H.

For Kathy Onorato,
for being my keeper

'Tis to create, and in creating live
A being more intense, that we endow
With what form our fancy, gaining as we give
The life we image.

—BYRON

Chapter One

The storm ripped over the mountains, gushing torrents of rain that struck the ground with the sharp ring of metal on stone. Lightning strikes spat down, angry artillery fire that slammed against the cannon roar of thunder.

There was a gleeful kind of mean in the air, a sizzle of temper and spite that boiled with power.

It suited Malory Price's mood perfectly.

Hadn't she asked herself what else could go wrong? Now in answer to that weary, and completely rhetorical, question, nature—in all her maternal wrath—was showing her just how bad things could get.

There was an ominous rattling somewhere in the dash of her sweet little Mazda, and she still had nineteen payments to go on it. In order to make those payments, she had to keep her job.

She hated her job.

That wasn't part of the Malory Price Life Plan, which she had begun to outline at the age of eight. Twenty years later, that outline had become a detailed and organized checklist, complete with headings, sub-headings, and cross-references. She revised it meticulously on the first day of each year.

She was supposed to *love* her job. It said so, quite clearly, under the heading of CA-REER.

She'd worked at The Gallery for seven years, the last three of those as manager, which was right on schedule. And she had loved it—being surrounded by art, having an almost free hand in the displaying, the acquiring, the promotion, and the setup for showings and events.

The fact was, she'd begun to think of The Gallery as hers, and knew full well that the rest of the staff, the clients, the artists and craftsmen felt very much the same.

James P. Horace might have owned the

smart little gallery, but he never questioned Malory's decisions, and on his increasingly rare visits he complimented her, always, on the acquisitions, the ambience, the sales.

It had been perfect, which was exactly what Malory intended her life to be. After all, if it wasn't perfect, what was the point?

Everything had changed when James ditched fifty-three years of comfortable bachelorhood and acquired himself a young, sexy wife. A wife, Malory thought with her blue-steel eyes narrowing in resentment, who'd decided to make The Gallery her personal pet.

It didn't matter that the new Mrs. Horace knew next to nothing about art, about business, about public relations, or about managing employees. James doted on his Pamela, and Malory's dream job had become a daily nightmare.

But she'd been dealing with it, Malory thought as she scowled through her dark, drenched windshield. She had determined her strategy: she would simply wait Pamela out. She would remain calm and self-possessed until this nasty little bump was past and the road smoothed out again.

Now that excellent strategy was out the

window. She'd lost her temper when Pamela countermanded her orders on a display of art glass and turned the perfectly and beautifully organized gallery upside down with clutter and ugly fabrics.

There were some things she could tolerate, Malory told herself, but being slapped in the face with hideous taste in her own space wasn't one of them.

Then again, blowing up at the owner's wife was not the path to job security. Particularly when the words *myopic, plebeian bimbo* were employed.

Lightning split the sky over the rise ahead, and Malory winced as much in memory of her temper as from the flash. A very bad move on her part, which only showed what happened when you gave in to temper and impulse.

To top it off, she'd spilled latte on Pamela's Escada suit. But that *had* been an accident.

Almost.

However fond James was of her, Malory knew her livelihood was hanging by a very slim thread. And when the thread broke, she would be sunk. Art galleries weren't a dime a dozen in a pretty, picturesque town like Pleasant Valley. She would either have to find another area of work as a stopgap or relocate.

Neither option put a smile on her face.

She loved Pleasant Valley, loved being surrounded by the mountains of western Pennsylvania. She loved the small-town feel, the mix of quaint and sophisticated that drew the tourists, and the getaway crowds that spilled out of neighboring Pittsburgh for impulsive weekends.

Even when she was a child growing up in the suburbs of Pittsburgh, Pleasant Valley was exactly the sort of place she'd imagined living in. She craved the hills, with their shadows and textures, and the tidy streets of a valley town, the simplicity of the pace, the friendliness of neighbors.

The decision to someday fold herself into the fabric of Pleasant Valley had been made when she was fourteen and spent a long holiday weekend there with her parents.

Just as she'd decided, when she wandered through The Gallery that long-ago autumn, that she would one day be part of that space.

Of course, at the time she had thought her paintings would hang there, but that was one item on her checklist that she'd been forced to delete rather than tick off when it was accomplished.

She would never be an artist. But she had to be, *needed* to be, involved with and surrounded by art.

Still, she didn't want to move back to the city. She wanted to keep her gorgeous, roomy apartment two blocks from The Gallery, with its views of the Appalachians, its creaky old floors, and its walls that she'd covered with carefully selected artwork.

But the hope of that was looking as dim as the stormy sky.

So she hadn't been smart with her money, Malory admitted with a windy sigh. She didn't see the point of letting it lie in some bank when it could be turned into something lovely to look at or to wear. Until it was used, money was just paper. Malory tended to use a great deal of paper.

She was overdrawn at the bank. Again. She'd maxed out her credit cards. Ditto. But, she reminded herself, she had a great wardrobe. And the start of a very impressive art collection. Which she would have to sell, piece by piece and most likely at a loss, to keep a roof over her head if Pamela brought the axe down.

But maybe tonight would buy her some time and goodwill. She hadn't wanted to attend the cocktail reception at Warrior's Peak. A fanciful name for a spooky old place, she thought. Another time she would've been thrilled at the opportunity to see the inside of the great old house so high on the ridge. And to rub elbows with people who might be patrons of the arts.

But the invitation had been odd—written in an elegant hand on heavy, stone-colored paper, with a logo of an ornate gold key in lieu of letterhead. Though it was tucked in her evening bag now along with her compact, her lipstick, her cell phone, her glasses, a fresh pen, business cards, and ten dollars, Malory remembered the wording.

The pleasure of your company is desired
for cocktails and conversation
Eight P.M., September 4
Warrior's Peak
You are the key. The lock awaits.

Now how weird was that? Malory asked herself, and gritted her teeth as the car shimmied in a sudden gust of wind. The way her luck was going, it was probably a scam for a pyramid scheme.

The house had been empty for years. She knew it had been purchased recently, but the details were sparse. An outfit called Triad, she recalled. She assumed it was some sort of corporation looking to turn the place into a hotel or a mini resort.

Which didn't explain why they'd invited the manager of The Gallery but not the owner and his interfering wife. Pamela had been pretty peeved about the slight—so that was something.

Still, Malory would have passed on the evening. She didn't have a date—just another aspect of her life that currently sucked—and driving alone into the mountains to a house straight out of Hollywood horror on the strength of an invitation that made her uneasy wasn't on her list of fun things to do in the middle of the workweek.

There hadn't even been a number or a contact for an R.S.V.P. And that, she felt, was arrogant and rude. Her intended response of ignoring the invitation would have been equally arrogant and rude, but James had spotted the envelope on her desk.

He'd been so excited, so pleased by the idea of her going, had pressed her to relay all the details of the house's interior to him. And he'd reminded her that if she could discreetly drop the name of The Gallery into conversation from time to time, it would be good for business.

If she could score a few clients, it might offset the Escada mishap and the bimbo comment.

Her car chugged up the narrowing road that cut through the dense, dark forest. She'd always thought of those hills and woods as a kind of Sleepy Hollow effect that ringed her pretty valley. But just now, with the wind and rain and dark, the less serene aspects of that old tale were a little too much in evidence for her peace of mind.

If whatever was rattling in her dash was serious, she could end up broken down on the side of the road, huddled in the car listening to the moans and lashes of the storm and imagining headless horsemen while she waited for a tow truck she couldn't afford.

Obviously, the answer was not to break down.

She thought she caught glimpses of lights beaming through the rain and trees, but her windshield wipers were whipping at the highest speed and were still barely able to shove aside the flood of rain.

As lightning snapped again, she gripped the wheel tighter. She liked a good hellcat storm as much as anyone, but she wanted to enjoy this one from someplace inside, anyplace, while drinking a nice glass of wine.

She had to be close. How far could any single road climb before it just had to start falling down the other side of the mountain? She knew Warrior's Peak stood atop the ridge, guarding the valley below. Or lording itself over the valley, depending on your viewpoint. She hadn't passed another car for miles.

Which only proved that anyone with half a brain wasn't out driving in this mess, she thought.

The road forked, and the bend on the right streamed between enormous stone pillars. Malory slowed, gawked at the life-size warriors standing on each pillar. Perhaps it was the storm, the night, or her own jittery mood, but they looked more human than stone, with hair flying around their fierce faces, their hands gripping the hilts of their swords. In the shimmer of lightning she could almost see muscles rippling in their arms, over their broad, bare chests.

She had to fight the temptation to get out of the car for a closer look. But the chill that tripped down her spine as she turned through the open iron gates had her glancing back up at the warriors with as much wariness as appreciation for the skill of the sculptor.

Then she hit the brakes and fishtailed on the crushed stone of the roadbed. Her heart jammed into her throat as she stared at the stunning buck standing arrogantly a foot in front of the bumper, with the sprawling, eccentric lines of the house behind him.

For a moment she took the deer for a sculpture as well, though why any sane person would set a sculpture in the center of a driveway was beyond her. Then again, sane didn't seem to be the operative word for anyone who would choose to live in the house on the ridge.

But the deer's eyes gleamed, a sharp

sapphire blue in the beam of her headlights, and his head with the great crowning rack turned slightly. Regally, Malory mused, mesmerized. Rain streamed off his coat, and in the next flash of light that coat seemed as white as the moon.

He stared at her, but there was nothing of fear, nothing of surprise in those glinting eyes. There was, if such things were possible, a kind of amused disdain. Then he simply walked away, through the curtain of rain, the rivers of fog, and was gone.

"Wow." She let out a long breath, shivered in the warmth of her car. "And one more wow," she murmured as she stared at the house.

She'd seen pictures of it, and paintings. She'd seen its silhouette hulking on the ridge above the valley. But it was an entirely different matter to see it up close with a storm raging.

Something between a castle, a fortress, and a house of horrors, she decided.

Its stone was obsidian black, with juts and towers, peaks and battlements stacked and spread as if some very clever, very wicked child had placed them at his whim. Against that rain-slicked black, long, narrow windows, perhaps hundreds of them, all glowed with gilded light.

Someone wasn't worried about his electric bill.

Fog drifted around its base, like a moat of mist.

In the next shock of lightning, she caught a glimpse of a white banner with the gold key madly waving from one of the topmost spires.

She inched the car closer. Gargoyles hunched along the walls, crawled over the eaves. Rainwater spewed out of their grinning mouths, spilled from clawed hands as they grinned down at her.

She stopped the car in front of the stone skirt of a wide portico and considered, very seriously, turning back into the storm and driving away.

She called herself a coward, a childish idiot. She asked herself where she'd lost her sense of adventure and fun.

The insults worked well enough that she soon was tapping her fingers on the car's door handle. At the quick rap on her window, a scream shot out of her throat.

The bony white face surrounded by a

black hood that peered in at her turned the scream into a kind of breathless keening.

Gargoyles do not come to life, she assured herself, repeating the words over and over in her head as she rolled the window down a cautious half inch.

"Welcome to Warrior's Peak." His voice boomed over the rain, and his welcoming smile showed a great many teeth. "If you'll just leave your keys in the car, miss, I'll see to it for you."

Before she could think to slap down the locks, he'd pulled her door open. He blocked the sweep of wind and rain with his body and the biggest umbrella she'd ever seen.

"I'll see you safe and dry to the door."

What was that accent? English? Irish? Scots?

"Thank you." She started to climb out, felt herself pinned back. Panic dribbled into embarrassment as she realized she had yet to unhook her seat belt.

Freed, she huddled under the umbrella, struggling to regulate her breathing as he walked her to the double entrance doors. They were wide enough to accommodate a semi and boasted dull silver knockers, big as turkey platters, fashioned into dragons' heads.

Some welcome, Malory thought an instant before one of the doors opened, and light and warmth poured out.

The woman had a straight and gorgeous stream of flame-colored hair—it spilled around a pale face of perfect angles and curves. Her green eyes danced as if at some private joke. She was tall and slim, garbed in a long gown of fluid black. A silver amulet holding a fat, clear stone hung between her breasts.

Her lips, as red as her hair, curved as she held out a hand sparkling with rings.

She looked, Malory thought, like someone out of a very sexy faerie tale.

"Miss Price. Welcome. Such a thrilling storm, but distressing, I'm sure, to be out in it. Come in."

The hand was warm and strong, and stayed clasped over Malory's as the woman drew her into the entrance hall.

The light showered down from a chandelier of crystal so fine that it resembled spun sugar sparkling over the twists and curves of silver.

The floor was mosaic, depicting the warriors from the gate and what seemed to be a number of mythological figures. She couldn't kneel down and study it as she might have liked and was already struggling to hold back an orgasmic moan at the paintings that crowded walls the color of melted butter.

"I'm so glad you could join us tonight," the woman continued. "I'm Rowena. Please, let me take you into the parlor. There's a lovely fire. Early in the year for one, but the storm seemed to call for it. Was the drive difficult?"

"Challenging. Miss—"

"Rowena. Just Rowena."

"Rowena. I wonder if I could take a moment to freshen up before joining the other guests?"

"Of course. Powder room." She gestured to a door tucked under the long sweep of the front stairs. "The parlor is the first door on your right. Take your time."

"Thank you." Malory slipped inside and immediately decided that "powder room" was a very poor label for the plush, spacious area.

The half dozen candles on the marble counter streamed out light and scent. Burgundy hand towels edged in ecru lace were arranged beside the generous pool of the sink. The faucet gleamed gold in the fanciful shape of a swan.

Here the floor mosaic showed a mermaid, sitting on a rock, smiling out at a blue sea as she combed her flame-colored hair.

This time, after double-checking to make certain that she'd locked the door, Malory did kneel down to study the craftsmanship.

Gorgeous, she thought, running her fingertips over the tiles. Old, certainly, and brilliantly executed.

Was there anything more powerful than the ability to create beauty?

She straightened, washed her hands with soap that smelled faintly of rosemary. She took a moment to admire the collection of Waterhouse's nymphs and sirens framed on the walls before digging out her compact.

There was little she could do for her hair. Though she'd drawn it back and anchored it at her nape with a rhinestone clip, the weather had played havoc with the dark blond curls. It was a look, she thought, as she dusted her nose. Sort of arty and carefree. Not elegant like the redhead, but it suited her well enough. She reapplied her lipstick, satisfied that the pale rose had been a good investment. Subtle worked best with her milkmaid coloring.

She'd paid too much for the cocktail suit. Of course. But a woman was entitled to a few weaknesses, she reminded herself as she straightened the slim satin lapels. Besides, the slate blue was right for her eyes, and the tailored lines pulled it all together into a style both professional and elegant. She closed her bag, lifted her chin.

"Okay, Mal, let's go drum up some business."

She stepped out, forced herself not to tiptoe back down the hall to drool over the paintings.

Her heels clicked briskly on the tile. She always enjoyed the sound of it. Powerful. Female.

And when she stepped through the first arch to the right, the thrilled gasp escaped before she could block it.

She'd never seen its like, in or out of a museum. Antiques so lovingly tended that their surfaces gleamed like mirrors; the rich, deep colors that demonstrated an artist's flair; rugs, pillows, and draperies that were as much art forms as the paintings and

statuary were. On the far wall was a fireplace she could have stood in with her arms
stretched out at her sides. Framed in mala-
chite, it held enormous logs that snapped
with tongues of red and gold fire.

This was the perfect setting for a woman
who looked like she'd stepped out of a
faerie tale.

She wanted to spend hours there, to wal-
low in all that marvelous color and light. The
uneasy woman who had huddled in her car
in the rain was long forgotten.

"It took five minutes for my eyes to stop
bugging out of my head after I walked in."

Malory jolted, then turned and stared at
the woman who stood framed in the side
window.

This one was a brunette, with dense
brown hair skimming between her jawline
and shoulders in a stylish swing. She was
perhaps six full inches taller than Malory's
compact five-four, and had the lush curves
to match the height. Both were set off with
trim black pants and a knee-length jacket
worn over a snug white top.

She held a champagne flute in one hand
and extended the other as she walked
across the room. Malory saw that her eyes

were deep, dark brown and direct. Her nose was narrow and straight, her mouth wide and unpainted. The faintest hint of dimples fluttered in her cheek when she smiled.

"I'm Dana. Dana Steele."

"Malory Price. Nice to meet you. Great jacket."

"Thanks. I was pretty relieved when I saw you drive up. It's a hell of a place, but I was getting a little spooked rattling around by myself. It's nearly quarter after." She tapped the face of her watch. "You'd think some of the other guests would be here by now."

"Where's the woman who met me at the door? Rowena?"

Dana pursed her lips as she glanced back toward the archway. "She glides in and out, looking gorgeous and mysterious. I'm told our host will be joining us shortly."

"Who is our host?"

"Your guess is as good as mine. Haven't I seen you?" Dana added. "In the Valley?"

"Possibly. I manage The Gallery." For the time being, she thought.

"That's it. I've come to a couple of show-ings there. And sometimes I just wander in and look around avariciously. I'm at the li-brary. A reference librarian."

They both turned as Rowena walked in. Though glided in, Malory thought, was a better description.

"I see you've introduced yourselves. Lovely. What can I get you to drink, Miss Price?"

"I'll have what she's having."

"Perfect." Even as she spoke, a uniformed maid came in bearing two flutes on a silver tray. "Please help yourselves to the canapés and make yourselves at home."

"I hope the weather isn't keeping your other guests away," Dana put in.

Rowena merely smiled. "I'm sure everyone who's expected will be here shortly. If you'll excuse me just another moment."

"Okay, this is just weird." Dana picked a canapé at random, discovered it was a lobster puff. "Delicious, but weird."

"Fascinating." Malory sipped her champagne and trailed her fingers over a bronze sculpture of a reclining faerie.

"I'm still trying to figure out why I got an invitation." Since they were there, and so was she, Dana sampled another canapé. "No one else at the library got one. No one else I know got one, for that matter. I'm starting to wish I'd talked my brother into coming with me after all. He's got a good bullshit barometer."

Malory found herself grinning. "You don't sound like any librarian I've ever known. You don't look like one either."

"I burned all my Laura Ashley ten years ago." Dana gave a little shrug. Restless, moving toward irritated, she tapped her fingers on the crystal flute. "I'm going to give this about ten more minutes, then I'm booking."

"If you go, I go. I'd feel better heading back into that storm if I drove to the Valley behind someone else."

"Same goes." Dana frowned toward the window, watched the rain beat on the other side of the glass. "Crappy night. And it was an extremely crappy day. Driving all the way here and back in this mess for a couple of glasses of wine and some canapés just about caps it."

"You too?" Malory wandered toward a wonderful painting of a masked ball. It made her think of Paris, though she'd never been there except in her dreams. "I only came tonight in hopes of making some contacts for The Gallery. Job insurance," she added, lifting her glass in a mock toast.

"As my job is currently in a very precarious state."

"Mine too. Between budget cuts and nepotism, my position was 'adjusted,' my hours trimmed back to twenty-five a week. How the hell am I supposed to live on that? And my landlord just announced that my rent's going up first of next month."

"There's a rattle in my car—and I spent my auto-maintenance budget on these shoes."

Dana looked down, pursed her lips. "Terrific shoes. My computer crashed this morning."

Enjoying herself, Malory turned away from the painting and raised a brow at Dana. "I called my boss's new wife a bimbo and then spilled latte on her designer suit."

"Okay, you win." In the spirit of good fellowship, Dana stepped over and clinked her glass against Malory's. "What do you say we hunt up the Welsh goddess and find out what's going on around here?"

"Is that what the accent is? Welsh?"

"Gorgeous, isn't it? But be that as it may, I think . . ."

She trailed off as they heard that distinctive click of high heels on tile.

The first thing Malory noticed was the hair. It was black and short, with thick bangs cut so blunt they might have required a ruler. Beneath them, the tawny eyes were large and long, making her think of Water-house again, and his faeries. She had a tri-angular face, glowing with what might have been excitement, nerves, or excellent cos-metics.

The way her fingers kneaded at her little black bag, Malory went with the nerves.

She wore red, stoplight red, in an abbre-viated dress that clung to her curvy body and showed off terrific legs. The heels that had clicked along the tile were a good four inches high and sharp as stilettos.

"Hi." Her voice was breathy and her gaze was already flicking around the room. "Um. She said I should come right in."

"Join the party. Such as it is. Dana Steele, and my equally baffled companion this eve-ning, Malory Price."

"I'm Zoe. McCourt." She took another cautious step into the room, as if she was waiting for someone to tell her there'd been a mistake and boot her out again. "Holy cow. This place, it's like a movie. It's, um, beautiful and all, but I keep expecting that scary guy in the smoking jacket to come in."

"Vincent Price? No relation," Malory said with a grin. "I take it you don't know any more about what's going on than we do."

"No. I think I got invited by mistake, but—" She broke off, ogling a bit when a servant entered with another flute on a tray. "Ah . . . thanks." She took the crystal gingerly, then just smiled down at the bubbling wine. "Champagne. It *has* to be a mistake. But I couldn't pass up the chance to come. Where is everybody else?"

"Good question." Dana angled her head, charmed and amused as Zoe took a small, testing sip of champagne. "Are you from the Valley?"

"Yes. Well, for the last couple years."

"Three for three," Malory murmured. "Do you know anyone else who got an invitation for tonight?"

"No. In fact, I asked around, which is probably why I got fired today. Is that food just to take?"

"You got fired?" Malory exchanged a look with Dana. "Three for three."

"Carly—she owns the salon where I work. Worked," Zoe corrected herself and walked toward a tray of canapés. "She heard me talking about it with one of my customers and got bent out of shape. Boy, these are terrific."

Her voice had lost its breathiness now, and as she appeared to relax, Malory detected the faintest hint of twang.

"Anyway, Carly's been gunning for me for months. I guess the invite, seeing as she didn't get one, put her nose out of joint. Next thing I know, she's saying there's twenty missing from the till. I never stole anything in my life. Bitch."

She took another, more enthusiastic gulp of champagne. "And then *bam!* I'm out on my ear. Doesn't matter. It's not going to matter. I'll get another job. I hated working there anyway. God."

It mattered, Malory thought. The sparkle in Zoe's eyes that had as much fear to it as anger said it mattered a great deal. "You're a hairdresser."

"Yeah. Hair and skin consultant, if you want to get snooty. I'm not the type who gets invited to fancy parties at fancy places, so I guess it's a mistake."

Considering, Malory shook her head. "I

don't think someone like Rowena makes mistakes. Ever."

"Well, I don't know. I wasn't going to come, then I thought it would cheer me up. Then my car wouldn't start, again. I had to borrow the baby-sitter's."

"You have a baby?" Dana asked.

"He's not a baby anymore. Simon's nine. He's great. I wouldn't worry about the job, but I've got a kid to support. And I didn't steal any goddamn twenty dollars—or twenty cents, for that matter. I'm not a thief."

She caught herself, flushed scarlet. "Sorry. I'm sorry. Bubbles loosening my tongue, I guess."

"Don't worry about it." Dana rubbed a hand up and down Zoe's arm. "You want to hear something strange? My job, and my paycheck, just got cut to the bone. I don't know what the hell I'm going to do. And Malory thinks she's about to get the axe at her job."

"Really?" Zoe looked from one face to the other. "That's just weird."

"And nobody we know was invited here tonight." With a wary glance toward the doorway, Malory lowered her voice. "From the looks of things, we're it."

"I'm a librarian, you're a hairdresser, she runs an art gallery. What do we have in common?"

"We're all out of work." Malory frowned. "Or the next thing to it. That alone is strange when you consider the Valley's got a population of about five thousand. What are the odds of three women hitting a professional wall the same day in the same little town? Next, we're all from the Valley. We're all female, about the same age? Twenty-eight."

"Twenty-seven," Dana said.

"Twenty-six—twenty-seven in December." Zoe shivered. "This is just too strange." Her eyes widened as she looked at her half-empty glass, and she set it hastily aside. "You don't think there's anything in there that shouldn't be, do you?"

"I don't think we're going to be drugged and sold into white slavery." Dana's tone was dry, but she set her glass down as well. "People know we're here, right? My brother knows where I am, and people at work."

"My boss, his wife. Your ex-boss," Malory said to Zoe. "Your baby-sitter. Anyway, this is Pennsylvania, for God's sake, not, I don't know, Zimbabwe."

"I say we go find the mysterious Rowena and get some answers. We stick together, right?" Dana nodded at Malory, then Zoe.

Zoe swallowed. "Honey, I'm your new best friend." To seal it, she took Dana's hand, then Malory's.

"How lovely to see you."

Their hands were still joined as they turned and looked at the man who stood in the archway.

He smiled, stepped inside the room. "Welcome to Warrior's Peak."

Chapter Two

For a moment Malory thought one of the warriors from the gate had come to life. He had the same fierce male beauty in his face, the same powerful build. His hair, black as the storm, waved back in wings from that strong, sculpted face.

His eyes were midnight blue. She felt the power of them, a flash of heat along her skin, when they met hers.

She wasn't a fanciful woman. Anything but, she told herself. But the storm, the house, the sheer ferocity of that gaze made her feel as though he could see everything in her mind. Everything that had ever been in her mind.

Then his gaze left hers, and the moment passed.

"I am Pitte. Thank you for gracing what is, for now, our home."

He took Malory's free hand, lifted it to his lips. His touch was cool, the gesture both courtly and dignified. "Miss Price." She felt Zoe's fingers go lax on hers, then Pitte was moving to her, lifting her fingers in turn. "Miss McCourt." And Dana's. "Miss Steele."

A boom of thunder had Malory jolting, and her hand groped for Zoe's again. He was just a man, she assured herself. It was just a house. And someone had to get everything back on an even keel.

"You have an interesting home, Mr. Pitte," she managed.

"Yes. Won't you sit? Ah, Rowena. You've met my companion." He took Rowena's arm when she came to his side.

They fit, Malory decided, like two halves of a coin.

"By the fire, I think," Rowena said, gesturing toward the fireplace. "Such a fierce night. Let's be comfortable."

"I think we'd be more comfortable if we understood what's going on." Dana planted her high-heeled boots and stood her ground. "Why we were asked here."

"Certainly. But the fire's so lovely. There's nothing quite like good champagne, good fellowship, and a nice fire on a stormy night. Tell me, Miss Price, what do you think of what you've seen of our art collection?"

"Impressive. Eclectic." With a glance back at Dana, Malory let Rowena lead her toward a chair near the fire. "You must have spent considerable time on it."

Rowena's laugh rippled like fog over water. "Oh, considerable. Pitte and I appreciate beauty, in all its forms. In fact, you could say we revere it. As you must, given your choice of profession."

"Art is its own reason."

"Yes. It's the light in every shadow. And Pitte, we must make certain Miss Steele sees the library before the evening's over. I hope you'll approve." She gestured absently at the servant who entered with a crystal champagne bucket. "What would the world be without books?"

"Books are the world." Curious, cautious, Dana sat.

"I think there's been a mistake." Zoe hung back, looking from face to face. "I don't know anything about art. Not real art. And books—I mean, I read, but—"

"Please, sit." Pitte nudged her gently into a chair. "Be at home. I trust your son is well."

She stiffened, and those tawny eyes went tiger-bright. "Simon's fine."

"Motherhood's a kind of art, don't you think, Miss McCourt? A work in progress of the most essential, most vital kind. One that requires valor and heart."

"Do you have children?"

"No. I haven't been given that gift." His hand brushed Rowena's as he spoke, then he lifted his glass. "To life. And all its mysteries." His eyes gleamed over the rim of the glass. "There's no need to fear. No one here wishes you anything but health, happiness, and success."

"Why?" Dana demanded. "You don't know us, though you seem to know a great deal more about us than we do about you."

"You're a seeker, Miss Steele. An intelligent, straightforward woman who looks for answers."

"I'm not getting any."

He smiled. "It's my fondest hope that you'll find all the answers. To begin, I'd like to tell you a story. It seems a night for stories."

He settled back. Like Rowena's, his voice was musical and strong, faintly exotic. The sort, Malory thought, designed for telling tales on stormy nights.

Because of it, she relaxed a little. What else did she have to do, after all, besides sit in a fantastic house by a roaring fire and listen to a strange, handsome man weave a tale while she sipped champagne?

It beat eating takeout while reconciling her checkbook hands down.

And if she could wheedle a tour of the place, and nudge Pitte toward The Gallery as a vehicle to expand his art collection, she might just save her job.

So she settled back as well and prepared to enjoy herself.

"Long ago, in a land of great mountains and rich forests, lived a young god. He was his parents' only child, and well beloved. He was gifted with a handsome face and strength of heart and muscle. He was destined to rule one day, as his father before him, and so he was reared to be the god-king, cool in judgment, swift in action.

"There was peace in this world, since

gods had walked there. Beauty, music and art, stories and dance were everywhere. For as long as memory—and a god's memory is infinite—there had been harmony and balance in this place."

He paused to sip his wine, his gaze tracking slowly from face to face. "From behind the Curtain of Power, through the veil of the Curtain of Dreams, they would look on the world of mortals. Lesser gods were permitted to mix and mate with those of the mortal realm at their whim, and so became the faeries and sprites, the sylphs and other creatures of magic. Some found the mortal world more to their tastes and peopled it. Some, of course, were corrupted by the powers, by the world of mortals, and turned to darker ways. Such is the way of nature, even of gods."

Pitte eased forward to top a thin cracker with caviar. "You've heard stories of magic and sorcery, the faerie tales and fantasies. As one of the guardians of stories and books, Miss Steele, do you consider how such tales become part of the culture, what root of truth they spring from?

"To give someone, or something, a power greater than our own. To feed our need for heroes and villains and romance." Dana shrugged, though she was already fascinated. "If, for instance, Arthur of the Celts existed as a warrior king, as many scholars and scientists believe, how much more enthralling, more potent, is his image if we see him in Camelot, with Merlin. If he was conceived with the aid of sorcery, and crowned high king as a young boy who pulled a magic sword out of a stone."

"I love that story," Zoe put in. "Well, except for the end. It seemed so unfair. But I think . . ."

"Please," Pitte said, "go on."

"Well, I sort of think that maybe magic did exist once, before we educated ourselves out of it. I don't mean education's bad," she said quickly, squirming as everyone's attention focused on her. "I just mean maybe we, um, locked it away because we started needing logical and scientific answers for everything."

"Well said." Rowena nodded. "A child often tucks his toys in the back of the closet, forgetting the wonder of them as he grows to manhood. Do you believe in wonder, Miss McCourt?"

"I have a nine-year-old son," Zoe replied.

"All I have to do is look at him to believe in wonder. I wish you'd call me Zoe."

Rowena's face lit with warmth. "Thank you. Pitte?"

"Ah, yes, to continue the tale. As was the tradition, upon reaching his majority the young god was sent beyond the Curtain for one week, to walk among the mortals, to learn their ways, to study their weaknesses and strengths, their virtues and flaws. It happened that he saw a young woman, a maid of great beauty and virtue. And seeing, loved, and loving, wanted. And though she was denied to him by the rules of his world, he pined for her. He grew listless, restless, unhappy. He would not eat or drink, nor did he find any appeal in all the young goddesses offered to him. His parents, disturbed at seeing their son so distressed, weakened. They would not give their son to the mortal world, but they brought the maid to theirs."

"They kidnapped her?" Malory interrupted.

"They could have done." Rowena filled the flutes again. "But love cannot be stolen. It's a choice. And the young god wished for love."

"Did he get it?" Zoe wondered.

"The mortal maid chose, and loved, and gave up her world for his." Pitte rested his hands on his knees. "There was anger in the worlds of gods, of mortals, and in that mystical half-world of the faeries. No mortal was to pass through the Curtain. Yet that most essential rule was now broken. A mortal woman had been taken from her world and into theirs, married to and bedded by their future king for no reason more important than love."

"What's more important than love?" Mallory asked and earned a slow, quiet look from Pitte.

"Some would say nothing, others would say honor, truth, loyalty. Others did, and for the first time in the memory of the gods, there was dissension, rebellion. The balance was shaken. The young god-king, crowned now, was strong and withstood this. And the mortal maid was beautiful and true. Some were swayed to accept her, and others plotted in secret."

There was a whip of outrage in his voice, and a sudden cold fierceness that made Malory think of the stone warriors again.

"Battles fought in the open could be

quelled, but others were devised in secret chambers, and these ate at the foundation of the world.

"It came to pass that the god-king's wife bore three children, three daughters, demi-goddesses with mortal souls. On their birth, their father gifted each with a jeweled amulet, for protection. They learned the ways of their father's world, and of their mother's. Their beauty, their innocence, softened many hearts, turned many minds. For some years there was peace again. And the daughters grew to young women, devoted to each other, each with a talent that enhanced and completed those of her sisters."

He paused again, as if gathering himself. "They harmed no one, brought only light and beauty to both sides of the Curtain. But there remained shadows. One coveted what they had that no god could claim. Through sorcery, through envy, despite all precautions, they were taken into the half-world. The spell cast plunged them into eternal sleep, a living death. And sleeping, they were sent back through the Curtain, their mortal souls locked in a box that has three keys. Not even their father's power can break the locks. Until the keys turn, one, by two, by three, the daughters are trapped in an enchanted sleep and their souls weep in a prison of glass."

"Where are the keys?" Malory asked. "And why can't the box be opened by enchantment since it was locked by it?"

"Where they are is a puzzle. Many magicks and spells have been cast to unlock the box, all have failed—but there are clues. The souls are mortal, and only mortal hands can turn the keys."

"My invitation said I was the key." Malory glanced at Dana and Zoe, got nods of confirmation. "What do we have to do with some mythological legend?"

"I have something to show you." Pitte rose, gestured toward the archway. "I hope it interests you."

"The storm's getting worse." Zoe sent a wary look toward the windows. "I need to start home."

"Please, indulge me."

"We'll all leave together." Malory gave Zoe's arm a reassuring squeeze. "Let's just see what it is he wants to show us first. I hope you'll invite me back at some point," she continued as she walked to the doorway to join Pitte and Rowena. "I'd very much like to see more of your art collection, and perhaps repay the favor by giving you a private tour of The Gallery."

"You'll certainly be welcome back." Pitte took her arm lightly and led her down the wide hall. "It would be a pleasure for Rowena and me to discuss our collection with someone who understands and appreciates it."

He turned toward another archway. "I hope you'll understand and appreciate this particular piece of it."

Over another fireplace that roared with flame was a painting that towered to the ceiling.

The colors were so vivid, so rich, the style so bold and strong, that Malory's art lover's heart took one fast leap. The portrait was of three women, young, beautiful, in flowing gowns of sapphire, of ruby, of emerald. The one in blue, with golden curls rioting to her waist, sat on a bench that circled a pool. She held a small gold harp.

Seated on the silver tiles at her feet, the girl in red had a scroll and quill in her lap and her hand on her sister's—for surely they were sisters—knee. Beside them, the girl in green stood, a chubby black puppy in the crook of her arm and a short silver sword at her hip. A heartbreak of flowers spilled around them.

There were trees with jeweled fruit dripping from the branches, and in the cerulean sky both birds and faeries were on the wing.

Enthralled, Malory was halfway across the room for a closer look when her heart gave another, harder knock. The girl in blue had her face.

Younger, she thought as she came to an abrupt halt. Certainly more beautiful. The skin was luminous, the eyes deeper, bluer, the hair more luxurious and romantic. But there was no mistaking the power of the resemblance, nor, she saw as she steadied herself, the resemblance between the others in the portrait and the other two guests at Warrior's Peak.

"Magnificent work. A master's work," Malory said, and was amazed at how calm her voice sounded through the buzzing in her ears.

"They look like us." There was wonder in the words as Zoe moved beside Malory. "How can they?"

"Good question." And suspicion in

Dana's. "How did the three of us come to be used as models for what is, obviously, a portrait of the three sisters in the story you just told us?"

"It was painted before you were born. Before your parents, your grandparents, and those who sired them were born." Rowena walked toward the portrait, stood below it with her hands folded at her waist. "Its age can be verified through tests. Isn't that so, Malory?"

"Yes. Its approximate age can be authenticated, but whatever its age, you haven't answered Zoe's question."

The smile that spread on Rowena's face seemed to hold both approval and amusement. "No, I haven't. What else do you see in the painting?"

Malory reached in her purse, took out a pair of black-framed, rectangular glasses. She slipped them on and made a more thorough study.

"A key, in the right corner of the sky. It seems to be a bird until you look closely. A second one there, on the branch of a tree, almost hidden by the leaves and fruit. And the third, just visible under the surface of the pool. There's a shadow there, in the trees. In the form of a man, maybe a woman. Just the hint of something dark watching them. Another shadow, just sliding onto the silver tile at the edge. A snake. Ah, and here, in the far background."

She lost herself in the painting, forgot herself and stepped up onto the hearth. "There's a couple—a man and a woman—embracing. The woman is robed, richly, with the purple symbolizing a woman of rank. And the man is garbed like a soldier. A warrior. There's a raven in the tree just above them. A symbol of impending doom. Just as the sky here is darker, with storm lights. A threat. The sisters are unaware of the threat. They look forward, grouped together, the crown of their ranks glinting in the sunlight that washes this area of the foreground. There's a sense of companionship and affection between them, and the white dove here, on the edge of the pool, is their purity. Each wears an amulet, the same shape and size, with the jewel reflecting the color of their gown. They are a unit, yet individuals. It's magnificent work. You can almost see them breathe."

"You have a discerning eye." Pitte

touched Rowena's arm as he nodded at Malory. "It's the prize of the collection."

"And still," Dana pointed out, "you haven't answered the question."

"Magick couldn't break the spell that locked the souls of the king's daughters in a box of glass. Sorcerers were called, and wizards and witches from all the worlds. But no magicks could unbind the curse. So another was cast. In this world, in every generation, three women are born who will come together in one place, at one time. They are not sisters, they are not gods, but mortal women. And they are the only ones who can release the innocents."

"And you want us to believe that we're those women?" Dana's brows arched. There was a tickle in her throat, but it didn't feel like laughter. "That we just happen to look like the women in this painting?"

"Nothing just happens. And whether you believe or not changes little." Pitte held out his hands toward them. "You are the chosen, and I am charged to tell you."

"Well, you've told us, so now—"

"And to make you this offer," he continued before Dana could finish. "You will each have, in turn, one phase of the moon to find one of the three keys. If within the twenty-eight days the first fails, the matter is done. If the first succeeds, the second's time begins. But if the second fails within her time, the matter is done. If all three keys are brought to this place, before the end of the third moon, you will be given a boon."

"What sort of boon?" Zoe asked.

"One million dollars. Each."

"Get out of town!" Dana snorted, then stared at her two companions. "Oh, come on, ladies. This is just screwy. Easy for him to toss money around like confetti when we'd be off on some wild-goose chase for a trio of keys that don't exist in the first place."

"And if they did—" Her eyes brilliant, Zoe turned toward Dana. "If they did, wouldn't you want a chance to find them? The chance for that kind of money?"

"What chance? It's a great big world out there. How do you expect to find a little gold key?"

"You will be given, each in turn, a guide." Rowena gestured to a small chest. "This we can do, if all agree. You may work together. In fact, we hope that you will. You must all agree. If one refuses the challenge, it's done. If all accept the challenge and the terms, you'll each be given twenty-five thousand dollars. It remains yours whether you fail or succeed."

"Wait a minute, wait a minute." Malory held up a hand, then pulled off her glasses. "Wait a minute," she repeated. "You're saying if we agree to look for these keys, just to look for them, we get twenty-five K? Free and clear?"

"The amount will be deposited in an account of your choosing. Immediately," Pitte stated.

"Oh, my God!" Zoe clasped her hands. "Oh, my God," she repeated and sat down heavily. "This has got to be a dream."

"A scam, you mean. What's the catch?" Dana questioned. "What's the fine print?"

"If you fail, any one of you, the penalty for all will be a year of your lives."

"What, like in jail?" Malory demanded.

"No." Rowena motioned to a servant to enter with a coffee cart. "A year of your life will not exist."

"Poof!" Dana snapped her fingers. "Like magic."

"The keys exist. Not in this house," Rowena murmured, "but in this world, this place. This we are able to do. More we are not allowed to say, although we may offer a little guidance. The quest isn't simple, so you will be rewarded for the attempt. Should you succeed, the reward is greater. Should you fail, there is penalty. Please, take this time to discuss it. Pitte and I will give you some privacy."

They walked out of the room, and Rowena turned back to slide the wide pocket doors shut.

"This," Dana said as she plucked a tiny cream puff from the dessert tray, "is a nuthouse. And if either of you is actually considering playing along with these fruitcakes, you belong in this nuthouse."

"Let me just say one thing." Malory poured a cup of coffee, stirred in two lumps of sugar. "Twenty-five thousand dollars. Each."

"You don't really believe they're going to plunk down seventy-five large because we say, oh, sure, we'll look for the keys. The ones that unlock the box holding the souls of a trio of demigoddesses."

Malory debated over a mini éclair. "Only one way to find out."

"They look like us." Ignoring the coffee

and pastries, Zoe stood beneath the painting, staring up. "So much like us."

"Yes, they do, and that's just creepy." Dana nodded when Malory held up the coffeepot. "Why paint the three of us together that way? We've never met before tonight. And the idea of somebody watching us, taking pictures or sketches or whatever so they could put this portrait together, spooks me."

"It wasn't something painted on a whim, or quickly." Malory handed Dana the coffee cup. "It's a masterpiece—the skill, the scope, the detail. Someone poured himself or herself into that piece, someone with incredible talent. And it took an incredible amount of work. If this is a scam, it's an elaborate one. Plus, what's the point? I'm broke. You?"

Dana puffed out her cheeks. "Close enough."

"I've got some savings," Zoe put in. "But I'm going to go through them pretty quick if I don't get another job, and fast. I don't know a lot about it, but it doesn't look like these people would be after the little bit of money we've got."

"Agreed. You want some coffee?"

"Thanks." She turned back to them and spread her hands. "Look, you all don't know me, and you've got no reason to care, but I could really use this money." Zoe came forward. "Twenty-five thousand would be like a miracle. Security for my son, a chance maybe to do what I've always wanted. Have my own little salon. All we have to do is say yes. So we look for some keys. It's not illegal."

"There are no keys," Dana insisted.

"What if there are?" Zoe put her cup down without drinking. "I have to say, the idea of twenty-five thousand dollars really helps open my mind to possibilities. And a million?" She gave a quick, baffled laugh. "I can't even think about it. It makes my stomach hurt."

"It'd be like a treasure hunt," Malory murmured. "It could be fun. God knows, it could be profitable. Twenty-five thousand would really close the gap for me, and that's a very practical priority just now. I might be able to have my own place, too. Not like The Gallery, but just a little place that spotlights artists and craftspeople."

It was a full ten years before that was due

KEY OF LIGHT 51

in the order of her life plan, but she could be flexible.

"Nothing's that simple. Nobody hands you money because you say you'll do something." Dana shook her head. "There's got to be more under all this."

"Maybe they believe it. The story," Malory added. "If you believed it, twenty-five thousand would be chump change. We're talking souls here." Unable to help herself, she looked back at the portrait. "A soul's worth more than twenty-five thousand dollars."

Excitement bounced inside her like a bright red ball. She'd never had an adventure, certainly not a paying adventure. "They've got money, they're eccentric, and they believe it. The fact is, going along with it sort of feels like we're the ones pulling the scam. But I'm going to get over that."

"You'll do it?" Zoe grabbed her arm. "You're going to do it?"

"It's not every day you get paid to work for the gods. Come on, Dana, loosen up."

Dana's brows drew together, her forehead forming a stubborn, vertical line between them. "It's asking for trouble. I don't know where or how, but it just feels like trouble."

"What would you do with twenty-five thousand?" Malory purred it, then offered another cream puff.

"Invest what I could so I could have my own little bookstore." Her sigh was wistful, and a sign that she was weakening. "I'd serve tea in the afternoons, wine in the evenings. Have readings. Oh, boy."

"It's strange how we're all having a job crisis, and that the thing we all want is to have our own place?" Zoe sent a wary look at the portrait again. "Don't you think it's strange?"

"No more strange than being here in this fortress and talking about going on a treasure hunt. Well, I'm in a fix," Dana muttered. "I say no, it kills it for both of you. Saying yes makes me feel like an idiot. I guess I'm an idiot."

"Yes?" With a hoot of laughter, Zoe threw her arms around Dana. "This is great! This is amazing!"

"Take it easy." Chuckling, Dana patted Zoe on the back. "I guess this is the time to pull out the right quote. 'One for all, and all for one.' "

"I got a better one." Malory picked up her

cup again, lifted it in a toast. " 'Show me the money.' "

As if on cue, the doors opened. Rowena entered first. "Shall we sit?"

"We've decided to accept the . . ." Zoe trailed off, looked at Dana.

"The challenge."

"Yes." Rowena crossed her legs. "You'll want to look over the contracts."

"Contracts?" Malory echoed.

"Naturally. A name has power. The writing of one's name, the promise of it, is necessary for all. Once you're satisfied, we'll select for the first key."

Pitte took papers out of a desk, handed one set to each woman. "They're simple, I believe, and cover the terms already discussed. If you'll write in where you wish the money to be sent, it will be done."

"Doesn't it matter to you that we don't believe in them?" Malory lifted a hand toward the portrait.

"You'll give your word that you'll accept the terms. That's enough for now," Rowena told her.

"Pretty straightforward for such an odd business," Dana commented. And promised herself she would take the contract to a lawyer the next day to see if it was binding.

Pitte handed her a pen. "As you are straightforward. If and when your turn comes, I know you'll do all you can."

Lightning sizzled along the window glass as the contracts were signed, then countersigned.

"You are the chosen," Rowena said as she rose again. "Now it's in your hands. Pitte?"

He walked back to the desk, picked up a carved box. "Inside are three disks. One has a figure of a key. The one who chooses that disk begins the quest."

"I hope it's not me." With a shaky laugh, Zoe wiped her damp palms on her skirt. "I'm sorry, I'm just really nervous." She closed her eyes, reached into the box. Keeping the disk clutched in her fist, she looked at Malory and Dana. "Let's all look at the same time. Okay?"

"Fine. Here goes." Dana reached in, kept the disk palmed against her side as Malory reached for the final one.

"Okay."

They stood in a circle, facing each other. Then held out the disks. "Wow." Malory cleared her throat. "Lucky me," she whispered as she saw the gold key etched into the white disk she had selected.

"You are the first," Rowena said, walking to her. "Your time starts at sunrise tomorrow and ends at midnight on the twenty-eighth day thereafter."

"But I get a guide, right. A map or something?"

Rowena opened the small chest and withdrew a paper, which she offered to Malory. She then spoke the words written on it.

"You must seek beauty, and truth and courage. One alone will never stand. Two without the third is incomplete. Search within and know what you have yet to know. Find what the dark covets most. Search without, where the light conquers shadows, as love conquers sorrow. Silver tears fall for the song she makes there, for it springs from souls. Look beyond and between, see where beauty blooms and the goddess sings. There may be fear, there may be grief, but the true heart vanquishes both. When you find what you seek, love will break the spell, and the heart will forge the key and bring it to light."

Malory waited a beat. "That's it? That's supposed to be a clue?"

"I'm so glad I didn't have to go first," Zoe said.

"Wait—can't you tell me anything else? You and Pitte already know where the keys are, right?"

"This is all we are allowed to give you, but you have all you need to have." Rowena laid her hands on Malory's shoulders, then kissed her cheeks. "Blessings on you."

Later Rowena stood, letting the fire warm her hands as she stared up at the painting. She felt Pitte come in to stand behind her, turned her face into his hand when he touched her cheek.

"I had higher hopes before they came," he told her.

"They're bright, resourceful. None are chosen who aren't capable."

"Yet we remain in this place, year by century by millennium."

"Don't." She turned, slid her arms around his waist, pressed herself to him. "Don't despair, my dearest love, before it really begins."

"So many beginnings, but never an end." He bent his head, touched his lips to her brow. "How this place crowds me."

"We've done all that can be done." She laid her cheek on his chest, comforted by the steady sound of his heartbeat. "Have a little faith. I liked them," she added, and took his hand as they started toward the doors.

"They're interesting enough. For mortals," he replied.

As they passed through the archway, the roaring fire vanished and the lights snapped off, leaving behind a trail of gold in the dark.

Chapter Three

She couldn't say she hadn't seen it coming. And James was certainly gentle, even paternal. But the boot was the boot however it was administered.

Being prepared, even having the miraculous cushion of the twenty-five thousand dollars now tucked away in her account—a fact that she had confirmed that morning—didn't make being fired any less horrible and humiliating.

"Things change." James P. Horace, natty as always in his bow tie and rimless glasses, spoke in modulated tones.

In all the years Malory had known him, she'd never heard him raise his voice. He could be absentminded, occasionally negligent about practicalities when it came to business, but he was unfailingly kind.

Even now his face held a patient and serene expression. A little like an aged cherub, Malory thought.

Though the office door was closed, the rest of The Gallery's staff would know, very shortly, the outcome of the meeting.

"I like to think of myself as a kind of surrogate father, and as such I want only the best for you."

"Yes, James. But—"

"If we don't move in some direction, we stand still. I feel that though this may be difficult for you initially, Malory, you'll soon see it's the best thing that could happen."

How many clichés, Malory wondered, could one man use when lowering the boom?

"James, I know Pamela and I haven't seen eye to eye." I'll see your cliché, and raise you. "As the new kid on the block, she's bound to be a bit defensive, while I tend to be territorial. I'm so terribly sorry I lost my temper. Spilling the coffee was an accident. You know I'd never—"

"Now, now." He waved his hands in the air. "I'm sure it was. I don't want you to give that another thought. Water under the bridge. But the point is, Malory, Pamela wants to take a more active role in the business, to shake things up a bit."

Desperation slithered into her belly. "James, she moved everything in the main room, jumbled pieces in from the salon. She brought fabric in—gold lamé, James—and draped it over the Deco nude like a sarong. Not only was the flow interrupted by the placements, but the result was, well, just tacky. She doesn't understand art, and space. She—"

"Yes, yes." His voice never changed pitch, his face never altered its placid expression. "But she'll learn. And I believe that teaching her will be enjoyable. I appreciate her interest in my business, and her enthusiasm—just as I've always appreciated yours, Malory. But the fact is, I really think you've outgrown us here. It's time for you to stretch yourself. Broaden your horizons. Take some risks."

Her throat closed, and her voice sounded thick when she managed to speak. "I love The Gallery, James."

"I know you do. And you're always welcome here. I feel it's time for me to give you a nudge out of the nest. Naturally, I want you to be comfortable while you're deciding what you'd like to do next." He took a check out of his breast pocket. "A month's severance should help keep the wolf from the door."

What will I do? Where will I go? Frantic questions flew around her brain like terrified birds. "This is the only place I've ever worked."

"Which makes my point." He set the check on the desk. "I hope you know how fond I am of you, and that you can come to me anytime, anytime at all, for advice. Though it would probably be best if we kept that between ourselves. Pamela is a little annoyed with you just now."

He gave her an avuncular peck on the cheek, a pat on the head, then strolled out.

Patient and placid he might be, but he was also weak. Weak, and though she hated to admit it—hated to realize it after all these years—selfish. It took a selfish weakness to fire an efficient, creative, loyal employee on the whim of his wife.

She knew it was useless to cry, but she

cried a little anyway as she stood in the small office that she'd decorated herself and boxed up her personal things. Her lifetime, career-wise, fit into a single storage box.

That was efficient again, practical. And, Malory decided, pathetic.

Everything was going to be different now, and she wasn't ready. She had no plan, no outline, no list for what came next. She wouldn't be getting up tomorrow, eating a light, sensible breakfast, dressing for work in the outfit carefully selected tonight.

Day after day without purpose, without plan, stretched out in front of her like some bottomless canyon. And the precious order of her life was strewn somewhere down there in the void.

It terrified her, but marching along with the fear was pride. So, she repaired her makeup and kept her chin up, her shoulders back, as she carried the box out of the office and down the stairs. She did her best to muster up a smile when Tod Grist rushed to the base of the stairs.

He was short and trim, clad in his signature black shirt and pants. Two tiny gold hoops glinted in his left earlobe. His hair was a shoulder-length streaky-blond, which Malory had always envied. The angelic face that it framed drew middle-aged and elderly ladies like the sirens' song drew sailors.

He'd started at The Gallery the year after Malory arrived and had been her friend, confidant, and bitching partner ever since.

"Don't go. We'll kill the bimbo. A little arsenic in her morning latte and she's history." He grabbed at the storage box. "Mal, love of my life, you can't leave me here."

"I got the boot. A month's severance, a pat on the head, and a pack of homilies." She fought to keep the tears from blurring her vision as she looked around the lovely, wide foyer, the streams of filtered light spilling over the glossy oak floor. "God, what am I going to do tomorrow when I can't come here?"

"Aw, baby. Here, give me that." He took the box, gave her a little nudge with it. "Outside, so we can blubber."

"I'm not going to blubber anymore." But she had to bite her lip when it quivered.

"I am," he promised and kept nudging until she was out the door. He set the box down on one of the iron tables on the pretty covered porch, then flung his arms around her. "I can't stand it! Nothing's going to be the same without you here. Who will I gossip with, who'll soothe my broken heart when some bastard breaks it? You notice this is all about me."

He made her laugh. "You'll still be my best bud, right?"

"Sure I will. You're not going to do something crazy, like move to the city?" He eased back to study her face. "Or fall in with bad companions and work in a strip mall gift shop?"

A lead weight landed—*ka-boom*—in her stomach. Those were the only two reasonable choices she had if she was going to make a living. But because he looked as if he might cry, she waved them away to bolster him. "Perish the thought. I don't know what I'm going to do, exactly. But I've got this thing—" She thought of her odd evening, and the key. "I'll tell you about it later. I've got something to keep me occupied for a while, then . . . I don't know, Tod. Everything's out of kilter."

Maybe she was going to blubber a little after all. "Nothing's the way it's supposed to be, so I can't see how it *will* be. Getting fired was not in the Malory Price Life Plan."

"It's just a blip," he assured her. "James is in some sort of sexual haze. He could still come to his senses. You could sleep with him," he added, inspired. "I could sleep with him."

"I have one thing to say to both of those suggestions. Ick."

"Profound, and true. How about if I come by tonight, bring you Chinese and a cheap bottle of wine?"

"You're a pal."

"We'll plot Putrid Pamela's demise and plan your future. Want me to walk you home, sweetie pie?"

"Thanks, but I'll be fine. Give me time to clear my head. Say good-bye to . . . everybody. I just can't face it now."

"Don't you worry."

She tried not to worry as she walked home. She tried to ignore the panic that dogged her with every step she took away from routine and closer to that wide, wide canyon.

She was young, educated, hardworking. She had money in the bank. Her whole life was ahead of her, like blank canvas. All she had to do was choose her paints and get on with it.

But right now, she needed to think of something else. Anything else. She had a month to decide. And an intriguing task to perform in the meantime. It wasn't every day you were asked to find a mysterious key and play a part in saving souls.

She would play along with that until she figured out the rest of her life. She'd given her word, after all, so she'd best get started on keeping it. Somehow. Right after she went home and buried her sorrows in a pint of Ben and Jerry's.

As she came to the corner, she looked back, mistily, miserably, toward The Gallery. Who was she kidding? That had been home.

On a long sigh, she took a step. And landed hard on her butt.

Whatever had collided with her sent her box of possessions flying, then fell on top of her. She heard a grunt, and what sounded like a yip. With the breath knocked out of her, and what felt like a minor mountain pressing on her chest, she stared up into a hairy black face.

Even as she fought for the breath to scream, an enormous tongue rolled out and slurped her face.

"Moe! Stop, heel, get the hell off! Jeez. Jesus, I'm sorry."

Malory heard the voice, the light panic in it, as she gagged and turned her head to try to avoid the tongue. Abruptly, the huge black mass pinning her down grew arms. Then a second head.

This one was human, a great deal more attractive than the first, despite the sunglasses that slid down a sharp, straight nose and the grim set to the mouth.

"Are you all right? Are you hurt?"

He shoved the massive weight away, then squeezed his body between them, like a defensive wall. "Can you sit up?"

The question was moot, as he was already pulling her from her ungainly sprawl to a sitting position. The dog tried to nose in but was elbowed back. "You lie down, you big sloppy idiot. Not you," he added with a quick, charming grin as he brushed Malory's hair back from her face. "I'm sorry. He's harmless, just clumsy and stupid."

"What . . . what is it?"

"Moe's a dog, or that's the rumor. We think he's a cross between a cocker spaniel and a woolly mammoth. I'm really sorry. My fault. I wasn't paying enough attention, and he got away from me."

She slid her gaze to the right, where the dog, if it *was* a dog, was hunkered down, thumping a tail as thick as her arm and looking as innocent as anything that homely could manage.

"You didn't hit your head, did you?"

"I don't think so." She found Moe's owner staring at her with a quiet intensity that made heat rush over her skin. "What?"

She was as pretty as a bakery-shop pastry. All that tumbled blond hair, the top-cream skin, the rosy, bottom-heavy mouth that was in a sexy little sulk. Her eyes were big, blue, and beautiful, despite the temper flames shooting out of them.

He nearly licked his lips when she scowled at him and lifted her hand to shove it through that terrific tangle of hair. "What are you staring at?"

"Just making sure you don't have little X's in your eyes. You went down pretty hard. Great eyes, by the way. I'm Flynn."

"And I'm tired of sitting on the sidewalk. Do you mind?"

"Oh. Yeah." He stood, took both her

hands in both of his, and pulled her to her feet.

He was taller than she'd realized, and she automatically stepped back so she didn't have to tip her face up to keep an eye on him. The sun was streaming over his hair— a lot of thick, wavy brown hair with hints of chestnut. His hands were still clasping hers, firmly enough that she felt the ridge of callus on them.

"You sure you're all right? Steady? You went down pretty hard."

"I'm aware of that." Painfully aware in the portion of her anatomy that had hit the sidewalk first. She crouched and began gathering what had spilled out of the box.

"I'll get this stuff." He crouched beside her, then stabbed a finger at the dog who was trying to inch his way toward them with the same stealth as an elephant tiptoeing across the African plain. "Stay, or there's no treat for you."

"Just get your dog. I don't need any help here." She snatched up her emergency cosmetic bag, tossed it in the box. And when she saw that she'd chipped a nail, she wanted to curl into a ball of self-pity and wail. Instead, she selected the temper button.

"You have no business being out on a public street with a dog of that size if you can't control him. He's just a dog, he doesn't know any better, but you're supposed to."

"You're right. You're absolutely right. Um . . . this must be yours."

He held out a strapless black bra.

Mortified, Malory grabbed it out of his hand, stuffed it in the box. "Go away now. Go very, very far away."

"Listen, why don't you let me carry that—"

"Carry your silly dog," she snapped and, hefting the box, strode away with as much dignity as she could muster.

Flynn watched her go as Moe lumbered over to press his considerable weight against his master's side. Absently, Flynn patted the massive head and enjoyed the indignant sway of feminine hips in a short skirt. He doubted that run in her stocking had been there before her encounter with Moe, but from his perspective it did nothing to detract from a pair of great legs.

"Pretty," he said aloud as she slammed

into a building halfway down the block. "And pretty steamed." He glanced down at the hopefully grinning Moe. "Nice job, jerkface."

After a hot shower, a change of clothes, and a medicinal bowl of cookie dough ice cream, Malory headed for the library. She hadn't made any firm arrangements with her—she supposed they were her partners—the night before. As she was the first, she would have to be in charge.

They needed to have some sort of meeting, to go over the clue, to plot out a plan of action. She didn't hold out any real hope of winning a million dollars, but she wasn't going to shrug it off or go back on her word.

She couldn't remember the last time she'd actually been in the library. For some reason, going in made her feel like a student again, full of naïveté, hope, and an eagerness to learn.

The main area wasn't large, and the tables were mostly unoccupied. She saw an older man reading the newspaper, a few people wandering the stacks, a woman with a toddler in tow at the checkout counter.

The place was so hushed, the ringing of a phone was like a shout. She glanced toward the sound, and the central island of counter. Dana sat there, a phone at her ear while her fingers clicked on a keyboard.

Pleased that she wouldn't have to search the building to find her, Malory walked over. She wagged her fingers as Dana nodded at her and finished the call.

"I was hoping you'd come by. Didn't expect you this soon."

"I'm now a woman of leisure."

"Oh." Sympathy softened Dana's face. "You got canned?"

"Canned, booted, axed, then knocked on my ass by an idiot and his dog on the way home. All in all, it's been a lousy day, even with the expansion of my bank account."

"I have to say, I didn't believe it. Those two up on the Peak are certifiable."

"Lucky for us. But still, we have to earn it. I'm first up, so I figure I need to get started. Somewhere."

"I'm ahead of you. Jan? Will you take the desk?" As she rose, Dana gathered a stack of books from under the counter. "Come with me," she told Malory. "There's a nice table by the window where you can work."

"Work at what?"

"Research. I've got several books on Celtic mythology, gods and goddesses, lore and legend. I'm going with the Celts since Rowena's from Wales and Pitte's Irish."

"How do you know he's Irish?"

"I don't. He sounded Irish. At this point I know little or nothing about Celtic myths, and I figure it's the same for you and Zoe."

"I don't have a clue."

Dana set the books down with a muffled thud. "So, we need to get one. I'm off in a few hours, then I can give you a hand. And I can call Zoe in if you like."

Malory stared at the stack of books. "Maybe that's a good idea. I don't know where to start."

"Pick one. I'll get you a notebook."

After an hour Malory needed an aspirin as well. When Zoe rushed up to sit at the table beside her, she took off her glasses and rubbed her tired eyes. "Good. Reinforcements." She shoved a book across the table.

"I'm sorry it took me so long. I was running errands. I bought Simon this video game he's been wanting. I know I probably shouldn't have spent the money, but I wanted to get him something, just for fun. I've never had so much money in my life," she whispered. "I know I have to be careful with it, but if you can't do a little something fun, what's the point?"

"You don't have to sell me. And after you've been at this for a while, you'll know you earned it. Welcome to the wacky world of the Celts. Dana's probably got another notebook."

"I brought my own." Out of an enormous bag, Zoe pulled a fresh notebook, thick as a brick, and a pack of pencils already sharpened to saber points. "It's sort of like going back to school."

Zoe's eager optimism cut through Malory's foul mood. "Want to pass notes and talk about boys?"

Zoe just grinned and opened a book. "We're going to find that key. I just know it."

By the time Dana joined them, Malory had written reams of notes in the modified shorthand she'd developed in college, had drained her pen and borrowed two of Zoe's pencils.

"Why don't we move this to my brother's place?" Dana suggested. "It's right around the corner. He's at work, so he won't be in the way. We can spread out a little, and you can give me the highlights."

"Fine with me." Stiff from sitting, Malory got to her feet.

"I can only stay for about an hour. I like to be there when Simon gets home from school, when I can."

"Then let's get started. These books are on me," Dana said as she began gathering some up. "Anybody takes one home for personal research, I need it back in a timely fashion and in the same condition it was in when you took it."

"She really is a librarian." Malory tucked books under her arm.

"Bet your ass." Dana led the way out. "I'm going to see what I can get off the Net, and through interlibrary loan."

"I don't know how much we're going to get out of books."

Dana slipped on her sunglasses, then tipped them down and peered at Malory over the tops. "Anything worth anything can be found in books."

"Okay, now you're heading toward Scary Library Lady. What we need to do is figure out the clue."

"Without information on the story, the characters in it, we've got no base."

"We've got four whole weeks," Zoe put in, and dragged sunglasses out of her shoulder bag. "That's enough time to find out a lot of stuff, look in a lot of places. Pitte said the keys were around here. So it's not like we have the whole world to worry about."

"Around here could mean the Valley, or the highlands. It could mean the entire state of Pennsylvania." Malory shook her head at the sheer scope and disorder. "Pitte and pal left it pretty wide open. Even if it's close by, it could be in someone's dusty drawer, on the bottom of the river, in a bank vault, or buried under a rock."

"If it was easy, somebody else would have found it by now," Zoe pointed out. "And the grand prize wouldn't be three million dollars."

"Don't be sensible while I'm crabbing."

"Sorry, but there's one other thing I was wondering. I couldn't sleep last night, going over and over the whole evening in my head. It's all so unreal. But even if you set all that aside for a minute, even if we're optimistic and say you find the key, how do we know it's *your* key, and not one of the other two?"

"Interesting." Malory shifted her load of books as they turned the corner. "How come the Weird Twins didn't think of that?"

"I figure they did. See, first you have to say it's all real."

Dana shrugged. "We've all got money in the bank, and we're walking along with a load of books on Celtic myths. That's real enough for me."

"If it's all real, then Malory can only find the first key. Even if the other two were right in front of her, she wouldn't find them. And we wouldn't either, not before it's our turn to look."

Dana stopped, angling her head as she studied Zoe. "Do you really believe all this?"

Zoe flushed but gave a careless shrug. "I'd like to. It's so fantastic and important. I've never done anything fantastic or important." She looked up at the narrow three-story Victorian painted a soft slate blue with creamy gingerbread trim. "Is this your brother's house? I've always thought it was so pretty."

"He's been fixing it up bit by bit. Kind of a hobby."

They started up the brick walk. The grass was green and trim on either side, but it needed flowers, Malory thought. Color and shape and texture. And an old bench on the porch, next to a big copper pot full of interesting sticks and grasses.

The house looked lonely without them, like a perfectly attractive woman, she thought, who'd been stood up for a date.

Dana took out a key, unlocked the door. "The best I can say about the inside is it'll be quiet." She stepped in, and her voice echoed. "And private."

The foyer was empty but for a few boxes shoved into a corner. The stairway leading up was a lovely, fanciful curve with a griffin head as its newel post.

The foyer spilled into a parlor, where the walls were painted a rich, shady-river green that went well with the warm honey-toned pine of the floor. But the walls, like the yard, were naked.

There was a huge sofa in the middle of the floor, the sort that shouted to Malory, A man bought me! Despite the fact that some of the green in it matched the walls, it was a hideous plaid, clunky of style and too large for the charm potential of the room.

Some sort of crate stood in as a table.

There were more boxes, one of which sat on the hearth of a delightful little fireplace with an ornately carved mantel that she could envision dressing up with a fabulous painting.

"So . . ." Zoe turned in a circle. "I guess he's just moving in."

"Oh, yeah. For the last year and a half." Dana laid her books on the crate.

"He's lived here for over a year?" It hurt, simply hurt Malory's heart. "And his single piece of furniture is this really ugly couch?"

"Hey, you should've seen his room at home. At least this is neat. Anyway, he's got some halfway decent stuff upstairs. That's where he lives. There's probably not any food, but there'll be coffee, beer, Coke. Anybody?"

"Diet Coke?" Malory asked.

Dana sneered. "He's a guy."

"Right. I'll live dangerously and have the real thing."

"Coke's fine," Zoe agreed.

"Coming up. Go ahead and sit. The couch is an eyesore but it's comfortable."

"All this wonderful space wasted," Malory decided, "on a man who would actually pay money for something like this." She dropped down on the couch. "Okay, it's comfortable. But it's still ugly."

"Can you imagine living in a place like this?" Zoe turned a quick circle. "It's like a doll's house. Well, a really big doll's house, but just as sweet. I'd spend all my free time playing with it, hunting for treasures to put in it, fussing with paint and fabric."

"So would I." Malory tilted her head. At her very best, she thought, she would never look as hip and exotic as Zoe managed to do in simple jeans and a cotton shirt. And she'd done the math, calculating how old Zoe had been when she'd had her baby. At that same age, Malory had been shopping for the perfect prom dress and preparing for college.

And yet, here they were, together in a largely empty room of a stranger's house and having nearly identical thoughts.

"It's strange how much we have in common. Strange, too, that we live in a relatively small town and never met before last night."

Zoe sat on the opposite end of the couch. "Where do you get your hair done?"

"Carmine's, out at the mall."

"That's a good salon. Hair Today, here in

town, where I worked? It's mostly women who want the same do week after week after week." She rolled her big, tawny eyes. "Can't blame you for heading out of town. You've got great hair. Did your stylist ever suggest that you take a couple inches off?"

"Cut?" Instinctively Malory's hand went to her hair. "Cut?"

"Just a couple inches, take some of the weight off. It's a terrific color."

"It's mine. Well, I get it punched up a bit." She laughed and dropped her hand. "I get the feeling you're looking at my hair the way I'm looking at this room. Wondering just what I could do with it if I had a free hand."

"Cokes *and* cookies." Dana brought in a trio of cans and a bag of store-bought chocolate chip cookies. "So, what have we got so far?"

"I didn't find anything that mentions three daughters of a young god and a mortal woman." Malory popped the top and sipped, though she would have preferred a glass and some ice. "Jesus, this stuff is so sweet when you're not used to it. I also didn't find anything about trapped souls or keys. A lot of strange-looking names like

Lug and Rhianna, Anu, Danu. Tales of battles—victories and death."

She took out her notebook, flipped it open to the first neatly arranged page. One look at it had Dana's dimples popping out.

"I bet you were an A student all the way through school. Honor roll, Dean's list. Fucking the curve for the rest of the class."

"Why?"

"You're too organized not to be. You made an outline and everything." She snatched the notebook, turned pages. "And time lines! Charts."

"Shut up." Laughing at herself, Malory grabbed the notebook back. "As I was saying before being snickered at for my organized research style, Celtic gods die—they appear to pop back, but they can actually be killed. And unlike what I know about the gods in Greek and Roman mythology, these don't live on some magic mountaintop. They inhabit the earth, live among people. Lots of politics and protocol."

Dana sat on the floor. "Anything that could be a metaphor for the keys?"

"If there was, it was over my head."

"Artists were gods, and warriors," Zoe added. "Or the other way around. I mean art—music, storytelling, all that—was important. And there were mother-goddesses. Motherhood was important. And the number three. So, it's like, Malory's the artist—"

It was a quick and painful twist in Malory's heart. "No, I sell art."

"You know art," Zoe said. "Like Dana knows books. I know about being a mother."

"That's good." Dana beamed at her. "That gives each of us our role in this. Pitte said beauty, truth, courage. In the painting, Malory—let's simplify by calling them by our names for now—Malory was playing an instrument. Music-art-beauty. I was holding a scroll and quill—book-knowledge-truth. And Zoe had the sword and the puppy. Innocence-protection-courage."

"Which means?" Malory demanded.

"We could say the first key, your key, is somewhere that has to do with art and/or beauty. That goes along with the clue."

"Great. I'll pick it up on my way home." Malory nudged a book with her toe. "What if they just made it up? The whole story?"

"I refuse to believe they made the whole thing up just to have us scrambling around looking for keys." Thoughtfully, Dana bit into a cookie. "No matter what we believe, *they* believe it's true. So there's got to be some root, some basis for this legend or myth or story they told us last night. If there's a root, it's in a book. Somewhere."

"Actually . . ." Zoe hesitated, then went on, "the book I was reading talked about how a lot of the Celtic mythology and legends didn't get written down. They were passed orally."

"Those damn bards," Dana muttered. "Look, Pitte and Rowena heard it somewhere, and whoever told them heard it from someone else. The information is out there, and information is my god."

"Maybe what we have to do is get information on Pitte and Rowena. Who the hell are they?" Malory spread her hands. "Where do they come from? Where do they get the kind of money that allows them to pass it out like cupcakes?"

"You're right." Annoyed with herself, Dana blew out a breath. "You're absolutely right, and I should've thought of that before. It happens I know somebody who can help us with that while we're looking into the myth." She glanced toward the doorway as she heard the front door open. "And here he comes now."

They heard a thud, a slam, a scramble, and a curse.

It was just familiar enough to have Malory pressing her fingers to her temples. "Holy Mother of God."

Even as she spoke, the huge black dog raced in. His tail swung like a demolition ball, his tongue lolled. And his eyes went bright as stars as he spotted Malory.

He let out a series of ear-shattering barks, then leaped into her lap.

Chapter Four

Flynn saw three things when he charged into the room after his dog: his sister sitting on the floor laughing like a lunatic; a sharp-looking brunette standing at the end of the couch heroically trying to dislodge Moe; and, to his surprise and delight, the woman he'd been thinking about for the better part of the day, mostly buried under Moe's bulk and insane affections.

"Okay, Moe, down. I mean it. That's enough." He didn't expect the dog to listen. He always tried; Moe never listened. But it seemed the right thing to do as he gripped the dog around the barrel of his belly.

He had to lean down—well, maybe not quite as far as he did. But she had the prettiest blue eyes, even when they were shooting daggers at him. "Hi. Nice to see you again."

Muscles jumped in her jaw when she clenched it. "Get him off!"

"Working on it."

"Hey, Moe!" Dana shouted. "Cookie!"

That did the trick. Moe leaped over the crate, nipped the cookie out of the hand Dana held in the air, then landed. It might have been a graceful landing if he hadn't skidded several feet over the uncarpeted floor.

"Works like a charm." Dana lifted her arm. Moe loped back, the cookie already history, and insinuated his bulk under it.

"Wow. He's really a big dog." Zoe eased over, held out a hand, then grinned when Moe licked it lavishly. "Friendly."

"Pathologically friendly." Malory brushed at the dog hair that had transferred itself to her once pristine linen shirt. "That's the second time today he's landed on me."

"He likes girls." Flynn took off his sunglasses, tossed them on the crate. "You never told me your name."

"Oh, so you're the idiot and his dog. Should've known. This is Malory Price,"

Dana said. "And Zoe McCourt. My brother, Flynn."

"Are you Michael Flynn Hennessy?" Zoe crouched to stroke Moe's ear, looked up at Flynn under her bangs. "M. F. Hennessy, with the *Valley Dispatch*?"

"Guilty."

"I've read a lot of your articles, and I never miss your column. I liked the one last week on the proposed ski lift up on Lone Ridge and the environmental impact."

"Thanks." He reached down for a cookie. "Is this a book club meeting, and will there be cake?"

"No. But if you've got a minute, maybe you could sit down." Dana patted the floor. "We'll tell you what it is."

"Sure." But he sat on the couch. "Malory Price? The Gallery, right?"

"Not anymore," she grimaced.

"I've been in a couple times, must've missed you. I don't cover arts and entertainment. I see the error of my ways."

His eyes, she noted, were the same color as the walls. That lazy-river green. "I doubt we have anything to offer that could complement your decor."

"You hate the couch, right?"

" 'Hate' is much too mild a word."

"It's very comfortable."

He glanced over at Zoe's comment and smiled. "It's a napping couch. You nap, your eyes are closed, so you don't care what it looks like. *Celtic Mythology,*" he read, angling his head to read the titles on the books scattered over the crate. *"Myths and Legends of the Celts."* He picked one up, turned it in his hands as he studied his sister. "What gives?"

"I told you I was going to that cocktail party at Warrior's Peak?"

His face went hard the instant the affable smile faded. "I thought you weren't going because I said there had to be something off about that since nobody I talked to got an invitation."

Dana picked up her Coke can, gave him a mildly interested look. "Do you actually think I listen to you?"

"No."

"Okay, then. Here's what happened."

She'd barely begun when he turned away from her and those green eyes sharpened on Malory's face. "You got an invitation?"

"Yes."

"And you." He nodded at Zoe. "What do you do, Zoe?"

"Right now I'm an unemployed hair-dresser, but—"

"Married?"

"No."

"Neither are you," he said as he looked at Malory again. "No ring. No 'I'm married' vibe. How long have the three of you known each other?"

"Flynn, stop doing a damn interview. Just let me tell you what happened."

Dana started again, and this time he boosted a hip off the couch, took a note-book out of his back pocket. Doing her best to appear as if she wasn't the least bit inter-ested in what he was doing, Malory slid her gaze to the left and down.

He used shorthand, she realized. And *real* shorthand, not any sort of bastardized ver-sion, as she did.

She tried to decipher it as Dana spoke, but it made her a little dizzy.

" 'The Daughters of Glass,' " Flynn mut-tered and kept scribbling.

"What?" Without thinking, Malory reached over and clamped her fingers on his wrist. "You know this story?"

"A version of it, anyway." Since he had her attention, he shifted toward her. His knee bumped hers. "My Irish granny told me lots of stories."

"Why didn't you recognize it?" Malory asked Dana.

"She didn't have my Irish granny."

"Actually, we're steps," Dana explained. "My father married his mother when I was eight."

"Or my mother married her father when I was eleven. It's all point of view." He reached up to toy with the ends of Malory's hair, grinned easily when she batted his fingers aside. "Sorry. There's just so much of it, it's irresistible. Anyway, my granny liked to tell stories, so I heard plenty of them. This one sounds like 'The Daughters of Glass.' Which doesn't explain why the three of you were invited up to the Peak to listen to a faerie tale."

"We're supposed to find the keys," Zoe put in, and snuck a peek at her watch.

"You're supposed to find the keys to unlock their souls? Cool." He stretched out to prop his feet on the crate, crossed his ankles. "Now it's my duty to ask how, when, and why."

"If you'd shut up for five minutes, I'd tell you." Dana reached for her Coke and drained it. "Malory goes first. She has twenty-eight days, starting today, to find the first key. When she does, either Zoe or I goes next. Same drill. Then the last of us gets her shot."

"Where's the box? The Box of Souls?"

Dana frowned as Moe deserted her to sniff Malory's toes. "I don't know. They must have it. Pitte and Rowena. If they don't the keys won't do them any good."

"You're telling me you're buying this? Miss Steeped-in-Reality? And you're going to spend the next few weeks looking for keys that open a magic glass box that holds the souls of three goddesses."

"Demigoddesses." Malory nudged Moe with her foot to discourage him. "And it isn't a matter of what we believe. It's a business deal."

"They paid us twenty-five thousand each." Dana offered. "In advance."

"Twenty-five thousand *dollars*? Get out!"

"The money's been deposited in our bank accounts. It's been verified." Forgetting herself, Malory reached for a cookie. Moe immediately dropped his heavy head on her knee. "Could you call off your dog?"

"Not as long as you've got cookies. These two people, whom you don't know, gave each of you twenty-five grand to look for magic keys? Did they have any beans for sale? A golden goose, maybe?"

"The money's real," Malory said stiffly.

"And what if you don't deliver? What's the penalty?"

"We lose a year."

"You're, what, indentured to them for a year?"

"A year gets taken away from us." Zoe looked at her watch again. She really had to go.

"What year?"

She gave him a blank look. "Well, I . . . The last year, I guess. When we're old."

"Or this year," he said and pushed to his feet. "Or next. Or ten years back, if we're being weird, which we sure as hell are."

"No, that can't be." Pale now, Zoe shook her head. "It can't be from before. That would change everything. What if it's the year I had Simon, or the year I got pregnant? That can't be."

"No, it can't, because none of this can

be." He shook his head and looked down at his sister. "Where's your head, Dana? Didn't it occur to you that when you don't come up with the goods these people might hurt you? Nobody dumps that kind of money on strangers. Which means you're not strangers to them. For whatever reason, they know you. They've looked into you."

"You weren't there," Dana said. "Eccentric is definitely apt in their case. Psychotic isn't."

"Besides, there's no motive for them to hurt us."

He spun back to Malory. No, he wasn't affable now, she realized, but annoyed. And working his way rapidly to irate. "And there is one for them to dump big gobs of money on you?"

"I've got to go." Zoe's voice shook as she grabbed her bag. "I have to get to Simon. My son."

She streaked out, and Dana leaped to her feet. "Nice job, Flynn. Very nice job scaring the single mother witless." She bolted after Zoe, hoping to calm her.

He jammed his hands in his pockets, stared hard at Malory. "You scared?"

"No, but I don't have a nine-year-old boy

to worry about. And I don't believe Pitte or Rowena wants to hurt us. Besides, I can take care of myself."

"Why do women always say that after they've gotten themselves in a really big jam?"

"Because men usually come along and make things worse. I'm going to look for the key, as I agreed to do. We all are. So would you."

She had him there. He jingled the change in his pocket, considered. Cooled off. "What did they tell you would happen if you found the keys?"

"The souls would be unlocked. And we'd each get a million dollars. And yes, I know how ridiculous that sounds. You had to be there."

"When you add that these three goddesses are currently sleeping in crystal beds in a castle behind the Curtain of Dreams, I guess you did have to be there."

"They have a painting of the Daughters of Glass. They look like us. It's a brilliant painting. I know art, Hennessy, and this is no paint-by-numbers deal. It's a goddamn masterpiece. It has to mean something."

His face sharpened with interest. "Who painted it?"

"It wasn't signed, not that I could see."

"Then how do you know it's a master-piece?"

"Because I *know.* It's what I do. Whoever painted it has an amazing talent, and a great love and respect for the subject mat-ter. That sort of thing shows. And if they'd wanted to hurt us, why didn't they do something last night, when we were all there? Dana was there, alone with them, before I arrived. Why not bash her over the head and chain her in the dungeon, then do the same with me, with Zoe. Or drug the wine? I've already thought about all that, al-ready asked myself all the questions. And I'll tell you why. Because they believe every-thing they told us."

"And this eases your mind? Okay, who are they? Where do they come from? How did they get here? Why did they come here? This isn't exactly Mystic Central."

"Why don't you find out instead of scar-ing people?" Dana demanded as she re-turned.

"Is Zoe okay?" Malory asked her.

"Sure, she's just great now that she has

visions of somebody using her kid as a human sacrifice." She punched Flynn in the shoulder.

"Hey, if you didn't want somebody to point out the flaws in the plan, you shouldn't have had your party at my place. So, tell me everything you know about this Rowena and Pitte."

He took more notes, managing to hold back any scathing comments on the lack of information.

"Anybody still got the invitation?"

He took the one Malory pulled out of her bag. "I'll see what I can find out."

"Did your grandmother's story say anything about where the keys were hidden?"

"No, just that they couldn't be turned by the hand of the gods. Which leaves a pretty open field."

Flynn waited until Malory left, then crooked a finger so Dana would follow him into the kitchen.

As rooms went it was a sad statement, with its ancient coppertone appliances, white-with-gold-speckled countertops and fake-brick linoleum floor.

"When are you going to do something about this room? It's awful."

"All in good time, my pretty, all in good time." He got a beer out of the fridge, wagged it at her.

"Yeah, why not?"

He got out a second, popped the tops on the wall opener that was in the shape of a bikini-clad blonde with a toothy grin.

"Now, tell me what you know about the very sexy Malory Price of the big blue eyes."

"I just met her last night."

"Uh-uh." He held back the beer. "Women know stuff about women. Like telepathically. The more a woman likes or dislikes another woman, the more she knows. There have been several scientific studies to verify this phenomenon. Give, or no beer for you."

She hadn't particularly wanted the beer, until he'd used it as a hammer. "Why do you want to know about her specifically? Why not Zoe?"

"My interest in Zoe is more academic. I can hardly start the wild and passionate affair I have in mind with Malory until I know all her secrets and desires."

"You're going to make me sick, Flynn."

He merely tipped up his beer, took a long, slow sip, while holding hers out of reach.

"I'm not your silly dog who'll beg for cookies. I'm only going to tell you so I can sit back and laugh derisively when she blows you off. I do like her," she added and held out a hand for the beer. "She strikes me as smart, ambitious, open-minded without being naive. She worked at The Gallery, just got canned over a dispute with the owner's new trophy wife. Since Malory called the new wife a bimbo, to her face, I'd say she doesn't always rate high on the tact and diplomacy scale, but calls 'em like she sees 'em. She likes good clothes and knows how to wear them—spends too much on them, which is why she was broke before this morning's windfall. She's not currently in a relationship and would like to own her own business."

"You really buried the lead." He took a long, slow sip. "So, she's not dating anyone. And she's gutsy. Not only does she tell off the boss's wife, but she drives alone, at night, to the spookiest house in western Pennsylvania."

"So did I."

"I can't have a mad, passionate affair with you, sweetie. It would just be wrong."

"Now, there, you have made me sick."

But she smiled when he leaned over and kissed her cheek. "Why don't you move in here for a couple weeks?"

Her dark chocolate eyes went baleful. "Stop looking out for me, Flynn."

"Can't do it."

"If I wouldn't move in when I was broke, why would I now that I'm flush? You know I like my own space, and you do too. Such as it is. And the goblins of Warrior's Peak are not going to come down and spirit me away in the night."

"If they were goblins, they wouldn't worry me." But because he knew her, he eased off. "How about telling your new pal Malory what an amazing man I am. All brainy and sensitive and buff."

"You want me to lie to her?"

"You're mean, Dana." He gulped down more beer. "You're just mean."

When he was alone, Flynn settled down in his upstairs study. He preferred the term "study" to "office," as an office meant work. No way around it. In a study, you could, well, study, or nap or read, or stare into space thinking long thoughts. You could certainly work, but it wasn't a requirement.

He'd outfitted the room with a big, brawny desk and a couple of wide leather chairs that he thought felt as if you might sink into them until you disappeared.

He had files as well, but he disguised them with manly-looking chests. One wall was covered with framed prints of pinup girls from the forties and fifties.

If all else failed, he could kick back, study them, and pass an enjoyable hour in solitude.

He booted up his computer, stepped over Moe, who had already flopped in the middle of the floor, and pulled a second beer out of the mini fridge he'd installed under a work counter.

He'd considered that idea pretty damn clever.

Then he sat, rolled his head as a boxer might before a round, and got down to some serious surfing.

If there was anything in the cyberworld about the new residents of Warrior's Peak, he would find it.

As always, he got sucked into the sirens' song of information. His beer went warm.

One hour passed into two, two headed toward three, before Moe solved the matter by giving the desk chair a push that shot it and Flynn halfway across the room.

"Damn it, you know I hate that. I just need a few more minutes."

But Moe had heard that one before, and he protested by plopping massive paws and a great deal of body weight onto Flynn's thighs. "So, maybe we'll take a walk. And if we happen to wander by a certain blonde's door, we could just stop in and share currently gathered information. And if that doesn't work, we'll pick up some pizza so it won't be a complete loss."

The word "pizza" had Moe tearing to the doorway. By the time Flynn made it downstairs, the dog was by the front door, his leash clamped between his teeth.

It was a nice evening for a walk. Quiet, balmy, with his little postcard town basking under the late-summer sun. At such moments, when the air was soft, the breeze fragrant, he was glad he'd made the decision to take over the *Dispatch* from his mother rather than heading out to make his mark at some big-city paper.

A lot of his friends had gone to the city,

and the woman he'd thought he loved had chosen New York over him.

Or he'd chosen the Valley over her.

It depended, he supposed, on your point of view.

Maybe the news here didn't have the scope or the edge of the news in Philly or New York, but there was still plenty of it. And what happened in the Valley, in the hills and mountains that surrounded it, mattered.

And just now he scented a story that would be bigger and juicier than anything the *Dispatch* had reported in the sixty-eight years since its presses began to run.

If he could help three women, one of whom was a sister he loved very much, flirt with an incredibly attractive blonde, *and* expose a major con . . . well, that would be a hell of a hat trick.

"You have to be charming," he told Moe as they approached the trim brick building that he'd watched Malory enter that morning. "You act like a dog, we'll never get through the door."

As a precaution, Flynn wrapped the leash twice around his fist before going into the twelve-unit building.

He considered it good luck that M. Price
was on the ground floor. Not only would he
not have to drag Moe up steps or pull him
into an elevator, but the building's ground
level had little patios.

That gave him the option of bribing Moe
with the cookie he'd stuffed in his pocket
and staking him outside.

"Charming," he said again, sotto voce,
giving Moe a narrow stare before he
knocked on Malory's door.

Her greeting, when she answered, wasn't
what he could call flattering.

She took one look at him and Moe. "Oh,
my God. You've got to be kidding."

"I can put him outside," Flynn said
quickly. "But we really need to talk."

"He'll dig up my flowers."

"He doesn't dig." Please God, don't dig.
"I've got a—I can't say the C word, or he'll
get excited. But I've got one in my pocket.
I'll just put him out there, out of the way."

"I don't—" Moe's nose arrowed straight
into her crotch. "Christ." In defense she
skipped back, which was all the invitation
Moe required.

He was through the door, dragging Flynn
merrily over an antique Turkish carpet,

barely missing slapping his lethal tail into a Deco vase filled with late-summer lilies.

Terrified, Malory made a dash for her patio door, yanked it open. "Out, out, straight out."

It was a word Moe knew. And he objected to going out when he'd just come in to so many fascinating scents. He simply dropped his wide butt on the floor and dug in.

With dignity no longer an option, Flynn hooked both hands in Moe's collar and dragged him bodily across the room and out the door.

"Oh, yeah, that was charming." Out of breath, Flynn looped the leash around the trunk of a tree. And as Moe began to howl, he dropped to his knees. "Stop it. Have you no pride? Have you no sense of masculine solidarity? How am I going to get my hands on that woman if she hates us?"

He pushed his face into Moe's. "Lie down and be quiet. Do this for me, and the world is yours. Starting with this."

He pulled out the cookie. The howling stopped instantly, and the tail began to thump.

"Screw this up and next time I leave you home."

He stood up and sent what he hoped was an easy smile toward Malory, who stood warily on the other side of the door.

He figured it was a major victory when she opened it and let him in.

"Have you tried obedience school?" she demanded.

"Ah, well, yeah, but there was an incident. We don't like to talk about it. This is a great place."

Stylish, arty, and female, he decided. Not delicate-little-trinket female but bold-unique-fascinating female.

The walls were a deep, rich rose, a strong background for the paintings. She favored antiques, or reproductions that looked enough like the real thing to pass. Soft fabrics and sleek sculpture.

And everything tidy as a shiny new pin.

It smelled female, classily so, from the lilies and the dried flower petals that women were forever putting in bowls. And, he supposed, from the woman herself.

She had music on low. What was that . . . Annie Lennox, crooning slyly about sweet dreams.

It seemed to Flynn that the entire place spoke of very specific, very high-toned taste.

He wandered over to a painting of a woman rising up out of a dark blue pool. There was a sense of speed about it, of sexuality, and of power.

"She's beautiful. Does she live in the sea or on the land?"

Malory arched her brow. At least he'd asked an intelligent question.

"I think she has yet to choose." She pondered him as he wandered around. He seemed more . . . well, male, she supposed, here in her place than he had on the sidewalk or stalking around the largely unfurnished room in his own house.

"What are you doing here?"

"First, I came because I wanted to see you again."

"Why?"

"You're really pretty." Because he found it both relaxing and entertaining to look at her, he hooked his thumbs in his front pockets and did just that. "You might think that's a shallow reason, but I like to think it's simply basic. If people didn't like looking at attractive things, we wouldn't have any art."

"How long did it take you to think of that one?"

His grin was fast and appreciative. "Not long at all. I'm pretty quick. Have you had dinner?"

"No, but I have plans. Why else are you here?"

"Let's do this part first. You haven't had dinner tomorrow night yet. Would you like to have dinner with me?"

"I don't think that's a good idea."

"Because you're annoyed with me? Or because you're not interested?"

"You're pretty annoying."

Those lazy-river eyes flirted. "Not once you get to know me. Ask anybody."

No, she had a feeling he wouldn't stay annoying. He'd be entertaining and interesting. And trouble. Plus, however attractive he was, he was anything but her type. "I've got enough on my plate without dating a man who has terrible taste in furniture and questionable taste in pets."

She glanced toward the patio as she said it, then couldn't stop the laugh as she saw Moe's ugly face pressed hopefully against the glass.

"You don't really hate dogs."

"Of course I don't hate dogs. I like dogs."
She angled her head to study the furry face.
"I don't think that is a dog."

"They swore he was when I got him from
the pound."

Her eyes went soft. "You got him from the
pound."

Aha, a chink in the defensive wall. He
stepped over so they could study Moe together. "He was a lot smaller then. I went in
to do a story on the shelter, and he sort of
came, well, gamboling up to me, looked at
me like he was saying, Okay, I've been waiting for you to show. Let's go home. I was a
goner."

"What does 'Moe' stand for? 'Mountain'?"

"He looks like Moe. You know, Moe
Howard." When her face stayed blank,
Flynn sighed. "Women, they don't know
what they're missing when it comes to the
courageous comedy and wit of The Three
Stooges."

"Yes, yes, we do know what we're missing. We miss it on purpose." Realizing they
were standing close, she took a deliberate
step back. "Was there something else?"

"I started running down these people you

guys are tangled up with. Liam Pitte, Rowena O'Meara. At least those are the names they're using."

"Why shouldn't those *be* their names?"

"Because when I used my incredible skills and talents, I found no record of anyone under those names that jibes with the new owners of Warrior's Peak. No social security numbers, no passport numbers, no driver's licenses, business licenses. No corporate paper trail for this Triad. At least none that connects to them."

"They're not American," she began, then blew out a breath. "Okay, no passport numbers. Maybe you didn't find it yet, or maybe they've used different names to buy the house."

"Maybe. It'll be interesting to find out, because right now it's looking like they popped out of thin air."

"I'd like to know more about the Daughters of Glass. The more I know about them, the better chance I have of finding the key."

"I'll call my grandmother, get more details of the legend. I can fill you in over dinner tomorrow."

She considered him, then looked back toward the dog. He was willing to help, and she only had four weeks. On a personal front, she would keep it simple. Friendly, but simple. At least until she'd decided what to do about him.

"Would that be a table for two or for three?"

"Two."

"All right. You can pick me up at seven."

"Great."

"And you can go out that way." She pointed toward the patio door.

"No problem." He walked to the door, glanced back. "You really are pretty," he said, then eased the door open just enough to squeeze out.

She watched him unhook the dog, watched him stagger under the weight when Moe leaped up to lavishly kiss his face. She waited until they'd trotted off before she chuckled.

Chapter Five

Malory found Zoe's little house easily enough. It was a tiny box on a narrow stamp of lawn. But it had been painted a cheerful yellow with bright white trim. A colorful patch of flowers bloomed vigorously along either side of the door.

Even if Malory hadn't been sure of the address, hadn't recognized Zoe's car parked at the curb, she'd have known the house by the boy in the yard, tossing a ball high in the air, then racing to catch it.

He looked almost eerily like his mother. The dark hair, the long-lidded eyes in a pixie face. He had a slight build clad in ripped jeans and a Pittsburgh Pirates T-shirt.

When he spotted Malory, he stood, legs

apart, flipping the ball lightly into the pocket of his glove.

He had the cautious and somewhat arrogant stance of a boy who'd had "don't talk to strangers" drummed into his head, and thought he was old enough, smart enough, to handle himself with one anyway.

"You must be Simon. I'm Malory Price, a friend of your mother's." She kept a smile on her face as the boy sized her up—and she wished she knew more about baseball than that it involved a number of men throwing, hitting, and trying to catch a ball and running around a field.

"She's in the house. I can get her." His way of doing so was to trot toward the door and shout, "Mom! There's a lady out here to see you!"

Moments later, Zoe opened the screen door, stood there wiping her hands on a dish towel. Somehow, despite the baggy shorts, old shirt, and bare feet, she still managed to look exotic.

"Oh. Malory." She lifted a hand to fiddle with one of the buttons of her shirt. "I wasn't expecting . . ."

"If this is a bad time—"

"No, no, of course not. Simon, this is

Miss Price. One of the ladies I'm going to be working with for a while."

"Okay. Hi. Can I go over to Scott's now? I finished mowing the lawn."

"Looks great. Do you want a snack first?"

"Nuh-uh." At her arch look, he grinned, showing a missing tooth and sudden, dazzling charm. "I mean, no thanks."

"Go ahead, then. Have a good time."

"Yes!" He started to race off, then skidded to a halt when she spoke his name in a tone that Malory assumed mothers developed through hormonal changes during gestation.

He rolled his eyes, but made sure his back was to Zoe as he did. Then he gave Malory a quick and easy smile. "Nice to meet you, and all."

"Nice to meet you, and all too, Simon."

He dashed off, like an inmate escaping the prison walls.

"He's gorgeous."

At Malory's statement, Zoe's face lit up with pride and pleasure. "He really is, isn't he? Sometimes I'll sneak to the window while he's out in the yard and just look at him. He's my whole world."

"I could see that. And now you're worried

that what we've done could hurt him some-how."

"Worrying about Simon is part of my job description. Listen, I'm sorry, come in. I used to spend Saturdays at the salon, so I thought I'd take advantage of having this one off and dig in around here."

"You've got a pretty house." She stepped inside the door, looked around. "A *very* pretty house."

"Thanks." Zoe looked around as well, grateful that she'd finished buffing up the living room. The pillows were plumped on the bright and cheery blue slipcovers of the sofa, and the old coffee table she'd an-tiqued was free of dust and held a trio of bottles filled with late-summer daisies snipped from her own little flower bed. The rug her grandmother had hooked when Zoe herself was a child was freshly vacuumed.

"These are great." Malory wandered over to look at the framed prints of foreign lo-cales grouped on a wall.

"They're just postcards I matted and framed. I always ask customers to pick me up a postcard when they go on a trip."

"They're really clever, and fun."

"I like to, you know, put things together.

Find stuff at yard sales or flea markets and haul it home, fix it up. It makes it yours that way, plus it doesn't cost a lot of money. Ah, would you like something to drink?"

"I would, if I'm not holding you up."

"No. I don't think I've had a Saturday off in . . ." She skimmed her fingers through her hair. "Ever," She decided. "It's nice to be home, and to have company."

Malory had a feeling that she was about to be invited to sit down while Zoe went back to the kitchen. To avoid that, she walked over and angled herself toward the doorway. "Did you plant the flowers yourself?"

"Simon and I did." With no choice, Zoe led the way into the kitchen. "I don't have any soft drinks. Sorry, but I can't keep them around with Simon. I've got some lemonade."

"That's great."

She'd obviously caught Zoe in the midst of a major kitchen cleaning, but still the room exuded the same casual charm as the living area.

"I love this." She trailed a finger over the mint-green paint of a cupboard. "It really shows what someone can do with imagination, taste, and time."

"Wow." Zoe took a squat glass pitcher out of the refrigerator. "That's quite a compliment coming from somebody like you. I mean, somebody who knows art. I wanted to have pretty things but still make a place where Simon could run around like a boy. And it's just the right size for us. I don't care about the million dollars."

She set her company glasses on the counter, shook her head. "Boy, does that sound stupid. Of course I *care* about the million dollars. What I mean is I don't need a million. I just want enough so we're secure. I only got into this because it seemed so interesting, and because the twenty-five thousand was like a miracle."

"And because that night, up at Warrior's Peak, was so compelling, so dramatic? Like we were all the stars of our own movie."

"Yes." Zoe let out a laugh as she poured. "I got caught up in the idea of it all, but I never considered, not for a minute, that we'd be taking any kind of risk."

"I don't know that we are. I'm not going to worry about that until we know more. But I don't have a child to consider. I wanted to come by and say that if you want to back out, I understand."

"I've been thinking about it. One of the advantages of serious cleaning is it's good thinking time. Do you want to take these out in the back? I've got some chairs out there. It's kind of a nice spot."

They walked out, and it was a nice spot—that tidy little yard, the two Adirondack chairs painted the same sunny yellow as the house, and a big, shady maple tree.

Once they were seated, Zoe took a deep breath. "If Pitte and Rowena are some kind of lunatics who've targeted us for some reason, there's no backing out. It won't matter. And if they are, doing whatever we can to find the keys makes the most sense. If they're not, then we should keep our word."

"It sounds like we're on the same track. I'm toying with going back up there to talk to them again, get another impression. In a day or two," Malory nodded, "after we—I hope—find out a little more. I know Dana will be zeroing in on the books, and Flynn's already heating up the Internet. If he finds anything, he'll tell me at dinner tonight."

"Dinner? You're going out with Flynn?"

"Apparently." Malory frowned into her

lemonade. "Five minutes after he left my apartment I was wondering how he talked me into it."

"He's awfully cute."

"Any guy would look cute beside that big, ugly dog."

"And he was flirting with you." Zoe gestured with her glass so that the ice clinked. "Big time."

"That I got. Flirting isn't on the agenda for the next few weeks if I'm going to focus on finding the first key."

"Flirting with a cute guy's a nice side benefit." Zoe sighed, sat back and wiggled toes that she'd painted poppy pink. "Or at least I seem to recall it was, from the dim, dark past."

"Are you kidding?" Surprised, Malory looked back at Zoe's sexy faerie face. "Men must hit on you all the time."

"The initial sortie usually stops dead when they find out I've got a kid." She shrugged. "And I'm not interested in the let's-get-naked-and-keep-it-casual deal. I've been there."

"Right now, I'm not interested in the let's-get-naked-and-make-it-serious deal. I have to figure out what I'm going to do with the rest of my life. My current windfall isn't going to last forever, but it does give me time to decide if I really want my own business, and how to go about it if I do."

"That's something else I was thinking about today. I'm going to have to get back to work. But the thought of starting a new job, with new people, out at the mall . . ." Zoe puffed out her cheeks and blew a hard breath. "And the last thing I want is to try to run a salon out of the house. Nobody takes you seriously when you do that. They start thinking hair's your hobby instead of your job. Plus, where you live isn't home anymore, and I'm not taking that away from Simon the way it was taken away from me."

"Your mother did hair out of your house?"

"Trailer." Zoe shrugged. "She did the best she could, considering we lived a couple miles outside Nowhere, West Virginia. My daddy took off when I was twelve, and I was the oldest of four."

"That's rough. I'm sorry."

"Rough on all of us, but like I said, she did the best she could. I'm just hoping to do better."

"I'd say making a pretty house and home

for you and your son means you're doing absolutely fine."

Color washed into her face. "Thanks. Anyway, I thought I'd start scouting around, see if I could find a place for rent that I could outfit for a salon."

"If you find one, see if you can find a nice storefront for me and my artworks shop." With a laugh, Malory set her glass aside. "Or maybe we should just combine the two and go into business together. Art and beauty, one-stop shopping. I've got to go."

She rose. "I'm going to swing by and see Dana, then go home and see if I get a brainstorm over that stupid clue. You want to plan for the three of us to get together one day early next week? A powwow."

"Fine with me, as long as we can work around Simon's schedule."

"We can do that. I'll call you."

She didn't know if it qualified as a brainstorm, but it was at least a direction.

Malory studied the clue line by line, searching for metaphors and hidden meanings, double entendres, loose connections.

Then she stepped back again to look at it as a whole.

There were mentions of the goddess. And the keys themselves were reputed to unlock imprisoned souls. Put all that together, she decided, and you had a sort of religious reference.

With that in mind, she spent the rest of the day going through every church and temple in the Valley.

She came home empty-handed, but she felt she'd done something positive with her day.

She dressed for dinner, keeping it simple with a sleeveless black top and black cropped pants, topped with a tailored jacket the color of strawberries.

At exactly seven, she was sliding into heeled sandals and preparing to wait. In her experience she was the only one who habitually made it a point to be on time.

So it was a surprise, a pleasant one, to hear the knock on her door even as she was checking the contents of her purse.

"You're prompt," she said to Flynn when she opened the door.

"Actually, I was here ten minutes ago, but I didn't want to seem anxious." He handed her a small bouquet of baby roses, nearly the same color as her jacket. "You look amazing."

"Thanks." She eyed him as she sniffed the rosebuds. He *was* cute, she thought. Dog or no dog. "I'll put these in water. Very nice touch, by the way."

"I thought so. Moe wanted to go for candy, but I held out for flowers."

She stopped. "He's not out there, is he?"

"No, no, he's home, making do with kibble and the Bugs Bunny marathon on the Cartoon Network. Moe's nuts about Bugs."

"I bet." She arranged the flowers in a clear glass vase. "Do you want a drink before we go?"

"Depends. Can you walk three blocks in those shoes or would you rather drive it?"

"I can walk three miles in heels. I'm a professional female."

"Can't argue with that. And because I can't, I'd like to do what I've been thinking about doing since I landed on top of you."

He moved in. That's what Malory would think later, when her brain started to function normally again. He simply moved into her, ran his hands up the sides of her body, over her shoulders, along her throat, then cupped her face in them.

It was all very slow, all very smooth. Then his mouth was on hers, taking its own sweet time. Somehow she was backed against the counter, pressed snugly between it and his body. Somehow her hands were gripping his hips, her fingers digging in.

And somehow she was sliding into the kiss without a single murmur of protest.

His fingers threaded back into her hair, and he nipped, not so playfully, at her bottom lip. When her breath caught, the tone of the kiss changed from flirty warmth to flashing heat.

"Whoa. Wait." She managed to catch the fading echo of warning bells ringing in her head, but her body stayed plastered against his.

"Okay. In a minute."

He needed another minute of her, of the taste of her, and the feel of her. There was more here than he'd expected, and he'd expected quite a punch.

There was something erotically sharp about the flavor of her, as if her mouth was a rare delicacy that he'd only just been allowed to sample. And something so soft about her texture, all those clouds of gilded hair, all those lovely curves and dips.

He gave her lips one last rub with his, then eased back.

She stared at him, those blue eyes he'd decided were irresistible, now wide and wary.

"Maybe . . ." She hoped the long, slow breath would level her voice again. "Maybe we should just start walking now."

"Sure." He offered a hand, and found himself flattered when she not only evaded it, but skirted around him to get her purse. "I figured if I kissed you now, I wouldn't be thinking about it all during dinner and lose track of the conversation."

He went to the door, opened it for her. "The trouble is, now that I have kissed you, I'm probably going to be thinking about kissing you again all during dinner and lose track of the conversation. So if you notice that my mind wanders, you'll know where and why."

"You think I don't know why you just said that." She walked out into the shimmering evening light with him. "By saying that, you'll plant the seed in my head so I'll be thinking about you kissing me all through dinner. Or that's the plan."

"Damn, you're good. If you're quick enough to unravel the dastardly plots of men regarding sex, the puzzle of the key ought to be child's play to you."

"You'd think so, wouldn't you? But the simple fact is I've had more experience with the dastardly plots of men regarding sex than I have with puzzles regarding goddesses and mythological spells."

"I don't know why"—he caught her hand in his, grinned at the sidelong look she sent him—"but I find that very exciting. If I ply you with wine at dinner, will you tell me about those experiences? There may be some plots I've missed along the way."

"You're going to buy me a martini, then we'll see."

He'd chosen one of the town's prettiest restaurants and had arranged for a table on the back terrace with a view of the mountains.

By the time she was sipping her martini, she was relaxed again. "I'd like to discuss the key. If I find your attention wandering, I'll kick you under the table."

"So noted. I'd just like to say one thing first."

"Go ahead."

He leaned toward her, breathed deep. "You smell terrific."

She leaned toward him. "I know. Now, would you like to know what I did today?" She waited a beat, then kicked him lightly on the ankle.

"What? Yes. Sorry."

She lifted her glass for another sip to hide her amusement. "First I went to see Zoe."

She relayed the gist of their conversation, pausing when the first course was served.

"The little yellow house." Flynn nodded as he brought the look of it into his mind. "Used to be dog-shit brown. She's really fixed it up. I've seen the kid in the yard, now that I think about it."

"Simon. He looks just like her. It's almost spooky."

"Now that you mention it, I would've put that together when I met her if I'd been able to take my eyes off you for two minutes."

Her lips twitched, and damn it, she was flattered. "You're very good at that—both timing and delivery."

"Yeah, it's a gift."

"Then I went to see Dana at her apartment. She was buried in books and brooding."

"Two of her best things."

"She hasn't been able to track down a version of the Daughters of Glass story yet, but she's working on it. Then I got this idea. Goddesses equal worship. All the reading I've been doing indicates that a lot of churches were built on pagan worship sites. Most Christian holy days coincide with the early pagan holy days, which were based on seasons, agriculture, that sort of thing. So I went to church. In fact I went to every church and temple in a twenty-mile radius."

"That's an interesting connection. Good, clear thinking."

"That's one of my major skills. I kept going over and over the clue. Look within, look without, singing goddess, and so on. So I went looking. Didn't expect to walk in and see the key waiting for me on a pew. But I thought maybe I'd see the symbol of it, you know? Something worked into a stained-glass window or a molding. But I didn't."

"It was still a good idea."

"A better one might be to go back to that house and talk to Rowena and Pitte again."

"Maybe. Want to know what I found out?"

"I do."

He waited while their entrées were served, then studied her fish and his steak. "How do you feel about surf and turf?"

"Amenable." They cut off portions, passed them.

"You know, this could develop into a serious deal. You and me? A lot of people are fussy about sharing food. I never get that." He sampled the steak. "I mean, it's food. You're supposed to eat it. What's the difference if it was on somebody else's plate first?"

"That's an interesting element to factor into a potential relationship. Now, what did you find out?"

"I talked to my grandmother about the story. There were some details I didn't remember clearly. First, there was dissension in the ranks over the god-king making a mortal his queen. It was okay to fool around with mortals, but he brought her behind the Curtain of Power—or the Curtain of Dreams. It's called both. And he took her as his wife. Because of this, some of the gods set themselves apart from the young king and his mortal wife, established their own rule."

"Politics."

"Can't get away from it. Naturally, this didn't sit too well with the king. There are other stories, full of war and intrigue and heroics, and that brings us to the daughters. Beloved by their parents, and by those loyal to the king and his wife. Each had beauty, as you'd expect, and each had power—a talent. One was an artist, one a bard, and one a warrior. Devoted to each other, they grew up in the kingdom, taught by a young goddess of magic, guarded by the king's most trusted warrior god. Either the teacher or the guard was to be with them at all times, to keep them safe from the plots surrounding them."

"In the painting there were two figures, a man and a woman, in the background. They seemed to be in an embrace."

Flynn gestured with his fork, then speared more steak. "That fits with what's coming. The king's advisers were campaigning to have the daughters marry three gods of rank from the opposing faction. To unite the kingdom again. But the self-proclaimed king of the opposing faction didn't like the idea of giving up his throne. Power had corrupted him, and his thirst for more, for complete dominance of this, let's say, netherworld, and the mortal one, consumed him. He wanted to kill the daughters, but he knew that if he did, all but his most devoted followers would turn against him. So he devised a plot, and the two who were closest to the daughters aided him, by falling in love."

"They betrayed the daughters?"

"Not purposely." He tipped more wine into their glasses. "By distraction. By looking at each other rather than looking after their charges. And as the daughters were young women, fond of their keepers, they made it easy for the lovers to slip away from time to time. And one day when they were unprotected, the spell was cast."

"Their souls were stolen."

"It's more than that. Are you going to eat the rest of that steak?"

"Hmm." She glanced down at her plate. "No. Do you want it?"

"For Moe. I go back empty-handed, he'll sulk." He asked the waiter to box up the leftovers, then smiled at Malory. "Dessert?"

"No, just coffee. Tell me the rest."

"Two coffees, a crème brûlée, and two spoons. You'll never hold out against the crème brûlée," he said to Malory, then leaned forward to finish the tale. "The bad king's a clever guy, and a sorcerer. He doesn't take heat for slaying innocents, and he turns the good king's choices and policy against him. If a mortal is fit to be queen, if three half-mortals are worthy of rank, then let the mortals prove it. Only mortals can break the spell. Until that's done, the daughters will sleep—unharmed. If mortal women, one to represent each daughter, can find each of the three keys, then the Box of Souls will be unlocked, the daughters' souls restored, and the kingdoms united."

"And if they fail?"

"The most popular version, according to my granny, has the bad king setting a time limit. Three thousand years—one millennium for each daughter. If the keys aren't found and the box unlocked within that time, he alone rules, both the god-world and the mortal."

"I never understand why anyone wants to rule the world. Seems like one big headache to me." She pursed her lips when the dish of crème brûlée was set between them. Flynn was right, she decided. She wasn't going to be able to hold out against it. "What happened to the lovers?"

"A couple of versions of that, too." He dipped his spoon in at one end of the dish while Malory dipped into the other. "My grandmother's pick is the one that has the grieving king sentencing the lovers to death, but his wife intervened, asking for mercy. Instead of execution, banishment. They were cast out through the Curtain of Dreams, forbidden to return until they found the three mortal women who would unlock the box of souls. And so they wander the earth, gods living as mortals, in search of the triad who will release not only the souls of the daughters but their own as well."

"Rowena and Pitte think they're the teacher and the warrior?"

It pleased him that their conclusions meshed. "That would be my take. You've got a couple of weirdos on your hands, Malory. It's a nice faerie tale. Romantic, colorful. But when people start casting themselves and others in the roles, you're edging into psychoville."

"You're forgetting the money."

"No, I'm not. The money worries me. Seventy-five thousand means it's not a game to them, not a little role-playing entertainment. They're serious. Either they actually believe the myth or they're seeding the ground for a con."

She toyed with another spoonful of the crème brûlée. "With the twenty-five thousand, I now have approximately twenty-five thousand, two hundred and five dollars, which includes the twenty I found in a jacket pocket this morning. My parents are fairly average middle-class people. They're not rich or influential. I don't have any rich or influential friends or lovers. I've got nothing worth conning."

"Maybe they're looking for something else, something you haven't thought of. But back to those lovers for a minute. Do you have any poor ones?"

She sipped her coffee, measuring him over the rim. The sun had set while they'd had dinner. Now it was candlelight that flickered between them. "Not at the moment."

"Here's a coincidence. Neither do I."

"I'm in the market for a key, Flynn, not a lover."

"You're assuming the key exists."

"Yes, I am. If I didn't assume that, I wouldn't bother to look for it. And I gave my word I would."

"I'll help you find it."

She set her cup down again. "Why?"

"A lot of reasons. One, I'm just a naturally curious guy, and however this thing works out, it's an interesting story." He skimmed a fingertip over the back of her hand, and the little thrill danced straight up her arm. "Two, my sister's involved. Three, I'll get to be around you. The way I figure it, you won't be able to hold out against me any more than you could hold out against the crème brûlée."

"Is that confidence or conceit?"

"Just fate, sweetie. Look, why don't we go back to my place and . . . Well, hell, I wasn't thinking about kissing you again until you gave me that snotty look. Now I've lost my train of thought."

"I'm not having any trouble following that train."

"Okay, that wasn't my track, but I'm willing to jump on board. What I was going to say was we could go back and do some research. I can show you what I've got so far, which is basically nothing. I can't dig up any data on your benefactors, at least not under the names they used to buy the Peak, or any variations of those names."

"I'll leave the research to you and Dana for now." She shrugged. "I've got some other trails to follow."

"Such as?"

"Logic. Goddesses. There are a couple of New Age shops in the area. I'm going to check them out. Then there's the painting. I'm going to find out who painted that portrait, see what else he or she has done, and where those paintings might be. Who owns them, how they acquired them. I need to take another trip up to Warrior's Peak, have another talk with Pitte and Rowena, and get another look at that painting. A better look."

"I'll go with you. There's a story here, Malory. This could be a huge scam, which would make it big news and my duty to report it."

She stiffened up. "You don't have any proof that Rowena and Pitte aren't legitimate—possibly loony, yes, but not crooks."

"Easy." He held up a hand for peace. "I'm not writing anything until I have all the facts. I can't get all the facts until I meet all the players. I need an entrée to that house. You're it. In exchange you get the benefit of my keen investigative skills and dogged reporter's determination. I go with you, or I talk Dana into taking me up there."

She tapped a finger on th table while she considered her options. They might not talk to you. In fact, they may not like it that we've brought you into this, even on a peripheral level."

"Leave that part to me. Getting into places where I'm not wanted is part of my job description."

"Is that how you got into my apartment last night?"

"Ouch. Why don't we run up there tomorrow morning? I can pick you up at ten."

"All right." What harm could it do to have him along?

"There's no need to walk me all the way to the door," Malory said as they approached her apartment building.

"Sure there is. I'm just an old-fashioned guy."

"No, you're not." She muttered it as she

opened her purse for her key. "I'm not asking you in."

"Okay."

She slanted him a look as they stepped up to the door. "You say that like you're an affable, easygoing man. You're not that, either. It's a ploy."

He grinned. "It is?"

"Yes. You're stubborn and pushy and more than a little arrogant. You get away with it because you put on that big, charming smile and that I-wouldn't-hurt-a-fly demeanor. But they're just tools to help you get what you want."

"God, you see right through me." Watching her, he twirled a lock of her hair around his finger. "Now I either have to kill you or marry you."

"And being appealing on some screwy level doesn't make you less annoying. Therein lies the flaw."

At those words he caught her face in his hands and crushed his lips enthusiastically to hers. The heat shot straight up from her belly and seemed to burst out the top of her head.

"Neither does that," she managed. She shoved her key in the lock, pushed the door open. Then shut it in his face. Half a beat later, she yanked it open. "Thanks for dinner."

He rocked gently on his heels when the door shut in his face a second time. When he strolled away, he was whistling, and thinking Malory Price was the kind of woman who made a man's life really interesting.

Chapter Six

Dana gulped down her first cup of coffee while standing naked in her tiny kitchen, eyes closed, brain dead. She drained it, hot, black, and strong, before letting out a soft whimper of relief.

She downed half the second cup on the way to the shower.

She didn't mind mornings, mainly because she was never awake enough to object to them. Her routine rarely varied. Her alarm buzzed, she slapped it off, then rolled out of bed and stumbled into the kitchen, where the automatic coffeemaker already had the first pot ready.

One and a half cups later, her vision was clear enough for a shower.

By the time she was done, her circuits were up and running, and she was too awake to sulk about being awake. She drank the second half of the second cup and listened to the morning news report while she dressed for the day.

With a toasted bagel and her third cup of coffee, she settled down with her current breakfast book.

She'd turned only the second page when the knock on her door interrupted her most sacred of rituals.

"Damn it."

She marked her place. Her annoyance faded, a little, when she opened the door to Malory.

"Aren't you the bright-and-early girl?"

"Sorry. You said you were working this morning, so I thought you'd be up and around by now."

"Up, anyway." She leaned on the jamb a moment and studied the minute green checks of the soft cotton shirt that precisely matched the color of Malory's pleated trousers. Just as the dove-gray slides she wore exactly matched the tone and texture of her shoulder bag.

"Do you always dress like that?" Dana wondered.

"Like what?"

"Perfect."

With a little laugh, Malory looked down at herself. "I'm afraid so. It's a compulsion."

"Looks good on you, too. I'll probably end up hating you for it. Come on in anyway."

The room was a compact, informal library. Books stood or were stacked on the shelves that ran along two walls from floor to ceiling, sat on the tables like knickknacks, trooped around the room like soldiers. They struck Malory as more than knowledge or entertainment, even more than stories and information. They were color and texture, in a haphazard yet somehow intricate decorating scheme.

The short leg of the L-shaped room boasted still more books, as well as a small table that held the remains of Dana's breakfast.

With her hands on her hips, Dana watched Malory's perusal of her space. She'd seen the reaction before. "No, I haven't read them all, but I will. And no, I don't know how many I have. Want coffee?"

"Let me just ask this. Do you ever actually use the services of the library?"

"Sure, but I need to own them. If I don't have twenty or thirty books right here, waiting to be read, I start jonesing. That's my compulsion."

"Okay. I'll pass on the coffee, thanks. I already had a cup. Two, and I'm wired."

"Two, and I can just manage to form complete sentences. Bagel?"

"No, but go ahead. I wanted to catch you before you left for work. Fill you in."

"Fill away." Dana gestured to the second chair at the table, then sat to finish her breakfast.

"I'm going back up to Warrior's Peak this morning. With Flynn."

Dana's lip curled. "I figured he'd horn in. And hit on you."

"Are either of those things a problem for you?"

"No. He's smarter than he comes across. That's one of the ways he gets people to spill their guts to him. If he hadn't horned in, I'd have baited him until he helped out. As for hitting on you, I had to figure he'd go for either you or Zoe. Flynn really likes women, and they really like him."

Malory thought of the way he'd moved in on her in her kitchen, the way she'd gone pliant as putty when he had. "There's a definite chemical reaction there, but I haven't decided if I like him or not."

Dana crunched on her bagel. "Might as well give in to it. He'll just wear you down, which is another thing he's really good at. He's like a damn Border collie."

"Excuse me?"

"You know how they herd sheep?" She used her free hand, zagging it right and left to demonstrate. "How they keep heading them off, working them around until the sheep end up going where the collie wants them to go? That's Flynn. You'll think, nope, I want to go over here, and he's thinking, well, you'll be better off over there. So you end up over there before you realize you've been herded."

She licked cream cheese off her finger. "And the hell of it is, when you find yourself there you almost always realize you *are* better off. He stays alive by never saying I told you so."

She'd gone to dinner with him, hadn't she? Malory considered. Kissed him—

twice. Three times if she was going to be technical. And he was not only coming with her to Warrior's Peak, he was driving her. Huh.

"I don't like being maneuvered."

Dana's expression was a combination of pity and amusement. "Well, we'll see how it goes." She rose, gathering her dishes. "What are you hoping for with Rowena and Pitte?"

"I don't expect to get much from them. It's the painting." Malory followed Dana into the little kitchen. It didn't surprise her to find books here as well, stacked in an open-fronted pantry where the average cook would have stored food staples.

"The painting's important somehow," she continued while Dana rinsed off the dishes. "What It says, and who said it."

She took a moment to explain the rest of the tale as Flynn had relayed it to her over dinner.

"So they're taking on the roles of the teacher and the guard."

"That's the theory," Malory confirmed. "I'm interested in how they'll react when I broach it. And I can use Flynn to distract them long enough to give me time to get another look at the painting and take a couple of pictures of it. That could lead to other paintings with similar themes. It might be helpful."

"I'll do a search on mythological art this morning." Dana checked her watch. "I've got to go. The three of us should get together on this as soon as we can."

"Let's see what we come up with today."

They walked out together, and Malory stopped on the sidewalk. "Dana. Is it just crazy to do all this?"

"Damn right. Call me when you get back from the Peak."

It was a more pleasant, if less atmospheric, drive on a sunny morning. As a passenger, Malory could indulge herself with the scenery and wonder what it was like to live high on a ridge where the sky seemed only a hand span away and the world was spread out like a painting below.

A fitting view for gods, she supposed. Lofty and dramatic. She had no doubt Rowena and Pitte had chosen it for its power as much as for the privacy.

In another few weeks, when those ele-
gantly rolling hills felt the chill of fall, the colors would stun the eye and catch the
breath.

Mists would hover in the morning, sliding
into those folds and dips between the hills,
spreading like sparkling pools until the sun
dissolved them.

And still the house would stand, black as
midnight, with its fanciful lines etched
against the sky. Guarding the valley. Or
watching it. What did it see, she wondered,
year after year across the decades?

What did it know?

The question brought on a shudder, a
sudden sharp sense of dread.

"Cold?"

She shook her head, and rolled down her
window. All at once the car seemed hot and
stuffy. "No. I'm spooking myself, that's all."

"If you don't want to do this now—"

"I want to do it. I'm not afraid of a couple
of rich eccentrics. In fact, I liked them. And I
want to see the painting again. I can't stop
thinking about it. Whatever direction my
mind goes off in, I keep coming back to the
painting."

She glanced out her window, into the

deep, leafy woods. "Would you want to live up here?"

"Nope."

Intrigued, she looked back at him. "That was fast."

"I'm a social animal. I like having people around. Moe might like it." He gazed into the rearview mirror to see Moe, nose jammed into the narrow window opening, floppy ears flying.

"I can't believe you brought the dog."

"He likes to ride in the car."

She angled around, studied Moe's blissful expression. "Obviously. Have you ever considered getting him clipped so his hair isn't in his eyes?"

"Don't say clipped." Flynn winced as he muttered the word. "We're still not over the whole neutering deal."

He slowed as they drove along the wall that edged the estate. Then stopped to study the twin warriors who flanked the iron gate.

"They don't look friendly. I camped up here a couple of times with some friends when I was in high school. The house was empty then, so we climbed over the wall."

"Did you go into the house?"

"There wasn't enough courage in a six-pack of beer for that, but we had a hell of a time freaking ourselves out. Jordan claimed he saw a woman walking on the parapet or whatever you call it. Swore he did. He wrote a book about her later, so I guess he saw something. Jordan Hawke," Flynn added. "You might've heard of him."

"Jordan Hawke wrote about Warrior's Peak?"

"He called it—"

"*Phantom Watch.* I read that book." As a ripple of fascination raced up her spine, she stared through the bars of the gates. "Of course. He described it all perfectly, but then he's a wonderful writer." She looked back at Flynn, suspiciously. "You're friends with Jordan Hawke?"

"Since we were kids. He grew up in the Valley. I guess we were sixteen—me, Jordan, and Brad—sucking down beers in the woods, slapping mosquitoes the size of sparrows, and telling very inventive lies about our sexual prowess."

"It's illegal to drink at sixteen," Malory said primly.

He shifted, and even through the shaded lenses of his sunglasses, she could see his eyes laughing. "Really? What were we thinking? Anyway, ten years later, Jordan's got his first bestseller, and Brad's off running the family empire—that would be lumber and the HomeMakers chain for Bradley Charles Vane IV, and I'm planning on heading to New York to be a hotshot reporter for the *Times.*"

Her eyebrows winged up. "You worked for the *New York Times*?"

"No, I never went. One thing and another," he said with a shrug. "Let's see what I can do about getting us through this gate."

Even as he started to step out of the car, the gate opened with a kind of otherworldly silence that sent a chill dancing along the nape of his neck. "Must really keep it lubed," he murmured. "And I guess somebody knows we're out here."

He slid back behind the wheel and drove through.

The house looked just as strange and stark and stunning in daylight as it had in a night storm. There was no magnificent stag to greet her, but the flag with its key emblem flew high and white, and rivers of flowers ran below. Gargoyles clung to the stone, and looked, to Malory's mind, as if they were considering leaping, not so playfully, on any visitor.

"I never got this close in the daylight." Slowly Flynn stepped out of the car.

"It's spooky."

"Yeah, but in a good way. It's terrific, like something you expect to see on a cliff above a raging sea. Too bad there's no moat. That would really top it off."

"Wait until you see the inside." Malory moved up beside him, and didn't object in the least when Flynn took her hand. The tickle at the back of her throat made her feel foolish and female.

"I don't know why I'm so nervous." She caught herself whispering it, then her hand jerked in Flynn's when the big entrance door opened.

Rowena stood framed in the towering doorway. She wore simple gray pants with a roomy shirt the color of the forest. Her hair spilled over her shoulders, her lips were unpainted, her feet bare. But however casual the outfit, she managed to look exotic, like some foreign queen on a quiet holiday.

Malory caught the glint of diamonds at her ears.

"How lovely." Rowena held out a hand on which rings sparkled elegantly. "How nice to see you again, Malory. And you've brought me such a handsome surprise."

"Flynn Hennessy. He's Dana's brother."

"Welcome. Pitte will be right along. He's just finishing up a call." She gestured them inside.

Flynn had to resist gawking at the foyer. "It doesn't seem like the kind of place you'd find telephones."

Rowena's chuckle was low, almost a purr. "We enjoy the advantages of technology. Come, we'll have tea."

"We don't want to put you to any trouble," Malory began, but Rowena waved her off.

"Guests are never any trouble."

"How did you find out about Warrior's Peak, Miss . . ."

"Rowena." She slid an arm silkily through Flynn's as she walked them to the parlor. "You must call me Rowena. Pitte always has an ear to the ground for an interesting spot."

"You travel a lot?"

"We do, yes."

"For work or pleasure?"

"Without pleasure, there's little point in work." She trailed a fingertip playfully down his arm. "Won't you sit? Ah, here's the tea."

Malory recognized the servant from her first visit. She brought the tea cart in silently, and left the same way.

"What business are you in?" Flynn asked.

"Oh, we do a bit of this and that, and some of the other. Milk?" she asked Malory as she poured. "Honey, lemon?"

"A little lemon, thank you. I have a lot of questions."

"I'm sure you do, as does your very attractive companion. How do you like your tea, Flynn?"

"Black's fine."

"So American. And what is your business, Flynn?"

He took the delicate cup she offered. His gaze was direct, and suddenly very cool. "I'm sure you already know. You didn't pick my sister's name out of a hat. You know everything you need to know about her, and that would include me."

"Yes." Rowena added both milk and honey to her own tea. Rather than looking insulted or chagrined, she looked pleased. "The newspaper business must be very interesting. So much information to be gathered, and dispersed. I imagine it takes a clever mind to know how to do both well. And here is Pitte."

He entered a room, Flynn thought, like a general. Measuring the field, gauging his ground, outlining his approach. However genial his smile, Flynn was certain there was a steely soldier behind it.

"Miss Price. What a pleasure to see you again." He took her hand, brought it to within an inch of his lips in a gesture that seemed too fluid not to be natural.

"Thanks for seeing us. This is Flynn—"

"Yes. Mr. Hennessy." He inclined his head. "How do you do?"

"Well enough."

"Our friends have questions and concerns," Rowena told him as she passed the cup of tea she'd already prepared.

"Naturally." Pitte took a seat. "You're wondering, I imagine, if we're . . ." He turned that mildly curious look to Rowena.

"Lunatics," she supplied, then lifted a plate. "Scones?"

"Ah, yes, lunatics." Pitte helped himself to a scone and a generous dollop of clotted cream. "I can assure you we're not, but then again, so would I if we were. So that's very little help to you. Tell me, Miss Price, are you having second thoughts about our arrangement?"

"I took your money and gave you my word."

His expression softened, very slightly. "Yes. To some that would make little difference."

"It makes all the difference to me."

"That could change," Flynn put in. "Depending on where the money comes from."

"Are you implying we could be criminals?" Now temper showed in the flush that swept Rowena's ice-edged cheekbones. "It shows considerable lack of courtesy to come into our home and accuse us of being thieves."

"Reporters aren't known for their courtesy, and neither are brothers when they're looking out for their sisters."

Pitte murmured something quiet and foreign, skimmed his long fingers over the back of Rowena's hand, the way a man might soothe a cat who was about to spit and claw. "Understood. It happens I've some skill in monetary matters. The money comes to us through perfectly legal means. We're neither lunatics nor criminals."

"Who are you?" Malory demanded before Flynn could speak again. "Where do you come from?"

"What do you think?" Pitte challenged softly.

"I don't know. But I think you believe you represent the teacher and the warrior who failed to protect the Daughters of Glass."

An eyebrow arched slightly. "You've learned more since you were here last. Will you learn more yet?"

"I intend to. You could help me."

"We're not free to help in that way. But I will tell you this. Not only teacher and warrior but companions and friends to those precious ones, and so only more responsible."

"It's only a legend."

The intensity in his eyes dimmed, and he leaned back again. "It must be, as such things are beyond the limits of your mind and the boundaries of your world. Still, I can promise you the keys exist."

"Where is the Box of Souls?" Flynn asked him.

"Safe."

"Could I see the painting again?" Now Malory turned to Rowena. "I'd like Flynn to see it."

"Of course." She rose and led the way into the room dominated by the portrait of the Daughters of Glass.

Malory heard Flynn catch his breath, then they were moving together closer to the painting. "It's even more magnificent than I remembered. Can you tell me who painted this?"

"Someone," Rowena said quietly, "who knew love, and grief."

"Someone who knows Malory. And my sister, and Zoe McCourt."

Rowena let out a sigh. "You're a cynic, Flynn, and a suspicious one. But as you've put yourself in the role of protector, I'll forgive you for it. We don't wish Malory, Dana, or Zoe any harm. Quite the opposite."

Something in her tone made him want to believe her. "It's pretty disconcerting to see my sister's face up there."

"You'd do whatever needed to be done to keep her safe and well. I understand that kind of loyalty and love. I admire and respect it. She's in no danger from me or Pitte. I can swear that to you."

He turned now, zeroing in on what hadn't been said. "But from someone else?"

"Life's a gamble," was all Rowena said. "Your tea's getting cold."

She turned toward the door just as Pitte stepped to it. "There seems to be a very large, very unhappy dog of some sort outside."

The temper and sharp words hadn't ruffled Flynn a bit, but that single statement made him wince. "He's mine."

"You have a dog?" The change in Rowena's tone was almost girlish. Everything about her seemed to go light and bright, then bubble out as she gripped Flynn's hand.

"He calls it a dog," Malory said under her breath.

Flynn merely gave her a sorrowful look before speaking to Rowena. "You like dogs?"

"Yes, very much. Could I meet him?"

"Sure."

"Ah, while you're introducing Rowena and Pitte to Moe, at their peril, could I take a minute to freshen up?" Casually, Malory gestured toward the powder room. "I remember where it is."

"Of course." For the first time since Malory had met her, Rowena seemed distracted. She already had a hand on Flynn's arm as they started down the hall. "What kind of a dog is he?"

"That's debatable."

Malory slipped into the powder room and counted to five. Slowly. Heart pounding, she opened the door a crack and did her best to peer up and down the corridor. Moving quickly now, she dashed back to the portrait, dragging out the little digital camera in her purse as she ran.

She took half a dozen full-length shots, then some of smaller details. With a guilty look over her shoulder, she shoved the camera back into the purse and pulled out her glasses, a plastic bag, and a small palette knife.

With her ears buzzing, she stepped up on the hearth and carefully, gently, scraped flakes of paint into the bag.

The entire process took less than three

minutes, but her palms were slick with sweat, her legs loose and wobbly by the time she'd finished. She took another moment to compose herself, then strolled—with what she hoped was casual ease—out of the room and out of the house.

The instant she stepped outside, she stopped dead. There was the regal and magnificent Rowena sitting on the ground with a mountain of dog sprawled over her lap.

And she was giggling.

"Oh, he's wonderful. Such a big sweetheart. What a good boy you are." She bent her head and nuzzled Moe's fur. His tail beat like a jackhammer. "What a kind, pretty boy." She looked up at Flynn and beamed. "Did he find you or did you find him?"

"It was sort of mutual." One dog lover recognized another. Tucking his thumbs in his pockets, Flynn scanned the expansive lawns, the slices of woods. "Big place like this, lots of room to run. You could have a pack of dogs."

"Yes. Well." Rowena lowered her head again and rubbed Moe's belly.

"We travel considerably." Pitte laid a hand on Rowena's hair, stroked it.

"How long do you plan to stay here?"

"When the three months is up, we'll move on."

"To?"

"That will depend. *A ghra.*"

"Yes. Yes." Rowena cuddled Moe another moment, then with a wistful sigh got to her feet. "You're very lucky to have such goodness in your life. I hope you treasure him."

"I do."

"I see you do, yes. You may be cynical and suspicious, but a dog like this knows a good heart."

"Yeah," Flynn agreed. "I believe that."

"I hope you'll bring him if you come back. He can run. Good-bye, Moe."

Moe sat up and lifted one massive paw with unaccustomed dignity.

"Wow. That's a new one." Flynn blinked as Moe politely allowed Rowena to shake his paw. "Hey, Mal! Did you see—"

As he said her name, Moe's head swiveled, and he was off at a sprint in Malory's direction, bringing a distressed yip to her throat as she braced for the onslaught.

Rowena called out, a single indecipherable word in a calm, brisk tone. Moe skidded to a halt inches from Malory's feet, plopped onto his butt. And once more lifted his paw.

"Well." Malory expelled a relieved breath. "That's more like it." She reached down, obligingly shook the offered paw. "Good for you, Moe."

"How the hell'd you do that?" Flynn wanted to know.

"I have a way with animals."

"I'll say. What was that, Gaelic?"

"Mmmm."

"Funny that Moe would understand a command in Gaelic when he mostly ignores them in plain English."

"Dogs understand more than words." She held out a hand for Flynn's. "I hope you'll all come back. We enjoy company."

"Thanks for your time." Malory walked to the car with Moe trotting happily beside her. The minute she sat, she tucked her purse on the floor like a guilty secret.

Rowena laughed, but the sound was a bit watery as Moe stuck his head out of the backseat window. She lifted a hand in a wave, then leaned against Pitte as Flynn drove away.

"I have real hope," she murmured. "I can't remember the last time I felt real hope. I—it frightens me. It actually frightens me to feel it."

Pitte wrapped an arm around her, drew her tighter to his side. "Don't weep, my heart."

"Foolish." She dashed a tear away. "To cry over a stranger's dog. When we get home . . ."

He shifted her, cupped her face in his hands. His tone was gentle, yet somehow urgent. "When we get home, you'll have a hundred dogs. A thousand."

"One will do." She rose on her toes to brush her lips across his.

In the car Malory let out a long, long breath.

"I take that sound of relief to mean you got the pictures."

"I did. I felt like an international art thief. I guess I have to give Moe points for being the main distraction. So, tell me what you thought of them."

"They're slick, smart, and full of secrets. But they don't seem crazy. They're used to money—real money. Used to drinking tea out of antique cups brought in by a servant. They're educated, cultured, and a little

snobby with it. The place is full of stuff—
fancy stuff. They've only been here a few
weeks, so they didn't furnish those rooms
locally. They had it shipped in. I should be
able to track that."

Frowning, he tapped his fingers on the
steering wheel. "She went goony on Moe."

"What?"

"She turned into a puddle the minute she
saw him. I mean, he's got a lot of charm,
but she melted. I have this impression of
her from inside. Cool, confident, aloof. The
kind of woman who's sexy because she
knows she's in charge. Strolling up Madison
Avenue with a Prada bag on her arm, or
running a board meeting in L.A. Power,
money, brains, and looks all wrapped up in
sex."

"I get it. You thought she was sexy."

"Last checkup, I had a pulse, so, yeah.
But you should've seen her face when Moe
jumped out of the car. All that polish, that
sheen just vanished. She lit up like Christ-
mas morning."

"So, she likes dogs."

"No, it was more. It wasn't the coochee-
coo that some fancy women do with dogs.
It was fall down on the ground, roll in the

grass, and gut-laugh. So why doesn't she have one?"

"Maybe Pitte won't have one around."

Flynn shook his head. "You're more observant than that. The guy would slice open a vein for her if she asked him to. Something strange about the way she got Moe to shake hands. Something strange about the whole deal."

"No argument. I'm going to concentrate on the painting, at least until one of us comes up with a different angle. I'll leave you to try to pin down Rowena and Pitte."

"I've got to cover a town hall meeting tonight. How about we get together tomorrow?"

He maneuvers. He herds. She remembered Dana's words and shot him a quick, suspicious look. "Define 'get together.' "

"I'll adjust the definition any way you want."

"I've got four weeks—less now—to find this key. I'm currently unemployed and have to figure out what I'm going to do, at least professionally, for the rest of my life. I recently ended a relationship that was going nowhere. Add up all the above, and it's very

clear I don't have time for dating and exploring a new personal relationship."

"Hold on a minute." He pulled off to the
side of the windy road, unhooked his seat
belt. He leaned over, took her shoulders,
and eased her over as far as her own belt
would allow while his mouth ravished hers.

A rocket of heat shot up her spine and left
its edgy afterburn in her belly.

"You've, ah, really got a knack for that,"
she managed when she could breathe
again.

"I practice as often as possible." To prove
it, he kissed her again. Slower this time.
Deeper. Until he felt her quiver. "I just
wanted you to add that to your equation."

"I was an art major. Math isn't my strong
suit. Come back here a minute." She
grabbed his shirt, yanked him to her, and let
herself go.

Everything inside her sparked. Blood and
bone and brain.

If this was what it meant to be herded,
she thought dimly, she could be flexible
about her direction.

When his hands clenched in her hair, she
felt a stir of power and anxiety that was as
potent as a drug.

"We really can't do this." But she was tugging his shirt out of his waistband, desperate to get her hands on flesh.

"I know. Can't." He fumbled with the buckle of her seat belt. "We'll stop in a minute."

"Okay, but first . . ." She brought his hand to her breast, then moaned as her heart seemed to tip into his palm.

He shifted her, cursed when he rapped his elbow on the steering wheel. And Moe, delighted with the prospect of a wrestling match, squeezed his head between the seats and slathered both of them with sloppy kisses.

"Oh, God!" Torn between laughter and shock, Malory scrubbed at her mouth. "I really, *really* hope that was your tongue."

"Ditto." Struggling to get his breath back, Flynn stared down at her. Her hair was sexily tousled, her face flushed, her mouth just a little swollen from the assault of his.

With the flat of his hand, he shoved Moe's face away and snapped out a curt order to sit. The dog flopped back on his seat and whined as if he'd been beaten with a club.

"I wasn't planning on moving this fast."

Malory shook her head. "I wasn't planning on moving at all. And I've *always* got a plan."

"Been a while since I tried this in a car parked on the side of the road."

"Me, too." She slid her gaze toward the pathetic sounds coming from the backseat. "Under the circumstances . . ."

"Yeah. Better not. I want to make love with you." He drew her up. "To touch you. To feel you move under my hands. I want that, Malory."

"I need to think. Everything about this is complicated, so I have to think about it." She certainly had to think about the fact that she'd nearly torn the man's clothes off in the front seat of a car, on the side of a public road, in broad daylight.

"My life's a mess, Flynn." The thought depressed her enough to have her pulse calming again. "Whatever the equation, I've screwed things up, and I have to get back on track. I don't do well with messy situations. So, let's slow this down a little."

He hooked a finger in the V of her blouse. "How much is a little?"

"I don't know yet. Oh, I can't stand it." She scooted around, leaned over the seat.

"Don't cry, you big baby." She ruffled the fur between Moe's ears. "Nobody's mad at you."

"Speak for yourself," Flynn grumbled.

Chapter Seven

I feel the sun, warm and somehow fluid like a quiet waterfall gliding from a golden river. It pours over me in a kind of baptism. I smell roses, and lilies, and some spicier flower that cuts the sweetness. I hear water, a playful trickle and plop as it rises up, then falls back into itself.

All these things slide over me, or I slide into them, but I see nothing but a dense white. Like a curtain I can't part.

Why am I not afraid?

Laughter floats toward me. Bright and easy and female. There's a youthful cheer in it that makes me smile, that brings a tickle of laughter to my own throat. I want to find the source of that laughter and join in.

Voices now, that quick bird-chatter that is again youth and female.

The sounds come and go, ebb and flow. Am I drifting toward it or away?

Slowly, slowly, the curtain thins. Only a mist now, soft as silken rain with sunlight sparkling through it. And through it, I see color. Such bold, rich color it sears through that thinning mist and stuns my eyes.

Tiles are gleaming silver and explode with sunlight in blinding flashes where the thick green leaves and hot-pink blossoms of trees don't shade or shelter. Flowers swim in pools or dance in swirling beds.

There are three women, girls, really, gathered around the fountain that plays its happy tune. It's their laughter I hear. One has a small harp in her lap, and the other a quill. But they're laughing at the wriggling puppy the third holds in her arms.

They're so lovely. There is about them a touching innocence that's so perfectly suited to the garden where they spend this bright afternoon. Then I see the sword sheathed at one's hip.

Innocent perhaps, but strong. There is power here; I can feel the tingle of it now sparking on the air.

And still I'm not afraid.

They call the puppy Diarmait, and set it down so it can romp around the fountain. Its excited yaps ring like bells. I see one girl slide her arm around the waist of another, and the third rest her head on the second's shoulder. There, they become a unit. A kind of triad. A whole of three parts that chatter about their new puppy, and laugh as he rolls gleefully in the flowers.

I hear them say names I know, somehow know, and look as they look. In the distance, in the shade of a tree that drips down with graceful branches heavy with jeweled fruit, are a couple caught in a passionate embrace.

He's tall and dark, and there's a strength to him I can sense might be terrible if roused. She's beautiful, and very slender. But there is about her, too, a sense of more.

They're desperately in love. I can feel that need, that heat inside me, throbbing like a wound.

Is love so painful?

The girls sigh over it. And they wish. Someday, they hope. Someday they will love like that—desire and romance, fear and joy all tied into one consuming entity. They

*will know the taste of a lover's lips, the thrill
of a lover's touch.*

Someday.

*We are, all of us, caught in that urgent
embrace, absorbed with our envy and our
dreams. The sky darkens. The colors dim. I
feel the wind now. Cold, cold as it spins
around and around. The sudden roar of it
screams in my ears. Blossoms tear from
branches, petals fly like bright bullets.*

*Now I'm afraid. Now I'm terrified even be-
fore I see the sly black shape of the snake
slither over those silver tiles, before I see the
shadow slink out of the trees and lift high
the glass box it holds in its black arms.*

*Words boom out. Though I press my
hands to my ears to block them, I hear them
inside my head.*

Mark this time and mark this hour when
I wield my awful power. Mortal souls of
daughters three forever will belong to
me. Their bodies lie in eternal sleep,
their souls imprisoned in this glass. The
spell will hold sure and deep unless
these things come to pass. Three keys
to find, to fit, only by mortal hands to
turn. Three thousand years in which to

learn. An instant more and souls will burn.

This test, this quest, to prove a mortal's worthiness. With these words I wind them, and with my art I bind them. These locks I seal and forge these keys, and here hurl them to the hand of destiny.

The wind dies, and the air goes still. There on those sun-washed tiles, the three girls lie, their eyes closed as if in sleep, their hands clasped. Three parts of one whole.

Beside them is a glass box, its clear panels leaded at the seams, its trio of locks glinting gold. Warm blue lights dance frantically inside it, seem to beat against the glass walls like trapped wings.

Three keys lie scattered around it.

And seeing them, I weep.

Malory was still shaky when she opened the door to Zoe.

"I got here as soon as I could. I had to get Simon off to school. You sounded so upset on the phone. What—"

"Dana's not here yet. I'd rather just go through this once. I made coffee."

"Great." Zoe put a hand on Malory's shoulder and simply lowered her into a chair. "I'll get it. You look like you still need to catch your breath. Kitchen that way?"

"Yeah." Grateful, Malory leaned back, rubbed her hands over her face.

"Why don't you tell me how your date with Flynn went the other night?"

"What? Oh. Good. Fine." She dropped her hands, then stared at them as if they belonged to someone else. "He seems almost normal without his dog. That must be Dana."

"I'll get it. Just sit." Zoe hurried out from the kitchen, heading Malory off before she could rise.

"Okay, where's the fire?" Dana demanded. Then stopped, sniffed. "Coffee. Don't make me beg for it."

"I'm getting it. Go sit with Malory," Zoe added under her breath.

Dana plopped down in a chair, pursed her lips, and gave Malory a long, hard stare. "You look terrible."

"Thanks so much."

"Hey, don't expect hugs and kisses when you get me out of bed and over here within twenty minutes and on one cup of coffee.

Besides, it's reassuring to know you don't roll out of bed looking perfect. What's up?"

Malory glanced over as Zoe came back with three thick white mugs of coffee on a tray. "I had a dream."

"I was having a damn good one myself. I think it involved Spike from *Buffy the Vampire Slayer* and a really big vat of dark chocolate, and then you called and interrupted it."

"Dana." Zoe shook her head, then sat on the arm of Malory's chair. "A nightmare?"

"No. At least . . . no. As soon as I woke up, I typed it out." She rose now and picked up papers from the table. "I've never had a dream with so much detail before. At least I've never remembered details so clearly after I woke up. I wrote it down because I wanted to make sure I didn't forget anything. But I'm not going to. Anyway, it'll be easier if you both just read it."

She handed them the typed pages, then took her own coffee and paced to the patio doors.

It was going to be another beautiful day, she mused. Another beautiful late-summer day with clear skies and warm breezes. People would walk around town, enjoying the weather, going about their business. Their normal, everyday chores in the normal, everyday world.

And she would never forget the sound of that dream-wind, the feel of that sudden, bitter cold.

"Wow. I can see why this shook you up." Dana set the pages aside. "But It's pretty clear where it came from. Flynn told me you guys went up to see the painting again yesterday. All of this is on your mind, and your subconscious just flipped you into it."

"It's scary." Zoe rushed to finish the last few sentences before she got up. Walking over, she rubbed her hands on Malory's shoulders. "No wonder you were so upset. I'm glad you called us."

"It wasn't just a dream. I was there." She warmed her chilled hands on the coffee mug as she turned. "I walked into that painting."

"Okay, honey, take it down a notch or two." Dana held up a hand. "You're over-identifying, that's all. A strong, vivid dream can really suck you in."

"I don't expect you to believe me, but I'm going to say out loud what's been in my head since I woke up."

Woke up, she remembered, shaking with cold, with the sound of that terrible wind still ringing in her ears.

"I was there. I could smell the flowers and feel the heat. Then the cold and the wind. I heard them screaming." She closed her eyes and fought a fresh surge of panic.

She could still hear them screaming.

"And I felt this, this charge in the air, this pressure. When I woke, my ears were still ringing from it. They were speaking Gaelic, but I understood them. How could I?"

"You just thought—"

"No!" She shook her head fiercely at Zoe. "I *knew*. When the storm came, when everything went crazy, I heard them calling out for their father. *Chi athair sinn.* Father, help us. I looked it up this morning, but I knew. How could I know?"

She took a steadying breath. "Their names were Venora, Niniane, and Kyna. How would I know?"

She walked back to sit. The relief of saying it all calmed her. Her pulse leveled, as did her voice. "They were so afraid. One minute they were just young girls playing with their puppy in a world that seemed so perfect and peaceful. And the next, what made them human was being torn out of them. It hurt them, and there was nothing I could do."

"I don't know what to think about this," Dana said after a moment. "I'm trying to be logical here. The painting's drawn you from the first, and we know the legend is Celtic in origin. We look like the girls in the painting, so we identify with them."

"How did I know the Gaelic? How do I know their names?"

Dana frowned into her coffee. "I can't explain that."

"I'll tell you something else I know. Whatever locked those souls away is dark, and it's powerful, and it's greedy. It won't want us to win."

"The box and the keys," Zoe interrupted. "You saw them. You know what they look like."

"The box is very simple, very beautiful. Leaded glass, a high, domed lid, three locks across the front. The keys are like the logo in the invitations, like the emblem on the flag flying on the house. They're small. Only about three inches long, I'd say."

"It still doesn't make sense," Dana insisted. "If they had the keys, why hide them? Why not just hand them to the right people, and game over?"

"I don't know." Malory rubbed her temples. "There must be a reason."

"You said you knew the names they called the couple making out under the tree," Dana reminded her.

"Rowena and Pitte." Malory dropped her hands. "Rowena and Pitte," she repeated. "They couldn't stop it either. It happened so quickly, so violently."

She took a long, long breath. "Here's the kicker. I believe it all. I don't care how crazy it sounds, I believe it all. It happened. I was taken into that painting, through the Curtain of Dreams, and I watched it happen. I have to find that key. Whatever it takes, I have to find it."

After a morning staff meeting that included jelly doughnuts and a pissed-off reporter who'd had her article on fall fashion cut by two inches, Flynn escaped to his office.

As his staff consisted of fewer than thirty people, including the eager sixteen-year-old he paid to write a weekly column from the teenage perspective, having one reporter in a snit was a major staff glitch.

He flipped through his messages, punched up a feature on Valley nightlife, approved a couple of photos for the next day's edition, and checked the accounting on ads.

He could hear the occasional ring of a phone, and even with his door shut, the muffled clatter of fingers on keyboards. The police radio on top of his file cabinet beeped and hummed, the television squeezed between books on a shelf was set on mute.

He had the window open and could hear the light whoosh of morning traffic, the sporadic thump of bass from a car stereo playing too loud.

Now and then he heard a door or drawer slam from the room beyond. Rhoda, the society/fashion/gossip reporter, was still making her annoyance known. Without looking through the glass, he could see her in his mind, spitting darts at him.

She, along with more than half the staff, had worked for the paper since he'd been a boy. And plenty of them, he knew, continued to see the *Dispatch* as his mother's paper.

If not his grandfather's.

There were times when he resented it, times when he despaired of it, and times when it simply amused him.

He couldn't decide which reaction he was having at the moment. All he could think was that Rhoda scared the hell out of him.

The best he could do was not think about it, or her, and settle in to polish his article on the meeting he'd attended the night before. A proposed stoplight at Market and Spruce, a debate over the budget and the need to repair the sidewalks on Main. And a rather spirited argument regarding the highly controversial notion of installing parking meters on Main to help pay for those repairs.

Flynn did what he could to inject a little energy into the subject matter and still stay true to the reporter's code of objectivity.

The *Dispatch* wasn't exactly the *Daily Planet,* he reflected. But then again, he wasn't exactly Perry White. Nobody around here would ever call him Chief. Even without Rhoda's periodic snits, he wasn't certain that anyone, including himself, really believed he was in charge.

His mother cast a very long shadow. Elizabeth Flynn Hennessy Steele. Even her name cast a very long shadow.

He loved her. Of course he did. Most of the time he even liked her. They'd butted heads plenty when he was growing up, but he'd always respected her. You had to respect a woman who ran her life and her business with equal fervor, and expected everyone else to do the same.

Just as you had to give her credit for stepping out of that business when necessity demanded it. Even if she had dumped it in her reluctant son's lap.

She'd dumped it all, including, he thought with a wary glance toward Rhoda's desk, surly reporters.

She was filing her nails instead of working, he noted. Baiting him. File away, he thought. Today's not the day we square off, you cranky old bat.

But that day soon will come.

He was deep into adjusting the layout on page 1 of section B when Dana walked in.

"Not even a cursory knock. No flirtatious little head peek in the door. Just stomp right in."

"I didn't stomp. I've got to talk to you,

Flynn." She threw herself into a chair, then glanced around. "Where's Moe?"

"It's backyard day for the Moe."

"Oh, right."

"And maybe you could go by, hang out with him for a while this afternoon. Then maybe you could throw together some dinner, so I'd come home to a hot meal."

"Sure, that'll happen."

"Listen, I've had a rough morning, I've got a goddamn headache, and I've got to finish this layout."

Dana pursed her lips as she studied him. "Rhoda sniping at you again?"

"Don't look," Flynn snapped before Dana could turn around. "You'll just encourage her."

"Flynn, why don't you just fire her ass? You take entirely too much crap off her."

"She's been with the *Dispatch* since she was eighteen. That's a long time. Now, while I appreciate you dropping in to tell me how to handle my employee problems, I need to finish this."

Dana just stretched out her endless legs. "She really stirred you up this time, huh?"

"Fuck it." He blew out a breath, then

yanked open his desk drawer to hunt up a
bottle of aspirin.

"You do a good job here, Flynn."

"Yeah, yeah," he muttered as he dug a
bottle of water out of another drawer.

"Shut up. I'm serious. You're good at
what you do. As good as Liz was. Maybe
better at some areas of It because you're
more approachable. Plus you're a better
writer than anybody you've got on staff."

He eyed her while he washed the aspirin
down. "What brought this on?"

"You look really bummed." She couldn't
stand to see him seriously unhappy. Irritated, confused, pissed off, or surly was
fine. But it hurt her heart to see misery
etched on his face. "Pleasant Valley needs
the *Dispatch,* and the *Dispatch* needs you.
It doesn't need Rhoda. And I bet knowing
that just sticks in her craw."

"You think?" The idea of that smoothed
out the raw edges. "The sticking-in-the-
craw part, I mean."

"You bet. Feel better?"

"Yeah." He capped the water bottle,
dropped it back in the drawer. "Thanks."

"My second good deed for the day. I've
just spent an hour at Malory's, and another

twenty minutes wandering around trying to decide if I should dump on you or just keep it between us girls."

"If it has to do with hairstyles, monthly cycles, or the upcoming Red Tag sale at the mall, keep it between you girls."

"That's so incredibly sexist, I'm not even going to . . . what Red Tag sale?"

"Watch for the ad in tomorrow's *Dispatch.* Is something wrong with Malory?"

"Good question. She had a dream, only she doesn't believe it was a dream."

Dana related the discussion before digging in her bag for the typed account Malory had given her. "I'm worried about her, Flynn, and I'm starting to worry about me, because she's got me half convinced that she's right."

"Quiet a minute." He read it through twice, then sat back in his chair, staring at the ceiling. "What if she is right?"

Exasperation spiked into her voice. "Do I have to start playing Scully to your Mulder? We're talking about gods and sorcery and the capture of souls."

"We're talking about magic, about possibilities. And possibilities should always be explored. Where is she now?"

"She said she was going to The Gallery, to do some research on the painting."

"Good. Then she's sticking with the plan."

"You didn't see her."

"No, but I will. What about you? Dig anything up?"

"I'm tugging a few lines."

"Okay, let's all meet at my place tonight. Let Zoe know, I'll tell Mal." When Dana frowned at him, he only smiled. "You came to me, honey. I'm in it now."

"I really owe you for this. . . ."

"Oh, sweetheart, any day I can do something behind the bimbo-nazi's back is a day of celebration."

Still, Tod cast a cautious look right and left before he opened the door to what had once been Malory's office and was now Pamela's domain.

"Oh, God, what has she done to my space?"

"Hideous, isn't it?" Tod actually shuddered. "It's like the walls vomited Louis XIV. My only satisfaction is that she actually has to look at this when she comes in."

The room was jammed full. The curvy desk, the tables, the chairs, and two tasseled ottomans all vied for space on a rug that screamed with red and gold. The walls were covered with paintings overpowered by thick, ornate gold frames, and statuary, ornamental bowls and boxes, glassware and whatnots crowded every flat surface.

Each piece, Malory noted, was a small treasure in itself. But packing it all together in this limited space made it look like someone's very expensive garage sale.

"How does she manage to get anything done?"

"She has her slaves and minions—meaning me, Ernestine, Julia, and Franco. Simone Legree sits up here on her throne and gives orders. You had a lucky escape, Mal."

"Maybe I did." But still, it had been a wrench to come through the front door again, knowing she no longer belonged.

Not knowing where she belonged.

"Where is she now?"

"Lunch at the club." Tod checked his watch. "You've got two hours."

"I won't need that much. I need the client list," she said as she headed for the computer on the desk.

"Oooh, are you going to steal clients from under her rhinoplasty?"

"No. Hmm, happy thought, but no. I'm trying to pin down the artist on a particular painting. I need to see who we have that buys in that style. Then I need our files on paintings with mythological themes. Damn it, she's changed the password."

"It's mine."

"She uses your password?"

"No—M-I-N-E." He shook his head. "She wrote it down so she wouldn't forget it—after she forgot two other passwords. I happened to, ah, come across the note."

"I love you, Tod," Malory exclaimed as she keyed it

"Enough to tell me what this is all about?"

"More than enough, but I'm in kind of a bind about that. A couple of people I'd have to talk to first." She worked fast, locating the detailed client list, copying it to the disk she'd brought with her. "I swear I'm not using this for anything illegal or unethical."

"That's a damn shame."

She chuckled at that, then opened her bag to offer him a look at the printout she'd made from the digital photo. "Do you recognize this painting?"

"Hmm, no. But something about the style."

"Exactly. Something about the style. I can't quite place it, but it's nagging at me. I've seen this artist's work before, somewhere." When the file was copied, she switched to another, put in a fresh disk. "If you remember, give me a call. Day or night."

"Sounds urgent."

"If I'm not having a psychotic episode, it may very well be."

"Does this have anything to do with M. F. Hennessy? Are you working on a story for the paper?"

She goggled. "Where did that come from?"

"You were seen having dinner with him the other night. I hear everything," Tod added.

"It doesn't have anything to do with him, not directly. And no, I'm not writing a story. Do you know Flynn?"

"Only in my dreams. He's very hot."

"Well . . . I think I might be dating him. I wasn't going to, but I seem to be."

"Lip lock?"

"Several of them."

"Rating?"

"Top of the scale."

"Sex?"

"Almost, but cooler heads prevailed."

"Damn."

"Plus he's funny and interesting and sweet. Pretty bossy in a really clever way so you barely notice until you've been bossed. Smart, and I think tenacious."

"Sounds perfect. Can I have him?"

"Sorry, pal, but I may have to keep him." She snatched out the disk, then carefully closed documents and shut down. "Mission accomplished with no loss of life. Thanks, Tod." She threw her arms around him, gave him a big, noisy kiss. "I've got to get to work on this."

She hunkered down in her apartment, systematically going through the data, cross-referencing, eliminating, until she had a workable list. By the time she left for Flynn's, she'd winnowed The Gallery's client list by seventy percent.

Dana was already there when she arrived. "Had dinner?"

"No." Malory looked, cautiously, for Moe. "I forgot."

"Good. We've got pizza coming. Flynn's out back with Moe for their daily romp. You're okay that I told him about your dream?"

"Yeah. We seem to have brought him into this."

"Okay. Go in and flop. We'll have some wine."

She'd barely done so when Zoe arrived with Simon in tow. "I hope it's all right. I couldn't get a sitter."

"I don't *need* a sitter," Simon declared.

"I need a sitter." Zoe hooked an arm around his neck. "He's got homework, so if there's a corner he can use. I brought the shackles."

Dana winked at him. "We'll use the dungeon. Can we torture him, then feed him pizza?"

"We've already had—"

"I could eat pizza," Simon interrupted. Then he let out a whoop as Moe charged in from the back of the house. "Wow! That's some dog!"

"Simon, don't—"

But boy and dog were already rushing together, caught in the throes of mutual love at first sight.

"Hey, Flynn, look what Zoe brought us. We get to make him do homework."

"I've always wanted to do that with somebody. You must be Simon."

"Uh-huh. This is a great dog, mister."

"The dog's Moe, I'm Flynn. Zoe, can Simon take Moe back out so they can run around like maniacs for a while?"

"Sure. Twenty minutes, Simon, then you hit the books."

"Sweet!"

"Straight out the back," Flynn told him. "There's a ball out there with toothmarks and drool all over it. He likes you to chase it and fetch it back to him."

"You're funny," Simon decided. "Let's go, Moe!"

"Pizza," Dana announced when the bell rang. "Want to call him back?"

"No, he's fine. He just finished eating three helpings of spaghetti."

"Flynn, be a man. Pay for the pizza."

"Why do I always have to be the man?" Then he zeroed in on Malory and grinned. "Oh, yeah. That's why."

Dana sat on the floor with a fresh notebook in her lap. "Let's be organized about this. The librarian in me demands it. Zoe, pour yourself some wine. We can each report what we've found or thought or speculated on since the last time we got together."

"I haven't found much." Zoe took a folder out of her canvas bag. "I typed up all my notes, though."

"Aren't you a good girl?" Delighted, Dana took the folder, then pounced on the first box of pizza when Flynn dropped two of them on the coffee table. "I'm *starving.*"

"There's news." He sat on the sofa beside Malory, turned her face toward him with his hand, then kissed her long and firm. "Hi."

"Gee, don't I get one of those?"

At Zoe's question, he shifted and leaned toward her, but she laughed and gave him a light shove. "I'd better settle for the wine."

"If Flynn's finished kissing girls," Dana began.

"Which won't be until I've drawn my last, gasping breath."

"Settle down," Dana ordered. "We know about Mal's experience. I have the typed report of it here, which I'll add to the collection of notes and other data."

"I've got more." Since it was there, Mallory took a slice of pizza from the box and dropped it onto a paper plate. "I have a list of people—clients through The Gallery—who've purchased or shown interest in classical and/or mythological subject matter in art. I've also started a search of like styles, but that's going to take some time. I intend to start making phone inquiries tomorrow."

"I could help," Zoe offered. "I was thinking that maybe we should do a search for paintings that include the element of a key. Like a theme."

"That's good," Malory acknowledged, and tore a sheet off the roll of paper towels that stood in for napkins.

"I've got some appointments tomorrow, but I'll work around them."

"I've been working on the clue itself." Dana picked up her wineglass. "I'm wondering if we should take some of the key phrases and do a search on place names. Like restaurants or shops. Take the Singing Goddess, for example. I didn't find anything on that, but it's the sort of thing that could be the name of a shop or a restaurant or a site."

"Not bad," Flynn said and helped himself to another slice of pizza.

"I've got some more." Still she said nothing as she reached into the box herself, topped off her wine. "I put in some Internet time running the three names Malory heard in her . . . in her dream. "Niniane" comes up a few times. Some legends have her as the sorceress who enchanted Arthur's Merlin and trapped him in the cave of crystal. There's another that has her as Merlin's mother. But when I put her together with the other two, I found one hit from this esoteric little site on goddess worship. It gives a variation on the Daughters of Glass—and calls them by those names."

"Those are their names. You can't think it's a coincidence that I dreamed those names and you found them today."

"No," Dana said carefully. "But isn't it possible you came across the same site and the names stuck in your head?"

"No. I would've written it down. I would've remembered. I never heard them before the dream."

"Okay." Flynn patted her knee. "First, I'll tell you I haven't found any record of a shipping or moving company that serviced Warrior's Peak. And no record of any company shipping furniture here for clients under Triad."

"They had to get all that stuff in there somehow," Dana protested. "They didn't just click the heels of their ruby slippers together."

"Just giving you the facts. The real-estate company didn't make the arrangements for them, either. At this point, I haven't found any trail leading Rowena or Pitte to the Peak. Not saying there isn't one," he continued before Dana could protest. "Just saying I haven't found one through the logical sources."

"I guess we have to look at the illogical ones."

He shifted to beam at Zoe. "There you go. But I've got one more logical step to take. Who do I know who collects art seriously, someone I could use as a source? The Vanes. So I gave my old pal Brad a call. It so happens he's heading back here in a couple of days."

"Brad's coming back to the Valley?" Dana asked.

"He's taking over the local headquarters for HomeMakers. Brad's got the Vanes' passion for art. I described the painting to him, or started to. I wasn't close to being finished when he gave me the title. *The Daughters of Glass.*"

"No, that can't be. I'd have heard of it." Malory pushed herself to her feet and began to pace. "Who's the artist?"

"Nobody seems to be sure."

"Just not possible," Malory continued. "A major talent like that, I'd have heard. I'd have seen more of the artist's work."

"Maybe not. According to Brad, nobody seems to know much about the artist. *The Daughters of Glass* was last seen in a private home in London. Where it was, by all accounts, destroyed during the Blitz. In 1942."

Chapter Eight

Malory closed herself in her apartment for two days. She submerged herself in books, telephone calls, E-mail. It was foolish, she'd decided, to run around chasing a dozen different angles and suppositions. Better—far better—to conduct the search with technology and systematic logic.

She couldn't function, simply couldn't *think,* in disorder. Which was why, she admitted as she carefully labeled yet another file, she'd failed as an artist.

Art, the creation of true art, required some mysterious, innate ability to thrive in chaos. Or that was her opinion. To be able to see and understand and *feel* dozens of shapes and textures of emotions at one time.

Then, of course, there was the little matter of possessing the talent to transfer those emotions onto a canvas.

She lacked the gift, on all levels, while the artist of *The Daughters of Glass* had it in spades.

The painting at Warrior's Peak, or one done by the same artist, was the path. She was sure of that now. Why else did she keep coming back to it? Why had she somehow in her dreams walked into it?

Why had she been chosen to find the first key, she thought, if not for her knowledge of and contacts in the art world?

She'd been told to look within and without. Within the painting, or another by the same artist? Did "without" mean to look at what surrounded the painting?

Opening a file folder, she studied the printout of the painting again. What surrounded the daughters? Peace and beauty, love and passion—and the threat to destroy it. As well as, she mused, the method to restore it.

A key in the air, in the trees, in the water.

She was damn sure she wasn't about to pluck a magic key out of the air or from a tree branch, so what did it *mean*? And which of those three was hers?

Too literal? Perhaps. Maybe "within" meant she was to look inside herself to her feelings about the painting, both the emotional and the intellectual response.

Where the goddess sings, she reflected as she rose from her piles of research to pace. No one had been singing in the dream. But the fountain had reminded her of music. Maybe it had something to do with the fountain.

Maybe water was her key.

And, she thought in frustration, she might not have left her apartment, but she was still running in circles.

There were only three weeks left.

Her heart jumped at the quick *rat-a-tat* on her glass patio doors. There stood the man and his dog on the other side. Instinctively she ran a hand over the hair she'd yanked back into a ponytail sometime that morning. She hadn't bothered with makeup or with changing out of the baggy cotton pants and tank she'd slept in.

Not only was she not looking her best, but she was pretty sure she'd dipped below her personal worst.

When she opened the door, she decided Flynn verified that when he took a good, hard look at her and said, "Honey, you need to get out."

She felt, actually felt, her face arrange itself in a sulk. "I'm busy. I'm working."

"Yeah." He glanced at the neat stacks of research materials on her dining room table, the pretty coffee carafe and china cup. There were small containers, all in matching red plastic, that held pencils, paper clips, Post-its.

A glass paperweight swirling with ribbons of color anchored a few typed pages. A storage box was tucked under the table, and he imagined she placed everything that related to her project inside it every night and took it out again every morning.

It was amazing to him, and oddly charming. Even alone and at work she kept things tidy.

Moe bumped her leg with his snout, then gathered himself to leap. Recognizing the signal now, Malory stuck out a hand. "No jumping," she ordered and had Moe quivering in his desire to obey.

As a reward she gave him a congratulatory pat on the head. "I don't have any—"

"Don't say it," Flynn warned. "Don't say any food words. He loses his head. Come on, it's great out." He caught Malory's hand in his. "We'll go for a walk."

"I'm working. Why aren't you?"

"Because it's after six, and I like to pretend I have a life outside of the newspaper."

"After six?" She glanced down at her watch, remembered she hadn't put it on that morning. It was just another sign that the efficient train of her life had jumped its tracks. "I didn't realize it was so late."

"Which is why you need to go for a walk. Fresh air and exercise."

"Maybe, but I can't go out like this."

"Why not?"

"I'm in my pajamas."

"They don't look like pajamas."

"Well, they are, and I'm not going out in them, and with my hair all horrible and no makeup on."

"There's no dress code for walking the dog." Still, he was a man who had a mother and a sister, and he knew the rules. "But if you want to change, we'll wait."

*   *   *

He'd dealt with enough women to know the wait could be anywhere from ten minutes to the rest of his life. Since he'd learned to think of the female grooming process as a kind of ritual, he didn't mind. It gave him a chance to sit out on the patio, with Moe flopped over his feet, and scribble ideas for articles in his notebook. In his opinion, time was only wasted if you didn't do something with it. If the something was staring off into space and letting the mind drift on whatever current was the strongest at that moment, that was fine.

But since that current was how he might get his hands on Malory again, he figured it would be more productive all around to channel his energies into work.

Since Brad was coming back to the Valley, the *Dispatch* would need a solid feature on him, on the Vanes, on HomeMakers. The history of the family and their business, the face of that business in today's economic climate, and any plans for the future.

He would handle that one himself, and combine his professional and personal interests. Just as he was doing with Malory. So he began to note down various aspects that described her.

"Blond, brainy, beautiful" headed his list.

"Hey, it's a start," he said to Moe. "She was picked for a reason, and the reason has to have something to do with who or what she is. Or isn't."

Organized. Arty.

He had never met anyone who managed to be both.

Single. Unemployed.

Huh. Maybe they should do an article on twenty- and thirtysomething singles in the Valley. The dating scene in small-town USA. If he gave that to Rhoda, she might start speaking to him again.

He glanced up when he caught a movement out of the corner of his eye, and watched Malory walk to the patio door. It hadn't taken her as long to transform herself as he'd figured it would.

He got to his feet, hooking a hand in Moe's collar before the dog could leap on Malory. "You look great. Smell even better."

"And I'd like to keep it that way." She leaned down, tapped a finger lightly on Moe's nose. "So, no jumping."

"Why don't we take a drive down to the river? Then he can run around like crazy."

* * *

She had to give him points. He'd managed to turn walking the dog into a date and had done it smoothly. So smoothly, she didn't realize she was on a date until they were sitting on a blanket by the river eating fried chicken while Moe raced around barking hopefully at squirrels.

But it was hard to complain when the air was cool and fresh, and the light softening as the sun sank lower in the west. When it dropped beneath those peaks, everything would go soft and gray and it would be cooler yet. She would need the light jacket she'd brought along—at least she would if they stayed to watch the stars come out.

And how long had it been since she'd watched the stars come out?

Now that she was here, she wondered if the enforced hibernation, however brief, had accomplished anything more than creating a logjam in her mind.

She wasn't an isolationist. She needed contact with people. Conversations, stimuli, sound and movement. And realizing that only made her understand how much she needed to be part of the workforce again.

If she grabbed the million dollars at the end of this strange rainbow, she would still need to work. Just for the day-to-day energy.

"I have to admit, I'm glad you got me out."

"You're not a cave dweller." He dug in the bucket for another drumstick when she frowned at him. "You're a social animal. Take Dana, she's more cave dweller than social animal. If you left her alone, she'd be perfectly happy holed up with mountains of books and a vat of coffee. At least for a few weeks. Then she'd need to come up for air. Me, I'd go nuts after a day or two. I need the charge. So do you."

"You're right. And I'm not sure how I feel about you figuring that out so soon."

"Soon's relative. I've spent, oh, about a year thinking about you in the past week. Given time and energy ratios. It's been a while since I've given that much thought to a woman, in case you're wondering."

"I don't know what I'm wondering. Yes, I do," she corrected. "Why haven't you brought up the key, or asked me what I'm doing about finding it?"

"Because you've had enough of that for

now. If you'd wanted to get into it, you'd have brought it up. You're not shy."

"You're right. Why did you bring me out here, away from town?"

"It's quiet. Nice view. Moe likes it. There's the slim chance I can get you naked on this blanket—"

"Try slim to none."

"Slim's enough to keep me going." He dipped a plastic fork into the fast-food potato salad. "And I wanted to see if Brad's moving in yet." He looked across the ribbon of water to the rambling two-story frame house on the opposite bank. "Doesn't look like it."

"You miss him."

"You got that right."

She plucked a blade of grass, ran it idly through her fingers. "I have some friends from college. We were so close, and I guess we all thought we'd be close forever. Now we're all scattered and hardly see each other. Once or twice a year if we can all manage it. We talk on the phone or through E-mail now and then, but it's not the same. I miss them. I miss who we were when we were friends, and that telepathy you develop so that you know what the other's thinking, or what she'd do in some situation. Is it that way for you?"

"Pretty much." He reached over, toyed with the ends of her hair in the same absent way she toyed with the blade of grass. "But we go back to being kids together. None of us are big on phone calls. Maybe because Brad and I end up on the phone through most of our workday. E-mail does the job. Jordan, he's the E-mail king."

"I met him for about ninety seconds at a book signing, in Pittsburgh, about four years ago. All dark and handsome, with a dangerous gleam in his eye."

"You want dangerous?"

It made her laugh. He was sitting on a ratty blanket eating bucket chicken while his big, silly dog barked at a squirrel that was ten feet up a tree.

Then she was flat on her back, his body pressed to hers, and the laugh died in her throat.

His mouth *was* dangerous. Foolish of her to have forgotten that. However affable and easy he appeared on the surface, there were storms inside him. Hot, whippy storms that could crash over the unwary before they could think about taking shelter.

So she didn't think at all, but let it rage.
And let that secret part of herself, that part
she'd never risked exposing, slide out. And
take, even as it was taken.

"How's this working for you?" he murmured as he fixed that amazing mouth on
her throat.

"So far, so good."

He lifted his head, looked down at her.
And his heart shuddered in his chest.
"Something here. Some big something
here."

"I don't think—"

"Yes, you do." Impatience, potent and
unexpected, snapped out. "You may not
want to think—I'm not real keen on it myself, but you do. I really hate using the obvious metaphor, but this is like turning a key
in a lock. I can hear the goddamn click."

He pushed up, dragged an unsteady
hand through his hair. "I'm not ready to hear
any goddamn click."

She sat up quickly, brushed fussily at the
front of her shirt. It threw her off balance
that she could find his temper both irritating
and arousing at the same time. "You think *I*
want to hear one? I've got enough on my
mind right now without you clicking around

in my head. I need to find the first key. I've got to work this out. I need to find a job. And I don't even want a stupid job. I want . . ."

"What? What do you want?"

"I don't *know.*" She scrambled to her feet. There was a fury inside her. She didn't know where it came from or where it needed to go. Turning away, she stared at the house across the river, folded her arms firmly over her chest. "And I always know what I want."

"You're one up on me there." He rose, but didn't go to her. Whatever was pumping inside him—anger, need, fear—was too unstable to risk touching her.

The breeze was playing with the ends of her hair, as he had. All those tumbling clouds the color of old gold, like something out of a painting. She looked so slim, so perfect, standing there, half turned away from him while the dying sun shot a thin line of fire along the rise of western hills.

"The only thing I've been absolutely sure I wanted . . . ever," he realized, "is you."

She glanced back as nervous wings began to stir in her belly. "I don't imagine I'm the only woman you've wanted to sleep with."

"No. Actually, the first was Joley Riden-becker. We were thirteen. And that particular desire was never fulfilled."

"Now you're making a joke of it."

"I'm not. Not really." He stepped toward her and his voice was gentle. "I wanted Joley, as much as I knew what that meant at thirteen. It was intense, even painful, and kind of sweet. Eventually I found out what that meant. I wanted other women along the way. I even loved one, which is why I know the difference between wanting a woman, and wanting you. If it was just sex, it wouldn't piss me off."

"It's hardly my fault you're pissed off." She scowled at him. "And you don't look or sound as if you are."

"I tend to get really reasonable when I'm seriously annoyed. It's a curse." He picked up the ball Moe spat at his feet, then threw it with a strong whiplash of arm. "And if you think it's a joy to be able to see both sides of an argument, to see the validity on each end, let me tell you, it's a pain in the ass."

"Who was she?"

He shrugged, then picked up the ball Moe returned, threw it again. "Doesn't matter."

"I'd say it does. And that she still does."

"It just didn't work out."

"Fine. I should be getting back now." She walked back to kneel on the blanket and tidy the remains of their impromptu picnic.

"That's a skill I admire, and nobody does it like a woman. The implied 'fuck you,' " he explained, then shot the ball in the air for Moe once more. "She left me. Or I didn't go with her. Depends on your point of view. We were together the best part of a year. She was a reporter for the local station, moved up to weekend anchor, then evening anchor. She was good, and we got to have all these arguments and discussions over the impact and value of our particular news medium. Which is sexier than it may sound. Anyway, we planned to get married, move to New York. Eventually, on the moving part. Then she got an offer from an affiliate up there. She went. I stayed."

"Why did you stay?"

"Because I'm George fucking Bailey." The ball burst out of his hand again like a rocket.

"I don't understand."

"George Bailey, giving up his dreams of travel and adventure to stay in his hometown and rescue the old savings and loan.

I'm no Jimmy Stewart, but the *Dispatch* sure as hell turned out to be my savings and loan. My stepfather, Dana's dad, had been ill. My mother shifted some of the responsibilities of editor in chief to me. I assumed it was temporary, until Joe got back on his feet. But the doctors, and my mother, wanted him out of the cold winters. And they wanted, deserved, to enjoy a retirement period. She threatened that if I didn't take over for her at the paper, she would shut it down. My mother doesn't make idle threats."

With a humorless laugh, he tossed the ball again. "You can bet your ass she doesn't. A Flynn runs the *Valley Dispatch* or there is no *Dispatch*."

Michael Flynn Hennessy, she thought. So Flynn was a family name *and* a legacy. "If she knew you wanted something different . . ."

He managed to smile. "She didn't want something different. I could've gone, just kicked the dust off my heels and gone with Lily to New York. And all the people who work at the paper would've been out of a job. Half of them, maybe more, wouldn't have been picked up by whoever started another paper. She knew I wouldn't go."

He studied the ball in his hand, turned it slowly, spoke softly. "She never did like Lily anyway."

"Flynn—"

He gave in to Moe's desperate excitement and heaved the ball. "Before I make it sound pitiful and pathetic—I did want to go, then. I loved Lily, then. But I didn't love her enough to pack up and go when she gave me the ultimatum. She didn't love me enough to stay, or to give me the time to work things out here and meet up with her."

Then you didn't love each other at all, Malory thought, but she remained silent.

"Less than a month after she'd landed in New York, she called and broke our engagement. She needed to concentrate on her career, couldn't handle the stress of a relationship, much less a long-distance one. I should be free to see other people and make a life, while she was going to be married to her job.

"And in six months she was married to an NBC news exec and moving steadily up the ladder. She got what she wanted, and in the end so did I."

He turned back to Malory. His face was calm again, the deep green eyes clear as if the fury had never been behind them. "My mother was right—and I really hate that part. But she was right. This is my place, and I'm doing exactly what I want to do."

"The fact that you see that says a lot more about you than about either one of them."

He threw the ball one last time. "I made you feel sorry for me."

"No." Though he had. "You made me respect you." She rose, walked to him and kissed his cheek. "I think I remember this Lily from the local news. Redhead, right? Lots of teeth."

"That'd be Lily."

"Her voice was entirely too nasal, and she had a weak chin."

He leaned over, kissed her cheek in turn. "That's a really nice thing to say. Thanks."

Moe raced back and spat out the ball on the ground between them. "How long will he do that?" Malory asked.

"For all eternity, or until my arm falls off."

She gave the ball a good boot with her foot. "It's getting dark," she said as Moe raced happily off. "You should take me home."

"Or I could take Moe home and we could—ah, I see by the way your eyebrows have arched and your lip has curled that your mind is in the gutter. I was going to say we could go to the movies."

"You were not."

"I certainly was. In fact, it so happens I have the movie section in the car, for your perusal."

They were all right again, she realized, and wanted to kiss him—this time in friendship. Instead, she fell into the rhythm and played the game out. "You have the entire paper in the car, because it's your paper."

"Be that as it may, I'll still let you pick the flick."

"What if it's an art film with subtitles?"

"Then I'll suffer in silence."

"You already know there aren't any such films playing at the local multiplex, don't you?"

"That's neither here nor there. Come on, Moe, let's go for a ride."

It had done her good, Malory decided, to step away from the puzzle and the problems for an evening. She felt fresher this morning, and more optimistic. And it felt good to be interested in and attracted to a complicated man.

He *was* complicated, she thought. Only more so because he gave the impression, at least initially, of being simple. And so that made him yet another puzzle to solve.

She couldn't deny that *click* he'd spoken of. Why should she? She wasn't a game player when it came to relationships—she was cautious. It meant she needed to find out if the click was merely sexual or tangled around something more.

Puzzle number three, she decided as she hunkered down to continue her research.

Her first phone call of the morning left her stunned. Moments after hanging up, she was tearing through her old college textbooks on art history.

The door of the Vane house was wide open. A number of burly men were hauling furniture and boxes in, or hauling furniture and boxes out. Just watching them gave Flynn a backache.

He recalled the weekend years before when he and Jordan had moved into an apartment. How they, with Brad's help, had carted a secondhand sofa that weighed as much as a Honda up three flights of stairs.

Those were the days, Flynn reminisced. Thank God they were over.

Moe leaped out of the car behind him and without waiting for an invitation raced straight into the house. There was a crash, a curse. Flynn could only pray that one of the Vane family antiques hadn't bit the dust as he hurriedly followed.

"Jesus Christ. You call this a puppy?"

"He was a puppy—a year ago." Flynn looked at his oldest friend, currently being greeted by and slobbered on by his dog. And his heart simply sang.

"Sorry about the . . . was that a lamp?"

Brad glanced at the broken china scattered in the foyer. "It was a minute ago. All right, big guy. Down."

"Outside, Moe. Chase the rabbit!"

In response, Moe let out a series of barks and bombed out the door.

"What rabbit?"

"The one that lives in his dreams. Hey."

Flynn stepped forward, crunching broken shards under his feet, and caught Brad in one hard hug. "Looking good. For a suit."

"Who's a suit?"

He couldn't have looked less like one in worn jeans and a denim work shirt. He looked, Flynn thought, tall and lean and fit. The Vanes' golden child, the family prince, who was as happy running a construction crew as he was a board meeting.

Maybe happier.

"I came by last evening, but the place was deserted. When did you get in?"

"Late. Let's get out of the way," Brad suggested as the movers carried in another load. He jerked a thumb and led the way to the kitchen.

The house was always furnished, and made available to execs or visiting brass from the Vane corporation. Once it had been their home in the Valley, a place Flynn had known as well as his own.

The kitchen had been redone since the days when he'd begged cookies there, but the view out the windows, off the surrounding deck, was the same. Woods and water, and the rising hills beyond.

Some of the best parts of his childhood

were tied up in this house. Just as they
were tied up in the man who now owned it.

Brad poured coffee, then led Flynn out on
the deck.

"How's it feel to be back?" Flynn asked
him.

"Don't know yet. Odd, mostly." He leaned
on the rail, looked out beyond.

Everything was the same. Nothing was
the same.

He turned back, a man comfortable in his
frame. He had a layer or two of big city on
him, and was comfortable with that as well.

His hair was blond that had darkened
with the years, just as the dimples in his
cheeks were closer to creases now. Much
to his relief. His eyes were a stone gray under straight brows. They tended to look intense, even when the rest of his face
smiled.

Flynn knew it wasn't the mouth that
showed Brad's mood. It was the eyes.
When they smiled, he meant it.

They did so now. "Son of a bitch. It's
good to see you."

"I never figured you for coming back, not
for any length of time."

"Neither did I. Things change, Flynn.

They're meant to, I guess. I've been itchy the last few years. I finally figured out I was itchy for home. How are things with you, Mr. Editor in Chief?"

"They're okay. I assume you'll be subscribing to our paper. I'll make arrangements for that," he added with a grin. "We put up a nice red box next to the mailbox on the road. Morning delivery out here usually hits by seven."

"Sign me up."

"I will. And I'm going to want to interview Bradley Charles Vane IV at his earliest convenience."

"Shit. Give me a while to settle in before I have to put on my corporate hat."

"How about next Monday? I'll come to you."

"Christ, you've become Clark Kent. No, worse, Lois Lane—without the great legs. I don't know what I've got going on Monday, but I'll have my assistant set it up."

"Great. How about we grab some beer and catch up tonight?"

"I can get behind that. How's your family?"

"Mom and Joe are doing fine out in Phoenix."

"Actually, I was thinking more about the delicious Dana."

"You're not going to start hitting on my sister again? It's embarrassing."

"She hooked up with anybody?"

"No, she's not hooked up with anybody."

"She still built?"

Flynn winced. "Shut up, Vane."

"I love yanking your chain over that one." And with a sigh, Brad was home. "Though it's entertaining, that's not why I asked you to come out. There's something I think you're going to want to see. I did some thinking when you told me about this deal Dana and her friends got themselves into."

"You know something about these people up at Warrior's Peak?"

"No. But I know something about art. Come on. I had them put it in the great room. I'd just finished uncrating it personally when I heard you drive up."

He walked along the deck, around the corner of the house to the double glass doors bordered by etched panels.

The great room boasted a towering ceiling with a circling balcony, a generous fireplace with hearth and mantel of hunter-green granite framed in golden oak. There was space for two sofas, one in the center of the room, the other tucked into a cozy conversation area along the far wall.

More space spilled through a wide arch, where the piano stood and where Brad had spent countless tedious hours practicing.

There, propped against the hearth of a second fireplace, was the painting.

The muscles in Flynn's belly went loose. "Jesus. Oh, Jesus."

"It's called *After the Spell.* I got it at an auction about three years ago. Do you remember I mentioned I'd bought a painting because one of the figures in it looked like Dana?"

"I didn't pay any attention. You were always razzing me about Dana." He crouched down now, stared hard at the painting. He didn't know art, but even with his limited eye, he'd have bet the farm that the same hand had painted this that had created the painting at Warrior's Peak.

There was no joy or innocence here, however. The tone was dark, a kind of grieving, with the only light, pale, pale light, glowing from the three glass coffins where three women seemed to sleep.

His sister's face, and Malory's, and Zoe's.

"I have to make a phone call." Flynn straightened and dug out his cell phone. "There's someone who has to see this right away."

Chapter Nine

She didn't like to be told to hurry, especially when she wasn't given a good reason why. So, on principle, Malory took her time driving to the Vane house.

She had a lot on her mind, and a little drive in the country was just the ticket, she decided, to line those thoughts up in some organized fashion.

And she liked tooling along in her little car over the windy road that followed the river, and the way the sun sprinkled through the leaves overhead to splatter patterns of light on the roadbed.

If she could paint, she would do a study of that—just the way light and shadow played on something as simple and ordinary as a country road. If she could paint, she thought again—which she couldn't, despite all the desire, all the study, all the years of trying.

But someone sure as hell could.

She should've tried to track down Dana and Zoe before driving out here. Really, she was supposed to be working with them, not with Flynn. He was . . . like an accessory, she told herself. A really attractive, sexy, interesting accessory.

Boy, she loved accessories.

Not a productive train of thought.

She switched the car radio off, steeped herself in silence. What she needed to do was find Dana and Zoe, tell them what she'd discovered. Maybe if she said it all out loud she, or they, could decipher what it meant.

Because at the moment she didn't have a clue.

All she knew, in her gut, was that it was important. Even vital. If not the answer, it was one of the bread crumbs that would lead to the answer.

She turned off the road and onto the private lane. No gates here. No circling walls. The Vanes were certainly wealthy enough to rate them. She wondered why they hadn't chosen to buy Warrior's Peak instead of building by the river, closer to town.

Then the house came into view and answered her question. It was beautiful, and it was wood. A lumber baron would hardly build or buy in stone or brick. He would, as he had, build to illustrate the art of his product.

The wood was honey gold, set off by copper trim that had gone dreamy green with age and weather. There was a complex arrangement of decks and terraces, skirting or jutting from both stories. Half a dozen rooflines peaked or sloped, all with a kind of artful symmetry that brought harmony to the whole.

The grounds were informal, as suited the site and the style, but she imagined that the placement of every shrub, every tree, every flower bed had been meticulously selected and designed.

Malory approved of meticulous design and execution.

She pulled up beside a moving van and was about to step out when she heard the wild, delighted barking.

"Oh, no, not this time. I've got your number, buddy." She reached into the box on the floor beside her and pulled out a large dog biscuit.

Even as Moe's homely face smooshed against the car window, she rolled it down. "Moe! Get the cookie!" And threw the dog biscuit as far as she could manage.

As he raced in pursuit, she nipped out of the car and made a dash for the house.

"Nice job." Flynn met her at the door.

"I'm a quick study."

"Counting on that. Malory Price, Brad Vane. Already called it," Flynn added in subtle warning as he saw the interest light in Brad's eye.

"Oh? Well, can't blame you." Brad smiled at Malory. "It's still nice to meet you, Malory."

"What are you talking about?"

"It's guy-speak," Flynn told her, and dipped his head to kiss her. "Just bringing Brad up-to-date. Dana and Zoe on the way?"

"No. Dana's working, and I couldn't reach Zoe. I left messages for both of them. What's this all about?"

"You're going to want to see it for yourself."

"See what? You drag me out here—no offense," she added to Brad, "you have a beautiful house—without any explanation. And I was busy. The time factor—"

"I'm starting to think time's a real factor." Flynn tugged her along toward the great room.

"Excuse the disorder. I've got a lot going out, a lot coming in today." Brad kicked aside a chunk of broken lamp. "Flynn tells me you managed the art gallery in town."

"Yes, until recently. Oh, what a fabulous room." She stopped, absorbed the space. It needed paintings, sculpture, more color, more texture. Such a wonderful space deserved art.

If she'd had a free hand and an unlimited budget she could've made this room a showcase.

"You must be eager to unpack your things, settle in, and . . . oh, my God."

The shock struck the instant she saw the painting. The stunning blast of discovery pumped straight into her blood, had her fumbling her glasses out of her purse and going down to her knees in front of it for a closer study.

The colors, the brushstrokes, the technique, even the medium. The same. The same, she thought, as the other. The three main subjects, the same.

"After the theft of the souls," she stated. "They're here, in this box on the pedestal in the foreground. My God, look at how the light and color seem to pulse inside the glass. It's genius. There, in the background, the two figures from the first painting, with their backs turned here. They're leaving. Banished. About to walk through that mist. The Curtain of Dreams. The keys."

She scooped her hair back, held the mass of it in one hand as she peered more closely. "Where are the keys? There! You can just see them, on a chain the female figure holds in her hand. Three keys. She's the keeper."

Wanting to see more detail, she fished a small silver-handled magnifying glass out of a felt bag in her purse.

"She carries a magnifying glass in her purse," Brad uttered in amazement.

"Yeah." Flynn grinned like a fool. "Isn't she great?"

Focused on the painting, she shut out the comments behind her and peered through the glass. "Yes, yes, it's the same design of

key. They're not worked into the background the way they are in the other painting. Not symbolism this time, but fact. She
has the keys."

She lowered the glass, eased back
slightly for an overview. "The shadow's still
in the trees, but farther back now. You can
barely see his shape. His work's done, but
still he watches. Gloats?"

"Who is *he*?" Brad wanted to know.

"Quiet. She's working."

Malory slipped the glass back into its
pouch, then returned it to her purse. "Such
a sad painting, such grief in the light, in the
body language of the two as they step toward that curtain of mist. The main subjects
in their crystal coffins look serene, but
they're not. It's not serenity, it's emptiness.
And there's such desperation in that light
inside the box. It's painful, and it's brilliant."

"Is it the same artist?" Flynn asked her.

"Of course. This is no student, no mimic,
no homage. But that's opinion." She sat
back on her heels. "I'm not an authority."

Could've fooled me, he thought. "Between you and Brad, I figure we've got all
the authority we need."

She'd forgotten Brad, and flushed a bit

with embarrassment. She'd all but lapped
the painting up, kneeling before it like a
supplicant. "Sorry." Still kneeling, she
looked up at him. "I got carried away. Could
you tell me where you acquired this?"

"At auction, in New York. A small house.
Banderby's."

"I've heard of them. The artist?"

"Unknown. You can just make out a par-
tial signature—an initial, really. Might be an
R, or a *P,* followed by the key symbol."

Malory bent lower to study the lower left
corner. "You had it dated, authenticated?"

"Of course. Seventeenth century. Though
the style has a more contemporary feel, the
painting was tested extensively. If you know
Banderby's you know it's both meticulous
and reputable."

"Yes. Yes, I know."

"And I had it tested independently. Just a
little habit of mine," Brad added. "The results coincided."

"I have a theory," Flynn began, but Malory waved him off.

"Can I ask you why you bought it? Banderby's isn't known for its bargains, and it's
an unknown artist."

"One reason is I was struck how much

the middle figure resembled Dana." It was true enough, Brad thought, if not the whole truth. "The overall painting, the power of it, caught me first, then that detail drew me in. And . . ." He hesitated, his gaze tracking across the painting. Then, feeling foolish, he shrugged. "You could say it spoke to me. I wanted it."

"Yes, I understand that." She took her glasses off, folded them and, slipped them carefully back in their case, then slid the case into her purse. "Flynn must have told you about the painting at Warrior's Peak."

"Sure, I told him. And when I saw this, I figured—"

"Ssh." Malory tapped him on the knee, then held up a hand for him to help her to her feet. "It has to be a series. There's another painting that comes before or after or in between. But there have to be three. It's consistently three. Three keys, three daughters. The three of us."

"Well, there are five of us now," Brad put in. "But, yeah, I follow you."

"You followed me when I said the same damn thing a half hour ago," Flynn complained. "My theory."

"Sorry." This time Malory patted him on

the arm. "It's all tumbling around in my head. I can almost make out the pieces, but I can't quite see the shape, or where they go. What they mean. Do you mind if we sit down?"

"Sure. Sorry." Immediately, Brad took her arm, led her to a sofa. "Can I get you something to drink?"

"Got any brandy? I know it's early, but I could really use just a little brandy."

"I'll find some."

Flynn sat beside her as Brad left the room. "What is it, Mal? You look a little pale all of a sudden."

"It hurts me." She looked toward the painting again, then closed her eyes as tears gathered in them. "Even as it dazzles my mind and my spirit, it hurts to look at it. I saw this happen, Flynn. I felt this happen to them."

"I'll put it away."

"No, no." She caught his hand, and the contact comforted her. "Art's supposed to touch you in some way. That's its power. What will the third be? And when?"

"When?"

She shook her head. "How flexible is your mind, I wonder? I'm just starting to find out how flexible mine is. You've told Brad all of it?"

"Yeah." Something here, he realized as he watched her. Something she wasn't quite sure she could say. "You can trust him, Malory. You can trust me."

"The question will be if either of you will trust me after I tell you both what I found out this morning and what I think it means. Your old friend might politely nudge me out the door and bolt it behind me."

"I never lock beautiful women out of the house." Brad walked back in with a snifter of brandy. He handed it to her, then sat on the coffee table, facing her. "Go ahead, knock it back."

She did just that, downing the brandy as she might a quick dose of medicine. It slid smoothly down her throat and soothed her jittery stomach. "It's a crime to treat a Napoleon that carelessly. Thanks."

"Knows her brandy," he said to Flynn. Color was seeping back into her cheeks. To give her a chance to recover more fully, he rapped Flynn with his elbow. "How the hell did you manage to get a woman with taste and class to look twice at you?"

"I had Moe knock her down, pin her to the ground. Better, Mal?"

"Yes." She blew out a breath. "Yes. Your painting's seventeenth century. That's absolutely conclusive?"

"That's right."

"I found out this morning that the painting at Warrior's Peak is twelfth century, possibly earlier but no later."

"If you got that from Pitte or Rowena—" Flynn began.

"No. I got that from Dr. Stanley Bower, of Philadelphia. He's an expert, and a personal acquaintance. I sent him scrapings of the painting."

"How'd you get scrapings?" Flynn wanted to know.

More color rose in her cheeks, but it wasn't the brandy that caused it. She cleared her throat, fussed with the clasp of her purse. "I took them when you went up there with me last week. When you and Moe distracted them. It was completely inappropriate, absolutely unethical. I did it anyway."

"Cool." Pure admiration shone in Flynn's tone. "So that means either Brad's experts or yours is off, or you're wrong about both being done by one artist. Or . . ."

"Or, the experts are right and so am I." Malory set her purse aside, folded her hands tight in her lap. "Dr. Bower would have to run more complex and in-depth tests to verify the date, but he wouldn't be off by centuries. I've seen both paintings, up close. Everything I know tells me they were done by the same hand. I know it sounds crazy. It *feels* crazy, but I believe it. Whoever created the portrait at Warrior's Peak did so in the twelfth century, and that same artist painted Brad's five hundred years later."

Brad slid his gaze toward Flynn, surprised that his friend wasn't goggling, or grinning. Instead, Flynn's face was sober and considering. "You want to believe that my painting was executed by a five-hundred-year-old artist?"

"Older, I think. Much older than that. And I think the artist painted both from memory. Rethinking bolting the door?" Malory asked him.

"I'm thinking both of you have gotten caught up in a fantasy. A romantic and tragic story that has no basis in reality."

"You haven't seen the painting. You haven't seen *The Daughters of Glass.*"

"No, but I've heard about it. All accounts place it in London, during the Blitz. Where it was destroyed. Most likely answer is that the one at the Peak is a copy."

"It's not. You think I'm being stubborn. I can be," Malory admitted, "but this isn't one of those times. I'm not a fanciful person either—or I haven't been."

She shifted her attention to Flynn, and her voice grew urgent. "Flynn, everything they told me, everything they told me and Dana and Zoe that first night was absolutely true. Even more amazing is what they didn't tell us. Rowena and Pitte—teacher and warrior—they're the figures in the background of each painting. They were there, in reality. And one of them painted both those portraits."

"I believe you."

Her breath shuddered out in relief at Flynn's simple faith. "I don't know what it means, or how it helps, but learning this— and believing it—is why I was picked. If I don't find the key, and Dana and Zoe don't find theirs after me, those souls will keep screaming inside that box. Forever."

He reached out, ran a hand over her hair. "We won't let that happen."

"Excuse me." Zoe hesitated at the entrance to the room. She was hard-pressed not to rub her hands over the satiny trim, or kick off her shoes to slide barefoot across the glossy floors.

She wanted to rush to the windows and study every view.

"The men outside said I should come right in. Um, Flynn? Moe's out there rolling around in something that looks a lot like dead fish."

"Shit. Be right back. Zoe, Brad." And he ran outside.

Brad got to his feet. He wasn't sure how he managed it when his knees had dissolved. He heard his own voice, a bit cooler than normal, a bit stilted, over the roar of blood in his head.

"Come in, please. Sit down. Can I get you something?"

"No, thanks. Sorry. Malory, I got your message and came right out. Is something wrong?"

"I don't know. Brad here thinks I've slipped a few gears, and I don't blame him."

"That's ridiculous." In her instant leap to

defend, she forgot the charm of the house, the aloof charm of the man. Her cautious and apologetic smile turned into a chilly scowl as she strode across the room to Malory's side. "And if you said any such thing, you're not only wrong, you're rude."

"Actually, I didn't get around to saying it yet. And as you don't know the circum- stances—"

"I don't have to. I know Malory. And if you're a friend of Flynn's, you should know better than to upset her."

"I beg your pardon." Where had that stiff, superior tone come from? How had his fa- ther's voice popped out of his mouth?

"It's not his fault, Zoe. Really. As to being upset, I don't know what I am." Malory shoved back her hair and, rising, gestured toward the painting. "You should take a look at this."

Zoe moved closer. Then clutched her throat. "Oh. Oh." And her eyes filled with hot tears. "It's so beautiful. It's so sad. But it belongs with the other. How did it get here?"

Malory slipped an arm around her waist so they stood joined together. "Why do you think it belongs with the other?"

"It's the Daughters of Glass, after the . . . the spell or the curse. The box, with the blue lights. It's just the way you described it, from your dream. And it's the same—the same . . . I don't know how to say it. It's like a set, or part of a set, painted by the same person."

Malory glanced over her shoulder at Brad, cocked a brow.

"Are you an art expert?" Brad asked Zoe.

"No." She didn't bother to look at him, and her tone was flat. "I'm a hairdresser, but I'm not stupid."

"I didn't mean to imply—"

"No, you meant to *say*. Will it help you find the key, Malory?"

"I don't know. But it means something. I have a digital camera out in the car. Can I take some pictures of it?"

"Be my guest." Brad jammed his hands into his pockets as Malory hurried out and left him alone with Zoe. "Are you sure I can't get you something? Coffee?"

"No, I'm fine. Thank you."

"I, ah, came in on this after the first reel," he began. "You might give me a little time to catch up."

"I'm sure Flynn will tell you everything you

need to know." She crossed the room, using the excuse of looking out for Malory as a chance to see the lovely river view.

What would it be like, she wondered, to be able to stand here whenever you wanted, to see the water and the light, the hills? Liberating, she imagined. And peaceful.

"Malory just told me she believes the Daughters of Glass exist, in reality. In some reality. And that the people you met at Warrior's Peak are several thousand years old."

She turned back, didn't so much as blink. "If she believes that, she has good reason. And I trust her enough to believe it too. Now would you like to tell me I've slipped a couple of gears?"

Irritation flickered over his face. "I never said that to her. I thought it, but I didn't say it. I'm not saying it to you either."

"But you're thinking it."

"You know, I only have two feet, but I'm managing to stay on the wrong one with you."

"Since I doubt we're going dancing anytime soon, I'm not really worried about your feet. I like your house."

"Thanks, so do I. Zoe—"

"I've done a lot of business at HomeMak-ers. I've found good values and excellent customer service in the local store."

"Good to know."

"I hope you're not planning on making any major changes there, but I wouldn't mind a little more variety on the seasonal stuff. You know, bedding plants, snow shovels, outdoor furniture."

His lips twitched. "I'll keep that in mind."

"And it wouldn't hurt to add a couple more cashiers on Saturdays. There's always a wait at the checkout."

"So noted."

"I'm starting my own business, so I pay attention to how things run."

"Are you opening your own salon?"

"Yes." She said it firmly, despite the way her stomach muscles clutched. "I was look-ing at space before I got Malory's message to come out here."

And why didn't Malory come back in? She was running out of steam now that her temper had leveled off. She didn't know what to talk about with a man who lived in a house like this, one who helped run an enormous national conglomerate. If "con-glomerate" was the word for it.

"In the Valley?"

"What? Oh, yes, I'm looking for a place in town. I'm not interested in a mall space. I think it's important to maintain a good downtown, and I want to be close to home so I can be more available to my son."

"You have a son?" His gaze zeroed in on her left hand, and he nearly sighed with relief at the lack of a wedding ring.

All Zoe saw was the quick look. She straightened her shoulders, stiffened them. "Yes. Simon's nine."

"Sorry it took me so long," Malory apologized as she came back in. "Flynn's got Moe tied to a tree in the side yard. He's hosing him down, for all the good that's going to do. He'll just be a wet incredibly smelly dog instead of only an incredibly smelly one. He said to ask if you had any shampoo or soap you could spare."

"I can come up with something. Go ahead and take your pictures."

Malory aimed the camera, waited until Brad's footsteps receded. "Talk about gods," she murmured to Zoe.

"What?"

"Bradley Charles Vane IV. His kind of

looks just smack a woman right in the hor-mones."

"Looks are genetic." Zoe very nearly sniffed. "Personality and manners are de-veloped."

"It was one fine day in the gene pool when he was made." She lowered the cam-era. "I gave you the impression he was giv-ing me a hard time. Really, he wasn't."

"Maybe, maybe not. But he's an arrogant snob."

"Wow." Malory blinked at the vehemence in Zoe's voice. "I didn't get that. I can't imagine Flynn being friends with anyone who fits the snob category. Arrogant is de-batable."

Zoe jerked a shoulder. "I've run into his type before. They're more interested in looking good than in being human. Anyway, he's not important. The painting is."

"I think it is. And what you said about them being a set, part of a set. I think that's true, and there's at least one more. I have to find it. Something in them, or about them, is going to point me toward the key. I'd better hit the books."

"Want some help?"

"All I can get."

"I'll head back now. There are a couple of things I need to do, then I'll swing by your place."

About the time Brad unearthed a bottle of shampoo he heard a car start. He went to the window, cursed under his breath as he watched Zoe and Malory head down his lane.

As far as first impressions went, he'd made a complete mess of it. He didn't usually alienate women on sight. But then again, the sight of a woman didn't usually slam into him like a hard, sweaty fist. Considering that, he supposed he could be excused for not being at his best.

He went downstairs, then detoured back into the great room instead of continuing to the outside. He stood staring at the painting as he had the first time he'd seen it at the auction house. The way he'd stared at it countless times since he'd acquired it.

He'd have paid any price for it.

It was true enough what he'd told Malory and Flynn. He'd bought it because it was magnificent, powerful, compelling. He'd been intrigued by the one figure's face, its resemblance to his childhood friend.

But it had been another face in the painting that had dazzled him, consumed him. Undone him. One look at that face, Zoe's face, and he'd fallen unreasonably in love.

Strange enough, he thought, when the woman had simply been a figure in a painting. How much more complicated and impossible was it now that he knew she was real?

He thought about it while he put some of his house in order. He continued to think about it later when he and Flynn climbed up to sit on the wall surrounding Warrior's Peak.

They each opened a beer and studied the exotic silhouette etched against a gloomy sky.

Lights glowed against the windows here and there, but as they drank their beers in silence, they saw no figure pass behind the glass.

"They probably know we're out here," Flynn said after a time.

"If we take your girlfriend's theory to

heart, and label them Celtic gods with a few thousand years under their belts, yeah, pretty safe bet they know we're out here."

"You used to be more open-minded," Flynn noted.

"Ah, no. Not really. Jordan would be the one inclined to bite on this kind of a story line and run with it."

"You see him lately?"

"A couple months ago. He's been doing a lot of traveling, so we don't manage to get together as often as we used to. Fuck it, Flynn." Brad flung an arm around Flynn's shoulder. "I've missed you assholes."

"Same goes. You going to tell me what you thought of Malory?"

"Classy, intellectual, and very, very hot— despite her dubious taste in men."

Flynn tapped the heels of his ancient tennis shoes against the stone of the wall. "I'm about half crazy about her."

"Serious crazy, or let's mambo crazy?"

"I don't know. Haven't figured it yet." He studied the house, and the quarter slice of moon that drifted over it. "I'm hoping it's door number two, because I'd just as soon not get serious crazy at this point."

"Lily was a social-climbing opportunist with a great rack."

"Jesus, Vane." He wasn't sure whether to laugh or give his friend a hard shove off the seven-foot wall. So he did neither and only brooded instead. "I was in love with her. I was going to marry her."

"Now you're not and you didn't. Lucky break for you. She wasn't worthy, Flynn."

Flynn shifted. He couldn't see Brad's eyes clearly. Their color blended into the night. "Worthy of what?"

"Of you."

"That's a hell of a thing to say."

"You'll feel better about the whole thing once you admit I'm right. Now back to current affairs. I liked her—your Malory—if you're keeping score."

"Even though you think she's whacked."

Boggy ground, Brad mused, even when you were walking it with a friend. "I think she's found herself in extraordinary circumstances and she's caught up in the mystique. Why wouldn't she be?"

Flynn had to smile. "That's just a diplomatic, bullshit way of saying she's whacked."

"You once punched me in the face for

saying Joley Ridenbecker had beaver teeth. I'm not heading meetings on Monday with a black eye."

"See, you are a suit. If I admit that Joley did indeed have teeth like a beaver, will you believe me if I tell you I've never known anyone with less of a whack quotient than Malory Price?"

"Okay, I'll take your word. And I'll admit the whole thing about the paintings is intriguing." Brad gestured with the beer, then drank again. "I'd like to get a look at the one in there myself."

"We can go up, knock on the door."

"In the daylight," Brad decided. "When we haven't been drinking."

"Probably better."

"Meanwhile, why don't you tell me more about this Zoe?"

"Haven't known her long, but I did some background checking. On her and Mal. Just in case Dana was getting sucked into some weird-ass scam. She moved to the Valley three years ago, with her kid."

"Husband?"

"Nope. Single parent. Looks like a good one to me. I met the kid. He's bright, normal, appealing. She worked at Hair Today, girly hair place on Market. Word is she's good at her profession, personable with customers, reliable. Got canned the same time Malory did, and around the same time they cut Dana's hours at the library to the bone. Another weird coincidence. She bought this little cardboard box of a house when she moved here. Apparently she's done most of the fixing-up work herself."

"Boyfriend?"

"Not that I know of. She . . . wait a minute. You ask two questions. Husband, boyfriend. My razor-sharp reporter's instinct leads me to the conclusion that you're thinking of the mambo."

"Or something. I should get back. I've got a hell of a lot to do in the next couple of days. But there's this one thing." Brad took another pull on the bottle. "How the hell are we going to get off this wall?"

"Good question." Flynn pursed his lips, studied the ground. "We could just sit here and keep drinking until we fall off."

Brad sighed, drained the bottle. "There's a plan."

Chapter Ten

Malory was barely out of the shower when she heard the knock on her front door. She belted her robe, snagged a towel, and wound it around her hair as she hurried to answer.

"Tod. You're up and about early."

"On my way to the coffee shop to ogle the nine-to-fivers before heading to work." He peered over her right shoulder, her left, then gave her a leer. "Got company?"

Malory swung the door wider in invitation. "No. All alone."

"Ah, too bad."

"You're telling me." She tucked up the ends of the towel more securely. "Want coffee here? I've already put the pot on."

"Not unless you can offer me a skinny mocha latte and a hazelnut muffin."

"Sorry, fresh out."

"Well, maybe I should just give you the good news, then be on my way." Still, he flopped into a chair.

"Oh! New boots?"

"Fabulous, aren't they?" He stretched out his legs, turned his feet right and left to admire them. "They're killing me, of course, but I couldn't resist them. I made a quick run through Nordstrom's on Saturday. Darling, you've got to go." He sat up, grabbed her hand as she curled on the end of the sofa. "The cashmere! There's a cowl neck in periwinkle that's calling your name."

"Periwinkle?" She sighed, long and deep, like a woman under the hands of a skilled lover. "Don't say periwinkle cashmere when I'm in the middle of a shopping moratorium."

"Mal, if you don't treat yourself, who will?"

"That's true. That's so true." She bit her lip. "Nordstrom's?"

"And there's a twinset in a strong peachy pink that was made for you."

"You know I have no defense against twinsets, Tod. You're killing me."

"I'll stop, I'll stop." He held up his hands. "But on to our morning bulletin. The Pamela has stepped in deep and stinky doo-doo."

"Oh, boy." Malory wiggled into the cushions. "Tell me everything. Don't spare the details."

"As if. Okay. We got in a Deco bronze— female figure wearing a flapper-style dress, feathered headband, pearls, gorgeous open-toed shoes, trailing a long scarf. She's absolutely charming. Witty, terrific details, with this sly 'let's you and me Charleston, big boy' smirk on her face. I fell in love."

"Did you call Mrs. Karterfield in Pittsburgh?"

"Ah, see!" He shot a finger in the air, as if proving a point. "Naturally you would assume that, or would have done so personally had you still been in charge. Which you should be."

"Goes without saying."

"I did, of course, call Mrs. Karterfield, who, as expected, asked us to hold it for her until she could come down personally to see it. Next week. And what happens when our darling Mrs. Karterfield from Pittsburgh comes into The Gallery to see a Deco figure?"

"She buys it. And often at least one other piece. If she comes in with a friend, which is usually the case, she harangues her companion until she buys something too. It's a good day when Mrs. Karterfield comes to town."

"Pamela sold it out from under her."

It took Malory ten seconds to find her voice. "What? What? How? Why? Mrs. K's one of our best customers. She *always* gets first look at Deco bronzes."

His lips folded into a thin, derisive smile. "A bird in the hand. That's what the twit told me when I found out. And how did I find out? I'll tell you," he said with a triumphant ring in his voice. "I found out when Mrs. K came in unexpectedly yesterday afternoon to see it. Just couldn't wait, she told me. And she brought *two* friends. Two, Mal. I could cry."

"What happened? What did she say?"

"I took her over to see it, and there's a Sold sign tucked under the base. I assumed it was a mistake, but I went to check. Pamela sold it that morning, apparently while I was in the back on the phone trying to soothe Alfred because Pamela the Putrid had accused him of overcharging for the crating for the marble nudes."

"Alfred? Overcharging?" Malory pressed her hands to her temples. "I can't keep up."

"It was horrible, just horrible. It took me twenty minutes to talk him down, and even then I wasn't sure he wouldn't stomp in and beat her with his hammer. Maybe I should've let him," Tod considered, then waved the thought away with both hands. "Anyway, while I was busy with Alfred, Pamela sold Mrs. K's Deco to a *stranger.* To some fly-by-night, some wanderer in off the street!"

He flopped back, splaying a hand over his chest. "I still can't believe it. Mrs. K was, naturally, very upset, and demanded to see you. Then I had to tell her you weren't with us any longer. And the doo-doo hit the fan. Big time."

"She asked for me? That's so sweet."

"It gets sweeter. Pamela came down. And they got into it. Boy, did they. Mrs. K asking how an item on hold for her could be sold. Pamela getting snippy and says how it's not gallery policy to hold a piece without a cash deposit. Can you *imagine*?"

"Cash deposit?" Horrified, Malory could only goggle. "From one of our oldest and most reliable clients?"

"Exactly! Then Mrs. K's all, Well, I've been patronizing The Gallery for fifteen years, and my word has always been good enough. And where is James? And Pamela's, I beg your pardon, but I'm in charge here. And Mrs. K shoots back that if James has put a moron in charge he's obviously gone senile."

"Oh, go, Mrs. K!"

"Meanwhile, Julia runs into the back and calls James to let him know there's a big, fat problem. Pamela and Mrs. K are practically coming to blows over the bronze when he comes rushing in. He's trying to calm them both down, but they're too into it. Mrs. K's saying she won't deal with *this woman.* I loved the way she said it. *This woman.* It sang. And Pamela's saying The Gallery's a business and can hardly run on one customer's whim."

"Oh, my God."

"James is frantic, promising Mrs. K he'll sort all this out, but she's furious. Her face is positively puce. She tells him she won't set foot in the place again as long as *that woman* is associated with The Gallery. And, you'll love this—if he let a jewel like Malory Price slip through his fingers he deserves to go out of business. And with that she sails out the door."

"She called me a jewel." Delighted, Malory hugged herself. "I love her. This is good stuff, Tod. It's really started my day off on a high note."

"There's even more. James is pissed. When's the last time you've seen James pissed?"

"Um. Never."

"Bingo." Tod punched a finger in the air. "He was pale as a sheet, his mouth was all tight and grim. And he told Pamela between clenched teeth"—Tod clamped his together to demonstrate—"'I need to speak with you, Pamela. Upstairs.'"

"What did she say?"

"Well, she stormed up, and he went behind her. Then he closed the door, which was very disappointing. I couldn't hear much of what he said, even though I went up and lurked around hoping to. But you could hear her clearly enough when she started raging. I'm making something out of this place, she tells him. You said I was in charge. I'm tired of having Malory Price thrown in my face every time I turn around. Why the hell didn't you marry her instead of me?"

"Oh." Malory thought about that scenario for a couple of seconds. "Eeuuw."

"Then she started crying, saying she was working so hard and nobody appreciated her. And she ran out. I barely scrambled away in time. It was all so exhausting, yet oddly exhilarating."

"Crying? Damn it." A little worm of sympathy crawled into Malory's chest. "Were they I'm-really-hurt-and-sad tears, or were they just I'm-really-pissed-off tears?"

"Pissed-off tears."

"Okay, then." She squashed the worm without mercy. "I'm probably going to hell, right, for getting such a charge out of all this?"

"We'll get a nice little condo together. But while we're still shuffling on this mortal coil, I think James is going to ask you to come back. In fact, Mal, I'm sure of it."

"Really?" Her heart gave a quick leap. "What did he say?"

"It's not so much what he said, as what he didn't say. He didn't go running after the weeping Pamela to dry her beady eyes. In fact, he stayed for the rest of the day, going over accounts. And he looked grim when he left. Absolutely grim. I'd say Pamela's reign of terror is at an end."

"This is a good day." Malory let out a long sigh. "A really good day."

"And I've got to get started on it. Not to worry," he said as he got up. "I'll keep you updated with bulletins. Meanwhile, the painting you were wondering about? The portrait?"

"The what? Oh, yes. What about it?"

"Remember how we both thought there was something familiar about it? It came to me. Do you remember, about five years ago, the oil on canvas, unsigned? Young Arthur of Britain, on the verge of drawing Excalibur from an altar of stone?"

Chilly fingers brushed the nape of her neck as the painting floated into her mind. "My God. I remember. Of course I remember. The color, the intensity, the way the light pulsed around the sword."

"Definitely the same style and school as the one you showed me. Might be the same artist."

"Yes . . . yes, it might. How did we ac-

quire it? Through an estate, wasn't it? In Ire-
land. James went to Europe for several
weeks to acquire. That was the best piece
he brought back with him. Who bought it?"

"Even my razor-sharp memory has its
limits, but I looked it up. Julia sold it to Jordan Hawke. The writer? Local boy, or was.
Lives in New York now, I think."

Her stomach did a long, slow roll. "Jordan Hawke."

"Maybe you can contact him through his
publisher if you want to talk to him about
the painting. Well, got to run, sugarplum."
He leaned down to give her a kiss. "Let me
know the minute James calls you to grovel.
I want all the deets."

There were half a dozen people at keyboards and phones when Malory reached
the third level of the *Dispatch,* where Flynn
had his office. She saw him immediately,
through the glass walls.

He paced back and forth in front of a
desk, tipping a bright silver Slinky from one
hand to the other. And appeared to be holding a conversation with himself.

She wondered how he could stand the

lack of privacy while he worked, that constant sensation of being on display. And the
noise, she thought. With all the clacking,
ringing, talking, and beeping, she would go
mad trying to formulate a single creative
thought.

She wasn't sure whom to speak with. No
one looked particularly like an assistant or
secretary. And despite the retro toy that
Flynn was currently playing with, it suddenly
dawned on Malory that he was a busy man.
An important man. Not a man she should
pop in on without notice.

As she stood, undecided, Flynn sat on
the corner of his desk, pouring the Slinky
from right hand to left and back again. His
hair was mussed, as if he'd spent some
time playing with it before he'd gotten hold
of the toy.

He wore a dark green shirt tucked into
casual khakis and very possibly the oldest
athletic shoes she'd ever seen.

There was a quick tingle in her belly, followed by a helpless little thud just under her
heart.

It was all right to be attracted to him, she
told herself. That was acceptable. But she
couldn't let this move to the level it was

headed for so quickly. That wasn't smart, it wasn't safe. It wasn't even . . .

Then he looked out through the glass, his eyes meeting hers for one fast, hot beat before he smiled. And the tingle, the thud, became more intense.

He flicked his wrist and the Slinky fell back into itself, then he gave her a come-ahead gesture with his free hand.

She wound her way through the desks and the din. When she stepped through the open office door, she saw with some relief that he hadn't been talking to himself, but on a speakerphone.

Out of habit, she closed the door behind her, then looked toward the sound of heroic snoring to see Moe sprawled belly-up between two filing cabinets.

What did you do about a man who brought his big, silly dog to work with him? she wondered. Maybe more to the point, how did you resist such a man?

Flynn held up a finger to signal one more minute, so she took the time to study his work area. There was a huge corkboard on one wall, jammed with notes, articles, photographs, and phone numbers. Her fingers itched to organize it, as well as the maze of papers on his desk.

Shelves were full of books, several of which seemed to be law and medical journals. There were phone books for a number of Pennsylvania counties, books of famous quotations, movie and music guides.

In addition to the Slinky, he had a yo-yo and a number of warlike action figures. There were several plaques and awards—to the paper and to Flynn personally, stacked together as if he hadn't gotten around to hanging them. She didn't know where she would have hung them either, as what little wall space he had was taken up by the corkboard and an equally large wall calendar for the month of September.

She turned around when he ended the call. Then stepped back as he moved toward her.

He stopped. "Problem?"

"No. Maybe. Yes."

"Pick one," he suggested.

"I got a tingle in my stomach when I saw you in here."

His grin spread. "Thanks."

"No. No. I don't know if I'm ready for that. I have a lot on my mind. I didn't come here to talk about that, but see—I'm already distracted."

"Hold that thought," he told her when his phone rang again. "Hennessy. Uh-huh. Uh-huh. When? No, that's no problem," he continued and scribbled on a pad that he unearthed from the rubble. "I'll take care of it."

He hung up, then unplugged the phone. "It's the only way to kill the beast. Tell me more about this tingle."

"No. I don't know why I told you in the first place. I'm here about Jordan Hawke."

"What about him?"

"He bought a painting from The Gallery about five years ago—"

"A painting? Are we talking about the same Jordan Hawke?"

"Yes. It's of young Arthur about to draw the sword from the stone. I think—I'm nearly sure—it's by the same artist as the painting at Warrior's Peak and the one your other friend owns. I need to see it again. It was years ago, and I want to be sure I'm remembering the details of it correctly and not just adding them in because it's convenient."

"If you're right, it's an awfully big coincidence."

"If I'm right, it's not a coincidence at all. There's a purpose to it. To all of it. Can you get in touch with him?"

Because his mind was racing through the details and possibilities, Flynn filled his hands with the Slinky again. "Yeah. If he's traveling, it might take a while, but I'll track him down. I didn't know Jordan had ever been in The Gallery."

"His name's not on our client list, so I'm assuming this was a one-shot deal. To my mind, that only makes it more important."

Excitement rose in her throat and bubbled out in her voice. "Flynn, I nearly bought that painting myself. It was beyond my budget at the time, but I was doing some creative math to justify the purchase. It was sold on my morning off, just before I was planning to go to James to ask him if I could buy it on a payment plan. I have to believe all this means something."

"I'll get in touch with Jordan. My take would be he bought it for somebody. He's not much on stuff, unlike Brad. He tends to travel light and keep the acquisitions to a minimum."

"I need to see the painting again."

"Got that. I'm on it. I'll find out what I can today and fill you in over dinner tonight."

"No, that's not a good idea. It's a really, really bad idea."

"Dinner's a bad idea? People have embraced the concept of the evening meal throughout history. There's documentation."

"Us having dinner is the bad part. I need to slow things down."

He set the toy down. He shifted his body, and when she would have countered to keep that distance between them, he grabbed her hand, tugged her forward. "Somebody rushing you?"

"More like something." Her pulse began to skip—in her wrists, in her throat, even at the back of her suddenly shaky knees. There was something about that cool calculation that came into his eyes, the sort that reminded her he tended to think two or three steps ahead. "Look, this is my problem, not yours, and . . . Stop," she ordered when his free hand cupped the back of her neck. "This is hardly the place for—"

"They're reporters." He inclined his head toward the glass wall between his office and the newsroom. "As such, they're aware that I kiss women."

"I think I'm in love with you."

She felt his hand jerk, then go limp. She saw the amusement and purpose on his face slide into blank shock. And twin demons of hurt and temper stabbed at her heart.

"There. Now I've made it your problem too." She pushed back from him—a simple matter, as he was no longer touching her.

"Malory—"

"I don't want to hear it. I don't need to hear you tell me it's too soon, too fast, you're not looking for this level of a relationship. I'm not stupid. I know all the brush-off lines. And I wouldn't be in this position right now if you'd taken no for an answer in the first place."

"Wait a minute now." Panic washed over his face, into his voice. "Let's take a second here."

"Take a second." Mortification was quickly outweighing the hurt and the anger. "Take a week. Take the rest of your life. Just take it someplace where I'm not."

She stormed out of his office. Since bloodcurdling terror still had a grip on him, he didn't consider going after her.

In love with him? She wasn't supposed to

fall in love with him. She was supposed to let him seduce her into bed, be sensible enough to keep things simple. She was supposed to be careful and practical and smart enough to keep *him* from falling in love with *her.*

He'd worked it all out, and now she was messing up the plan. He'd made himself very specific promises when his engagement had fallen apart. The first of which was to be sure he didn't put himself in that position again—a position where he was vulnerable to someone else's whims and wishes. To the point that his own ended up shattered around him.

His life was nothing like he'd thought it would be. Women—his mother, Lily—had shifted the lines on him. But damn it, he *liked* his life now.

"Women." Disgusted, he dropped into the chair behind his desk. "There's no figuring them."

"Men. They want everything their way."

Dana lifted her glass of wine in Malory's direction. "Sing it, sister."

Hours after she'd stalked out of Flynn's

office, Malory was soothing her wounded pride with a nice Pinot Grigio, female companionship, and salon treatments in the comfort of her own home.

There were a number of things to discuss, but she couldn't think about paintings and keys and destiny until she'd vented her spleen.

"I don't care if he is your brother. He's still a man."

"He is." Dana looked mournfully into her wine. "I'm sorry to say, but he is. Have some more potato chips."

"I will." With her hair pulled back from a face coated with a green-clay refining mask, Malory sipped and munched. She studied the folds of tinfoil Zoe was layering in Dana's hair. "Maybe I should have highlights too."

"You don't need them," Zoe told her and painted another section of Dana's hair. "You need shaping."

"Shaping involves scissors."

"You won't even know I've cut it, except it'll look and feel better."

"Let me drink a little more first. And see how it looks after you've whacked at Dana's."

"Don't say 'whack' in a sentence about my hair," Dana cautioned. "Are you going to tell us what you and Flynn fought about?"

Malory sniffed. "He just wants sex. Typical."

"Pig." Dana reached into the chip bowl. "I really miss sex."

"Me too." Zoe set another square of foil. "Not just the sex part, but the leading up to it and the coming down from it parts. The excitement and the nerves and the anticipation beforehand. Then all that skin and movement and discovery during, and the full and floating feeling after. I miss that a lot."

"I need another drink." Malory reached for the bottle. "I haven't had sex in four months."

"Got that beat." Dana raised her hand. "Seven and a half and counting."

"Sluts," Zoe said with a laugh. "Try a year and a half."

"Oh, ouch." Dana took the bottle, topped off her glass and Zoe's. "No, thanks all the same, but I don't think I want to try a year and a half of celibacy."

"It's not so bad if you keep busy. You're set for a while." Zoe patted Dana on the shoulder. "Just relax while I take off Malory's mask."

"Whatever you do to me, make sure I'm gorgeous. I want Flynn to suffer the next time he sees me."

"Guaranteed."

"It's really sweet of you to do all this."

"I like it. It's good practice."

"Don't say 'practice' when I've got a headful of tinfoil," Dana complained around a mouthful of chips.

"It's going to be great," Zoe assured her. "I want to have a full-service salon, and I need to be sure I can handle all the treatments I want to offer. I looked at this wonderful building today."

Her face went wistful as she cleaned and blotted Malory's skin. "It's way too big for what I need, but it was just great. Two stories with a big attic space. A frame house right on the border of business and residential on Oak Leaf Drive. It's got a wonderful covered porch, even a garden in the back where you could set tables and benches. High ceilings, solid hardwood floors that need work. The rooms all sort of tumble into each other on the first floor. A really nice flow of space that keeps it all intimate."

"I didn't know you were looking at houses," Malory said.

"I'm just looking. This is the first place I've seen that caught at me. You know?"

"Yeah, I know. If it's too big, and you really love it, maybe you could get somebody to take part of it for another business."

With the mask removed, Zoe began to stroke on a moisturizer. "I thought of that. Actually, I have this wild idea. Don't tell me I'm crazy until I finish. Each of us said what we really wanted was to have our own place."

"Oh, but—"

"Not till I'm finished." Zoe cut Malory off as she dabbed on eye cream. "The lower floor has two wonderful bow windows. Perfect for displays. There's a central hall, and on each side are those nice rooms. If someone was interested in opening a tasteful gallery for art and local crafts, she couldn't find a better place. At the same time, on the other side of that hall there's a wonderful set of parlors that would make a terrific bookstore, with room for a hip little bistro or tearoom."

"I didn't hear anything about a salon in

there," Dana pointed out, but she was listening.

"Upstairs. When someone comes in to get her hair or nails done, or enjoy any number of our wonderful treatments and services, she'll have to pass by the gallery and the bookstore, coming and going. Perfect time to select that lovely gift for Aunt Mary, or pick up a book to read while she's being combed out. Maybe even have a nice glass of wine or cup of tea before heading home. It's all there, in one fabulous setting."

"You really have been thinking," Malory murmured.

"I sure have. I even have a name for it. 'Indulgence.' People need to indulge themselves from time to time. We could do packages and cross-promotions. I know it's a big idea, especially when we haven't known each other very long. But I think it could work. I think it could be great. Just look at it before you say no."

"I'd like to see it," Dana said. "I'm miserable at work. And what's the point of being miserable?"

Malory could almost see the energy and enthusiasm for the idea pumping off Zoe in waves. There were a dozen rational comments she could make to point out why it wasn't just a big idea but a messy one.

She didn't have the heart to do that, but she felt obliged to ease carefully back. "I don't want to muck things up, but I'm pretty sure I'm going to be asked to come back to The Gallery. In fact, my old boss called this afternoon and asked if I'd come in and speak with him tomorrow."

"Oh. Well. That's great." Zoe stepped behind Malory's chair, began to run her fingers through Malory's hair to get a feel for the weight and the lines. "I know you love working there."

"It was like home." Malory lifted a hand, covered one of Zoe's. "I'm sorry. It did sound like a good idea. A fun one, but—"

"Don't worry about it."

"Hey." Dana waved a hand. "Remember me? I'm still interested. I can take a look at the place tomorrow. Maybe we can make it work between the two of us."

"Great. Mal, let's wet down your hair."

She felt too guilty to argue, and with her hair dampened, she sat stoically while Zoe snipped.

"I'd better tell you both why I went by the

newspaper this morning to see Flynn, to whom I'm no longer speaking."

Zoe continued to snip as she told them about the painting in The Gallery and her belief that it was done by the same artist.

"You'll never guess who bought it," she continued. "Jordan Hawke."

"Jordan Hawke?" Dana all but squeaked. "Goddamn it, now I want chocolate. You must have some."

"Emergency supply, deli drawer of the fridge. What's the problem?"

"We were semi-involved a million years ago. Damn it, damn it, damn it," Dana repeated as she yanked open the drawer and found two bars of Godiva. "Godiva's your emergency chocolate?"

"Why not have the best when you're feeling your worst?"

"Good point."

"You were involved with Jordan Hawke?" Zoe wanted to know. "Romantically?"

"It was years ago, when I was still young and stupid." Dana unwrapped the bar, took a big bite. "Bad breakup, he took off. End of story. Bastard, creep, asshole." She took another bite. "Okay, I'm done."

"I'm sorry, Dana. If I'd known . . . Well, I

don't know what I'd have done. I need to see the painting."

"Doesn't matter. I'm over him. I'm so over him." But she picked up the chocolate bar again, had another bite.

"I have to say something, and you might want the second emergency bar after I do. I can't buy coincidence on this. I can't rationalize it all. The three of us—and Flynn, your brother. Now Flynn's two best friends. And one of those friends is a former lover of yours. That makes a very tight circle."

Dana stared at her. "Just let me go on record as saying I really hate that part. Do you have another bottle of this wine?"

"I do. Rack above the fridge."

"I'll either walk home or call Flynn to pick me up. But I'm planning on being toasted by the time I leave."

"I'll drive you home," Zoe offered. "Go ahead and get toasted—as long as you're ready to leave by ten."

"Your hair looks fabulous." Swaying a little from trying to keep Dana company with wine consumption, Malory waved her fingers at Dana's new hair.

The subtle blond highlights accented Dana's dusky skin tone and dark eyes. And as a result of whatever else Zoe's magic fingers had done, the long, straight sweep looked sleeker, glossier.

"I'll have to take your word. I'm pretty blind."

"Mine looks fabulous too. Zoe, you're a genius."

"Yes, I am." Flushed with success, Zoe nodded at both of them. "Use that night cream sample I gave you for the next couple of days," she told Malory. "Let me know what you think. Come on, Dana, let's see if I can pour you into the car."

" 'kay. I really like you guys." With a drunk and sentimental smile, Dana threw her arms around each of them. "I can't think of anybody I'd rather be in the big mess with. And when it's over, we should have hair and drinking nights once a month. Like a book club."

"Good idea. 'Night, Mal."

"You want some help with her?"

"Nope." Zoe wrapped a supporting arm around Dana's waist. "I've got her. I'm stronger than I look. I'll call you tomorrow."

"Me too! Did I tell you Jordan Hawke is a jerk?"

"Only about five hundred times." Zoe guided Dana toward the car. "You can tell me again on the drive home."

Malory closed the door, carefully locked it, then wove her way to the bedroom. Unable to resist, she stood in front of the mirror and experimented with the new cut, tossing her hair, tilting her head at different angles.

She couldn't tell, not exactly, what Zoe had done, but whatever it was, it was right. Could be, she mused, it paid to keep her mouth shut for a change instead of directing the hairdresser's every snip.

Maybe she should feel guilty and drink wine every time she visited the salon.

She could try the combination in other areas of her life. The dentist, ordering in restaurants, men. No, no, not men. She scowled at herself in the mirror. If you didn't direct men, they directed you.

Besides, she wasn't going to think about men. She didn't need men. She didn't even like men at the moment.

In the morning, she would spend an hour working on the puzzle of the key. Then she

would dress, very carefully, very professionally. A suit, she decided. The dove gray with
the white shell. No, no, the red. Yes, the red
suit. Powerful *and* professional.

She raced to the closet, scanned her
wardrobe, which was arranged precisely
according to function and color. With the
red suit in hand, she danced back to the
mirror, held it in front of her.

"James," she began, trying out a sympa-
thetic yet aloof expression, "I'm so sorry to
hear that The Gallery is going to hell in a
handbasket without me. Come back? Well,
I don't know if that's possible. I have several
other offers. Oh, please, please, don't
grovel. It's embarrassing."

She fluffed her hair. "Yes, I know Pamela
is the devil. We all know that. Well, I suppose if things are *that* bad, I'll have to help
you out. Now, now, don't cry. Everything's
going to be fine. Everything's going to be
perfect again. Just as it should be."

She snickered and, pleased that all would
soon be right with her world again, turned
away to prepare for bed.

She undressed and lectured herself into
putting her clothes away instead of just
throwing them around the room. When she

heard the knock on her front door, she was wearing only a white silk sleep shirt. Assuming it was one of her friends who'd forgotten something, she turned off the locks and opened the door.

And blinked at a grim-faced Flynn.

"I want to talk to you."

"Maybe I don't want to talk to you," she responded, trying to enunciate each word instead of slurring them together.

"We need to work this out if we're going to . . ." He took a good look at her, the wonderfully tumbled hair, the glowing face, the slim curves under clingy white silk. And the vague and glassy look of her eyes.

"What? You're drunk?"

"I'm only half drunk, which is completely my business and my right. Your sister is fully drunk, but you've no cause for concern as Zoe, who is not in any way drunk, is driving her home."

"It takes countless beers or an entire bottle of wine to get Dana completely drunk."

"That seems to be correct, and in this case it was wine. Now that we've established that, I'll remind you I'm only half drunk. Come in and take advantage of me."

He let out what might've been a laugh

and decided the best place for his hands—
well, not the best but the smartest—was his
pockets. "That's a delightful invitation,
sweetie, but—"

She solved the problem by gripping his
shirt firmly and giving a good yank. "Come
on in," she repeated, then fixed her mouth
on his.

Chapter Eleven

Flynn found himself shoved back against the door, tripping over his own feet as it swung shut behind him. Most of the blood had drained out of his head by the time she'd gone to work on his throat with lips and teeth.

"Whoa, wait. Mal."

"Don't wanna wait." Her hands got as busy as her mouth. Had she actually thought she didn't like men? She certainly liked this one. So much that she wanted to gobble him up in quick and greedy bites.

"How come people always say you gotta wait? I want you to . . ." She clamped her teeth on his earlobe, then whispered a creative demand.

"Oh, God."

He wasn't entirely sure if it was a prayer of thanks or a plea for help. But he was sure his willpower had a very specific limit, and he was fast approaching it.

"Okay, okay, let's just calm down here a minute, Malory." She slid her body over his, and when her eager fingers danced down, down, he felt his eyes do a slow roll to the back of his head. "Now hold on."

"I am." She tipped her head back to send him a wicked grin.

"Ha, ha. Yeah, you are." He closed his hands over her wrists and with no little regret lifted her busy hands to his shoulders.

He was out of breath and hard as stone. "We've got a choice here. You can hate me in the morning, or I can." Her eyes sparkled up at him, and her lips were curved in a feline smile that had his throat going dry. "God, you're pretty when you're half plowed. You should go lie down now."

"Okay." She pressed herself against him, gave her hips a suggestive little grind. "Let's."

Slippery knots of lust tied and tangled in his belly. "I'm just going to back away from the beautiful drunk woman."

"Uh-uh." She rose on her toes to rub her lips over his again, felt the desperate plunge of his heart. "You'll never make it out the door. I know what I'm doing, and I know what I want. Does that scare you?"

"Pretty much, yeah. Honey, I came by to talk to you, about something I'm currently incapable of remembering. Why don't I make us some coffee and we'll . . ."

"I guess I have to do everything." In one fluid motion, she slid the sleep shirt over her head and tossed it aside.

"Oh, sweet Jesus."

Her body was pink and white—delicious—with that elegant cloud of hair tumbling down to tease her breasts. Her eyes, deeply blue and suddenly full of knowledge, fixed on his as she stepped close to him again.

Her arms had wound around his neck, and her mouth was a hot, silky temptation on his. "Don't be afraid," she whispered. "I'll take very good care of you."

"I bet." Somehow his hands had gotten lost in the sexy mass of her hair. His body was a maze of aches and needs, and reason couldn't find the exit. "Malory, I'm no hero."

"Who wants one?" With a laugh, she nipped at his jaw. "Let's be bad, Flynn. Let's be really bad."

"Since you put it that way." He swung her around, reversing their position so she was trapped between the door and his body. "I hope to God you remember whose idea this was, and that I tried to—"

"Shut up, and take me."

If he was going to hell, he'd make damn sure it was worth the trip. With his hands on her hips, he jerked her up to her toes, and caught the light of triumph on her face an instant before his mouth crushed hers.

It was like holding a lit fuse, all sizzle and spark, a dangerous woman who knew her own power. Who was testing his. Her skin was already flushed and hot, and as he took his hands over her the soft sounds she made in her throat weren't whimpers but urgings. Already desperate, he buried his face in her hair, pressed his hand between her thighs.

She erupted. A throaty cry, a bite of nails on his back, a lightning surge of hips. Then she was dragging his shirt over his head, scraping her teeth over his shoulder as her quick hands yanked at his jeans.

"In bed." Though he had wild, erotic visions of taking her against the door, the pleasure would end too soon that way. Instead he circled her, prying off his shoes as they bumped into a corner of the wall.

She didn't care where. She only wanted to go on feeling this wild whiplash of power, having these wonderful pulsing aches continue to dominate her body. She was spinning in some mad world of exquisite sensations, and every touch, every taste, added more.

She wanted to feel his muscles quiver, to feel the heat pumping out of his pores. And to know, deep inside, that she had caused it.

They fell on the bed, breathless and insane, and rolled, an erotic tangle of limbs on the pretty pastel covers.

She laughed when he clamped his hands on hers and yanked her arms over her head.

"Gotta slow down a little," he managed.

She arched up to him. "Why?"

"Because I'm going to do things to you, and that takes time."

She ran her tongue over her top lip. "Where would you like to start?"

His belly tightened to the edge of pain.

He lowered his head to start with her mouth. Plump and soft, hot and wet. He drugged himself with her until they both trembled. He slid his tongue over the hollow of her throat, where her pulse hammered. Then down, slowly, until he could taste the delicate, scented breasts. And when he caught her nipple between his teeth and tugged, she began to moan.

She gave herself over to the pleasure, the sheer bliss of being savored and exploited. Her body was open to him, to that ravenous mouth, those questing hands. When he took her up, she flew free, riding the hot punch of air, tumbling down again to draw him closer.

She could see him in the light that spilled from the hallway, and her heart leaped at the intensity on his face as he watched her. Love and delight raced through her. Here was an answer, the answer to at least one question.

He was for her. And she rose up, wrapping herself around him with a kind of giddy glee.

Their mouths met again in a deep, shuddering kiss that had his heart flipping over inside his chest.

She smelled of something secret, of seduction. Those quick, catchy gasps coming from her sliced through him like tiny silver knives. He wanted to bury himself inside her until the world ended. And when her hands cruised over him, when those soft sounds of approval hummed in her throat as she explored him, he wondered if it already had.

She scraped her nails over his belly and had him quivering like a stallion. "I want you. I want you inside me. Tell me you want me."

"I do. I want you." He lowered his mouth to hers once more. "Malory. From the first minute."

Her lips curved under his. "I know." She arched her hips. "Now."

He braced himself, then a sliver of sanity cut through the madness. "Oh, Christ. Condom. Wallet. Pants. Where are my pants?"

"Mmm. It's okay." She rolled over him, nipping at his shoulder as she pulled open the nightstand drawer. "Condom. Drawer. Nightstand."

"Have I mentioned that I love practical, prepared women?"

"Why don't I help you on with this?"

She took her sweet time so that he had to fist his hands in the tangled spread to keep himself from flying to the ceiling.

The woman had wicked hands, he thought and bit back a groan.

Wonderful, wicked hands.

She rose over him, shook her hair back. And smiled. "Now," she said.

He moved fast, flipping her onto her back, pinning her body with his. "Now," he repeated and drove deep inside her.

He watched the shock race over her face, felt the waves of it vibrate through him. They trembled there, each caught on some fine edge.

And with her eyes locked on his, she began to move. A rising up, a falling away, so smooth, so fluid it was like sliding through silk. Her name echoed in his head, like a song, or a prayer. He clung to the echo of it, clung to the frayed threads of control as she shattered around him.

She fell apart. Oh, God, the most wonderful sensation. A losing of self, then a gathering back. Her mind hazed. And with one last liquid sigh, she rode the final crest.

Locking him close, she took him with her.

*   *   *

He didn't want to think. Thinking under the current circumstances couldn't be productive. It would be much better for all involved if he kept his mind a solid blank and just enjoyed the superior sensation of having a soft, sexy woman under him.

If he didn't think, he might be able to keep her there long enough to make love with her again. Then there'd be another period of not-thinking.

Who knew how long he could keep up that pattern? Maybe indefinitely.

When she moved under him, a lazy kind of stretch, it seemed a very good possibility.

"I want some water." She stroked a hand down his back. "You thirsty?"

"Not if it means moving for the next five or ten years."

She gave his ass a light pinch. "*I'm* thirsty. So you have to move."

"Okay." But he nuzzled her hair a moment longer. "I'll get it."

"That's all right." She gave him a little shove and wiggled out from under him. "I'll get it."

She stopped by the closet on the way

out, and he had a glimpse of something thin and silky billowing out over that gorgeous body before she strolled out the door.

"Maybe I'm dreaming. Maybe this is just some wish-fulfillment fantasy, and I'm really in my own bed with Moe snoring on the floor."

Or maybe not.

He sat up, scrubbed his hands over his face. And unfortunately, began to think. He'd come over because he'd been churned up, pissed off, and generally confused by the scene they'd had in his office that morning.

And now he was in her bed, naked, and they'd just had incredible sex. When she'd been drunk. Well, maybe not drunk, but impaired.

He should've walked away. He should've found the moral fortitude to walk away from a naked, willing woman when that naked, willing woman's inhibitions had been erased by alcohol.

And what was he, a saint?

When she walked back in wearing nothing but a short red robe, he scowled at her.

"I'm a human being. I'm a man."

"Yes. I think we've established that beyond doubt." She sat on the side of the bed, offered him the glass she'd brought in.

"You were naked." He took the glass, gulped down water. "You were all over me."

She cocked her head. "And your point is?"

"If you regret this—"

"Why should I?" She took the glass back, swallowed the stingy sip he'd left behind. "I got you where I wanted you. I'd been drinking, Flynn, but I knew what I was doing."

"Okay, then. Okay. It's just that, after what you said this morning . . ."

"That I'm in love with you?" She set the glass on the coaster she kept on her nightstand. "I am in love with you."

Emotions ran through him, all too hot and fast to decipher. But layered over all of them was sheer, sweaty fear. "Malory." When she only continued to study him with a quiet patience, the fear began to trickle into his throat. "Listen, I don't want to hurt you."

"Then don't." She gave his hand a comforting little squeeze. "Actually, you've got a lot more to worry about than I do."

"I do?"

"Yes, you do. I love you, which means, naturally, I want you to love me back. I don't always get what I want, but I usually find a way to get it. Almost always, in fact. So to my way of thinking, you'll end up in love with me. Since the idea of that scares you, you've got more to worry about than I do."

She trailed a hand over his chest. "You're in really good shape for somebody who works at a desk."

He grabbed her hand before it could head south. "Let's stay focused here. The whole love deal just isn't in the cards for me."

"You had a bad experience." She leaned in to give him a light kiss. "That sort of thing's bound to leave a mark. Lucky for you, I can be patient. And gentle," she added as she shifted, then straddled him. "And very, very determined."

"Oh, boy. Malory—"

"Why don't you just lie back and enjoy the fringe benefits of being courted?"

Aroused, flustered, grateful, he let her nudge him back. "Sort of hard to argue with that."

"As well as a waste of time." She unbelted her robe, let it slide from her shoulders. She ran her hands up his chest, then caught his face in them before she kissed him senseless. "I'm going to marry you," she murmured. And laughed when his body jerked in shock. "Don't worry. You'll get used to the idea."

Still laughing, she smothered his unintelligible protest with her mouth.

She felt so *good.* Not just the sex, Malory thought as she sang in the shower. Though that could hardly be discounted. She always felt good, confident, directed, when she had a clear, well-defined purpose.

The quest for the key was so nebulous that it confused as much as it energized. But convincing Flynn that they belonged together was crystal clear. A goal she could get her teeth into.

She hadn't a clue why she'd fallen in love with him, and that's what told her it was real.

He certainly didn't fit her image of her dream man. He didn't cook gourmet meals or speak fluent French (or Italian) or love spending his free time in museums. He didn't wear tailored suits or read poetry.

At least, she didn't think he read poetry.

She'd always planned to fall in love with a

man who had some of those attributes. And, naturally, in her outline the right man would court her, charm her, seduce her, then pledge his undying love at the perfect romantic moment.

Before Flynn she had analyzed and dissected every relationship, picked at every flaw until she'd worked a dozen holes into the cloth of it.

And in the end, that hadn't mattered, because none of them had been right.

She had no desire to worry about the flaws with Flynn. She only knew her heart had gone splat when she'd least expected it. And she liked it.

She had to admit she also liked the idea that he was spooked. It was intriguing, and it was challenging to be the pursuer for a change. To be the aggressor, and to keep a man slightly off balance with honesty.

When he'd finally managed to stumble out of bed sometime around three in the morning, she'd sensed his fear and confusion just as much as she'd sensed his desire to stay.

Let him stew about it for a while, she decided.

She amused herself by calling the local

florist and ordering a dozen red roses to be delivered to his office. She almost danced out of her apartment to keep her appointment with James.

"Well, aren't we bright and sassy this morning," Tod commented when she swung into The Gallery.

"Aren't we just." She caught his face in her hand and gave him a noisy kiss. "Is he in?"

"Upstairs. He's expecting you. Sugarpie, you look fabulous. Good enough to eat."

"I feel good enough to eat." She patted his cheek, then glided up the steps. She knocked on the office door, stepped in. "Hello, James."

"Malory." He rose from the desk, both hands extended. "Thank you so much for coming in."

"Of course." She took the chair he gestured toward. "How are things?"

With a pained expression on his face, he sat. "I'm sure you've heard about the difficulty Pamela had with Mrs. K. A terrible misunderstanding, which I'm afraid may have cost The Gallery a valued client."

Malory forced herself to appear concerned even while her mind jumped with glee. "Yes, I'm so sorry that things have . . ." Don't say gone to hell in a hand-basket, she ordered herself, and continued without missing a beat. "Been a bit difficult during this transition."

"Yes. Difficult. Pamela's very enthusiastic about The Gallery, but I'm afraid she's still learning. I see now that I gave her too much autonomy too quickly."

To keep from punching her fists in the air, Malory sedately folded her hands on her knee. "She has a very precisely defined vision."

"Yes. Yes." He worried his gold pen, fiddled with his tie. "I think her strengths may lie in a more peripheral area than actual client-staff relations. I realize there's friction between the two of you."

Cool, she reminded herself. "I also had a very precisely defined vision, which unfortunately clashed with hers. So, yes, there was considerable friction."

"Well." He cleared his throat. "Perhaps I let Pamela influence me in that regard. I felt, sincerely, that it might be time for you to explore your talents, to experiment. However, I see I didn't take into consideration your affection and loyalty to The Gallery, or how being nudged out of the nest, as it were, might upset you."

"I admit it did." But she tempered her statement with the sweetest of smiles.

"I have considered all of this over the last couple of weeks. I'd very much like you to come back, Malory. To resume your managerial duties. At a ten percent increase in salary."

"This is so unexpected." She had to imagine her butt glued to the chair so she couldn't leap up and do a victory dance. "And I'm flattered. But . . . can I be frank?"

"Of course."

"The friction we spoke of is still going to be there. I have to admit I hadn't been happy here the last several months. Your . . . nudging me out of the nest," she said, "was painful and frightening. But once I was out, I had the opportunity to look back and realize that the nest had become . . . let's say a little crowded."

"I understand." He held up his hands, then clasped them together under his chin. "I can promise that Pamela won't interfere with your authority, or with the policies that have long been in effect here. You'll have the last word, barring mine, of course, on

KEY OF LIGHT 301

acquisitions and displays, on featured artists and so on. Just as before."

It was exactly what she'd wanted. More than, she realized when she calculated the bonus in salary. She would be back doing what she did best, and with considerable financial reward, and she would have the personal, if unattractive, satisfaction of putting Pamela's nose out of joint.

She would have won, without firing a shot.

"Thank you, James. I can't tell you how much it means to me to know you want me back, that you have confidence in me."

"Wonderful, wonderful." He beamed at her. "You can start right away, today if that's good for you. It'll be like the last two weeks never even happened."

Like they never even happened.

Her stomach gave a mighty pitch. Then, suddenly, it was as if sensible Malory stepped to the side and listened in shock as reckless Malory took charge.

"But I can't come back. I'll always be grateful for everything you taught me, all the opportunities you gave me—the last being pushing me out the door so I'd have to leave my comfort zone. I'm going to open my own business."

Oh, my God, she thought. I'm going to open my own business.

"It won't be anything as grand as The Gallery. Smaller, more . . ." She nearly said "accessible," then managed to backtrack. "Low-key," she continued. "I'm going to focus primarily on local artists and craftspeople."

"Malory, you must be aware how much time and energy that sort of thing consumes. And more, the financial risk involved." There was no doubt about it, James was panicking.

"I know. I don't seem to be as worried about taking risks as I used to be. In fact, I'm excited by the prospect of taking them. But thank you, thank you so much for all you've done for me. I really have to go now."

She got up quickly, afraid she would change her mind. Here was her safety net, spread out, ready to catch her. And she was swinging out beyond it to where the ground was very hard, and very far away.

"Malory, I wish you'd take some time to think this through."

"Do you know what happens when you always look before you leap?" She reached out and touched his hand before hurrying toward the door. "You hardly ever make the jump."

She didn't waste time. Malory hunted down the address Zoe had relayed, and pulled into a double driveway behind Dana's car.

Good location, she decided, sliding practical Malory back into place. There would be some pedestrian traffic, and reasonable parking for people who needed it.

The house was charming. Homey, she thought. And the three of them working together could certainly perk it up. Paint the porch, plant some trailing vines. Zoe probably already had a horde of ideas on that.

The walkway needed to be repaired or replaced. She noted that detail down on the clipboard she'd brought with her. Window boxes? Yes, planted seasonally.

And wouldn't it snazz up the entrance to have a stained-glass window replace the clear one over the front door? Something designed specifically for them. She had some contacts in that area.

Still making notes, she opened the front door.

The foyer could be a showcase for all three businesses. Yes, there was a way to do that with clever placement and displays, keeping it friendly and informal while advertising their goods and services.

The light was good, the floors a treasure once they were refinished. The walls, well, paint would solve that.

She wandered through, delighted with the rooms. They did seem to tumble together, she thought. Just as Zoe had said.

An excellent way to blend businesses.

After filling pages with notes she strolled back, just as Dana and Zoe came down the stairs.

"Eventually, I'd like to refit the master bath with a Swedish shower and aromatherapy station," Zoe was saying. "But for now . . . Malory, hi."

"Hi." Malory lowered her clipboard. "I'm in."

"I knew it!" With a whoop, Zoe flew down the stairs and grabbed her. "I just knew it. Did you see? Have you been through? Isn't it great? Isn't it perfect?"

"Yes, yes, and yes. I haven't been upstairs yet, but down here . . . I love it," she said.

Dana stood on the stairs, her lips pursed in speculation. "Why'd you change your mind?"

"I don't know. At least I don't know in any reasonable, logical sense. When James offered me my job back, with a raise, I thought, thank God, everything'll be back to normal now."

She let out a breath and, hugging the clipboard to her chest, spun in a circle. "Then, I don't know, I heard myself telling him I couldn't come back, I was starting my own business. I guess I realized I don't want everything to be back to normal. I want to do this, and I want to do it with both of you. That's all I know."

"We've all got to be really sure. Zoe, tell her what you told me. About the house."

"Well, the owner's willing to rent it, but they're looking for a buyer. The fact is, it makes more financial sense to buy it."

"Buy it?" The gorge she was leaping across suddenly widened. "How much?"

Zoe named a price, then hurried on when Malory paled. "But that's just the asking price. Plus, I've been doing some figuring, and if you compare the mortgage payment at current interest rates over a thirty-year term to the proposed monthly rent, it's not that much more. And it's equity. It's an investment. Then there's the tax break."

"Don't get her started on the tax break," Dana warned. "Your brains will start leaking out of your ears. Just take my word for it, she's got it covered."

"We need a lawyer to draw up a legal partnership," Zoe continued. "Then we pool our money. We have enough for the down payment, especially once we negotiate the asking price down. And still there's enough left over to hold us. We'll take a loan for the property and the start-up costs. We can do it."

"I believe you. I think that's why my stomach hurts." Malory pressed a hand to it, then looked at Dana. "Buy?"

"God help us. Buy," she agreed.

"I guess we should shake or something." Zoe held out a hand.

"Wait, before we do, I should tell you something." Malory cleared her throat. "I had sex with Flynn last night. Three times."

"Three?" Dana abruptly sat down on the stairs. "Ah, go, Flynn?"

"You're okay with that?"

"I'm his sister, not his mother." But she rubbed at her temple. "Weren't you drunk last night?"

"No, you were. I was just buzzed. I'll add that being aware I was buzzed, he attempted, pretty strongly, to be a gentleman and step back."

"That's so sweet," Zoe offered.

"Even after I got naked and jumped him."

"That's . . . Wow!"

With a laugh, Malory patted Zoe's shoulder. But Dana remained silent. "I didn't get naked and jump him just because I was buzzed and well, horny. I'm in love with him. I don't have the whys on that any more than I know why I want to own this house with the two of you. It just is, from somewhere deep inside me. It just is. I'm in love with him, and I'm going to marry him."

"Malory! This is wonderful." Leading with her romantic heart, Zoe flung her arms around her friend. "I'm so happy for you."

"Don't hand out the orange blossoms yet. I still have to convince him he can't live without me." She stepped forward. "I'm in love with him, Dana."

"I'm getting that."

"I know this might complicate our friendship, and any business relationship we might plan on having."

"And if it does?"

"Then I'm sorry. I'll back out of the friendship. I'll back out of the business plans. But I'm going to keep Flynn, whether he likes it or not."

Dana's lips twitched as she got to her feet. "I guess he's toast. We going to shake hands on this deal and get us a lawyer or what?"

Chapter Twelve

She didn't know what she was feeling. She wasn't sure what she was doing. But little snags like that had never stopped Dana before.

The minute she could manage it, she tracked down Flynn.

She missed him at the paper, followed his trail to the vet's, where she was told she'd missed him and Moe by fifteen minutes. The irritation of that had her deciding she was angry with him, though she had no concrete reason to be.

But by the time she arrived at his house, she was enjoying her temper.

She slammed the door and stalked into

the living room, where both her brother and his dog were sprawled out like the dead.

"I need to talk to you, Casanova."

"Don't yell." Flynn remained on the sofa. On the floor beside him Moe whimpered. "Moe needed his shots. We've both been traumatized. Go away. Come back tomorrow."

"Now, right now, before I find a sharp implement to stick in your rump. What's the idea of banging Malory when you know perfectly well she has to keep her mind on the goal?"

"I don't know. Might've had something to do with my tripping and falling over her naked body. And it wasn't banging. I object to the term 'banging,' which is beside the fact that it's none of your goddamn business."

"It's my business when she's just become my business partner. When prior to that we were partners of another sort, and it's my business because I like her a lot, and she's in love with you. This shows a remarkable lack of taste, but is nonetheless the way it is."

Guilt crept slyly into his belly. "It's not my fault she thinks she's in love with me."

"I didn't say 'thinks.' She's not an idiot, despite her lousy taste in men. She knows her own mind and heart. And if you're not taking her feelings into consideration before you unzip your fly—"

"For Christ's sake, give me a break." He sat up now, dropped his head in his hands. "She won't listen to me. And she did the un-zipping."

"You were just an innocent bystander."

"There's no point in blasting me about this. I've spent considerable time blasting myself, for all the good that's done. I don't know what the hell to do."

She sat on the table, leaned toward him. "What do you want to do?"

"I don't know. She sent me flowers."

"Excuse me?"

"She sent me a dozen red roses this morning. The card said, 'Think of me.' How the hell could I *not* think of her?"

"Roses?" The idea just tickled her. "Where are they?"

He squirmed. "Um. I put them up in the bedroom. Goofy. This role reversal, it's just not right. It's not natural. I think it flies in the face of countless rules of scientific order. I

need to put things back on track. Somehow. Back on track. Stop grinning at me."

"You're hooked."

"I am not hooked. And that's another
term I object to. Someone with a degree in
library science should be able to find more
appropriate terms."

"She's perfect for you." She kissed his
cheek. "Congratulations. I'm not mad at
you anymore."

"I don't care who you're mad at. And it's
not a matter of who's perfect for me. I'm not
perfect for anyone. I'm a slob. I'm inconsiderate and selfish. I like having my life loose
and unstructured."

"You're a slob, no question. But you're
neither inconsiderate nor selfish. It's that inconsiderate and selfish bitch Lily who put
that in your head. If you buy that, you're just
stupid."

"So, are you wishing a stupid slob on
your new pal?"

"Maybe. I love you, Flynn."

"Man, I'm getting a lot of that lately." He
tapped a finger on her nose. "Love you,
too."

"No. Say: 'I love you.'"

"Come on."

"All three words, Flynn. Choke them out."

"I love you. Now go away."

"I'm not finished."

He groaned and fell back on the couch. "We're trying to take a nap here, for our mental health."

"She never loved you, Flynn. She liked who you were in the Valley. She liked being seen with you, and she liked picking your brain. You may be stupid, but you're pretty smart in some areas. She used you."

"And that's supposed to make me feel better. Knowing I let myself be used?"

"It's supposed to make you stop blaming yourself for what happened with Lily."

"I'm not blaming myself. I hate women." He showed his teeth in a vicious smile. "I just want to bang them. Now will you go away?"

"You've got red roses in your bedroom."

"Oh, man."

"Hooked," she repeated and drilled a finger in his belly.

He took the sisterly poke like a man. "Let me ask you something. Did anybody like Lily?"

"No."

He hissed out a breath, stared up at the ceiling. "Just checking."

The knock on the door had him cursing and her bounding up. "I'll get it." She sang it out. "Maybe it's more flowers."

Amused, she pulled open the door. And it was her turn to curse, with more imagination and viciousness than Flynn had managed.

"Hey, nice mouth, Stretch."

Jordan Hawke, handsome as the devil and to Dana's mind twice as evil, gave her a wink and strolled back into her life.

She considered, for one brief, heady moment, tripping him. She grabbed his arm instead, imagined twisting it into cartoon taffy. "Hey. Nobody asked you in."

"You living here now?" He shifted his body in a slow, easy move. He'd always had moves. At six three he had five inches on her. She'd once found that fact exciting, but now it was simply irritating.

He hadn't gotten fat, or ugly, or fallen victim to male-pattern baldness. And wasn't that just too damn bad? No, he was still lanky and gorgeous, and all that thick black hair remained sexily rumpled around a tanned, rawboned face set off by sizzling blue eyes. His mouth was full and sculpted and, she had reason to know, very inventive.

It curved now in a lazy, mocking smile that made her want to bloody it.

"Looking good, Dane." He smoothed a hand over her hair, and had her head jerking back before she could stop herself.

"Hands off. And no, I'm not living here. What do you want?"

"A date with Julia Roberts, a chance to jam with Bruce Springsteen and the E Street Band, and a really cold beer. How about you?"

"To read the details of your slow, painful death. What are you doing here?"

"Annoying you, apparently. But that's just a side benefit. Flynn home?"

He didn't wait for an answer, but stepped away from her and headed for the living room. Moe roused himself, sent out a half-hearted growl.

"That's it, Moe," Dana said cheerfully. "Sic 'im."

Obviously unconcerned about being attacked by an enormous mass of canine, Jordan crouched down. "So this is the famous Moe."

Veterinary trauma forgotten, Moe scrambled up. He charged, flopped both front paws on Jordan's shoulders, and gave him a welcoming kiss.

Dana could only grind her teeth as Jordan's laugh joined Moe's happy bark.

"You're a big guy, aren't you? Look at that face." He rumpled Moe's fur, scratched his ears, then glanced over at Flynn. "How's it going?"

"Okay. Didn't know you were coming so soon."

"Had some time. Got a beer?"

"Sure."

"I hate to interrupt this emotional, heartfelt reunion." Dana's voice was an ice pick aimed at the nape of Jordan's neck. "But what the hell's he doing here?"

"Spending some time with friends, in my hometown." Jordan got to his feet. "Still okay to bunk here?"

"Absolutely." Flynn unfolded himself from the couch. "Man, it's good to see you."

"Same here. Big house. Great dog. Bad couch."

With a laugh, Flynn swung his arms around his oldest friend. "Really good to see you."

For a moment, just an instant, as she watched the two grown men hug, Dana's heart softened. Whatever else she could say about Jordan Hawke—and the list was long—he was and had always been Flynn's. As much brother, she supposed, as friend.

Then those hot blue eyes met hers and baked her heart hard again.

"How about that beer, Stretch? We can play catch-up and you can tell me how you got roped into looking for imaginary keys."

She shot her brother one accusatory look, then jerked her chin up. "Unlike the two of you, I actually have things to do."

"Don't you want to see the painting?"

That nearly stopped her, but giving in to curiosity would've spoiled her exit. She continued to the door and strode out without a backward glance.

She had things to do, all right. The first of which was to carve a wax doll in Jordan's image and stick pins in sensitive areas.

"Did you have to piss her off?" Flynn demanded.

"My breathing pisses her off." And knowing that put a little hole in his gut. "How come she's not living here? The house is big enough."

"She won't." With a shrug, Flynn led the way back to the kitchen. "Wants her own space and blah-blah. You know Dana. Once her mind's set you can't move her with a forklift."

"Tell me about it."

Because Moe was dancing around, Flynn dug out a dog biscuit and flipped it to him before getting the beers. "You brought the painting?"

"Yeah. I don't know what it's going to tell you."

"Me either. I'm hoping it tells Malory something."

"So when am I going to meet this Malory?" Jordan leaned back against the counter.

"I don't know. Soon."

"I thought there was a deadline on this deal," Jordan said.

"Yeah, yeah. We've still got a couple weeks."

"Problem, pal?"

"No. Maybe. We've gotten tangled up, and it's getting really serious really fast. I can't think."

"What's she like?"

"Smart, funny, sexy."

"You put sexy third." Jordan gestured with his beer. "That's serious. What else?"

"Goal-oriented, I'd say." He began to pace. "With a kind of tidy nature. Honest. Not much game-playing there. Grounded. You could say she's grounded, which is why her getting wound up in this key business makes it all seem possible. She's got blue eyes. Big blue eyes," Flynn sighed.

"Again, the physical falls well down the list. You're stuck on her."

Uneasy, Flynn lifted his beer. "There are degrees of being stuck."

"True enough, but if she's got you this worried I'd say you're already in to your knees, and sinking. Why don't you give her a call? She can come get a look at the painting, and I can get a look at her."

"Let's give it till tomorrow."

"You're scared of her. Make that up to your waist and sinking."

"Shut up. I just think it'd be smart for Brad to bring his painting over, let the three of us give them both a good look. See what we come up with, without the female element."

"Works for me. You got any food around here?"

"Not really. But I've got all the takeout and delivery places on speed dial. Take your pick."

"Surprise me. I'll go get my stuff."

It wasn't so different from their youth, unless you considered that the living room where they sprawled belonged to one of them rather than to a parent.

Since the choice had been left to Flynn, they were eating Italian, but the beer had been upgraded to a bottle of Johnnie Walker Blue that Brad had brought with him.

The paintings were propped side by side against the wall while the three of them sat on the floor. Moe took the couch.

"I don't know much about art," Flynn began.

"But you know what you like," Brad finished.

"I wasn't going to stoop to a cliché."

"Actually, it's a valid statement." Jordan agreed. "Art, by its very nature, is subjective. Warhol's *Campbell's Soup Can,* Dalí's *Melting Watch,* da Vinci's *Mona Lisa.* It's all in the eye of the beholder."

"As impossible to compare Monet's *Water Lilies* with Picasso's *Lady in Blue* as it is to compare Dashiell Hammett and Steinbeck. It's all in the style, purpose, and perception."

Flynn rolled his eyes toward Brad. "What I was going to say before the two of you went off on that little intellectual riff is that It seems to me that the same person painted both of these. Or if it was two different people, one was emulating the other's style."

"Oh." Brad swirled the liquor in his glass and grinned. "Okay, then. I'll go along with that. And what does that tell us?"

"It'll tell us a lot if we have Jordan's painting tested. We already know the one at Warrior's Peak and Brad's were done more than five hundred years apart. We need to know where Jordan's fits in."

"Fifteenth century."

Flynn turned his head, stared at Jordan. "You had it dated already?"

"A couple years after I bought it. I needed to get some stuff insured. Turned out it was worth several times what I paid for it. Kinda weird when you think of it, as The Gallery's got a rep for being pricey."

"Why'd you buy it?" Brad asked him.

"I don't know how many times I've asked myself that. I don't even know why I went in there that day. It wasn't one of my usual stops. Then I saw it, and it just grabbed me. That moment, that breath just before destiny, between innocence and power. He'll pull the sword free. You know it. And in that moment, the world changes. Camelot's born, Arthur's fate is sealed. He'll unite a people, be betrayed by a woman and a friend, and sire the man who'll kill him. In this moment, he's a boy. In the next, he'll be a king."

"Some would argue that he was born a king."

Jordan shook his head at Brad's statement. "Not until he put his hands on the hilt of the sword. He could have walked away from it. I wonder if he would have if he'd known what was coming. Glory and grandeur, sure, and a slice of peace, but then deceit, deception, war. And an early death."

"Well, that's cheerful." Flynn started to pour another drink. Then he stopped, looked back at the paintings. "Wait a minute. Maybe you're on to something. In the other, you've got the results after that moment of destiny you were talking about.

Would the god-king have married the mortal, conceived three daughters, if he'd known their fate? Is it about choices, which direction we take?"

"And if it is?" Brad put in. "It doesn't tell us much."

"It gives us a theme. And if we make the leap that the paintings are clues to the location of the keys, then we have to follow the theme. Maybe the first is in a place where a decision was made, one that changed the course of lives."

"Flynn." Jordan hesitated, swirled his drink. "You seriously believe these keys exist?"

"That's right. And if you guys had been around since the beginning of this, you'd have come around to that by now. There's no way to explain it, Jordan, no more than you can explain why that boy was the only person in the world who could pull Excalibur from the stone."

"How about you?" Jordan asked Brad.

"I'm trying to keep an open mind. You've got to add up the coincidences, or what appear to be coincidences. You and I own those paintings. We're all back in the Valley, and so are they. Flynn's involved, personally

involved with two of the women who were
invited to Warrior's Peak. Jordan and Dana
used to be an item. And I bought the painting because I was caught by that face—
Zoe's face. It just about knocked me on my
ass. And let's keep that little tidbit among
the three of us."

"You're interested in Zoe?" Flynn asked.

"Yeah, which is dandy, since she appears
to have taken an instant dislike to me.
Which I don't get," he added with some
heat. "Women don't dislike me right off the
bat."

"No, it usually takes a little time," Jordan
agreed. "Then they dislike you."

"On the contrary. I'm a very smooth oper-
ator. Usually."

"Yeah, I remember how smooth you were
with Marsha Kent."

"I was seventeen," Brad argued. "Fuck
you."

"Do you still have her footprint on your
ass?" Jordan wanted to know.

"You still got Dana's on your balls?"

Jordan winced. "Tit for tat there. Question. Does that painting look as much like
the other two as it does like Dana?"

"Oh, yeah," Flynn told him. "Different dos, but the faces are dead on."

"No question as to the age on it, Brad?"

"None."

Jordan sat silent a moment, nursing his drink, studying Dana's face. So still, so pale, so empty. "Okay, I'll take a side step out of logic and into the zone. There are six of us and three keys. And what, just over two weeks left to find the first one?" He reached for the bottle again. "It'll be a snap."

Beyond the puzzle to be solved, Flynn thought, it was good to have his friends back. Good to know even as he crawled into bed in the early hours of the morning that Jordan was crawling onto the mattress in the spare room. And Brad was already zonked out on the sofa downstairs, guarded by Moe.

It had always seemed to him that there'd been nothing they couldn't do together. Whether it had been fighting off imaginary alien invaders, learning how to unhook a girl's bra one-handed, or driving cross-country in a secondhand Buick. They'd always come through for each other.

When Jordan's mother had died, both he and Brad had been there, holding vigil during those endless nights at the hospital.

When Lily had dumped him, the one constant Flynn had been sure of was his friends.

Through good times and not so good times, he thought sentimentally, they'd been there for each other. Physical distance never meant a damn.

But it was better, a hell of a lot better, to have them here. Since they were, the first key was practically in the lock.

He closed his eyes and instantly fell asleep.

The house was dark, and bitterly cold. He could see his breath puff out in thin white vapors as he wandered aimlessly down dark corridors that turned, that twisted. There was a storm blasting, a crash and boom that shook the air and shot out fast, angry light, zigzagging in the dark.

In the dream he knew he walked the halls of Warrior's Peak. Though he could barely see, he recognized it and knew the turn of the corridor, the feel of the wall under his trailing fingers. Though he had never walked there before.

He could see the rain whipping outside the second-story window, could see the way it glowed blue in the lightning strikes. And he saw the ghost of his own face blurry in the glass.

He called out, and his voice echoed. On and on, like a rolling wave. There was no one to answer. And yet he knew he wasn't alone.

Something walked those halls with him. Lurking just behind. Out of sight, out of reach. Something dark that pushed him on, up the stairs.

Fear tripped into his heart.

Doors lined the corridor, but all of them were locked. He tried each one, turning, tugging the knob with fingers gone stiff with cold.

Whatever stalked him crept closer. He could hear it breathe now, horrible, some-how liquid pulls on the air that merged with his own rapid panting.

He had to get out, get away. So he began to run, loping through the storm-slashed dark while what pursued him followed, with rapid clicks on the wood like eager claws.

He burst out onto a parapet, into the storm where lightning speared down and set the stone to smoking. The air burned and froze, and the rain pelted him like shards of glass.

With nowhere left to run, with fear a cold snake crawling in his belly, he turned to fight.

But the shadow was so huge, so close. It covered him before he could raise his fists. The cold tore through him, drove him to his knees.

He felt something ripped from him—wild, unspeakable pain, dull, shocking horror. And knew it was his soul.

Flynn woke, shuddering with cold, clammy with the dregs of terror, and with the sun pouring in onto his face.

Struggling for breath, he sat up. He'd had his share of nightmares, but never one this intense. Never one where he'd actually felt pain.

Could still feel it, he thought as he gritted

his teeth against the sharp stabs in his chest and belly.

He tried to tell himself it was the combination of pizza and whiskey and late night. But he didn't believe it.

As the pain dulled, he slid gingerly out of bed, walked as cautiously as an old man to the bathroom, and turned the shower on hot. He was freezing.

He reached up to swing open the mirrored medicine cabinet for aspirin and caught a glimpse of his face.

The pallor of his skin, the glassy edge of shock in his eyes, were bad enough. But they were nothing compared to the rest.

He was soaking wet. His hair was drenched, his skin beaded with water. Like a man who'd been out in a storm, he thought, and lowered himself to the seat of the toilet as his legs gave way.

Not just a nightmare. He'd been inside Warrior's Peak. He'd been out on the parapet. And he hadn't been alone.

This was more than a quest for magic keys. More than a puzzle to be solved with the promise of a pot of gold at the end.

There was something else here. Something powerful. Dark and powerful.

He was going to find out what the hell was going on before any of them got in any deeper.

He stepped into the shower and let the hot water beat on him until it penetrated the chill in his bones. Then, calmer, he downed some aspirin, pulled his sweatpants on.

He would go down and make coffee, then he'd be able to think. Once his head was clear, he would roust both of his friends and get their take.

Maybe it was time for the three of them to go up to Warrior's Peak and get the truth out of Rowena and Pitte.

He was halfway down when the bell rang, and Moe raced out barking like the hounds of hell on speed.

"Okay, okay. Shut up." Johnnie Walker hadn't given Flynn a hangover, but the nightmare had stepped up to the plate and knocked one home. He grabbed Moe by the collar, yanked back as he pulled the door open with his other hand.

She looked like a sunbeam. It was his only clear thought as he stared at Malory. Dressed in a pretty blue suit that showed off her legs, she smiled at him. Then stepped forward, wrapped her arms around him.

"Good morning," she said, and by pressing her lips to his drained even that single thought out of his mind.

His fingers went limp on Moe's collar, then fell away from it to lift up, dive into her hair. The aches and dread he'd awakened with fell away as well.

In that one moment he felt as if nothing would ever be beyond his reach again.

Moe gave up trying to shoehorn himself between them, and settled on leaping and barking for attention.

"Christ Jesus, Hennessy, can't you get your dog to . . ." At the top of the stairs, Jordan trailed off. Below him stood his friend and the woman, bathed in morning sunlight. And drowning in each other.

The fact was, even when Flynn eased back from the embrace and glanced up, he had the look of a man going under for the third time. Blissfully.

"Morning. Sorry to interrupt. You must be Malory."

"Yes, I must be." Her brain was a bit muddled from the kiss, but she was pretty sure she was staring up at a great-looking guy wearing nothing but black boxer shorts. "I'm sorry. I didn't realize Flynn had company . . . oh." Her brain cleared. "You're Jordan Hawke. I'm a big fan."

"Thanks."

"Hold it." Flynn held up a hand as Jordan started down. "Maybe you could go put some pants on."

"Sure."

"Come on back. I need to let Moe out." Giving her hand a tug, Flynn managed to dislodge her from the spot she'd frozen in to stare at Jordan. But she dug in again at the living room entrance.

Brad was facedown on the couch, with one arm and one leg drooping off. He was dressed like Jordan, though his boxers were white.

It was interesting to note, Malory thought, that the scion of the Vane empire had an excellent butt.

"Slumber party?" she ventured.

"Guys don't have slumber parties. We just hang out. Moe!" Flynn called the dog, who'd wandered in to lick the portion of Brad's face that wasn't smashed into the cushions. "Brad's always been able to sleep through anything."

"So it would seem. It's nice to have your friends back in town."

"Yeah." He pulled her back to the kitchen. Moe beat them to it, and stood dancing at the back door as if he'd been waiting for hours. He streaked out the instant Flynn opened it.

"Why don't I make some coffee?" Malory offered.

"Yeah? You'll make it?"

"Just part of the service." Since the coffee can was already on the counter, she measured enough for a full pot. "If you marry me, I'd make the coffee every morning. Of course, I'd expect you to take out the trash every day." She tossed a grin over her shoulder. "I believe in sharing household chores."

"Uh-huh."

"And there's the unlimited access to sex."

"That's a big plus."

She laughed as she measured the water. "I like making you nervous. I don't think I've ever made a man nervous before. Then again . . ." She switched the pot on, turned around. "I've never been in love with one before. Not like this."

"Malory—"

"I'm a very determined woman, Flynn."

"Oh, yeah, that's coming through loud

and clear." He stepped back even as she moved in on him. "I just think we should . . ."

"What?" She trailed her hands up his chest.

"See? I can't remember once you start looking at me."

"I take that as a good sign." She touched her lips lightly to his.

"I'm already making a habit of this," Jordan said as he came in. "Sorry."

"It's all right." Malory brushed her hair back as she turned away to find clean coffee mugs. "I just stopped in to ask Flynn to marry me. It's nice to meet another of his friends. Are you in town for long?"

"Depends. What did he say when you asked him?"

"Oh, he has trouble making complete sentences when I bring up love and marriage. Odd, isn't it, seeing as he's a journalist."

"You know, I'm standing right here," Flynn pointed out.

"Is that coffee?" Brad stumbled in, blinked when he spotted Malory, then stumbled back out again. "Sorry."

Amused, she wiped out the mugs. "This

house is full of attractive men, and I've seen all of them without their clothes on. My life has certainly changed. How do you take your coffee, Jordan?"

"Black's fine." He leaned a hip on the counter while she poured. "Flynn said you were smart, funny, and sexy. He was right."

"Thanks. I've got to run. I've got an appointment to sign papers."

"For what?" Flynn asked.

"The partnership papers with Dana and Zoe. I thought Dana told you."

"Told me what?"

"That we're buying the house, going into business."

"What house? What business?"

"The house on Oak Leaf. And our business. Businesses, I suppose. My gallery, Dana's bookstore, Zoe's salon. We're calling it Indulgence."

"Catchy," Jordan decided.

"I can't believe I'm jumping in like this." She pressed a hand to her stomach. "So unlike me. I'm terrified. Well, I don't want to be late." She stepped over, caught Flynn's baffled face in her hands and kissed him again. "I'll call you later. We're hoping you'll do a story on our new enterprise. Nice meeting you, Jordan."

"Really nice meeting you." He watched her walk down the hall. "Nice legs, killer eyes, and bright enough to light up a cave. You got yourself a live wire there, buddy."

His lips were still vibrating from hers. "Now that I've got her, what am I going to do with her?"

"You'll figure it out." He moved over to top off his coffee. "Or she will."

"Yeah." Flynn rubbed a hand over his heart. There was a flutter in it. Maybe that's what came from handling a live wire. "I need more coffee, then I need to talk to you and Brad. You guys aren't going to believe the dream I had last night."

Chapter Thirteen

"I can't believe they didn't show it to you." Dana dug the key to Flynn's house out of her purse.

"Neither can I. I didn't even think," Malory added, as annoyance propelled her from the car to Flynn's front door. "I just assumed Jordan was having it shipped. Plus the three of them were half naked. It was distracting."

"Don't blame yourself." Zoe gave her a bolstering pat on the back. "And anyway, you'll get to see it now."

"They're up to something," Dana muttered. "I can just feel it. When the three of them get together, they're *always* up to something." She unlocked the door, pushed it open. Waited a beat.

"Nobody's home."

"They were just getting up when I was here a couple of hours ago." Malory walked inside without a qualm. "And now that I think about it, Flynn did look like he was up to something."

"They'll try to cut us out." Ready and willing to work herself into a rant on men in general, Dana tossed her keys back in her purse. "It's typical behavior for their species. Oh, we know better, don't you worry your pretty head, little lady."

"I hate that." Firing up, Zoe hissed a breath between her teeth. "You know how an auto mechanic always gives you that smirk and says he'll explain the problem to your husband?"

Dana sucked air through her nose. "That burns my ass."

"If you ask me, that Bradley Vane's at the bottom of it." Zoe set her fists on her hips. "He's just the type to try to run everything and everyone. I pegged him from the get-go."

"No, it'll be Jordan." Dana kicked a shoe out of her way. "He's an instigator."

"It's Flynn's responsibility," Malory disagreed. "It's his house, they're his friends, and . . . oh, my God."

Light slanted across both paintings as they stood propped carelessly against the wall just where Flynn had left them. Her heart squeezed with admiration and envy at the sight.

She walked toward them slowly, as she might a lover who both dazzled and titillated. Her throat ached as she knelt on the floor in front of them.

"They're beautiful," Zoe said from behind her.

"They're more." Gently, Malory lifted the portrait of Arthur, tilting it toward the light. "It's not just talent. Talent can be technical, achieve a kind of perfection of balance and proportion."

She came close to that, she thought, when she painted. Fell just short of technical perfection. And miles away from the magic that made an image art.

"It's genius when you're able to take that talent beyond technique and into emotion," she continued. "To message, or just to simple beauty. When you have that, you light up the world. Can't you feel his heart pounding?" she asked as she studied the young Arthur. "His muscles quivering as he takes the hilt? That's the power of the artist. I'd give anything—anything—to be able to create like this."

A shiver ran through her, twin snakes of hot and cold. For a heartbeat her fingers seemed to burn. And for that heartbeat something inside her opened, and lit, and she saw how it could be done. Must be done. How she could explode on canvas into art.

The knowledge filled her to bursting, left her breathless.

Then was gone in an instant.

"Mal? Malory?" Zoe crouched down, took her shoulders. "What's wrong?"

"What? Nothing. I got dizzy for a second."

"Your eyes went funny. They went huge and dark."

"It must've been the light." But she felt strangely queasy as she pulled her purse over and took out her magnifying glass.

Using the natural light, she began a slow, careful study of each painting.

There was the shadow, just the hint of a form lurking deep, deep in the green of the forest. And two figures—a man and a woman—watching the boy, the sword, the stone, from the far background. From a chain at the woman's waist hung three gold keys.

"What do you think?" Dana demanded.

"I think we've got a couple of choices." Considering them, Malory sat back, rolled her shoulders. "We can convince Brad and Jordan to have these sent to experts for verification of whether or not it's the same artist. And by doing so, we risk this entire business getting out."

"What's the other choice?" Zoe asked her.

"We can take my word for it. Everything I know, everything I've studied and learned tells me the same person painted both of these. The same person who painted the portrait at Warrior's Peak."

"If we go with that, what do we do with it?" Dana demanded.

"We figure out what the paintings are telling us. And we go back up to Warrior's Peak. We ask Rowena and Pitte how at least two of these works were done more than a century apart."

"There's another part that goes with

that," Zoe said quietly. "We accept the magic. We believe."

"I always have time to entertain three handsome men." Rowena all but purred it as she showed Flynn, Brad, and Jordan into the parlor where the portrait of the Daughters of Glass dominated.

She paused, waiting until all attention was focused on it. "I assume the painting interests you, Mr. Vane. Your family has quite an extensive and eclectic art collection, I'm told."

He stared at the portrait, at the figure carrying both a short sword and a little dog. Zoe's eyes stared back at him. "Yes, we do."

"And has the interest passed down to you?"

"It has. As a matter of fact, I believe I own another painting by this artist."

She sat, a secret smile playing around her mouth as she spread the long skirts of her white dress. "Is that so? What a small world."

"It gets smaller," Jordan put in. "I seem to

have another painting that may be by this artist."

"Fascinating. Ah." She gestured as a servant rolled a cart in. "Coffee? I assumed you'd prefer it to tea. American men aren't much on tea, are they?"

"You don't ask about the subject of the other paintings." Flynn sat beside her.

"I'm sure you'll tell me. Cream, sugar?"

"Black. Seems a waste of time when I'm pretty sure you already know. Who's the artist, Rowena?"

She poured the coffee with a steady hand, taking the liquid to within a half inch of the rim while her gaze stayed level with Flynn's. "Did Malory ask you to come here today?"

"No. Why?"

"The quest is hers, as are the questions. Such matters have rules. If she asked you to represent her, that's a different thing altogether. Did you bring your dog?"

"Yeah, he's outside."

Her face went wistful. "I don't mind if he comes in."

"White dress, big black dog. You might want to rethink that. Rowena, Malory didn't ask us to come, but she and the others know we're helping them look into things. It's okay with them."

"But you didn't tell them you were coming to speak with me. Men often make the mistake of assuming that a woman wishes to be relieved of responsibilities and details." Her face was open and friendly, her voice carrying the lilt of a laugh. "Why is that?"

"We didn't come here to discuss male-female dynamics," Jordan began.

"What else is there, really? Man to man, woman to woman, certainly," Rowena continued with an elegant spread of her hands. "But it all comes down to people, what they are to each other. What they'll do for and to one another. Even art is only a representation of that, in one form or another. If Malory has concerns or questions about the painting or paintings she must ask. You won't find the key for her, Flynn. It's not for you."

"I dreamed I was in this house last night. Only it wasn't a dream. It was more."

He watched her eyes change, go dark with shock. Or something else, something bigger.

"Such a dream isn't unusual under the circumstances."

"I've only been in the foyer and in two rooms in this place. Or had been until last night. I can tell you how many rooms are on the second floor, and that there's a stair-case on the east side leading to the third that has a newel post carved like a dragon. I couldn't see it well in the dark, but I felt it."

"Wait. Please."

She rose quickly and hurried from the room.

"This is some strange deal you've got go-ing here, Flynn." Jordan poked at the pretty cookies arranged on a glass plate. "There's something familiar about that woman. I've seen her somewhere before."

"Where?" Brad demanded.

"I don't know. It'll come to me. Hell of a looker. A face like that, you don't forget. And why should she freak over you having a dream? Because freak's just what she did, in her own classy way."

"She's afraid." Brad walked closer to the portrait. "She went from sly to scared in a heartbeat. She knows the answer to the paintings, and she was having a good time toying with us about that until Flynn dropped his dream adventure on her."

"And I didn't even get to the best part."

Flynn got to his feet to explore the room before Rowena got back. "Something's off here."

"You just getting that, son?"

Flynn spared a glance at Jordan as he opened a lacquered cabinet. "Not just the already established 'off.' That's a woman in control," he said with a jerk of his thumb toward the doorway. "Cool, confident, sure of herself. The woman who just took a flyer out of here wasn't any of those things. Man, there's some high-class booze in here."

"Would you care for a drink, Mr. Hennessy?"

Though he winced a little, Flynn turned toward the doorway and spoke equably to Pitte. "No, thanks. A little early for me yet." He closed the cabinet. "How's it going?"

Rowena laid a hand on Pitte's arm before he could respond. "Finish it," she ordered Flynn. "Finish the dream."

"Let's talk quid pro quo." Inclining his head, Flynn walked back to sit on the sofa. "You want to hear about the rest of the dream, and we want to know about the paintings. I show you mine, you show me yours."

"You bargain with us?"

Flynn was amazed at the stunned outrage in Pitte's voice. "Yeah."

"It's not permitted." Again Rowena laid a
hand on Pitte's arm. But from the hot, impatient look he sent her, Flynn didn't bank on
her restraining him for long. "We can't give
you answers just because you ask. There
are limits. There are paths. It's important
that we know what happened to you."

"Give me something back."

Pitte snapped something out, and though
the language was a mystery to Flynn, he
recognized an oath when he heard one. Following it was a bright flash, an electric slice
through the air. Warily, Flynn looked down
at his lap, and the banded stacks of hun-
dred-dollar bills that now rested there.

"Ah. Nice trick."

"You've got to be kidding." Jordan had
already leaped forward and now reached
down and plucked up a stack of bills. He
fanned them, then patted them against his
palm as he stared at Pitte. "Definitely time
for some answers."

"Do you require more?" Pitte demanded,
and Rowena turned on him with a kind of
stunning female fury.

The words they hurled at each other were

unintelligible. Gaelic, Flynn thought. Maybe Welsh. But the gist was clear enough. Their temper rocked the room.

"Okay, take five." With three determined strides, Brad moved forward, stepped between them. "This isn't getting us anywhere." His voice was calm and controlled, and had both of them snarling at him. Still, he stayed where he was and glanced back at Flynn. "Our host just pulled . . . how much?"

"Looks like about five thousand."

"Five grand out of thin air—and boy, have I got some stockholders who'd like to talk to you. He seems to think you want cash for information. Do you?"

"Tough as it is to turn down five thousand magic dollars, no." It stung, he could admit it, but Flynn set the stack on the table. "I'm worried about three women who haven't hurt anyone, and I'm a little worried about myself. I want to know what's going on."

"Tell us the rest, and we'll tell you what we can. Tell us freely," Rowena added as she moved back to Flynn. "I'd prefer not to make you tell us."

Irritated now, Flynn leaned forward. "Make me?"

Her voice was winter cool against the heat of his when she spoke. "My dear, I could make you quack like a duck, but as I imagine your brave and sensible friend would say, such an incident wouldn't accomplish anything. You think we wish harm to you, or to your women? We don't. We wish harm to none. That I can tell you freely, Pitte." She shifted, angled her head. "You've insulted our guest with this crass display. Apologize."

"Apologize?"

"Yes." She sat again, brushed at her skirts. Waited.

Pitte bared his teeth. He tapped his fingers restlessly on his thighs. "Women are a plague to man."

"Aren't they just?" Jordan agreed.

"I'm sorry to have offended you." Then he flicked a wrist. The money vanished. "Better?"

"There's no reasonable way to answer that question, so I'll ask one instead. Who the hell are you people?" Flynn demanded.

"We're not here to answer your questions." Pitte walked over to the silver pot, poured coffee into a Dresden cup. "Even a journalist—which I warned you would be an annoyance," he added as an aside to Rowena—"should be aware of certain rules of behavior when invited into someone's home."

"Why don't I just tell you who you are," Flynn began, then broke off as the delighted bark banged into the room seconds before Moe arrived. "Oh, shit."

"There he is!" Rowena simply spread her arms in welcome, and had them full of dog when the women walked into the room. "How nice, how lovely. It's like a party."

"Sorry to burst in on you this way." Malory scanned the room, then zeroed in on Flynn. "But there's an issue of certain people thinking they should take over from the womenfolk."

"That's not exactly true."

"Really? And what would be exactly true?"

"Just following a lead, that's all. You were busy rushing into business partnerships, buying houses."

"I've been rushing into a lot of things lately. Maybe we should debate the fact that I rushed you into bed."

The twin claws of embarrassment and annoyance pricked him as he got to his feet. "Sure, we can do that. Maybe we can find a more appropriate time and place for it."

"You want to talk about appropriate when you and your testosterone team try to take over my responsibilities, my business? Just because I'm in love with you, just because I sleep with you, doesn't mean I'll sit back and let you run my life."

"Who's running whose life?" Frustration had him flinging out his arms. "You're the one who has mine mapped out. I'm in this, Malory, whether I want to be or not. And I'm here to find out what that means. And if it's heading where I think it is, you're out. All of you." He shot scathing looks at Dana and Zoe. "Out."

"Who made you boss?" Dana demanded. "You couldn't tell me what to do when I was ten. You sure as hell can't pull it off now."

"Oh, you watch me. You made it seem like a game." He shot the accusation at Rowena. "Even some sort of romantic quest. But you didn't tell them what might be at stake."

"What are you talking about?" Malory jabbed at his shoulder.

"The dreams." Ignoring Malory, Flynn

continued to speak to Rowena. "They're warnings, aren't they?"

"You never finished telling us. Perhaps everyone should sit down, and you can start from the beginning."

"You had a dream? Like mine?" Malory jabbed at him again. "Why didn't you tell me?"

"Just shut it down a damn minute." Out of patience, he nudged her onto the couch. "Just be quiet," he ordered. "I don't want to hear anything out of you until I'm finished."

He started at the beginning, with him wandering the house, with the sensation of being watched, stalked. He related the experience on the parapet, the fear and pain, and ended with his waking in his own bed, drenched with rain.

"He—it—wanted my soul, was letting me know that that could be the price for being in this."

"This isn't the way." Pitte clamped a hand on Rowena's and spoke to her as if no one else was in the room. "This can't be the way. They aren't to be harmed. That was the first and most sacred promise."

"We can't know. If we're not allowed behind the Curtain, we can't know what situation now exists. If he's broken the vow, he must believe he can escape the consequences. He must believe . . . they are the ones," she said in a whisper. "It can be done, and they can succeed. He's opened the Curtain to stop them. He's come through."

"If they fail—"

"They cannot fail." She spun around, her face set with purpose. "We'll protect you."

"Will you?" Shaken, Malory folded her hands on her lap, squeezing her fingers until the pain cleared her head. "The way you protected the Daughters of Glass? Teacher and warrior. Somehow, you are." She got up, walked to the portrait. "You're here," she said, gesturing to the couple in the background. "And here, in this room. In this place. And you think that what's there, in the shadows of the trees is here too. You don't show his face."

"He has more than one." Rowena spoke in a matter-of-fact tone that was utterly chilling.

"You painted this, and the two that we have."

"Painting is one of my passions," Rowena

confirmed. "One of my constants. Pitte." She turned to him. "They know this much."

"I don't know a damn thing," Dana declared.

"Step over here, to the cynical side of the room," Jordan invited.

"It's what Malory knows that matters now." Rowena held out a hand. "All that I have will be used to keep you safe."

"Not good enough." Flynn shook his head. "She's out of it. They're all out of it. You want your money back, we'll—"

"Excuse me, I can speak for myself. This isn't a matter of a refund, is it?" she asked Rowena. "There's no turning back, no saying, uh-oh, the stakes are higher than I realized, game over."

"The agreement was made."

"Without full disclosure," Brad put in. "Whatever sort of contract these women signed with you won't hold up legally."

"The issue isn't legal," Malory said impatiently. "It's moral. And more than that, it's destiny. As long as I am, as long as I know, I'm part of it. Until the four weeks are up. And if I find the first key, one of them is next." She looked at Dana and Zoe. "One of them will be at risk for the next phase of the moon."

"Yes."

"You know where the keys are," Flynn exploded. "Just hand them over. End this."

"Do you think, if that were possible, we would remain in this prison?" In a gesture that mirrored both disgust and bitterness Pitte flung out his arms. "Year by century by millennium, trapped in a world not our own. Do you think we live with you out of *choice*? That we place our fates, the fates of those in our charge, in your hands because we wish it? We are bound here, bound by this single task. And now so are you."

"You can't go home." After the boom of Pitte's, Zoe's quiet voice was like a hammer blow. "We are home. You had no right to trick us into being part of this without telling us the risks."

"We didn't know." Rowena spread her hands.

"For a couple of gods, there's a hell of a lot you don't know and can't do."

Pitte's eyes went to smoke as he rounded on Flynn. "Perhaps you'd like a demonstration of what we can do."

Fists already clenched, Flynn stepped forward. "Bring it on."

"Gentlemen." Rowena's heavy sigh was like a flood of cool water, designed to lower the rising temperature of the room. "The male, regardless of his origins, remains woefully predictable in some areas. Your pride and manhood aren't at risk here, in either case. Flynn, whatever the world, there are laws woven through the fabric of it."

"Rip the fabric. Break the law."

"If it were within my power to hand out the keys at this moment, it would solve nothing."

"They wouldn't work," Malory stated and earned a nod of approval from Rowena.

"You understand."

"I think I do. If this spell . . . is it a spell?"

"That's the simplest word for it," Rowena agreed.

"If it's to be broken, it has to be by us. Women. Mortal women. Using our brains, our wits and energies, our resources in our world. Otherwise, no key opens the box. Because . . . we're the real keys. The answer's in us."

"You're so close to where you need to be." Emotions storming across her face,

Rowena rose, laid her hands on Malory's arms. "Closer than any have come before."

"But not close enough, not yet. And half my time is gone. I need to ask you some questions. In private."

"Hey, one for all here," Dana reminded her. Malory sent her a silent plea. "Okay, okay. We'll wait outside."

"I'll stay with you." Flynn laid a hand on Malory's shoulder, but she shrugged it off.

"I said this was private. I don't want you here."

His face went blank and cold. "Fine, then, I'll get out of your way."

With obvious regret, Rowena gave Moe a little nudge to send him along. She frowned at the sharp slam of the door behind Flynn. "Your man has a sensitive heart. More easily bruised than yours."

"Is he my man?" Before Rowena could speak, Malory shook her head. "First things first. Why was I taken behind the Curtain?"

"He wanted to show you his power."

"Who is he?"

Rowena hesitated, then when Pitte nodded, continued. "He is Kane, a sorcerer. The dark one."

"The one in the shadows, the one I saw in my dream. The stealer of souls."

"He showed himself to you so you would be frightened. There's no need to frighten you unless you can succeed."

"Why did he hurt Flynn?"

"Because you love him."

"Do I?" Malory's voice thickened with emotion. "Or have I been made to think I do? Is that just one more trick?"

"Ah." Rowena let out a soft breath. "Perhaps you're not as close as I thought. Don't you know your own heart, Malory?"

"I've known him two weeks, and I feel as if my life will never be quite right if he's not in it. But is it real? At the end of my four weeks, will I still feel that way?" She pressed a hand to her heart. "Or will it be taken away from me? Is it any worse to have your soul taken from you than your heart?"

"I think not, for one feeds the other. And I can't give you the answer, because you already have it. If you choose to look."

"Then tell me this. Will he be safe if I step away from him? If I close my heart to him, will he be safe?"

"You'd give him up to protect him?" Pitte asked.

"Yes."

Thoughtful, he walked to the lacquered cabinet, opened it to take out a bottle of brandy. "And you'd tell him this?"

"No, he'd never—"

"Ah, so you would deceive him." With a small smile, Pitte poured brandy into a snifter. "And justify the lie by saying that it was for his own good. Women, whatever their world, are predictable," he said, with a mocking bow to Rowena.

"Love," she corrected, "is a constant force in any universe. Your decisions, your choices, must be yours," she told Malory. "But your man won't thank you for any sacrifice you make to protect him." She gave Pitte a mocking bow in turn. "They never do. Go now." She touched a hand to Malory's cheek. "Rest your mind a while, until you can think clearly with it. And you have my word, whatever can be done to keep you, your man, your friends safe will be done."

"I don't know them." She pointed to the portrait. "But I know those people outside.

You should know, if it comes down to a choice, I'll choose those I know."

Pitte waited until they were alone before bringing Rowena a second snifter. "I have loved you through time and through worlds."

"And I you, my heart."

"But I've never understood you. You could have answered her question about love and eased her mind."

"She'll be the wiser, and the happier, for finding the answer herself. How much can we do for them?"

He leaned down, pressed his lips to her brow. "Our best."

Chapter Fourteen

She needed time, Malory admitted. She'd been on a roller coaster since the first of the month, and though there'd been a thrill in riding those fast dips and sharp turns, she needed a break.

Nothing in her life was the same as it had been, she thought as she let herself into her apartment. She'd always counted on consistency, and that single element had slipped through her fingers.

Or been tossed aside on impulse.

She didn't have The Gallery. She wasn't completely certain she had her sanity. On one of those dips and turns, she'd stopped being sensible, dependable Malory Price and had become irrational, emotional, fanciful Malory Price—a woman who believed in magic, in love at first sight.

All right, maybe third sight, she corrected as she closed her curtains and crawled onto her bed. But it was the same thing, essentially.

She'd taken money that could have seen her through several lean months and invested it in an enterprise with two women she'd known for less than four weeks.

And trusted implicitly, she decided. Without reservation.

She was about to embark on a business of her own, without any stock, any solid plan, any safety net. Against all logic, the idea of it made her happy.

And still her head was pounding, her stomach churning. Over the thought that she might not be in love at all. That the blissful confidence and pleasure she felt in Flynn was only an illusion.

If the illusion shattered, she was afraid she would grieve for the rest of her life.

She bunched the pillow under her head, curled into a ball, and begged for sleep.

*   *   *

It was sunny and warm when she woke, and the air smelled like summer roses. She snuggled in for a moment. Warm sheets carrying the faint scent of her man, the soft drift of silence.

She rolled over lazily, blinked. Something odd hung over her mind. Not really unpleasant, just odd.

The dream. The strangest dream.

She sat up and stretched, feeling the healthy pull of muscles. Naked, and easy with it, she slid out of bed, sniffed the butter-yellow roses on the dresser before picking up her robe. She paused by the window to admire her garden, draw in the fragrant air. She pushed the window open wider and let the sound of birdsong follow her out of the room.

The odd feeling was already fading—as a dream does on waking—as she glided down the stairs, trailing a hand over the silky wood of the banister. Jewel lights from the window over the door played on the floor. More flowers, exotic sprays of white orchids, speared out of the antique vase on the entrance table.

His keys were tossed beside them, in the

little mosaic bowl she'd bought just for that purpose.

She wound her way through the house to the kitchen, then grinned. He was at the stove, sliding a battered slice of bread into the skillet. There was a tray beside him, already topped with a flute of sparkling juice, a single rose in a bud vase, her pretty coffee cup.

The back door was open. Through it, she could hear the birds continuing to sing and the dog's occasional happy barks. Blissful, she crept forward, then wrapped her arms around his waist, pressed a kiss to the nape of his neck.

"Watch it. My wife could wake up any minute."

"Let's risk it."

He turned, caught her up in a long, hard kiss. Her heart leaped, her blood fired, even as she thought, Perfect. It's all so perfect.

"I was going to surprise you." Flynn ran his hands over her back as he eased her away. "Breakfast in bed. The Hennessy Special."

"Make it a better surprise, and have breakfast in bed with me."

"I could probably be persuaded. Hold

on." He grabbed a spatula, flipped the bread over.

"Mmm. It's after eight. You shouldn't have let me sleep so late."

"I didn't let you get much sleep last night." He winked at her. "Seemed only fair to let you catch a little this morning. You've been working so hard, Mal, getting ready for your show."

"I'm nearly done."

"And when it's over, I'm going to take my incredibly beautiful and talented wife on a well-deserved vacation. Do you remember that week we spent in Florence?"

Sun-drenched days, love-drenched nights. "How could I forget? Are you sure you can take the time off? I'm not the only one who's been busy around here."

"We'll make time." He flipped the French toast onto a plate. "Why don't you grab the paper, and we'll crawl back into bed for an hour . . . or two."

Sleepy cries began to sound from the baby monitor on the counter. Flynn glanced toward it. "Or maybe not."

"I'll get him. Meet me upstairs."

She hurried up, part of her mind acknowledging the paintings lining the walls. The street scene she'd done in Florence, the seascape from the Outer Banks, the portrait of Flynn sitting at his desk in his office.

She turned toward the nursery. The walls there were decorated with her paintings as well. The bright faerie-tale scenes she'd done the entire time she'd been pregnant.

And in the crib with its glossy spindle bars, her little boy cried impatiently for attention.

"There now, sweetheart. Mama's right here." She picked him up, cuddled him close.

He would have his father's hair, she thought, as she cooed and swayed. It was already coming in dark, with those hints of chestnut shining through when the light caught it.

He was so perfect. So absolutely perfect.

But as she carried him toward the changing table, her legs went weak.

What was his name? What was her baby's name? Panicked, she clutched him close, then whirled as she heard Flynn come to the door.

"You look so beautiful, Malory. I love you."

"Flynn." Something was wrong with her

eyes. It was as if she could see through him, as if he were fading away. "Something's wrong."

"Nothing's wrong. Everything's exactly right. Everything's just the way you wanted it to be."

"It's not real, is it?" Tears began to sting her eyes. "It's not real."

"It could be."

A light flashed, and she was standing in a studio awash with light. Canvases were stacked against the walls or rested on easels. She faced another, brilliant with color and shape. A brush was in her hand, and she was already daubing it on her palette.

"I've done this," she whispered as she stared at the canvas. It was a forest, misty with green light. The figure walking on the path was alone. Not lonely, she thought, but solitary. There was home at the end of the path, and a bit of time yet to enjoy the quiet and the magic of the woods.

Her hand had done that. Her mind, her heart. She could feel it, just as she could feel and remember every brush-stroke on every canvas in the room.

The power of that, the glory of it with all its pain and pleasure.

"I can do this." With a kind of frantic glee, she continued to paint. "I have to do this."

The joy was like a drug, and she was greedy for it. She knew how to mix just the right tone of color, when to sweep it on, when to switch for the fine, fine details.

How to create that light, that shadow so one might feel as if he or she could slip inside, walk that path, and find home at the end of it.

But even as she painted, tears began to run down her cheeks. "It's not real."

"It could be."

The brush clattered to the floor, splattering paint, as she whirled.

He stood beside her, with the sun's rays flooding over him. And still he was dark. His hair, black and glossy, spread like wings to his shoulders. His eyes were a strong stone gray. Sharp, high cheekbones hollowed his cheeks, and his mouth was full, appealingly wicked.

Beautiful, she thought. How could he be beautiful?

"Did you think I'd look like a demon? Like something out of a nightmare?" His amusement only added charm. "Why should I? They've made you think poorly of me, haven't they?"

"You're Kane." Fear was alive in her, with its cold hands closing around her throat. "You stole the souls from the Daughters of Glass."

"It needn't concern you." His voice was beautiful as well. Melodic, soothing. "You're an ordinary woman in an ordinary world. You know nothing of me or mine. I wish you no harm. The opposite, in fact." With a dancer's grace, he wandered the room, his soft boots silent on the paint-splattered floor. "This is your work."

"No."

"Oh, yes, you know it." He lifted a canvas, studied the sinuous lines of a mermaid lounging on a rock. "You remember painting this, and the others. You know now how it feels to have that power. Art makes gods out of men." He set the canvas down again. "Or women. What are we, in my world, but artists and bards, magicians and warriors? You want to keep the power, Malory?"

She swiped at the tears, saw her work through them. "Yes."

"You can have it, all of it, and more. The

man you want, the life, the family. I'll give them to you. The child you held in your arms? It can all be real, it can all belong to you."

"At what price?"

"So little." He slid a finger over her damp cheek, and the tear he stole flamed on its tip. "So very little. You've only to stay within this dream. To wake and sleep within it, to walk, to speak, to eat, to love. All you can wish for will be here for you. Perfection—without pain, without death."

She let out a shuddering breath. "There are no keys in this dream."

"You're a clever woman. Why care about keys, about bastard goddesses who have nothing to do with you? Why risk yourself and those you love for foolish girls who should never have been born? Would you give up your own dream for strangers?"

"I don't want a dream. I want my life. I won't trade my life for your illusions."

His skin went white, his eyes black. "Then lose all!"

She screamed as he reached for her, and again when the cold speared through her. Then she was pulled clear, tumbled free, to wake gasping in her own bed.

She heard the banging on the door, the shouting. Terror leaped out of bed with her. She made it to the living room at a stumbling run and spotted Flynn on the other side of her patio doors, about to smash one of her chairs through the glass.

He tossed it aside as she unlocked the door, shoved it open.

"Who's in here?" He grabbed her shoulders, lifted her right off her feet, and set her out of his way. "Who hurt you?"

"Nobody's here."

"You were screaming. I heard you screaming." He strode into the bedroom, fists ready.

"I had a nightmare. It was just a bad dream. No one's here but me. I have to sit down." She braced a hand on the couch, lowered herself.

His own legs felt a little shaky. She'd screamed as if something was tearing her to pieces. He'd had a good taste of terror the night before, but it had been nothing compared to what had pumped into him on the other side of that glass door.

He marched into the kitchen, poured a glass of water. "Here, drink some. Take it slow."

"I'll be okay in a minute. I woke up, and you were pounding and shouting. Everything's still confused."

"You're trembling." He glanced around, spotted a chenille throw. Wrapping it around her shoulders, he sat on the couch beside her. "Tell me about the dream."

She shook her head. "No. I don't want to talk about it, or think about it right now. I just want to be alone for a while. I don't want you here."

"That's the second time today you've said that to me. But this time you're not getting your way. In fact, I'm calling Jordan and letting him know I'm staying here tonight."

"This is my apartment. Nobody stays here unless I invite them."

"Wrong again. Get undressed, get in bed. I'll make you some soup or something."

"I don't want soup, I don't want you. And I certainly don't want to be coddled."

"Then what the hell do you want?" He lunged to his feet, vibrating with fury and frustration. "One minute you're all over me, telling me you're in love with me, you want to spend your life with me. Then the next you want me to hit the road. I'm sick to death of women and their mixed signals and capricious minds and their goddamn expectations of me. Right now, you're going to do what I want, and that's getting into bed while I make you something to eat."

She stared at him. A dozen vile and vicious words leaped into her throat. And she lost them all in a burst of tears.

"Oh, Christ." Flynn scrubbed his hands over his face. "Nice job. Take a bow, Hennessy."

He stalked to the window, stared out while she wept wildly behind him. "I'm sorry. I don't know what to do about you. I can't keep up. You don't want me here, fine. I'll call Dana. But I don't want you to be alone."

"I don't know what to do about me either." She reached in the drawer for a pack of tissues. "If I've sent you mixed signals, it hasn't been deliberately." She mopped at her face, but the tears simply wouldn't stop. "I don't have a capricious mind—at least I never used to. And I don't know what my goddamn expectations of you are. I don't even know what my goddamn expectations are of me anymore. I used to. I'm scared. I'm scared of what's happening around me and inside me. And I'm scared because I don't know what's real. I don't know if you're actually standing over there."

He came back, sat beside her again. "I'm here," he said as he took her hand firmly in his. "This is real."

"Flynn." She steadied herself by staring at their joined hands. "All my life I've wanted certain things. I wanted to paint. For as long as I can remember, I wanted to be an artist. A wonderful artist. I studied, and I worked. And I never came close. I don't have the gift."

She closed her eyes. "It hurt, more than I can tell you, to accept that." Steadier, she let out a breath, looked at him. "The best I could do was work with art, to be around it, to find some purpose for this love." She fisted a hand on her heart. "And that I was good at."

"Don't you think there's something noble about doing what we're really good at, even if it wasn't our first choice?"

"That's a nice thought. But it's hard to set a dream aside. I guess you know that."

"Yeah, I know that."

"The other thing I wanted was to love someone, to be loved by him. Absolutely. To know when I went to bed at night, woke in the morning, that this someone was with me. Understood me and wanted me. I never had much luck with that one either. I might meet someone, and we'd seem to click. But it never got inside me. I never felt that leap, or the burn that eases into that wonderful, spreading warmth. When you just know this is the one you were waiting for. Until you. Don't say anything," she said quickly. "I need to finish."

She picked up the water again, soothed her throat. "When you wait all your life for something and then you find it, it's like a miracle. All the parts inside you that've been on hold, they open up and start beating. You were okay before, you were good. You had purpose and direction, and everything was just fine. But now it's more. You can't explain what that more is, but you know, if you lose it, you'll never be able to fill those empty spaces in just the same way again. Not ever. That's terrifying. I'm afraid that what's inside me is just a trick. That I'll wake up tomorrow and what's beating in here will have stopped. It'll be quiet again. I won't feel this way. I won't feel the way I've waited all my life to feel."

Her eyes were dry again, her hand steady

as she set the water down. "I can stand you not loving me back. There's always the hope that you will. But I don't know if I can stand not loving you. It would be like . . . like having something stolen from inside me. I don't know if I can handle going back to the way I was."

He brushed a hand down her hair, then drew her close to his side so her head rested on his shoulder. "Nobody's ever loved me, not the way you're talking about. I don't know what to do about it, Malory, but I don't want to lose it either."

"I saw the way things could be, but it wasn't true. Just an ordinary day that was so perfect it was like a jewel in the palm of my hand. He made me see it and feel it. And want it."

He eased back, turning her to face him. "The dream?"

She nodded. "It hurt more than anything I've ever known to let it go. It's a hard price, Flynn."

"Can you tell me?"

"I think I have to. I was tired. I felt like I'd been through this emotional wringer. I just wanted to lie down, have it go away for a while."

She took him through it, the waking with that sensation of absolute well-being, of moving through a house that was full of love, finding him in the kitchen making her breakfast.

"That should've clued you in. Me, cooking? An obvious delusion."

"You were making me French toast. It's my favorite lazy-morning treat. We talked about going on vacation, and I remembered all the other places we'd gone, what we'd done. Those memories were inside me. Then the baby woke up."

"Baby?" He went icy pale. "We had— there was . . . a baby?"

"I went up to get him out of the crib."

"Him?"

"Yes, him. Along the walls on the way were paintings I'd done. They were wonderful, and I could remember painting them. Just as I could remember painting the ones in the nursery. I picked the baby up, out of the crib, and this love, this terrible love for him. I was full of it. And then . . . and then I didn't know his name. I had no name for him. I could feel the shape of him in my arms, and how soft and warm his skin was, but I didn't know his name. You came to the door, and I could see through you. I knew it wasn't real. None of it was real."

She had to stand up, to move. She walked over to open the curtains again. "Even as I started to hurt, I was in a studio. My studio, surrounded by my work. I could smell the paint and the turpentine. I had a brush in my hand, and I knew how to use it. I knew all the things I'd always wanted to know. It was powerful, like having the child who had come from me in my arms. And just as false. And he was there."

"Who was there?"

She drew in a sharp breath, turned back. "His name is Kane. The stealer of souls. He spoke to me. I could have it all—the life, the love, the talent. It could be real. If I just stayed inside it, I'd never have to give it up. We would love each other. We'd have a son. I'd paint. It would all be perfect. Just live inside the dream, and the dream's real."

"Did he touch you?" He rushed to her to run his hands over her as if to check for wounds. "Did he hurt you?"

"This world or that," she said, steady again. "My choice. I wanted to stay, but I couldn't. I don't want a dream, Flynn, no matter how perfect it is. If it's not real, it means nothing. And if I'd stayed, isn't that just another way of giving him my soul?"

"You were screaming." Undone, Flynn laid his forehead on hers. "You were screaming."

"He tried to take it, but I heard you shouting for me. Why did you come here?"

"You were upset with me. I didn't want you to be."

"Annoyed," she corrected and slid her arms around him. "I still am, but it's a little hard to get through everything else to my irritation. I want you to stay. I'm afraid to sleep, afraid I might go back and this time I won't be strong enough to come out again."

"You're strong enough. And if you need it, I'll help pull you out."

"This might not be real either." She lifted her mouth to his. "But I need you."

"It's real." He lifted her hands, kissed each one in turn. "That's the only thing I'm sure of in this whole damn mess. Whatever I'm feeling for you, Malory, it's real."

"If you can't tell me what you feel, then show me." She drew him to her. "Show me now."

All the conflicting emotions, the needs and doubts and wants, poured into the kiss.

And as she accepted them, accepted him, he felt himself settle. Tenderness spread through him as he picked her up, cradled her in his arms.

"I want to keep you safe. I don't care if it irritates you." He carried her to her room and laid her on the bed, began to undress her. "I'll keep getting in the way, if that's what it takes."

"I don't need someone to look out for me." She lifted a hand to his cheek. "I just need you to look at me."

"Malory, I've been looking at you from the beginning, even when you're not around."

She smiled, arched up so he could slip off her blouse. "That's a strange thing to say, but it's nice. Lie down with me."

They were side by side, faces close. "I feel pretty safe right now, and it's not particularly irritating."

"Maybe you're feeling a little too safe." He skimmed a fingertip over the swell of her breast.

"Maybe." She sighed when he began to nuzzle the side of her neck. "That doesn't scare me a bit. You're going to have to try a lot harder."

He rolled over, pinned her, then plundered her mouth with his.

"Oh. Nice work," she managed.

She was trembling, just enough to arouse him, and her skin was flushing warm. He could steep himself in her, in the tastes and textures. He could lose himself in that low, driving urge to give her pleasure.

He was tied to her. Perhaps he had been even before he'd met her. Could it be that all the mistakes he'd made, all the changes in direction, had been only to lead him to this time, and this woman?

Was there never any choice?

She sensed him drawing back. "Don't. Don't go away," she begged. "Let me love you. I need to love you."

She wound her arms around him, used her mouth to seduce. For now, she would trade pride for power without a qualm. As her body moved sinuously under his, she felt his quiver.

Hands stroked. Lips took. Breathy moans slid into air that had gone dim and thick. Long, lazy kisses built in intensity and ended on gasps of greed.

He was with her now, locked in a rhythm too primal to resist. The hammer blows of his heart threatened to shatter his chest, and still it wasn't enough.

He wanted to gorge on the flavors of her, to drown in that sea of needs. One moment she was pliant, yielding; the next, as taut as a bunched fist. When her breath sobbed out his name, he thought he might go mad.

She rose over him. Locking her hands in his, she took him into her, a slow, slow slide that tied his frantic system into knots.

"Malory."

She shook her head, leaning down to rub her lips over his. "Want me."

"I do."

"Let me take you. Watch me take you."

She arched back, stroking her hands up her torso, over her breasts, into her hair. And she began to ride.

Heat slapped him back, a furnace blast that had his muscles going to jelly, that scorched his bones. She rose above him, slim and strong, white and gold. She surrounded him, possessed him. Spurred him toward madness.

The power and pleasure consumed her. She drove them both faster, harder, until her vision was a blur of colors. Alive, was all she could think. They were alive. Blood burned in her veins, pumped in her frenzied heart. Good healthy sweat slicked her skin. She could taste him in her mouth, feel him pounding in the very core of her.

This was life.

She clung to it, clung even when the glory climbed toward the unbearable. Until his body plunged, and she let go.

He made good on the soup, though he could tell it amused her to have him stirring a pot at her stove. He put on music, kept the lights low. Not for seduction, but because he desperately wanted to keep her relaxed.

He had questions, a great many more questions, about her dream. The part of him that felt that asking questions was a human obligation warred with the part that wanted to tuck her up safe and quiet for a while.

"I could run out," he suggested, "grab some videos. We can veg out."

"Don't go anywhere." She snuggled closer to him on the couch. "You don't have to distract me, Flynn. We have to talk about it eventually."

"Doesn't have to be now."

"I thought a newspaperman dug for all the facts fit to print, and then some."

"Since the *Dispatch* isn't going to be running a story on Celtic myths in the Valley until all of this is finished, there's no rush."

"And if you were working for the *New York Times*?"

"That'd be different." He stroked her hair, sipped his wine. "I'd be hard-boiled and cynical and skewer you or anybody else for the story. And I'd probably be strung out and stressed. Maybe have a drinking problem. Be working toward my second divorce. I think I'd like bourbon, and I'd have a redhead on the side."

"What do you *really* think it'd be like if you'd gone to New York?"

"I don't know. I like to think I'd have done good work. Important work."

"You don't think your work here's important?"

"It serves a purpose."

"An important purpose. Not only keeping people informed and entertained, giving them the continuity of tradition, but keeping a lot of them employed. The people who work on the paper, deliver it, their families. Where would they have gone if you'd left?"

"I wasn't the only one who could run it."

"Maybe you were the only one who was supposed to run it. Would you go now, if you could?"

He thought about it. "No. I made the choice. Most of the time I'm glad I chose as I did. Just every once in a while, I wonder."

"I couldn't paint. Nobody told me I couldn't or made me give it up. I just wasn't good enough. It's different when you're good enough, but someone tells you you can't."

"It wasn't exactly like that."

"What was it like?"

"You have to understand my mother. She makes very definite plans. When my father died, well, that must've really messed up Plan A."

"Flynn."

"I'm not saying she didn't love him, or didn't mourn. She did. We did. He made her laugh. He could always make her laugh. I don't think I heard her laugh, not really, for a year after we lost him."

"Flynn." It broke her heart. "I'm so sorry."

"She's tough. One thing you can say about Elizabeth Flynn Hennessy Steele, she's no wimp."

"You love her." Malory brushed at his hair. "I wondered."

"Sure I do, but you won't hear me say she was easy to live with. Anyway, when she pulled herself out of it, it was time for Plan B. Big chunk of that was passing the paper to me when the time came. No problem for me there, since I figured that was way, way down the road. And that I would deal with it, and her, when I had to. I liked working for the *Dispatch,* learning not just about reporting but about publishing too."

"But you wanted to do that in New York."

"I was too big for a podunk town like Pleasant Valley. Too much to say, too much to do. Pulitzers to win. Then my mother married Joe. He's a great guy. Dana's dad."

"Can he make your mother laugh?"

"Yeah. Yeah, he can. We made a good family, the four of us. I don't know that I appreciated that at the time. With Joe around, I figured some of the pressure on me was off. I guess we all figured they'd work the paper together for decades."

"Joe's a reporter?"

"Yeah, worked for the paper for years. Used to joke that he'd married the boss. They made a good team too, so it looked like everything was going to work out fine and dandy. After college, I figured to build up another couple years' experience here, then give New York a break and offer my invaluable skills and services. I met Lily, and that seemed to be the icing on the cake."

"What happened?"

"Joe got sick. Looking back, I imagine my mother was frantic at the idea that she might lose somebody else she loved. She's not big on emotional displays. She's sort of contained and straightforward, but I can see it, hindsight-wise. And I can't imagine what it was like for her. They had to move. He had a better chance of copping more time if they got out of this climate, and away from stress. So either I stayed, or the paper closed."

"She expected you to stay."

He remembered what he'd said about expectations. "Yeah. Do my duty. I was pissed off at her for a year, then irritated for another. Somewhere in year three I hit resigned. I don't know exactly when that became . . . I guess you could say contentment. But around the time I bumped into contentment, I bought the house. Then I got Moe."

"I'd say you're off your mother's plan and on your own."

He let out a half laugh. "Son of a bitch. I guess I am."

Chapter Fifteen

There was very little that Dana dragged herself out of bed for. Work, of course, was the
primary incentive. But when she had the
morning off, her main choice for entertainment was sleep.

Giving that up at Flynn's request demonstrated, in her opinion, extreme sisterly affection. And should earn her major points,
to be redeemed in any future necessity.

She knocked on Malory's door at seven-
thirty, wearing a Groucho Marx T-shirt,
ripped jeans, and a pair of Oakleys.

Because he knew his sister, Flynn
opened the door and shoved a steaming
cup of coffee into her hands.

"You're a peach. You're a jewel. You are my personal treasure chest."

"Stuff it." She strode in, sat on the couch, and began to inhale the coffee. "Where's Mal?"

"Still sleeping."

"Got bagels?"

"I don't know. I didn't look. I should've looked," he said instantly. "I'm a selfish bastard, thinking only of myself."

"Excuse me, but I'd have liked to say that."

"Just saving you the time and energy. I've got to go. I need to be at the paper in . . . shit, twenty-six minutes," he said when he looked at his watch.

"Just tell me why I'm in Malory's apartment, drinking coffee and hoping there are bagels, when she's asleep."

"I don't have time to get into it. She had a rough one, and I don't want her to be alone. At all, Dana."

"Jesus, Flynn, what? Did somebody beat her up?"

"You could say that. Emotionally speaking. And it wasn't me," he added as he headed for the door. "Just stick with her, will you? I'll shake loose as soon as I can, but I've got a full slate today. Let her sleep, then, I don't know, keep her busy. I'll call."

He was out the patio door and loping away while Dana scowled after him. "For a reporter, you're sure stingy with the deets." Deciding to make the best of it, she got up to raid Malory's kitchen.

She was taking the first enthusiastic bite of a poppy-seed bagel when Malory came in.

Heavy-eyed, Dana noted. A little pale. Considerably rumpled. She imagined the rumpled part was on Flynn. "Hi. Want the other half?"

Obviously groggy, Malory just blinked. "Hi, yourself. Where's Flynn?"

"He had to run. Go stand for journalism and all that. Want some coffee instead?"

"Yes." She rubbed her eyes and tried to think. "What're you doing here, Dana?"

"Don't have a clue. Flynn called me, at the ungodly hour of about forty minutes ago, and asked me to come over. He was short on details but long on pleading, so I hauled my ass over here. What's up?"

"I guess he's worried about me." She

considered it, then decided she didn't mind very much. "That's sort of sweet."

"Yeah, he's sugar. Why is he worried about you?"

"I think we'd better sit down."

She told Dana everything.

"What did he look like?" Dana demanded.

"Well . . . strong face, leaning toward the ascetic side. Wait a minute—I think I can sketch it."

She got up to take a pad and pencil from a drawer, then sat down again. "He had very well-defined features, so it won't be too hard. But more than how he looked was the way he felt. Compelling. Even charismatic."

"What about the house you were in?" Dana pressed while Malory worked.

"I just got impressions. It seemed so familiar in the dream, the way your home does. So you don't notice a lot of details. Two-story with a lawn in the back, a pretty garden. Sunny kitchen."

"It wasn't Flynn's house?"

Malory looked up then. "No," she said slowly. "No, it wasn't. I didn't think of that.

Wouldn't you assume it would be? If it's my fantasy, why weren't we living in his house? It's a great house, it's already in my head."

"Maybe he couldn't use Flynn's house because it's already occupied, and . . . I don't know. It's probably not important."

"I think everything's important. Everything I saw and felt and heard. I just don't know how yet. Here . . ." She turned the pad around. "It's rough, but that's the best I can do. It's a pretty decent impression of him anyway."

"Wow!" Dana pursed her lips, whistled. "So Kane the sorcerer's a hottie."

"He scares me, Dana."

"He couldn't hurt you, not really. Not when it came right down to it."

"Not this time. But he was in my head. It was like an invasion." She pressed her lips together. "A kind of rape. He knows what I feel, and what I wish for."

"I'll tell you what he didn't know. He didn't know you'd tell him to kiss your ass."

Malory sat back. "You're right. He didn't know I'd refuse, or that I'd understand— even in the dream—that he wanted me trapped somewhere, however wonderful, where I couldn't find the key. Both of those things surprised and irritated him. And that means he doesn't know everything."

With considerable reluctance, Dana tagged along when Malory decided to work at Flynn's house. It made sense, as the two paintings were there. But so was Jordan Hawke.

Her hopes that he would be out some-where were quashed when she saw the vin-tage Thunderbird in Flynn's driveway.

"Always had a thing about cars," she muttered, and though she sniffed at the T-Bird, she secretly admired its lines, the sweep of tail fins and the sparkle of chrome.

She'd have paid money to get behind the wheel and open that engine up on a straightaway.

"Don't know why the jerk has to have a car when he lives in Manhattan."

Malory recognized the tone, both the sulkiness and the bitterness, and paused at the door. "Is this going to be a problem for you? Maybe we can make arrangements to see the paintings again when Jordan's not here."

"No problem for me. He doesn't exist in my reality. I long ago drowned him in a vat of ebola. It was a messy, yet oddly satisfying, task."

"Okay, then." Malory lifted a hand to knock, but Dana nudged her aside.

"I do *not* knock on my brother's door." She shot her key into the lock. "No matter what morons he might have staying with him."

She strode in, prepared for a confrontation. Unwilling to be so easily deflated when she didn't see him, she slammed the door.

"Dana."

"Oops. Slipped." Hooking her thumbs in her pockets, she strolled into the living room. "Just where we left them," she said with a nod at the paintings. "And you know what, I don't see anything different about them either. Job's done for today. Let's go shopping or something."

"I want to do a more thorough study of them, and I want to go through all the research notes. But there's no reason for you to hang around."

"I promised Flynn."

"Flynn's a worrywart."

"Well, yeah, but I promised." Sensing movement in the doorway behind her, she stiffened. "And unlike some, I keep my promises."

"And hold a grudge with equal fervor," Jordan commented. "Hello, ladies. What can I do for you?"

"I'd like to go over the paintings and my notes again," Malory told him. "I hope you don't mind."

"Who's he to mind? It's not his house."

"True enough." Jordan, tall and tough in black jeans and black T-shirt, leaned against the doorjamb. "Help yourself."

"Haven't you got something better to do than lurk?" Dana tossed out. "A book to pretend to write, a publisher to skin."

"You know us commercial fiction hacks. We just knock 'em out in a couple weeks, then lounge around on our royalties."

"I don't mind if the two of you want to fight, really, I don't." Malory dumped her briefcase, fat with notes, on the crate. "But maybe you could take it to another room."

"We're not fighting," Jordan replied. "This is foreplay."

"In your dreams."

"Stretch, in my dreams you're usually wearing a lot less. Let me know if I can help you out with anything, Malory." He straightened, then strolled away.

"Be right back." Dana was after him like a rocket. "In the kitchen, hotshot." She streamed by, then gritted her teeth while she waited for him to catch up.

He moved at his own pace, she thought, and always had. Her temper sparked as he wandered in. She was readying the first salvo when he stepped right up, gripped her hips, and covered her shocked mouth with his.

The blast of heat blew straight through her.

That had always been, as well.

Fire and flash and promise all balled together in some sort of molten comet that exploded in the brain and left the system wrecked.

Not this time, not this time. Not ever again.

With considerable force she shoved him back a step. She wouldn't slap. Too predictable and female. But she very nearly punched.

"Sorry. I thought that was what you called me out here for."

"Try that again, and you'll be bleeding from various fatal wounds."

He shrugged, sauntered over to the coffeepot. "My mistake."

"Damn right. Any rights you had to touch me expired a long time ago. You may be part of this thing because you happened to buy that damn painting, and I'll tolerate you because of that. And because you're Flynn's friend. But as long as you're here, you'll abide by the rules."

He poured two mugs of coffee, set hers on the counter. "Spell them out for me."

"You don't ever touch me. If I'm about to step in front of a damn bus, you don't so much as reach out to pull me back to the curb."

"Okay. You'd rather be run over by a bus than have me touch you. Check. Next?"

"You're a son of a bitch."

Something that might have been regret flashed across his face. "I know it. Look, let's step back a minute. Flynn's important to both of us, and this is important to Flynn. That woman out there's important to him, and she's important to you. We're all connected here, whether we want to be or not. So let's try to figure it out. He was in and out of here in about three minutes flat this morning. I didn't get much more out of him then, or when he called last night, than that Malory's in trouble. Fill me in."

"If Malory wants you to know, she'll tell you."

Hand her an olive branch, he thought, and she rams it down your throat. "Still a hard-ass."

"It's private stuff," she snapped. "Intimate stuff. She doesn't know you." Despite a thousand vows, she felt her eyes fill. "Neither do I."

That single tearful look punched a hole in his heart. "Dana."

When he stepped toward her, she snatched a bread knife off the counter. "Put your hands on me again, I'll hack them off at the wrist."

He stayed where he was, slid his hands into his pockets. "Why don't you just stick it in my heart and get it over with?"

"Just stay away from me. Flynn doesn't want Malory left alone. You can consider this your shift, because I'm leaving."

"If I'm going to be guard dog, it would help to know what I'm guarding against."

"Big, bad sorcerers." She yanked open the back door. "Anything happens to her, I'll not only jam that knife in your heart, I'll cut it out and feed it to the dog."

"Always were good with imagery," he drawled after she'd slammed out.

He rubbed a hand over his stomach. She'd tied it in knots—something else she was damn good at. He looked at the coffee she hadn't touched. Though he knew it was foolishly symbolic, he picked up the cup and poured the coffee down the sink.

"Down the drain, Stretch. Just like us."

Malory studied the paintings until her vision blurred. She made more notes, then stretched out on the floor to stare at the ceiling. She jumbled what she knew in her head, hoping it would form a new, clearer pattern.

A singing goddess, shadows and light, what was within herself and outside herself. To look and see what she hadn't seen. Love forged the key.

Hell.

Three paintings, three keys. Did that mean there was a clue, a sign, a direction in each painting for each key? Or was there a compilation in the three paintings for the first key? For hers?

Either way, she was missing it.

There were common elements in each portrait. The legendary subject matter, of course. The use of forest and shadows. The figure cloaked by them.

That would be Kane.

Why was Kane in the portrait of Arthur? Had he actually been there at the event, or was his inclusion, and Rowena's and Pitte's, symbolic?

But still, even with those common elements, the Arthurian portrait didn't seem part of what she was certain was a set. Was there another painting, to complete the triad, of the Daughters of Glass?

Where would she find it, and what would it tell her when she did?

She rolled over, examined the portrait of young Arthur once more. The white dove at the right top. A symbol for Guinevere? The beginning of the end of that shining moment?

Betrayal by love. The consequences of love.

Wasn't she dealing with consequences of love now, within herself? The soul was as much a symbol of love and beauty as the heart was. Emotions, poetry, art, music. Magic. Soulful elements.

Without a soul, there were no consequences, and no beauty.

If the goddess could sing, didn't that mean she still had her soul?

The key might be in a place where there was art, or love. Beauty or music. Or where the choice to keep them or discard them was made.

A museum, then? A gallery? The Gallery, she thought and bolted to her feet.

"Dana!"

She dashed toward the kitchen, pulling up short when she saw Jordan sitting at the scarred table working on a small, sleek laptop.

"Sorry. I thought Dana was in here."

"She took off hours ago."

"Hours?" Malory passed a hand over her face as if coming out of a dream. "I lost track of time."

"Happens to me regularly. Want some

coffee?" He glanced toward the empty pot on the counter. "All you have to do is make it."

"No, I really need to . . . You're working. I'm sorry to interrupt."

"No problem. I'm having one of those days where I fantasize about having an alternate profession. Like being a lumberjack in the Yukon or a bartender at a tropical resort."

"Pretty disparate choices."

"Either of which seems like more fun than what I'm doing."

She noted the empty coffee cup, the half-full ashtray set beside the jazzy laptop on a secondhand picnic table in a stupendously ugly kitchen.

"Could be the ambience isn't particularly conducive to creativity."

"When things are going well, you can be in a sewer with a notebook and a Ticonderoga."

"I suppose that's true, but I'm wondering if you're set up in this . . . unfortunate room because you're watching out for me."

"Depends." He eased back, fiddled with his dwindling pack of cigarettes. "If that's okay with you, sure. If it's going to piss you off, then I'm afraid I don't know what you're talking about."

She cocked her head. "And if I said I had to leave now, that there's something I want to check out?"

He gave her an easy smile, one she thought might pass for innocent on a less wicked face. "I'd say, is it okay if I tag along? It might do me good to get out of the house for a while. Where are we going?"

"The Gallery. It occurred to me that the key must be attached to art, to beauty, to the paintings. It's the most logical place in the area to look."

"Uh-huh. So, you're going to walk into a public place of business, during business hours, and nobody's going to mind if you go on a scavenger hunt through the stock and/or office areas."

"Well, when you put it that way." Deflated, she sat across from him. "Do you think this whole thing is just some kind of lunacy?"

Jordan recalled watching several thousand dollars appear and disappear. "Not necessarily."

"And if I said I might have a way to get into The Gallery *after* business hours?"

"I'd say you wouldn't have been picked to be a part of this unless you were a creative woman with a flexible mind who's willing to take some chances."

"I like that description. I don't know if it always applied, but it does now. I need to make some phone calls. And, Jordan? I think it shows a strong sense of character and loyalty for a man to waste his day looking after a stranger because a friend asked him to."

Malory took the keys from Tod and gave him a huge hug in return. "I owe you big."

"I'll say, but I'll settle for any sort of an explanation."

"As soon as I can. I promise."

"Honeybun, this is all getting really weird. You get fired, then you hack into Pamela's files. You turn down the invitation to come back to home and hearth with a substantial raise. And now you're going to skulk around the place after closing."

"You know what?" She jingled the keys in her hand. "That's not the really weird part. All I can tell you is I'm doing something important, and with the best intentions. I'm not going to do The Gallery or James, or most especially you, any harm."

"I'd never think you would."

"I'll have these back to you tonight. First thing in the morning at the latest."

Tod glanced out the window to see Flynn loitering on the sidewalk. "This doesn't have anything to do with sexual fetishes or fantasies?"

"No."

"Well, that's a shame. I'm walking away. I'm going to have a lovely martini, maybe two, and put all this completely out of my mind."

"Do just that."

He started out, then stopped and looked back at her. "Whatever you're doing, Mal, be careful."

"I will. Promise."

She waited, watched Tod stop to speak to Flynn before sauntering off. She opened the door, gestured Flynn in, then locked it, set the security code. "What did Tod say to you?"

"That if I got you into any sort of trouble he'd hang me up by my balls and then snip off various other body parts with manicure scissors."

"Ouch. Good one."

"You bet." He peered out the window to make sure Tod was gone. "And let me tell you, if I was thinking about getting you into any sort of trouble, that image would be a very strong deterrent."

"I guess, when it comes down to it, I'm the one who could be getting you in trouble. There's the legal angle, the criminal angle, and your reputation as publisher and editor in chief of the *Dispatch* on the line here. You don't have to do this."

"I'm in. Manicure scissors are those little pointy ones that curve, right?"

"That's right."

He hissed out a breath. "Yeah, I was afraid of that. Where do we start?"

"Upstairs, I think. We can work our way down. Assuming the keys in the painting are in proportion, it'll be about three inches long."

"Little key."

"Yes, a fairly little key. The business end is a single, simple drop," she continued and handed him a small sketch. "The other end is decorative, this complex pattern. It's a Celtic design, a triple spiral called a *triske-*

les. Zoe found the pattern in one of Dana's books."

"You three make a good team."

"It feels like it. It's gold, probably solid gold. I can't imagine we won't recognize it when we see it."

He glanced toward the main showroom with its vaulted ceilings and generous space. There were the paintings, of course, and the sculpture and other artworks. Display cases and tables. Drawers and chests and counters with infinite cubbyholes.

"A lot of places a key might hide in here."

"Wait until we get into the storage and shipping areas."

They started in the offices. Malory set aside her guilt at going through drawers, riffling through personal items. This wasn't any time for delicacy, she told herself. She crawled around James's desk, searching under it.

"Do you really think people like Rowena and Pitte, or whatever god's in charge of hiding the keys, would tape the secret key to the bottom of a desk drawer?"

She sent him a sulky look as she slid the drawer back in place. "I don't think we can afford to overlook any possibility."

She looked so cute, he thought, sitting on
the floor with her hair tied back from her
face and her mouth all pouty. He wondered
if she'd worn black because she felt it
suited the circumstances.

It would be just like her.

"Fair enough, but wo'd get through those
possibilities faster if we called the whole
team in."

"I can't have a pack of people running
around here. It's just not right." And the guilt
of what she was doing scraped her conscience like ragged fingernails. "It's bad
enough you're here. You can't use anything
you see here in a story."

He crouched down with her, stared into
her face with eyes that had gone winter
cool. "Is that what you think?"

"It doesn't seem unreasonable that the
thought crossed my mind." She rose to take
a painting off the wall. "You're a journalist,"
she continued as she checked the frame,
tested the backing. "I owe something to this
place, to James. I'm just saying that I don't
want him involved."

She rehung the painting, chose another.

"Maybe you should write up a list of what

is and isn't appropriate for me to write about. In your opinion."

"There's no need to get testy."

"Oh, yeah, there is. I've invested a lot of my time and energy in this, and I haven't printed a word. Don't question my ethics, Malory, just because you're questioning your own. And don't ever tell me what I can or can't write."

"It's just a matter of saying this is off the record."

"No, it's not. It's a matter of you trusting and respecting someone you claim to love. I'm going to start in the next room. I think we'll do better separately."

Just how, she wondered, had she managed to screw that one up so completely? She took the last painting off the wall, ordered herself to concentrate.

Obviously Flynn was oversensitive. She'd made a perfectly reasonable request, and if he wanted to get huffy about it, it was his problem.

She spent the next twenty minutes going over every inch of the room, and comforting herself with her conviction that he'd overreacted.

They didn't speak for the next hour, and

though they were two people performing the same task in the same space, they managed to avoid contact.

By the time they started on the main level, they'd developed a rhythm, but they still weren't speaking.

It was tedious, frustrating work. Checking every painting, every sculpture, every pedestal and objet d'art. Going over the stairs tread by tread, crawling along the trim.

Malory took herself off to the storeroom. It was both painful and thrilling to come across newly acquired pieces, or to see others that had been sold since she'd left The Gallery and were waiting to be crated and shipped.

Once she'd been privy to every step and stage, and had been granted the right to acquire items and negotiate a price. In her heart The Gallery had been hers. She couldn't count the times she'd been inside it after hours like this. No one would have questioned her presence then. There would have been no need to beg the keys from a friend, or to feel guilt.

To question her ethics, she admitted.

She wouldn't have felt this awful grief,

she realized. Grief that this part of her life had been taken away from her. Maybe she was crazy for refusing the offer to take it back. Maybe she was making a huge mistake by deviating from the sensible, the *tangible*. She could go back and speak to James, tell him she'd changed her mind. She could slide back into routine again, have what she'd always had.

And it would never be the same.

That was the grief. Her life was changed, irrevocably. And she hadn't taken the time to mourn the loss. She did so now, with every piece she touched, every minute she spent in the space that had once been the most important part of her life.

She revisited a thousand memories, so many of them part of the day-to-day routine that had meant nothing at the time. And everything once it had been taken away.

Flynn pulled open the door. "Where do you want to—" He broke off when she turned toward him. Her eyes were dry, but devastated. She held a rough stone sculpture in her arms as she might a child.

"What is it?"

"I miss this place so much. It's like something's died." Very gently, she replaced the sculpture on a shelf. "I acquired this piece, about four months ago. It's a new artist. He's young, with all the fire and temperament you'd expect from the feel of his work. He's from a small town in Maryland, and he's had a little local luck, but no major gallery showed any interest. It felt good to give him his first real break, and to think of what he might do, what *we* might do in the future."

She ran a fingertip over the stone. "Someone bought this. I didn't have anything to do with that part, don't even recognize the name on the invoice. It's not mine anymore."

"It wouldn't have been here or have been sold if it wasn't for you."

"Maybe, but those days are over. I don't have a place here anymore. I'm sorry for what I said before. Very sorry I hurt your feelings."

"Forget it."

"No." She drew a breath. "I'm not going to say I didn't have some concerns about how you might handle this whole thing eventually. I can't claim that I have absolute trust in you. That conflicts with loving you, and I can't explain it. No more than I can explain how I know the key's not here. How I knew that the minute I walked in to get the keys from Tod. I still have to look, have to finish what I started. But it's not here, Flynn. There's nothing here for me now."

Chapter Sixteen

Flynn closed the door of his office, a signal that he was writing and was not to be disturbed. Not that anybody paid a great deal of attention to the signal, but it was the principle of the thing.

He let the idea for the column simply flow out initially, a kind of serpentine river of thought that he would channel into a more disciplined form on the second pass.

What defined the artist? Were artists only those who created what was perceived as the beautiful or the shocking, those who formed some piece of work that delivered a visceral punch? In painting, in music, in literature or theater?

If so, did that make the rest of the world

nothing more than the audience? Passive observers whose only contribution was applause or criticism?

What became of the artist without the audience?

Not his usual sort of column, Flynn mused, but it had been kicking around in his head since the night he and Malory had searched The Gallery. It was time to let it out.

He could still see the way she'd looked in that storeroom. A stone figure in her arms and grief swimming in her eyes. In the three days since, she'd kept him and everyone else at arm's length. Oh, she paid lip service to being busy, to following different angles on her quest, to putting her life back in order.

Though from his point of view there'd never been any real disorder to it.

Still, she refused to come out. And she wouldn't let him in.

Maybe the column was a kind of message to her.

He rolled his shoulders, tapped his fingers on the edge of his desk until his mind shifted back and found the words.

Wasn't the child who first learned to form

his own name with letters a kind of artist? One who was exploring intellect, coordination, and ego. When the child held that fat pencil or bright crayon in his fist, then drew those letters on paper, wasn't he creating a symbol of himself with lines and curves? This is who I am, and no one else is quite the same.

There is art in the statement, and in the accomplishment.

What about the woman who managed to put a hot meal on the table in the evening? To a Cordon Bleu chef, this might be a pedestrian feat, but to those who were baffled by the directions on a can of condensed soup, having that meat loaf, mashed potatoes, and string beans hit the table in unison was a great and mysterious art.

"Flynn?"

"Working," he snapped without looking up.

"You're not the only one." Rhoda shut the door at her back, marched over and sat in a chair. She folded her arms across her chest and stared holes at Flynn through her square-framed glasses.

But without the audience, ready and willing to consume the art, it becomes con-gealed leftovers to be dumped . . . "Damn it."

He shoved back from his keyboard. "What?"

"You cut an inch from my feature."

His hands itched to pick up his Slinky. And wrap its coils around Rhoda's skinny throat. "And?"

"You said it was running a full twelve inches."

"And what you had was eleven solid inches, and an inch of fill. I cut the fill. It was a good piece, Rhoda. Now it's a better piece."

"I want to know why you're always pick-ing on me, why you're always cutting my pieces. You barely put a mark on John's or Carla's, and they're all over my work."

"John handles sports. He's been handling sports for over a decade. He's got it down to a science."

Art and science, Flynn thought and made a quick shorthand note to remind himself to work it into the column. And sports . . . If anyone watched the way a pitcher sculpted the dirt on the mound with his feet until it was exactly the shape, the texture, the slope he—

"Flynn!"

"What? What?" He snapped back, rewound the tape in his mind. "And I do edit Carla when and if she needs it. Rhoda, I'm on a deadline myself here. If you want to get into this, let's schedule some time tomorrow."

Her mouth pruned. "If we don't resolve this now, I won't be coming in tomorrow."

Instead of reaching for his action figure of Luke Skywalker and imagining the Jedi knight drawing his light saber and blasting the superior smirk off Rhoda's face, Flynn sat back.

The time had come, he decided, to do the blasting himself.

"Okay. First, I'm going to tell you I'm tired of you threatening to walk. If you're not happy here, not happy with the way I run the paper, then go."

She flushed scarlet. "Your mother never—"

"I'm not my mother. Deal. I run the *Dispatch.* I've been running it for nearly four years now, and I intend to run it for a long time. Get used to it."

Now her eyes filled, and since Flynn considered tears fighting dirty, he struggled to ignore them. "Anything else?" he asked coolly.

"I've been working here since before you could read the damn paper."

"Which may be our problem. It suited you better when my mother was in charge. Now it suits you better to continue to think of me as a temporary annoyance, and an incompetent one at that."

Rhoda's mouth dropped open in what appeared to be sincere shock. "I don't think you're incompetent. I just think—"

"That I should stay out of your work." The genial tone was back in his voice, but his expression remained frigid. "That I should do what you tell me instead of the other way around. That's not going to happen."

"If you don't think I do good work, then—"

"Sit down," he ordered as she started to rise. He knew the drill. She would storm out, slam things around, glare at him through the glass, then make sure her next piece slid in only minutes before deadline.

"It so happens I think you do good work. Not that it matters a hell of a lot coming from me because you don't have any confidence in or respect for my skill or my authority. I guess that makes it tough for you because you're a journalist, we're the only game in town, and I'm in charge. I don't see any of those factors changing. Next time I ask for twelve inches, give me a solid twelve and we won't have a problem." He tapped the tip of his pencil against the desk while she gaped at him.

Perry White, he mused, might've handled it better, but he figured he was in the ballpark. "Anything else?"

"I'm going to take the rest of the day off."

"No, you're not." He swiveled back to his keyboard. "Have that piece on the elementary school expansion on my desk by two. Close the door on your way out."

Flynn went back to typing, pleased when he heard the door click closed instead of slam. He waited thirty seconds, then shifted in his chair enough to look through the glass wall. Rhoda was sitting at her desk as if paralyzed.

He hated confrontations like that. The woman used to sneak him gumdrops when he would come into the offices after school. It was hell, he decided, rubbing his temple and pretending to concentrate on his work. Just hell being a grown-up.

He escaped for an hour in the afternoon to meet Brad and Jordan at the Main Street Diner. It hadn't changed much since the three of them had gathered there regularly after football games or for late-night bullshit sessions that had revolved around girls and life plans.

The air was still ripe with the smell of the diner's signature chicken-fried steak, and the counter still held a four-tiered display rack of that day's pies. As Flynn looked down at the burger he'd ordered out of habit, he wondered if it was the diner that had gotten stuck in the past, or himself.

He frowned at Brad's club sandwich. "Trade me."

"You want my sandwich?"

"I want your sandwich. Trade me." To solve the matter, Flynn switched the plates himself.

"If you didn't want a burger, why'd you order one?"

"Because. I'm a victim of habit and tradi-tion."

"And eating my sandwich is going to solve that?"

"It's a start. I also started breaking habit by reaming Rhoda out at the paper this morning. Once she comes out of shock, I'm pretty sure she'll start planning my demise."

"How come you wanted his sandwich instead of mine?" Jordan asked.

"I don't like Reubens."

Jordan considered, then switched his plate with Brad's.

"Jesus, are we finished playing musical plates now?" Brad scowled at the Reuben, then decided it actually looked pretty good.

Though he was already wishing he had his burger back, Flynn picked at the club sandwich. "Do you think staying in your hometown all your life keeps you too attached to the past, too resistant to change and growth, and thereby inhibits your ability to function as a mature adult?"

"I didn't know this was going to be a philosophical discussion." But willing to play, Jordan considered the question as he squeezed ketchup on the burger. "It could be said that staying in your hometown means you're comfortable there and have created strong roots and ties. Or that you're just too lazy and complacent to get your ass out."

"I like it here. Took me a while to come to that. Up until recently I'd been pretty complacent about how things were going. Complacency's taken a backseat since around the first of the month."

"Because of the keys?" Brad asked. "Or Malory?"

"One goes with the other. The keys, that's an adventure, right? Sir Galahad and the Holy Grail, Indiana Jones and the Lost Ark."

"Elmer Fudd and Bugs Bunny," Jordan put in.

"Right, same deal." You could always count on Jordan to get your drift, Flynn thought. "None of our lives are going to suffer if we don't find them. Not really."

"One year," Brad said. "That's a pretty stiff penalty clause to my way of thinking."

"Okay, yeah." Flynn plucked a potato chip from the little mound beside his sandwich. "But I'm having a hard time seeing either Rowena or Pitte punishing these women."

"They may not be the ones who do the messing," Jordan commented. "They may simply be the conduit, so to speak, to reward or punishment. Why do we assume they have a choice either?"

"Trying to think positive here," Flynn replied. "And the idea that we will find the keys, and what happens then, is compelling."

"Besides the fact that it's a puzzle, and it's damn hard to walk away from a puzzle."

Flynn nodded at Brad, shifted in his seat. "Then there's the magic. The acceptance that magic, some kinds of magic, are real. Not an illusion, but an actual kick in the ass of the natural order. I mean, how cool is that? That's the kind of thing we give up when we become adults. The casual belief in magic. This has given it back."

"You want to look at it as a gift or a burden?" Jordan wondered. "Could go either way."

"Thanks again, Mr. Bright Side. But yes, I know that too. We're coming up on deadline here. A little more than a week. If we don't find it, maybe we'll pay, maybe we won't. But we'll never *know.*"

"You can't dismiss the potential consequences of failure," Brad pointed out.

"I'm trying to believe that nobody's going

to screw up the lives of three innocent women because they tried and failed."

"You go back to the beginning of this, and the lives of three innocent women—demigoddesses or not—were screwed up simply because they existed." Jordan dashed salt on what had been Flynn's fries. "Sorry, pal."

"Add in that the women in the portrait look like the women we know." Brad drummed his fingers on the table. "There's a reason for that, and the reason puts them at the core of it all."

"I'm not letting anything happen to Mal-ory. Or any of them," Flynn responded.

Jordan picked up his glass of iced tea. "Just how stuck on her are you?"

"That's another question. I haven't fig-ured it out."

"Well, we'll help you there." Jordan winked at Brad. "What're friends for? How's the sex?"

"Why's that always first with you?" Flynn demanded. "That's a lifelong pattern."

"Because I'm a guy. And if you don't think women rate sex high on the list, you're a sad and pitiful fool."

"It's great." Flynn met Jordan sneer for

sneer. "You only wish you were having this level of sex with a beautiful woman. But it's not like that's the only thing going on between us. We have actual conversations, with and without clothes on."

"Including phone conversations?" Brad asked. "That last over five minutes?"

"Yeah, so?"

"Just making the list. Have you cooked her anything? Not just nuking something, but using an actual stove."

"I just made her some soup when—"

"That counts. Take her to any chick flicks?"

Frowning, Flynn picked up a triangle of sandwich. "I don't know that it qualified as a chick flick." He set it down again. "Okay, yes. Once, but it was—"

"No explanations, this part of the quiz is true or false. We can move on to our essay section," Jordan assured him. "Picture your life in, let's say five years. That work?" he asked Brad.

"Some require ten, but I think we can be more lenient. Five works for me."

"Okay, picture your life in five years. Can you structure the visual without her being in it?"

"I don't know how I'm supposed to picture five years from now when I'm not sure what I'll be doing in five days."

But he could, he could see his house, with some of the long-term plans he had for it in place. He could see himself at the paper, walking Moe, hanging out with Dana. And he could see Malory at every angle. Walking down the stairs in the house, coming by the paper to meet him, chasing Moe out of the kitchen.

He went a little pale. "Oh, man."

"She's in there, isn't she?" Jordan asked.

"She's in there all right."

"Congratulations, son." Jordan slapped him on the shoulder. "You're in love."

"Wait a minute. What if I'm not ready?"

"Tough luck," Brad replied.

Brad knew all about luck and decided his was in when he stepped out of the diner and spotted Zoe stopped at the traffic light.

She was wearing dark wraparound sunglasses and moving her lips in a way that made him assume she was singing along with the car stereo.

It wasn't stalking, exactly, if he just happened to hop in his car, zip out into traffic and follow. The fact that he cut off a pickup truck was completely incidental.

It was reasonable, even important, that they get to know each other better. He could hardly help Flynn if he didn't know the women Flynn was connected to.

That made sense.

It had nothing to do with obsession. Just because he'd bought a painting with her face in it, just because he couldn't get that face out of his mind, all that didn't mean he was obsessed.

He was merely interested.

And if he was practicing various opening lines under his breath, it was only because he understood the value of communication. He certainly wasn't nervous about speaking to a woman. He spoke to women all the time.

Women spoke to *him* all the time, if it came to that. He was considered one of the top eligible bachelors—and God, did he hate that term—in the country. Women went out of their way to talk to him.

If Zoe McCourt couldn't spare five minutes for some polite conversation, well, that was her loss.

By the time she pulled into a driveway, he'd worked himself into a mass of nerves and irritation. The vaguely annoyed glance she sent him when he pulled up behind her put a cap on it.

Feeling foolish and insulted, he climbed out.

"Are you following me?" she demanded.

"Excuse me?" In defense, his voice was flat and cold. "I think you're overestimating your charms. Flynn's worried about Malory. I saw you and thought you'd be able to tell me how she's doing."

Zoe continued to observe him warily as she unlocked her trunk. Her jeans were tight enough to afford him an intriguing view of firm female butt. She wore a short, snug red jacket with an equally snug striped top that stopped a full inch above the waistband of the jeans.

He noted with some fascination that her belly button was pierced and sported a tiny silver bar. He actually felt his fingertips grow warm with the urge to touch it.

"I stopped by to see her before."

"Huh? Who? Oh, Malory." Now the back of his neck grew warm and he cursed himself. "How is she?"

"She looks tired, and a little down on her-self."

"I'm sorry." He stepped forward as she began to unload the trunk. "Let me give you a hand."

"I can get it."

"I'm sure you can." He solved the matter by taking the two heavy sample books of wallpaper from her. "But I don't see any reason you should. Redecorating?"

She took out a paint sample book, a small toolbox—which he pulled away from her—a notebook, and some tile chips. "We contracted for this house. We're going to open the business here. It needs work."

He walked ahead, leaving her to slam the trunk. Yes, it did need work, but it had a sturdy look, and the lot was nicely estab-lished. Solid location, decent parking.

"Looks like it has good bones," he com-mented. "You have the foundation checked out?"

"Yes."

"Wiring up to code?"

She dug out the keys she'd picked up from the realtor. "Just because I'm a woman doesn't mean I don't know how to buy a house. I looked at a number of properties, and this was the best value, with the best location. Most of the work it needs is cosmetic."

She shoved open the door. "You can just dump them on the floor. Thanks. I'll tell Mallory you asked about her."

Brad just kept walking so that she had to step back. Though it took some effort, he refused to let his gaze drift down to her navel again. "Are you always irritated when someone tries to help you?"

"I'm irritated when someone thinks I can't handle myself. Look, I don't have that much time to do what I'm here to do. I need to get started."

"Then I'll stay out of your way."

He studied the ceiling, the floor, the walls as he wandered through the entrance area. "Nice space."

He didn't detect any damp, but there was a definite chill. He wasn't sure if it was a faulty furnace or the woman who was blowing cold. "Which part are you taking?"

"Upstairs."

"Okay." He started up, nearly amused now by her impatient indrawn breath. "Nice stairs. Can't go wrong with white pine."

Some of the trim needed to be replaced,

he noted. And the double-hung window at the top of the steps had yet to be upgraded. She'd need to see to that, get herself a double-glazed for insulation.

The walls had gone dingy, and there were a few cracks from settling. But that was easily seen to.

He liked the way the rooms split off and ran together, and wondered if she would remove some of the hollow-core doors altogether or replace them with something more solid and in tune with the feel of the house.

And what was she going to do about lighting? He didn't know anything about salons, but it seemed logical that good, strong lighting would be essential.

"Excuse me. I need my toolbox."

"What? Oh, sorry." He handed it to her, then ran his fingers over the chipped and peeling window trim. "You know, you could go with cherry for contrast here. Different woods, leaving the natural grain, going with warm tones. You're not going to cover these floors, are you?"

She took out her measuring tape. "No."

Why didn't he go away? She had work to do, thinking to do. And most of all she'd

wanted to be alone in her wonderful building, planning and deciding and dreaming
about how it was all going to be when she'd
finished.

The colors, the textures, the tones, the
smells. Everything.

And here he was, in her way, wandering
around. All male and gorgeous and distracting in his perfect suit and his expensive
shoes. He smelled, oh so subtly, of high-
end soap and aftershave.

He probably paid more for a cake of soap
than she had for the jeans and shirt she was
wearing. And he thought he could just mill
around, wafting in *her* air, making her feel
clumsy and inferior.

"What are your plans for this room?"

She wrote down her measurements and
kept her back to him. "This is the main salon. It's for hair, manicures, and makeup."
When he didn't respond, she was com-
pelled to look over her shoulder. He was
staring contemplatively at her ceiling.
"What?"

"We have these mini track lights. Very
practical, but with a fun look. They have the
advantage of being able to be set in a num-

ber of directions. You going for fun or elegant in here?"

"I don't see why it can't be both."

"Good point. Soft colors or bold?"

"Bold here, soft in the treatment rooms. Look, Bradley—"

"Ouch. That sounded like my mother." He'd already crouched down to flip through a sample book, and cast her a quick grin. "Do you guys have like a training center where you learn how to develop that withering tone?"

"Men aren't allowed to have that information. If I told you, I'd have to kill you. And I just don't have the time. We're going to close on the property in a month, and I want to have my plans outlined so I can start on them the minute we do."

"I can help you."

"I know what I'm doing and how I want to do it. I don't know why you assume—"

"Hold on. Boy, are you touchy." Wouldn't you think a woman who wore skintight jeans and decorated her navel would be a little more approachable? "I'm in the business, remember?" He tapped the Home-Makers logo on the sample book. "Not only that, but I like helping a building meet its potential. I can give you a hand with some labor and material."

"I'm not looking for a handout."

He set the book aside, slowly got to his feet. "I said a hand, not a handout. What is it about me that puts your back up?"

"Everything. That's unfair." She shrugged. "But it's true. I don't understand people like you, so I tend to distrust them."

"People like me?"

"Rich, privileged people who run American empires. I'm sorry, I'm sure you have some very nice qualities or you wouldn't be Flynn's friend. But you and I have nothing in common. Plus, I have a lot on my plate right now and no time to play games. So let's clear this up, then we can move on. I'm not going to have sex with you."

"Okay, well, obviously my life is no longer worth living."

She wanted to smile at that, nearly did. But she had reason to know his sort was very tricky. "Are you going to tell me that you're not hoping to sleep with me?"

He took a careful breath before speaking. She'd hooked the earpiece of her sunglasses in the V of her shirt, and those long, tawny eyes were staring very directly into his. "You and I both know there's no way for me to answer that question correctly. It's the mother of trick questions. Others in this category are, Do I look fat in this? Do you think she's pretty? And if you don't know, I'm certainly not going to tell you."

Now she had to bite the inside of her lip to hold back the laughter. "The last isn't a question."

"It's still a mystery and a trap. So why don't I just say I find you very attractive. And we have more in common than you seem to think, starting with a circle of friends. I'm willing to help you, Malory, and Dana with this place. None of you has to have sex with me in return. Though if the three of you wanted to get together and organize a nice tasteful orgy I wouldn't say no. Meanwhile, I'll let you get back to work."

He started out, then said casually as he walked down the stairs, "By the way, HomeMakers is having a sale on wall treatments—paper and paint—next month. Fifteen to thirty percent off all stock."

Zoe hurried to the top of the steps. "When next month?"

"I'll let you know."

So, she wasn't going to have sex with him. Brad shook his head as he walked to his car. That had been an unfortunate statement on her part. Obviously, she wasn't aware that the one thing no Vane could resist was a direct challenge.

His only plan had been to ask her out to dinner. Now, he decided as he studied the windows on the second level, he'd have to take a little time and work out a strategy.

Zoe McCourt was about to go under siege.

Zoe had other things on her mind. She was running late, but that was nothing new. There always seemed to be another flood of things to do or remember or fix right before she walked out the door.

"You give those cookies to Chuck's mother. She'll divvy them up." Zoe turned the car into the driveway two blocks from her own house, then sent her son a stern look. "I mean it, Simon. I don't have time to take them in myself. If I go to the door she'll keep me there for twenty minutes, and I'm already late."

"Okay, okay. I coulda walked."

"Yeah, but then I wouldn't've been able to do this." She grabbed him, dug her fingers into his ribs to make him squeal.

"Mom!"

"Simon!" she said in the same exasperated tone.

He was laughing as he got out and dragged his duffel from the backseat.

"You mind Chuck's mother, and don't keep everybody up all night. You've got Malory's number?"

"Yes, I've got Malory's number. And I know how to dial nine-one-one, and to run out of the house if I set it on fire when I play with matches."

"Smart guy. Come over here and give me a kiss."

He made a show of dragging his feet, keeping his head dipped to hide his grin as he approached her car window. "Make it quick. Somebody might see us."

"Just tell them I wasn't kissing you. I was yelling at you." She gave him a kiss, resisted hugging him. "See you tomorrow. Have a good time, baby."

"You, too, baby." He snickered, then raced for the house.

With a mother's skill, she backed out of

the drive while watching her boy until he
was safely inside.

Then she headed off to Malory's, and her
first grown-up sleepover.

Chapter Seventeen

Malory knew what was going on. Nobody wanted her to be alone, and her new friends were worried about her. Zoe had been so enthusiastic about the brainstorm of an all-girl sleepover that Malory hadn't been able to refuse.

The very fact that she'd wanted to refuse, had wanted to burrow into her cave alone, forced her to admit she needed a change.

She'd never been a loner, nor had she been much of a brooder in the past. When she was troubled, she went out, saw people. Bought things, gave a party.

Zoe's request for an all-nighter gave Malory the push to do all of that. She bought food and pretty new candles with citrusy scents. And fragrant soaps and fussy new guest towels, then some good wine.

She cleaned the apartment she'd been neglecting, spilled spicy potpourri into bowls. And groomed herself in the meticulous way that women groomed for other women.

By the time Dana arrived, she had cheese and fruit and fancy crackers set out, the candles lit and music set on low.

"Wow, pretty elegant around here. I should've dressed up some."

"You look great." Determined to be cheerful, Malory leaned in to kiss Dana's cheek. "I appreciate you guys doing this."

"Doing what?"

"Hanging out with me, giving me a boost. I've been feeling down the last couple of days."

"None of us figured on the energy drain this deal would be." She passed Malory a grocery bag, then set down her overnight case. "I bought extra supplies. Wine, Cheez-Its, chocolate truffles, and popcorn. You know, the four basic food groups." Dana flipped through the movie selection next to the entertainment center. "Did you rent every chick flick ever made?"

"Every one currently available on DVD. How about some wine?"

"You don't have to twist my arm. New perfume?"

"No, must be the candles."

"Nice. That's Zoe. Better pour another glass."

Zoe came in through the patio doors, loaded down with bags. "Cookies," she said a little breathlessly. "Videos, aromatherapy, and coffee cake for the morning."

"Nice job." Dana took one of the bags from her and handed her a glass of wine. Then she leaned closer and said, "How do you get your lashes to look like that? All sooty and spiky?"

"I'll show you. This is fun. I went by the house today to do some measuring and to look at some samples there in the space and light. I've got wallpaper books and paint chips in the car if we want to look later. Bradley Vane caught me while I was there. What's his story?"

"Golden boy with a social conscience." Dana attacked the Brie. "Star athlete, high school and college. Track a specialty. Honor student but not a nerd. Semi-engaged a couple of times, but always managed to wiggle out before it stuck. Been friends with Flynn just about from birth. Excellent body, which I've been fortunate enough to see through various stages. Interested in seeing it yourself?"

"Not that way. I haven't had much luck with men, so the only one who's going to be in my life for the time being is Simon. Oh, I love this song." She slipped out of her shoes to dance. "So, Mal, how's it going with Flynn?"

"Well, I love him, so it's pretty irritating. I wish I could dance like that."

"Like what?"

"All long legs and loose hips."

"Come on, then." Zoe set her wine down, held out her hands. "We'll work on it. You do one of two things. Pretend nobody's watching or pretend that this guy, this incredibly sexy guy, is watching. Either way, depending on your mood, you just let go."

"How come girls always end up dancing with girls?" Malory wondered as she tried to get her hips to move independent of the rest of her body, as Zoe's seemed to do.

"Because we're better at it."

"Actually," Dana said, helping herself to a

little tree of green grapes, "it's a kind of social, sexual ritual. The female performs,
tempts, and teases, the male observes, fan-
tasizes, and selects. Or is selected. Jungle
drums or the Dave Matthews Band, it
comes down to the same thing."

"Are you going to dance?" Malory asked
her.

"Sure." Popping one more grape, Dana
got up. Hips and shoulders went into a sinuous rhythm as she moved toward Zoe.
They slithered into a dance that was, to
Malory's mind, both sexy and free.

"Now I'm totally outclassed."

"You're doing fine. Loosen your knees.
And speaking of rituals, I have some ideas.
But . . ." Zoe grabbed her wine again. "I
think we should have some more wine before I bring it up."

"You can't do that," Dana complained. "I
hate that. What's the idea?" She took Zoe's
glass, had a hurried sip. "Look, I drank
more. Tell me."

"Okay. Let's sit down."

Remembering her role as hostess, Malory
brought the wine and the tray of food to the
coffee table. "If this ritual has anything to do

with leg waxing, I need much more wine first."

"No." Zoe laughed. "But I have an almost painless technique with hot wax. I can give you a Brazilian without anyone shedding a tear."

"A Brazilian?"

"Tidy up the bikini area. It leaves just a neat little strip so you can wear the tiniest thong without looking, well, unkempt."

"Oh." Instinctively Malory folded her hands over her crotch. "Not even if you use morphine and shackles."

"Honest, it's all in the wrist," Zoe explained. "Well, so . . . back to what I was saying," she continued. "I know we've all been reading and researching and trying to come up with theories and ideas to help Malory find the first key."

"And you've both been great. Really. I just feel like I'm missing something, some little thing that could open it all up."

"Maybe we've all missed something," Zoe countered. "The legend itself. Mortal woman mates with Celtic god and becomes queen. Female power. She has three daughters. Female again. One of their guardians is a female."

"Well, it is a fifty-fifty shot," Dana pointed out. "Even for gods."

"Wait. So when their souls are stolen and trapped *by a man,* it's said that three mortals, mortal *women,* have to find and turn the keys."

"Sorry, Zoe, I'm not following you. We already know all this." Malory reached half heartedly for a grape.

"Let's take it a little further. Gods, in Celtic lore, are, well, earthier than say the Greek or Roman ones. They're more like wizards and sorcerers than . . . what's the word? Um, omniscient beings. Is that right?" she asked Dana.

"Yeah."

"They have ties to the earth, to nature. Like, well, witches. There's black magic and white, but they both use natural elements and forces. And here's where you sort of have to step out of the box."

"We haven't been in the box since September the fourth," Dana pointed out.

"What if we were chosen because we're . . . well, because we're witches?"

Malory frowned at the level of wine in Zoe's glass. "How much did you have to drink before you got here?"

"No, just think about it. We look like them. Maybe we're somehow related to that . . . bloodline or something. Maybe we have power, but we just never knew it."

"The legend says mortal women," Malory reminded her.

"Witches aren't necessarily immortal. They're just people with more. I've been reading up. In Wicca the female witch has three stages. The maiden, the mother, the crone. And they pay homage to the goddess. They—"

"Wicca is a young religion, Zoe," Dana said.

"But its roots are old. And three, that's a magic number. There are three of us."

"I really think I'd know if I were a witch." Malory considered it as she sipped her wine. "And if this has somehow escaped my notice for nearly thirty years, what am I supposed to do about it now? Conjure something, cast a spell?"

"Turn Jordan into a horse's ass. Sorry," Dana shrugged when Malory stared at her. "Just daydreaming."

"We could try it. Together. I bought some things." Zoe jumped up, pulled open her bag. "Ritual candles," she said, digging through. "Incense. Table salt."

"Table salt?" Baffled, Malory picked up the dark blue box of Morton's and studied the cheerful girl with her umbrella.

"You can make a protective circle with it. It wards off evil spirits. Ash wands. Sort of wands. I bought a baseball bat and cut it up to make them."

"Martha Stewart meets Glenda the Good Witch." Dana picked up the thin wooden wand, waved it. "Shouldn't it sprinkle fairy dust?"

"Drink more wine," Zoe ordered. "Crystals. Amethyst and rose quartz and this really great ball." She held up the globe.

"Where'd you get all this loot?" Malory demanded.

"New Age shop at the mall. Tarot cards— Celtic ones because it seemed right. And—"

"A Ouija board!" Dana pounced on it. "Man, oh, man, I haven't seen one of these since I was a kid."

"I found it at the toy store. They don't carry them in the New Age place."

"We had this pj party when I was a kid. Got all toked up on Pepsi and M&Ms and lit candles. Everybody asked the name of the guy they'd marry. Mine came up PTZBAH." Dana gave a sentimental sigh. "It was really sweet. Let's do the Ouija first," Dana suggested. "For old times' sake."

"Okay, but we've got to do it right. Take it seriously." Zoe rose to turn off the lights and music.

"I wonder if Ptzbah is still out there." Dana slid to the floor, opened the box.

"Wait. We have to set up the ritual. I got a book."

They sat in a circle on the floor.

"We have to cleanse our minds," Zoe instructed. "Visualize opening our chakras."

"I never open my chakras in public." Dana giggled, unrepentant, until Malory slapped her knee.

"And we light the ritual candles. White for purity. Yellow for memory. Purple for power." Zoe bit her lip as she carefully ignited the tapers. "Place the crystals. Amethyst for . . . shoot." She reached for her book, flipped pages. "Here. Amethyst for intuition. And the incense. Rose quartz for psychic power and divination."

"It's pretty," Malory decided. "Soothing."

"I think we should all take turns with the

Tarot cards, and maybe try some chants, but let's make Dana happy and do this first." Zoe set the board between them and placed the pointer in its center.

"We have to concentrate," she said. "Focus our minds and our powers on one question."

"Can it be about the love of my life? I pine for Ptzbah."

"No." Zoe swallowed a laugh and tried to look stern. "This is serious business. We want the location of the first key. Malory should do the asking, but you and I need to think it."

"We should close our eyes." Malory rubbed her fingers on her pants, took a deep breath. "Ready?"

They laid fingertips on the pointer, sat in silence.

"Should we call on the Otherworld or something?" Malory whispered. "Pay our respects, ask for guidance? What?"

Zoe opened one eye. "Maybe you should call on the ones behind the Curtain of Dreams."

"Denizens," Dana suggested. "That's a good word. Call on the denizens behind the Curtain of Dreams for guidance."

"Okay, here goes. Everybody quiet, everyone be calm. Concentrate." Malory waited ten seconds in silence. "We call on the denizens behind the Curtain of Dreams, to aid and to guide us in our, um, in our quest."

"Tell them you're one of the chosen ones," Zoe said out of the corner of her mouth and was shushed by Dana.

"I am one of the chosen, one of the seekers of the keys. Time is short. I ask you to show me the way to the key so that we can free the souls of . . . Dana, no pushing the pointer."

"I'm not. Really."

Mouth dry, Malory opened her eyes and watched the pointer shudder under their fingertips.

"The candles," Zoe whispered. "Oh, jeez, look at the candles."

The flames shot up, a trio of slim gold edged with red. Light began to throb, like a pulse. Something blew cold through the room and set those flames dancing.

"This is wild!" Dana exclaimed. "I mean seriously wild."

"It's moving." The pointer jerked, with Malory's fingers trembling on it. She heard nothing but the roar of blood in her own head as she watched it slide from letter to letter.

YOUR DEATH

Her gasp was still strangled in her throat when the room suddenly burst with light and wind. She heard someone scream, threw up an arm to shield her eyes as a form coalesced out of a whirlpool of air.

The board shattered as if made of glass.

"What are you playing at?" Rowena stood in the center of them, the sharp heel of her shoe digging into a shard of the board. "Have you no more sense than to open a door to such things as you cannot understand or defend against?"

With an annoyed sigh, she stepped gracefully out of the circle and picked up the wine. "I'd like a glass, please."

"How did you get here? How did you know?" Malory pushed herself up on rubbery legs.

"It's fortunate for you that I did both." She picked up the salt, and upended the box over the remains of the board.

"Oh, now, just a damn minute."

"Sweep it up together," Rowena ordered Zoe. "Then burn it. I'd very much appreciate a glass of wine." She handed the bottle to Malory, then sat on the sofa.

Outraged, Malory stalked into the kitchen, yanked a wineglass from the cupboard. She marched back and shoved the glass into Rowena's hand. "I didn't invite you into my home."

"On the contrary, you invited me and whoever else chose to come through the opening."

"Then we are witches."

Rowena's expression changed as she looked over at Zoe's rapt face. "No, not the way you mean." Her tone was more gentle now, patient teacher to eager student. "Though every woman has some magic. Still, together your powers are trebled, and you had just enough skill, just enough desire to issue an invitation. I'm not the only one who answered it. You felt him," she said to Malory. "You've felt him before."

"Kane." She cupped her elbows and shuddered as the memory of the cold seeped into her. "He moved the pointer, not us. He was playing with us."

"He threatened Malory." The thrill forgotten, Zoe was on her feet now. "What are you going to do about it?"

"All I can."

"Maybe that's not good enough." Dana reached up to link her hand with Malory's. "I heard you scream. I saw your face when you did. You felt something Zoe and I didn't, and it was real terror. It was real pain."

"It's the cold. It's . . . I can't describe it."

"The absence of all warmth," Rowena murmured. "All hope, all life. But he can't touch you unless you allow it."

"Allow it? How the hell did she . . ." Zoe broke off, looked down at the broken board at her feet. "Oh, God. I'm so sorry. Mal, I'm so sorry."

"It's not your fault. It's not." She took Zoe's hand, so for a moment the three of them were linked.

Seeing them, Rowena smiled into her wine.

"We were looking for answers, and you had an idea. Which is more than I've had the last couple of days. We tried something. Maybe it was the wrong something," she added as she whipped back to Rowena, "but that doesn't give you the right to slap at us for it."

"You're absolutely right. I apologize." She leaned forward to spread Brie on a cracker, then tapped a finger against the Tarot deck. Light flickered over them, then was gone. "These will do you no harm. You may develop a skill for readings, or even find you have a gift for them."

"You . . ." Zoe pressed her lips together. "If you hadn't come when you did . . ."

"It's my duty, and my wish, to keep you from harm. When and how I can. Now I should go, leave you to your evening." Rowena rose, looked around the room. "You have a pretty home, Malory. It suits you."

Feeling ungracious and childish, Malory huffed out a breath. "Why don't you stay, finish your wine?"

Surprise ran across Rowena's face. "That's very kind of you. I'd like that. It's been a very long time since I've sat in the company of women. I've missed it."

It wasn't very strange, after the initial awkwardness, to have a woman who'd lived for thousands of years sitting in her living room drinking her wine.

And it became apparent by the time they started on the truffles that women—goddess or mortal—were the same under the skin.

"I rarely fuss with it," Rowena said while Zoe worked her mane of hair into an elegant upsweep. "It's not one of my talents, so I tend to wear it down. I've cut it occasionally, but I always regret it."

"Not everyone can wear it simply as you do, and still look regal."

Rowena studied herself in the hand mirror as Zoe worked, then tilted the glass to study her stylist. "I'd love to have your hair. It's so striking."

"Couldn't you? I mean if you wanted to look a certain way, couldn't you just . . ." Zoe fluttered her fingers and made Rowena laugh.

"That isn't my gift."

"What about Pitte?" Dana rolled over on the couch. "What's his deal?"

"He's a warrior, full of pride and arrogance and will. He's maddening and exciting." She lowered the mirror.

"Zoe, you're an artist."

"Oh, I just like playing with hair." She stepped in front of Rowena and released a few tendrils around her face. "A great look for that important board meeting or the after-Oscars bash. Sexy, female, and powerful. Well, you give that off no matter what the do."

"Excuse me, but I just have to ask," said Dana, "what's it like to be with the same guy for, well, basically forever?"

"He's the only man I want," Rowena answered.

"Oh, come on, come, on. You've got to have had a few hundred fantasies about other men in the last couple of millennia."

"Of course." Rowena set the mirror down, and her lips bowed into a dreamy smile. "There was a young waiter once, in Rome. Such a face and form. With eyes so dark it seemed I could see worlds drowning in them. And he served me coffee and a bun. He called me *bella donna* with such a knowing smile. While I ate my bun I imagined biting into his tasty bottom lip."

She pressed her own together, then laughed. "I painted him in my studio, and let him flirt with me outrageously. And when I nudged him along after a session, I would drag Pitte away from whatever he might be doing and seduce him."

"You never cheated."

"I love my man," Rowena said simply. "We're bound, body, heart, soul. There's magic in that, more potent than any spell, more wicked than any curse." She reached up, laid a hand over Zoe's. "You loved a boy, and he gave you a son. For that, you'll always love him, even though he was weak and betrayed you."

"Simon's my world."

"And you've made it a bright and loving world. I so envy you your child. You." She rose, stepped closer to trail her fingers over Dana's hair. "You loved one who was no longer a boy, yet not quite a man. For that, you've never forgiven him."

"Why should I?"

"There's a question," Rowena replied.

"What about me?" Malory asked, and Rowena sat on the arm of the sofa, touched a hand to her shoulder.

"You love the man so much, so fast and fierce, it makes you doubt your own heart. For that, you can't trust him."

"How can I trust what doesn't make sense?"

"As long as you need to ask, you won't have the answer." She leaned down, pressed her lips to Malory's brow. "Thank you for having me in your home, for sharing yourselves with me. Here, take this."

She held out her hand, offered Malory the pale blue stone in the palm. "What is it?"

"A small charm. Put it under your pillow tonight. You'll sleep well. I must go." She smiled a little, lifting her hand to her hair as she rose and crossed to the glass door. "I wonder what Pitte will think of my hair. Good night." She opened the door and slipped into the night.

Zoe waited three seconds, then scurried to the door. Framing her face with her hands, she pressed it close to the glass. "Shoot. I thought she'd go poof or something, but she's just walking. Like a normal person."

"She seems pretty normal." Dana shifted around to reach the popcorn. "You know, for a goddess with a few thousand years under her belt."

"But sad." Malory turned the blue stone over in her hand. "There's all that sophistication and cool amusement on the surface, but there's this terrible sadness under it. She meant it when she said she was envious of you for having Simon, Zoe."

"It's funny to think about." Zoe wandered back, chose a brush, a rat-tail comb, and pins, then moved behind the sofa. "She lives in that big, well, castle, really, with all those beautiful things." She began to brush Dana's hair. "And she's beautiful, even wise, I think. She's rich and has a man she loves. She's traveled and she can paint those wonderful pictures."

Dividing sections of Dana's hair, she began to braid. "But she envies someone like me because I have a kid. Do you think she can't have children? I didn't want to ask, it's so personal. But I wonder why she couldn't. If she can do all the things she can do, why couldn't she have a baby?"

"Maybe Pitte doesn't want to have kids." Dana shrugged her shoulders. "Some people don't. What're you doing back there, Zoe?"

"New do. I'm mixing some skinny braids in. It should be young and kicky. Do you?"

"Do I what?"

"Want to have kids?"

Dana munched popcorn and considered. "Yeah. I'd like to have a couple. I figure if I don't find a guy I can stand being with for the long term in the next few years, I'll just do it on my own. You know, make love with medical science."

"You'd do that?" Fascinated, Malory reached into the bowl. "Raise a child on your own. I mean, on purpose," she added, looking up at Zoe. "You know what I mean."

"Sure, I would." Dana settled the bowl between them. "Why not? I'm healthy. I think I'd be good at the parenting thing, that I have a lot to offer a kid. I'd want to make sure I had solid financial security first, but if I'm cruising toward say, thirty-five and there's no guy in the picture, I'd do the deed."

"Sort of takes the romance out of it," Malory commented.

"Maybe, but it gets results. You've got to look at the big picture. If there's something you want, deep down want, you can't let anything stop you from getting it."

Malory thought of her dream, of the child she'd held in her arms. Of the light filling her world, her heart. "Even if you really, really want something, there are lines."

"Well, murder and a certain amount of mayhem are discouraged. I'm talking about making important choices, then going the distance and dealing with the results. What

about you, Zoe? Would you do it again?
The raise-a-kid-on-your-own part?" Dana
asked.

"I don't think I'd set out to do it again. It's
hard. There's nobody to share the load with,
and sometimes the load seems impossible
for one person. But more, there's nobody
who looks at the child and feels what you
feel. Nobody to share that love and pride
and, I don't know, surprise with."

"Were you scared?" Malory asked her.

"Yeah. Oh, yeah. I still get scared. I think
it's supposed to be scary because it's so
important. Do you want babies, Mal?"

"I do." She rubbed the stone gently between her fingers. "More than I realized."

By three, Dana and Zoe were sleeping in
her bed, and Malory was picking up the
worst of the debris, too restless to settle in
on the sofa. There were too many thoughts,
too many images flitting around in her mind.

She studied the little blue stone again.
Maybe it would work. She'd accepted bigger things than having a piece of rock under
her pillow as the cure for the insomnia that
was plaguing her.

Or maybe she hadn't. Maybe she really hadn't accepted any of it, not in that deep-down way Dana spoke of. She was exhausted, yet she wasn't putting the stone under her pillow and letting herself try.

She claimed to love Flynn, yet she was waiting, tucking a small part of herself safely away and waiting for the feeling to pass. And at the same time, she was annoyed and hurt that he didn't simply fall over in love with her and even things out.

After all, how could she keep her balance, outline plans, and keep it all tidy if everything between them wasn't equal?

Everything belongs in its place, doesn't it? Everything has its slot. And if it doesn't fit just right, well, you're not the one who's going to change. That's up to the other guy.

With a sigh, she dropped down on the couch. She'd pursued a career in art like a demon because while fate hadn't cooperated by giving her talent, she wasn't about to admit that all those years of study and work had been wasted.

She made it fit.

She'd stayed at The Gallery because it was comfortable, because it was sensible and convenient. She'd made noise about striking out on her own one day. But she hadn't meant it. Too big a risk, too messy. If Pamela hadn't come along, she would still be at The Gallery.

And why did she resent Pamela with every fiber of her being? All right, the woman was pushy and had all the taste of overcooked trout, but a more flexible woman than Malory Price would've found a way around that. She resented Pamela primarily because she'd shifted the balance, she'd changed the lines.

She just hadn't fit.

Now there was the business she and Dana and Zoe were starting. She'd been the one to drag her feet on that. Oh, she'd come through in the end, but how many times had she questioned that decision since? How many times had she considered backing out because it was too hard to see how it could all be neatly done?

And she hadn't moved forward on it. Hadn't gone back to the property or made any plans, put out any feelers for artists and craftspeople.

Hell, she hadn't even mailed off the application for her business license. Because once she did, she was committed.

She was using the key as an excuse not to take the final step. Oh, she was looking for it, giving the quest her time and her energy. One thing she took seriously was responsibility.

But here and now, alone and awake at three in the morning, it was time to admit one undeniable fact. Her life may have changed in a dozen strange and fascinating ways in three weeks' time, but she hadn't changed at all.

She put the stone under her pillow. "There's still time," she murmured, and curled up to sleep.

Chapter Eighteen

When she woke, the apartment was silent as a tomb. She lay still a moment, studying the lance of light that sneaked through the chink in the patio drapes and onto her floor.

Morning, she thought. Full morning. She didn't remember falling asleep. Better, much, much better, she didn't remember tossing and turning and worrying about sleep.

Slowly, she slid a hand under her pillow, feeling for the stone. She frowned, groping now, then sat up to lift the pillow. There was no stone under it. She searched under the cushions, on the floor, under the couch, before sitting down again with a huff of confusion.

Stones didn't just disappear.

Or maybe they did. When they'd served their purpose. She'd slept and slept well, hadn't she? Just as promised. In fact, she felt wonderful. As if she'd had a nice, relaxing vacation.

"Okay, thanks, Rowena."

She stretched out her arms, took a deep breath. And drew in the unmistakable scent of coffee.

Unless the gift included morning coffee, someone else was up.

She walked into the kitchen and found a pleasant surprise.

Zoe's coffee cake was on the counter, set on a pretty plate and protected with Saran Wrap. The coffeepot was on warm and was three-quarters full, and the morning paper was neatly folded and placed between.

Malory picked up the note tucked under the cake plate and read Zoe's somewhat exotic mix of cursive and printing.

Good morning! Had to get going—have a teacher's conference at ten.

Ten, Malory thought with an absent glance at the kitchen clock. Her mouth fell open when she saw that it was nearly eleven.

"That can't be right. Can it?"

Didn't want to wake either of you, tried to be quiet.

"You must move like a ghost," Malory said aloud.

Dana's got to be at work at two. Just in case, I set the alarm clock in your room for her. Set it for noon so she wouldn't have to rush and would have time for breakfast.

I had the best time. Just wanted to tell you, both of you, that whatever happens I'm so glad I found you. Or we found each other. However it worked, I'm just really grateful you're my friends.

Maybe next time we can get together at my place.

Love, Zoe.

"Looks like it's a day for gifts." Smiling, Malory set the note down where Dana would find it, too. Hoping to extend her good mood, she cut a sliver of cake, poured the coffee. She arranged them on a tray, added the paper and a small glass of juice, then carried it all out to her patio.

Fall was teasing the air. She'd always enjoyed the faint, smoky scent that autumn brought with it when the leaves began to take on hints of the vibrant colors to come.

She needed to pick up some potted mums, she noted as she broke off a piece of coffee cake. She was behind schedule on that. And some pumpkins and gourds for festive arrangements. She would gather some leaves, the maple ones once they'd turned scarlet.

She could pick up some extra things and do something fun for Flynn's front porch.

She sipped coffee while she skimmed the front page. Reading the morning paper was a different experience now that she'd met Flynn. She liked wondering how he decided what went where and how he juggled it all—stories, ads, pictures, typeface, tone—and made it one cohesive whole.

She nibbled and sipped her way through, then felt her heart give a quick jolt when she came to his column.

Odd, wasn't it, that she'd seen it before. Week after week. What had she thought? she wondered. Cute guy, nice eyes, or something just that casual and forgettable. She'd read his column, had either agreed or disagreed. She hadn't taken any notice of the work and effort he put into it, what turned his mind to whatever subject he wrote about that week.

It was different now that she knew him, now that she could hear his voice speaking the words she read. She could envision his face, its expressions. And have some insight into the workings of his very flexible mind.

What defines the artist? she read.

By the time she'd finished the column and was going back to read it through a second time, she'd fallen in love with him all over again.

Flynn sat on the corner of a desk and listened while one of his reporters pitched him an idea for an article about a local man who collected clowns.

Stuffed clown dolls, clown statues, clown pictures. Porcelain clowns, plastic clowns, clowns with dogs. Clowns that danced or sang or drove little clown cars.

"He's got more than five thousand clowns, not including clown memorabilia."

Flynn tuned out for a moment, as the very idea of five thousand clowns in one place at one time was slightly terrifying. He imagined them banding together in a clown army and waging war with seltzer bottles and rubber bats.

All those big red noses, all that maniacal laughter. All those huge, scary smiles.

"Why?" Flynn asked.

"Why?"

"Why does he have five thousand clowns?"

"Oh." Tim, a young reporter who habitually wore suspenders and too much hair gel, creaked back in his chair. "See, his father started the collection back in the twenties or something. It's like this generational deal. He started adding to it himself, you know, like in the fifties, then the whole bunch of them got passed to him when his father died. Some of his collection is like museum quality. This stuff goes for real bucks on eBay."

"Okay, give it a run. Take a photographer. I want a shot of the whole collection with the guy in it. And him with a couple of the more interesting pieces. Get him to give you the history or significance of specific pieces. Play up the father-son connection, but lead off with the numbers and a couple of pieces from each end of the money scale. It could work for the Weekender section. And Tim, try to edit out the 'you knows' and 'likes' when you interview him."

"Got it."

Flynn looked over to see Malory standing between the desks holding an enormous pot of rust-colored mums. Something about the sparkle in her eye made the rest of the room fade away.

"Hi. Doing some gardening?"

"Maybe. Is this a bad time?"

"No. Come on back. How do you feel about clowns?"

"Wrathful when they're painted on black velvet."

"Good one. Tim?" he called back. "Get some shots of any clown paintings on black velvet. Sublime to ridiculous and back again," Flynn added. "It could be good."

She stepped into the office ahead of him, continuing on to set the flowers on his window ledge. "I wanted to—"

"Wait." He held up a finger while he tuned in to the call coming out of his police scanner. "Hold that thought," he told her, and poked his head back out the door. "Shelly, there's a TA, five hundred block of Crescent. Local PD and EMTs responding. Take Mark."

"TA?" Malory repeated when he turned back to her.

"Traffic accident."

"Oh. I was thinking just this morning how much you have to juggle and weigh and shape to put out the paper every day." She bent down to pat the snoring Moe. "And you manage to have a life at the same time."

"In a manner of speaking."

"No, you have a very good life. Friends, family, work that satisfies you, a house, a silly dog. I admire that." She straightened. "I admire you."

"Wow. You must've had a really good time last night."

"I did. I'll tell you about that, but I don't want to—what is it—smother my lead."

"Bury the lead."

"Right." She stepped over the dog, laid her hands on Flynn's shoulders. And leaning in, kissed him. Long, long and warm. "Thank you."

His skin had started to hum. "What for? Because if it was really good, maybe you should thank me again."

"Okay." This time she linked her hands behind his head and added a bit of heat to the warmth.

Outside the office, applause broke out.

"Jesus, I've got to get blinds for this place." He tried the psychological angle of shutting the door. "I don't mind being the hero, but maybe you should tell me what dragon I slayed."

"I read your column this morning."

"Yeah? Usually if somebody likes my column they just say 'Nice job, Hennessy.' I like your way better."

" 'It isn't only the artist holding brush and vision who paints the picture,' " she quoted. " 'It's those who look and see the power and the beauty, the strength and the passion, who bring brushstroke and color to life.' Thank you."

"You're welcome."

"Every time I start feeling sorry for myself because I'm not living in Paris and setting the art world on its ear, I'm going to take out your column and remind myself what I've got. What I am."

"I think you're extraordinary."

"Today, so do I. I woke up feeling better than I have in days. Amazing what a good night's sleep will do—or a little blue stone under the pillow."

"You lost me."

"It's not important. Just something Rowena gave me. She joined our little sleepover last night."

"Yeah? What was she wearing?"

Laughing, she sat on the edge of his desk. "She didn't stay long enough for the pajama section of the night's entertainment, but you could say she arrived in the nick. The three of us were fooling around with a Ouija board."

"You've got to be kidding."

"No. Zoe had this theory that maybe the three of us were witches but didn't know it. Which is why we were chosen . . . and really, it made some sense at the time. In any case, things got very strange. Candle flames rising, wind blowing. And Kane, he got in. Rowena said we'd opened a door, like an invitation."

"Damn it, Malory. Goddamn it! What're you doing playing around with—with mystical forces? He's already had a shot at you. You could've been hurt."

He had such a face, she thought. Such a

great face. It could change from interested
to amused to furious in a split second.
"That's something Rowena made very clear
last night. There's no point in being angry
with me about it now."

"I didn't have the option of being angry
with you before now."

"True enough." She grunted when Moe,
awakened by the temper in Flynn's voice,
tried to jump in her lap. "You're absolutely
right that we shouldn't have played with
something we didn't understand. I'm sorry,
believe me, and it isn't something I plan on
trying again."

He reached over to give her hair a quick
tug. "I'm trying to have an argument here.
The least you could do is cooperate."

"I'm too happy with you to argue today.
Let's pencil something in for next week. Besides, I just came by to bring you the flowers. I've interrupted your day long enough."

He glanced at the mums—the second
bunch of flowers she'd brought to him.
"You're sure cheerful today."

"Why shouldn't I be? I'm a woman in
love, who's made what I feel are very good
decisions about . . ."

"About?" he prompted when her eyes went blank.

"Choices," she mumbled. "Moments of decision, moments of truth. Why didn't I think of that before? Maybe it was your house, but my dream perception of perfection turned it around. Made it all fit. More mine than yours. Or maybe that has nothing to do with it. And it's just you."

"What is?"

"The key. I need to search your house. Is that going to be a problem?"

"Ah . . ."

Impatient now, she waved away his hesitation. "Look, if you have anything personal or embarrassing tucked away like skin magazines or adventurous sex toys, I'll give you a chance to get them out. Or promise to ignore them."

"The skin mags and adventurous sex toys are all locked in the vault. I'm afraid I can't give you the combination."

She moved into him, trailed her hands up his chest. "I know it's a lot to ask. I wouldn't like anyone poking through my place when I wasn't there."

"Not that much to poke through. But I

don't want any grief about how I should spring for new underwear and use what I've got as dustrags."

"I'm not your mother. Will you let Jordan know I'm coming?"

"He's off somewhere today." Flynn pulled his keys out of his pocket, worked the house key off the chain. "You think you'll still be there when I get home?"

"Why don't I make sure I'm there when you get home?"

"Why don't you? Then I'll call Jordan, tell him to stay away. He can bunk with Brad tonight, and I can have you all to myself."

She took the key, bumped her lips lightly on his. "I'll look forward to being had."

The wicked gleam in her eye kept him grinning for an hour after she'd gone.

Malory jogged up the steps to Flynn's front door. She was going to be systematic, slow and thorough, she told herself.

She should have thought of this before. It was like connecting the dots.

The paintings reflected moments of change, of destiny. Certainly her life had changed when she'd fallen for Flynn. And this was Flynn's house, she thought as she stepped inside. Hadn't he said he'd bought it when he'd accepted *his* destiny?

Looking within and without, she remembered as she merely stood and tried to absorb the feel of the place. Inside the house, outside in the yard?

Or was it more metaphorical, in that she'd begun to see herself inside this space?

Light and shadows. The house was full of both.

She could only be grateful it wasn't full of things. Flynn's spartan style was going to make the search simpler.

She started in the living room, automatically wincing at the couch. She looked under the cushions, found eighty-nine cents in loose change, a Bic lighter, a paperback edition of a Robert Parker novel, and cookie crumbs.

Unable to stand it, she hunted up the vacuum cleaner and a dustrag and began to clean as she went.

This two-for-one process kept her in the kitchen for more than an hour. At the end of it she was sweaty and the kitchen sparkled, but she hadn't turned up anything resembling a key.

She switched gears and headed upstairs. She'd begun and ended her dream upstairs, she recalled. Maybe that was symbolic. And certainly there couldn't be anything up here in as deplorable shape as the kitchen.

One glance at the bathroom disabused her of that notion. Even love—of a man and of order—had its limits, she decided, and shut the door without going inside.

She stepped into his office and was immediately charmed. All the dark thoughts that had damned him for a pig vanished.

It wasn't neat. God knew, it needed a good dusting, and there was enough dog hair balled in the corners to knit an afghan. But the walls were sunny, the desk was a beauty, and the framed posters showed an eye for art and style that she hadn't given him credit for.

"You've got all these wonderful sides to you, don't you?" She trailed her fingers over the desk, impressed by the stack of files, amused by the action figures.

It was a good work space. A good thinking space, she imagined. He didn't give a

damn about the state of his kitchen. His
sofa was just a place to take a nap or
stretch out and read a book. But he took
care with his surroundings when it was important to him.

Beauty, knowledge, courage. She'd been
told she would need all three. In the dream
there had been beauty—love, home, art.
Then the knowledge that it was illusion. And
finally the courage to break that illusion.

Maybe that was a part of it.

And love would forge the key.

Well, she loved Flynn. She accepted that
she loved Flynn. So where was the damn
key?

She turned a circle, then wandered over
to take a closer look at his art collection.
Pinup girls. He was such a . . . guy, she decided. A very clever guy.

There was a sexual punch to the photographs, but an innocence underlying that.
Betty Grable's legs, Rita Hayworth's mane
of hair, Monroe's unforgettable face.

Legends, as much for their beauty as
their talent. Goddesses of the screen.

Goddesses.

Her fingers shook as she took the first
print from the wall.

She had to be right. This had to be it.

But she examined every print, every frame, then every inch of the room, and found nothing.

Refusing to be discouraged, she sat at his desk. She was close. A step off, one way or the other, but close. The pieces were all there, she was certain of it now. She just needed to find the right pattern and make them fit.

She needed to get out in the air for a while, let it turn over in her mind.

She would do something ordinary while it brewed in there.

No, not something ordinary. Something inspired. Something artful.

Flynn decided it was time to reverse the roles back to where they had started, and so he stopped off on the way home to buy her flowers. There was a bite of fall in the air, and its nip had already teased color into the trees. The surrounding hills were hazed with reds and golds and umbers over the green.

Over those hills, a three-quarter moon would rise tonight.

Did she think of that, he wondered, and worry?

Of course she did. It would be impossible for a woman like Malory to do otherwise. Still, she'd been happy when she came to his office. He meant to keep her that way.

He would take her out to dinner. Maybe drive into Pittsburgh for a change of scene. A long drive, a fancy dinner—that would appeal to her, keep her mind off . . .

The minute he stepped in the front door, he knew something was off.

It smelled . . . good.

A little lemony, he thought as he approached the living room. A little spicy. With female undertones. Did women just sort of exude scent when they'd been in a place for a few hours?

"Mal?"

"Back here! In the kitchen!"

The dog beat him by a mile and was already being given a biscuit, a stroke, and a firm nudge out the back door. Flynn wasn't sure what made his mouth water, the scents pumping out of the stove or the woman wearing a white bib apron.

God, who knew an apron could be sexy?

"Hi. What're you doing?"

"Cooking." She shut the back door. "I know it's an eccentric use for a kitchen, but call me crazy. Flowers?" Her eyes went soft, almost dewy. "They're pretty."

"You are too. Cooking?" He tossed his embryonic plans for the evening aside without a qualm. "Would that involve anything resembling dinner?"

"It would." She took the flowers, kissed him over them. "I decided to dazzle you with my culinary talents, so I went to the grocery store. You didn't have anything in here that qualified as actual food."

"Cereal. I have a lot of cereal."

"I noticed." Because he didn't own a vase, she filled a plastic pitcher with water for the flowers. The fact that she didn't cringe while doing so made her very proud of herself. "You also didn't appear to own any of the usual implements used in preparing actual food. Not a single wooden spoon."

"I don't understand why they make spoons out of wood. Haven't we progressed beyond carving tools out of trees?" He picked one up off the counter, then frowned. "Something's different in here. Something changed."

"It's clean."

Shock registered on his face as he stared around the room. "It *is* clean. What did you do, hire a brigade of elves? What do they charge by the hour?"

"They work for flowers." She sniffed at them, and decided they looked very sweet in the plastic pitcher after all. "You're paid in full."

"You cleaned. That's so . . . weird."

"Presumptuous, but I got carried away."

"No, 'presumptuous' isn't the word that springs to mind." He took her hand, kissed her fingers. "The word's 'wow.' Should I be really embarrassed?"

"I won't if you won't."

"Deal." He drew her close, rubbed his cheek against hers. "And you're cooking. In the oven."

"I wanted to take my mind off things for a while."

"So did I. I was going to play the let's-go-out-to-a-fancy-dinner card, but you trumped my ace."

"You can tuck the ace up your sleeve and play it anytime. Putting things in order helps clear my mind, and there was a lot to put in order around here. I didn't find the key."

"Yeah, I got that. I'm sorry."

"I'm close." She stared at the steam puffing out of a pot as if the answer might appear in it. "I feel like I'm just missing a step somewhere. Well, we'll talk about that. Dinner's about ready. Why don't you pour the wine. I think it'll complement the meat loaf."

"Sure." He picked up the wine she had breathing on the counter, then set it down again. "Meat loaf? You made meat loaf."

"Mashed potatoes too—shortly," she added as she set up the mixer she'd brought over from her own kitchen. "And green beans. It seemed harmonious, considering your column. And I assumed that since you used the meal, you must like meat loaf."

"I'm a guy. We live for meat loaf. Malory." Ridiculously moved, he caressed her cheek. "I should've brought you more flowers."

She laughed and got to work on the potatoes she'd boiled. "Those will do nicely, thanks. This is actually my first meat loaf. I'm more a toss-some-pasta-together or a sauté-some-chicken girl. But I got the recipe from Zoe, who swears it's foolproof and guy-friendly. She claims Simon inhales it."

"I'll try to remember to chew." Then he took her arm to turn her toward him and moved in, slowly, ran his hands up her body until his fingers skimmed her jaw. He laid his lips on hers, softly, sliding her into the kiss the way he might slide her into a feather bed.

Her heart did one long, lazy roll even as the mists shimmered over her brain. The rubber spatula she held slipped out of limp fingers as everything inside her melted against him, into him.

He felt it, that shudder and give, that surrender to self as much as to him. When he eased her back, her eyes were blue and blurry. It was woman, he realized, who had the power to make man feel like a god.

"Flynn."

His lips curved as he brushed them over her forehead. "Malory."

"I . . . I forgot what I was doing."

He bent down to retrieve the spatula. "I think you were mashing potatoes."

"Oh. Right. Potatoes." Feeling a bit drunk, she walked to the sink to wash the spatula.

"This has to be the nicest thing anyone's ever done for me."

"I love you." She pressed her lips together, stared out the window. "Don't say anything. I don't want to make things uncomfortable for either of us. I've been thinking about this a lot. I know I've rushed and I've pushed. Neither of which is much like me." She spoke briskly now as she went back to the mixer.

"Malory—"

"Really, you don't need to say anything. It'd be enough, more than enough for now, if you just accepted it, maybe enjoyed it a little. It seems to me love shouldn't be a weapon or a device or a weight. Its beauty is that it be a gift, with no strings attached to it. Just like this meal."

She smiled, though the steady way he watched her was unnerving. "So, why don't you pour the wine, then wash up? And we'll both just enjoy it."

"Okay."

It could wait, Flynn thought. Maybe it was meant to wait. In any case, the words in his head sounded off-key when compared with the simplicity of hers.

So they would enjoy each other, and the

meal she'd prepared in the awkward, homely kitchen with fresh flowers arranged in a plastic pitcher.

As beginnings went, this one had elements of both of them. Wasn't it interesting how one managed to complement the other?

"You know, if you made me a list of stuff I should have in here, I could pick it up."

She arched her brows, took the wine he offered, then pulled a little notepad out of her apron pocket. "This is already half full. I was planning to wait until you were lulled into complacency by meat and potatoes."

He flipped through the notebook and noted that items were listed under specific headings. Foodstuffs, Cleaning Supplies— with subheadings Kitchen, Bathroom, Laundry—Household Necessities.

Jesus, the woman was irresistible.

"Am I going to need to take out a loan?"

"Think of it as an investment." Taking the notebook from him, she tucked it into his shirt pocket, then concentrated on the potatoes. "Oh, by the way, I really like the art in your office upstairs."

"Art?" It took him a minute. "Oh, my girls. Really?"

"Clever, nostalgic, sexy, stylish. It's a great room altogether, which I admit was something of a relief to me, considering the rest of the house. Enough that I wasn't flattened by disappointment when my brainstorm about the key didn't pan out." She drained the beans that she'd dashed with basil into one of her serving bowls, handed it to him. "Monroe, Grable, Hayworth, and so on. Screen goddesses. Goddess, key."

"Good segue."

"Yeah, it seemed so, but no luck." She passed him the bowl of potatoes, then using the potholders she'd bought, took the meat loaf out of the oven. "Still, I think I'm on the right track, and it gave me the chance to see your thinking space."

She sat, scanned the table. "Hope you're hungry."

They dished up the meal. At the first bite of meat loaf, Flynn sighed. "Good thing you put Moe out. I'd hate to torment him with this, since he won't be getting much of it. My compliments to the artist."

There was pleasure, Malory discovered, in watching someone you loved eat what you'd prepared. Pleasure in sharing a simple meal at the kitchen table at the end of the day.

She'd never felt deprived eating dinner alone, or in the company of a friend. But now it was easy to see herself sharing this hour with him, night after night, year after year.

"Flynn, you said that when you accepted that you were meant to stay in the Valley, you bought this house. Did you—do you—have a vision for it? How you want it to look and feel?"

"I don't know if you'd call it a vision. I liked the look of it, the lines of it, and the big yard. Something about a big yard makes me feel prosperous and safe."

He went back for seconds. "I figure I'll have to gut this room sooner or later, rip it into the new millennium. Buy stuff for the rest of the place, eventually. But I never seem to get around to it. I guess because it's just me and Moe."

He poured more wine for both of them. "If you've got some ideas, I'm open to suggestions."

"I've always got ideas, and you should be careful before you get me started. But that wasn't why I asked. I had a vision for the property we bought—Dana and Zoe and I. As soon as I walked into that house I could see how it would work, what it needed from me, what I could bring to it. And I haven't been back since."

"You've been pretty busy."

"That's not it. I deliberately haven't been back. That's not like me. Usually when I have a project, I can't wait to get started, to start fiddling with things, lining them up, making lists. I took the step. I signed on the dotted line, but I haven't taken the next step."

"It's a big commitment, Mal."

"I'm not afraid of commitment. Hell, I thrive on it. But I've been a little afraid of this. I'm going to go over tomorrow, take a look at the place. Apparently the previous owners left a lot of stuff they didn't want in the attic. Zoe asked me to go through it before she started hauling things out."

"What kind of attic? A dark, spooky attic or a big, fun, Grandma's attic?"

"I have no idea. I haven't been up there." It shamed her to admit that. "I haven't been off the ground floor, which is ridiculous, as I own a third of the property. Or will. I'm going to change that. Change isn't my best thing."

"Want me to go with you? I'd like to see the place anyway."

"I was hoping you'd say that." She reached over to give his hand a squeeze. "Thanks. Now, since you asked about ideas on this house, I'd suggest you start in the living room, which by my definition is an area where you're supposed to live."

"You're going to insult my sofa again, aren't you?"

"I don't believe I have the skills to form the insult that sofa merits. But you might want to think about actual tables, lamps, area rugs, curtains."

"I was thinking I could just order a bunch of stuff out of a catalogue."

She sent him a very long, very dry stare. "You're trying to scare me, but it won't work. And since you've generously offered to help me out tomorrow, I'll return the favor. I'd be glad to give you a hand with turning that space into a room."

Since he'd all but licked his plate clean a second time, he resisted going for thirds. "Was that a trick, some clever ploy to drag me off to a furniture store?"

"It wasn't, but it sure circled around to it well, didn't it? I can give you some of my thoughts while we do the dishes."

She rose to stack dishes, but he put a hand over hers. "Let's just go in there now, and you can show me what's so wrong with my simple, minimalist approach."

"After the dishes."

"Uh-uh. Now." He began to pull her out of the room, amused at the struggle on her face as she glanced back at the table. "They'll still be there when we get back. Trust me. It's not going to hurt to do them out of the logical order."

"Yes, it does. A little. Five minutes, then. The condensed consultation. First, you did a good job with the walls. It's a good-sized room, and the strong color's a complement, which you could enhance with touches of other strong colors in curtains and . . . What're you doing?" she demanded when he began unbuttoning her shirt.

"Getting you naked."

"Excuse me." She tapped his fingers away. "I charge extra for naked decorating consults."

"Bill me." He swept her off her feet.

"This was just a trick, wasn't it? A ploy to

get my clothes off and have your way with me."

"Sure circled around nicely, didn't it?" He dumped her on the couch and dived on top of her.

Chapter Nineteen

He made her laugh as he nipped along her jawline, playfully wrestled her down when she tried to squirm away.

"You taste even better than meat loaf."

"If that's the best you can do, then *you're* the one who'll be washing dishes."

"Your threats don't scare me." He walked his fingers up her ribs toward her breast. "There's a dishwasher somewhere in that kitchen."

"Yes, there is. And you had a bag of dog food stored in it."

"Is that where that went to?" He nibbled at her earlobe.

"It's now in the utility closet, where it belongs." She turned her head slightly to give him easier access to her neck. "You're obviously unaware that there are very practical, even attractive, containers manufactured to store items such as dog food."

"No kidding? Looks like I've got my work cut out for me, getting these domestic worries out of your mind. But I like a challenge after a good meal. Let's just get this off."

He tugged at her shirt, then made a throaty sound as he smoothed a finger over the salmon-colored lace of her bra. "I like this. We'll leave that on a while."

"We could take this upstairs, you know. I cleaned under the cushions and learned just what this monster can swallow. We could be next."

"I'll protect you."

He replaced his fingertips with his lips, skimmed them over lace and flesh.

The enormous cushions gave under their weight, cradled them together as he sampled her. She wiggled and squirmed in mock resistance, an erotic game that aroused them both.

Her mind began to fog as he scraped his teeth down her torso. "What do you think of Brazilians?"

Baffled, he lifted his head. "What? The people, or the nuts?"

She stared at him, amazed that she'd spoken out loud, delighted with his response. Laughter shook her, rolled straight up from her belly as she grabbed him and rained kisses over his face. "Nothing. Never mind. There." She dragged his shirt over his head. "Now we're even."

She loved the feel of his skin under her hands, the sturdy shoulders, the play of muscles. She loved, oh, yes, the feel of his hands on her. Gentle or rough, rushed or patient.

And as the evening light slipped through the windows, as he roamed down her body, she closed her eyes and let sensation rule.

Flutters and tugs, heat and chills. Each was a separate thrill blending into a single, steady ache. His fingers danced over her belly, made it quiver, before he drew her pants down her hips and legs.

Then his tongue slid over her, down her, into her, and flashed her to peak.

She moaned his name when her body went bowstring taut under his. Sighed his name as she seemed to dissolve under his hands.

He wanted, as he'd wanted in that stunning moment in his kitchen, to give her anything. Everything she wanted, all she needed, more than she could imagine.

He'd never known what it was to be offered unconditional love, to know it waited for him. He'd never felt deprived of it because he'd never known it existed.

And now he held the woman who'd given it to him.

She was his miracle, his magic. His key.

He pressed his lips to her shoulder, her throat, rode on the punch of these huge new emotions when her arms came around him.

Words tumbled through his mind, but none of them were enough. He found her mouth with his, cupped her hips, and filled her.

Warm and loose and sleepy, she curled into him. She was more than willing to cocoon herself in this lovely sexual haze, to drift in it to the sound of her own skin humming. Chores could wait, forever if need be. As long as she could snuggle here, feeling Flynn's heart pound against hers.

She wondered why they didn't just drift off to sleep this way, warm, naked, and tangled with the bloom of lovemaking covering them both like soft, silky clouds.

She stretched luxuriously under his hand when he stroked her back. "Mmmm. Let's just stay here all night, like a couple of bears in a cave."

"You're happy?"

She tipped her face up to smile at him. "Of course I am." She snuggled back in. "So happy I'm pretending there aren't dishes waiting to be washed or leftovers to put away."

"You haven't been happy the last few days."

"No, I guess I haven't." She settled her head more comfortably on his shoulder. "I felt like I'd lost my direction, and everything around me was shifting and changing so fast I couldn't keep up. Then it occurred to me that if I didn't change, at least open myself to changing, the direction didn't matter. Because I was going nowhere."

"There are some things I want to tell you, if you can handle some more changes."

Uneasy, as his tone was so serious, she braced herself. "All right."

"About Lily."

He felt her tense, an instant tightening of muscles, and could all but feel her will herself to relax again. "This may not be the best moment to tell me about another woman. Especially one you loved and planned to marry."

"I think it is. We knew each other casually for several months, then intimately for the best part of a year. We clicked on a number of levels. Professionally, socially, sexually—"

Her lovely cocoon was now in shreds, and she began to feel the cold. "Flynn—"

"Hear me out. It was the longest adult relationship I'd had with a woman. Serious relationship with long-term planning. I thought we were in love with each other."

"She hurt you, I know. I'm sorry, but—"

"Quiet." He tapped a finger on the top of her head. "She didn't love me, or if she did, that love had specific requirements. So you couldn't call it a gift."

He was silent for a moment, selecting his words carefully. "It isn't easy looking in the mirror and accepting that you were missing some element, some *thing* that kept a person you wanted from loving you."

She tried to keep steady. "No, it's not."

"And even when you come to terms with it, when you realize it just wasn't right, that there was something missing from the other person, too, something missing from the whole, it still breaks your stride. It makes you a lot more hesitant about taking that kind of chance again."

"I understand that."

"And you end up going nowhere," he stated, echoing her earlier statement. "Jordan said something to me the other day that had me thinking, and thinking back. I asked myself if I'd ever really imagined life with Lily. You know, pictured how we'd be together a few years down the road. I could see the immediate future, the moving-to-New-York thing. How we'd get jobs in our chosen fields, find a place to live, and then I realized that was pretty much it. That was all I'd been able to see. Not how we would live or what we'd do beyond that vague picture, not how we'd look together in a decade. It wasn't hard to picture my life without her in it, maybe harder to pick up my life at the point she dumped me. Lots of bruises on the pride and ego. Lots of anger and hurt. And the by-product of feeling like I probably wasn't cut out for the whole love-and-marriage thing."

Her heart was twisting, for both of them. "You don't have to explain."

"I'm not finished. I was bumping along pretty well. Had my life in order—not so you'd think so, but it suited me. Then Moe knocked you flat on the sidewalk, and things began to change. No secret I was attracted to you from the get-go, and hoped we'd end up naked on this sofa sooner or later. But, initially, that's as far as I could see things, regarding you and me."

This time he tipped her face up. He wanted her to look at him now. Wanted to see her face. "I've known you less than a month. On a lot of basic points we come at it from opposite angles. But I can see my life with you, the way you can look through a window and see your own little world spread out. I can see how it could be a year from now, or twenty years from now, with you and me and what we make."

He skimmed his fingers along her cheek, just to feel the shape of it. "What I can't see is how I'd pick up my life from this point and make it without you."

He watched her eyes fill with tears,

watched them spill over. "I love you." He brushed away a tear with his thumb. "I don't have a master plan for what happens next. I just know I love you."

Emotions surged through her, so bright and rich she wondered that they didn't burst out of her in colored light. Terrified that she was about to fall apart, she struggled to smile. "I have to ask you for something important."

"Anything."

"Promise me you'll never get rid of this couch."

He laughed, nuzzled her cheek. "You're going to regret that."

"No, I won't. I'm not going to regret a thing."

With the two women who had become her friends and partners, Malory sat on the front porch of the house that would be one-third hers.

The sky had clouded up since she'd arrived, clouds stacking on clouds to make a multilayered sweep of grays.

Storm brewing, she figured, and found herself pleased with the idea of being inside with rain pounding on the roof. But first she wanted to sit while the electricity gathered in the air and those first puffs of wind bent the trees.

More than anything she'd needed to share her joy and her nerves with her friends.

"He loves me." She didn't think she would ever tire of saying it aloud. "Flynn loves me."

"It's so romantic." Zoe dug a tissue out of her purse and sniffled into it.

"It was. You know, there was a time I wouldn't have thought so. I'd have had a very detailed outline in my mind. Candle-light, music, with me and the perfect man in some elegant room. Or outdoors, in some spectacular setting. It would all have had to be arranged, just so."

With a shake of her head, she laughed at herself. "That's why I know it's the real thing. Because it didn't have to be just so, and elegant and perfect. It just had to be. It had to be Flynn."

"Jeez. It's hard for me to equate the stars in your eyes with Flynn." Dana rested her chin on her fist. "Nice and all, because I love him too. But it's Flynn, my favorite moron. I've never pictured him as a romantic figure." She turned toward Zoe. "What the hell's in that meat loaf? Maybe I should get the recipe."

"I'm going to take another look at it myself." She patted Malory's knee. "I'm really happy for you. I liked the way you two looked together right from the start."

"Hey, you moving in with him?" Dana perked up. "That would set Jordan out on his butt that much sooner."

"Sorry, we didn't get to that stage yet. We're just basking in the we're-in-love moment for now. And that, friends and neighbors, is a real change for me. I'm not making schedules and lists. I'm just going with it. God, I feel like I could take on the world! Which brings me to the next part of this session. I'm sorry I haven't contributed to any of the plans for the house here or done anything about moving forward with ideas for fixing it up, putting it all together."

"I wondered if you were going to bail," Dana admitted.

"I was thinking about it. I'm sorry I didn't tell you. I guess I had to work out for myself what I was doing and why. Now I know. I'm starting my own business because the longer you put off dreams, the less chance you have of making them real. I'm going into a partnership with two women I like a lot. Not only am I not going to let them down, but I'm not going to let me down either."

She got to her feet, and with her hands planted on her hips, turned to look at the house. "I don't know if I'm ready for this, but I'm ready to try. I don't know if I'm going to find the key in the time I have left, but I know I've tried there, too."

"I know what I think." Zoe rose to join her. "If it weren't for the key, you wouldn't be with Flynn now. We wouldn't be together, and we wouldn't have this place. Because of that I've got a chance to make something special, for myself, for Simon. I wouldn't have had that without the two of you."

"Let me start off saying we can skip the group hug." Still, Dana walked over to them. "But I feel the same way. I wouldn't have had the chance for this without both of you. My idiot brother has a classy lady in love with him. All that starts with the key. I say you're going to find it."

She looked up as rain began to splatter. "Now let's get the hell in out of the rain."

Inside, they stood in a loose semicircle.

"Together or separate?" Malory asked.

"Together," Zoe answered.

"Top or bottom?"

"Top." Dana glanced over, got assenting nods. "You said Flynn was coming by?"

"Yeah, he's going to slip over for an hour."

"We can use him as a pack mule, then, for anything we want to haul out of the attic."

"Some of the stuff up there is great." Zoe's face shone with enthusiasm as they started up. "I know it looks like junk at first glance, but I think once we get to it, we'll be able to use some. There's an old wicker chair that could be rewoven and painted. It'd look good on the porch. And there's a couple of those pole lamps. The shades are trash, but the poles could be cleaned up and antiqued."

Her voice faded away as Malory climbed the steps. The window at the top was wet with rain, dull with dust. And her heart began to thud like a fist against her ribs.

"This is the place," she whispered.

"Yeah, it is. This is it." Dana set her hands on her hips as she looked around the second floor. "It'll be ours and the bank's in a few weeks."

"No, this is *the* place. From my dream. This is the house. How could I be so stupid not to realize, not to understand?" Excitement pitched into her voice, rushing the words out. "It wasn't what was Flynn's, but what was mine. I'm the key. Isn't that what Rowena said?"

She whirled back to face them, her eyes brilliant and bright. "Beauty, knowledge, courage. That's the three of us, that's this place. And the dream, that was my fantasy, my idea of perfection. So it had to be my place."

She pressed a hand to her heart as if to keep it from leaping free. "The key's here. In this house."

In the next instant she was alone. The staircase behind her filled with a thin blue light. Like a mist, it rolled toward her, crawled along the floor at her feet until she stood ankle-deep in the damp chill of it. Rooted in shock, she called out, but her voice rang hollow in a mocking echo.

With her heart drumming, she looked at the rooms on either side of her. The eerie blue fog snaked and twined its way up the walls, over the windows, blocking even the gloomy light of the storm.

Run! It was a frantic whisper in her mind. Run. Get out now, before it's too late. This wasn't her fight. She was an ordinary woman leading an ordinary life.

She gripped the banister, took the first stop down. She could still see the door through that sheer blue curtain that so quickly ate the true light. Through the door was the real world. Her world. She had only to open that door and walk out for normalcy to click back into place.

That was what she wanted, wasn't it? A normal life. Hadn't her dream shown her that? Marriage and family. French toast for breakfast and flowers on the dresser. A pretty life of simple pleasures built on love and affection.

It was waiting for her, outside the door.

She walked down the steps like a woman in a trance. She could see beyond the door, somehow *through* the door, where the day was perfect with autumn. Trees a wash of color gilded by sunlight, air brisk and tart. And though her heart continued to gallop inside her chest, her lips curved in a dreamy smile as she reached for the door.

"This is wrong." She heard her own voice, oddly flat and calm. "This is another trick." A part of her shuddered in shock as she turned away from the door, turned from the perfect life waiting outside. "What's out there isn't real, but this is. This is our place now."

Stunned that she'd nearly deserted her friends, she called out for Dana and Zoe again. Where had he put them? What illusion had separated them? Fear for them had her rushing back up the steps. Her flight tore the blue mists, only to have it gather back into nasty ribbons behind her.

To orient herself she went to the window at the top of the stairs and rubbed away those frigid mists. Her fingertips went numb, but she could see it was still storming. Rain whipped down out of a bruised sky. Her car was in the drive, just where she'd left it. Across the street a woman with a red umbrella and a bag of groceries dashed toward a house.

That was real, Malory told herself. That was life, messy and inconvenient. And she would get it back. She'd find her way back. But first she had a job to do.

Chills crawled along her skin as she

turned to the right. She wished for a jacket, for a flashlight. For her friends. For Flynn. She forced herself not to run, not to rush blindly. The room was a maze of impossible corridors.

It didn't matter. Just another trick, one meant to confuse and frighten her. Somewhere in this house was the key, and her friends. She would find them.

Panic tickled her throat as she walked. The air was silent now, even her lonely footsteps were smothered by the blue mist. What was more frightening to the human heart than being cold and lost and alone? He was using that against her, playing her with her own instinct.

Because he couldn't touch her unless she allowed it.

"You're not going to make me run," she shouted. "I know who I am and where I am, and you're not going to make me run."

She heard someone call her name, just the faintest ripple through the thick air. Using it as a guide, she turned again.

The cold intensified, and the mists swirled with wet. Her clothes were damp, her skin chilled. The call could have been another trick, she thought. She could hear nothing now but the blood beating inside her own head.

It hardly mattered which direction she chose. She could walk endlessly in circles or stand perfectly still. It wasn't a matter of finding her way, or being misdirected now. It was, she realized, nothing more than a battle of wills.

The key was here. She meant to find it; he meant to stop her.

"It must be lowering to pit yourself against a mortal woman. Wasting all your power and skill on someone like me. And still, the best you can do is this irritating blue-light special."

An angry red glow edged the mist. Though Malory's heart plunged, she gritted her teeth and kept moving. Maybe it wasn't wise to challenge a sorcerer, but aside from the risk she realized another side effect.

She could see another door now where the red and blue lights merged.

The attic, she thought. It had to be. Not illusionary corridors and turns, but the true substance of the house.

She focused on it as she walked forward. When the mists shifted, thickened, swirled, she ignored them and kept the image of the door in her head.

At last, her breath shallow, she plunged a hand through the fog and clamped her fingers around the old glass knob.

Warmth, a welcome flood of it, poured over her as she pulled the door open. She started up, into the dark, with the blue mist creeping behind her.

Outside, Flynn navigated through the mean-tempered storm, edging forward in the driver's seat to peer through the curtain of rain that his wipers could barely displace.

In the backseat, Moe whimpered like a baby.

"Come on, you coward, it's just a little rain." Lightning pitchforked through the black sky, followed by a boom of thunder like a cannon blast. "And some lightning."

Flynn cursed and muscled the wheel in position when the car bucked and shuddered. "And some wind," he added. With gusts approaching gale force.

It hadn't seemed like more than a quick thunderstorm when he'd left the office. But it worsened with every inch of road. As

Moe's whimpers turned to pitiful howls, Flynn began to worry that Malory or Dana or Zoe, maybe all three of them, had gotten caught in the storm.

They should have been at the house by now, he reminded himself. But he would have sworn that the rage of the storm was worse, considerably worse, on this end of town. Fog had rolled down from the hills, blanketed them in gray as thick and dense as wool. His visibility decreased, forcing him to slow down. Even at a crawl, the car fishtailed madly on a turn.

"We'll just pull over," he said to Moe. "Pull over and wait it out."

Anxiety skated up his spine, but instead of easing when he nudged the car to the curb, it clamped on to the back of his neck like claws. The sound of the rain pounding like fists on the roof of the car seemed to hammer into his brain.

"Something's wrong."

He pulled out into the street again, his hands vising on the wheel as the wind buffeted the car. Sweat, born of effort and worry, snaked down his back. For the next three blocks he felt like a man fighting a war.

There was a trickle of relief when he spotted the cars in the driveway. They were okay, he told himself. They were inside. No problem. He was an idiot.

"Told you there was nothing to worry about," he said to Moe. "Now you've got two choices. You can pull yourself together and come inside with me, or you can stay here, quaking and quivering. Up to you, pal."

Relief drained away when he parked at the curb and looked at the house.

If the storm had a heart, it was there. Black clouds boiled over the house, pumped the full force of their fury. Even as he watched, lightning lanced down, speared like a fiery arrow into the front lawn. The grass went black in a jagged patch.

"Malory."

He didn't know if he spoke it, shouted it, or his mind simply screamed it, but he shoved open the car door and leaped into the surreal violence of the storm.

The wind slapped him back, a backhanded blow so intense that he tasted blood in his mouth. Lightning blasted like a mortar directly in front of him, and the air stank with burning. Blind from the driving rain, he bent over and lurched toward the house.

He stumbled on the steps and was calling her name, over and over like a chant, when he saw the hard blue light leaking around the front door.

The knob burned with cold and refused to turn under his hand. Baring his teeth, Flynn reared back, then rammed the door with his shoulder. Once, twice, and on the third assault, he broke it in.

He leaped inside, into that blue mist.

"Malory!" He shoved his dripping hair out of his face. "Dana!"

He whirled when something brushed his leg, and lifted his fists, only to lower them on an oath when it turned out to be wet dog. "Goddamn it, Moe, I don't have time to—"

He broke off when Moe growled deep in his throat, let out a vicious bark, and charged up the stairs.

Flynn sprinted after him. And stepped into his office.

"If I'm going to do a decent job covering the foliage festival, then I need the front page of the Weekender section and a sidebar on the related events." Rhoda folded her arms, her posture combative. "Tim's interview with Clown Guy should go on page two."

There was a vague ringing in his ears, and a cup of coffee in his hand. Flynn stared at Rhoda's irritated face. He could smell the coffee, and the White Shoulders fragrance that Rhoda habitually wore. Behind him, his scanner squawked and Moe snored like a steam engine.

"This is bullshit."

"You've got no business using that kind of language with me," Rhoda snapped.

"No, this is bullshit. I'm not here. Neither are you."

"It's about time I got treated with a little respect around here. You're only running this paper because your mother wanted to keep you from making a fool of yourself in New York. Big-city reporter, my butt. You're a small-time, small-town guy. Always have been, always will be."

"Kiss my ass," Flynn invited and threw the coffee, cup and all, in her face.

She let out one short scream, and he was back in the mist.

Shaken, he rounded once again toward the sound of Moe's barking.

Through that rolling mist, he saw Dana on her knees with her arms flung around Moe's neck.

"Oh, God, thank God. Flynn!" She sprang up, wrapped herself around him as she had the dog. "I can't find them. I can't find them. I was here, then I wasn't, now I am." Hysteria pitched and rocked in her voice. "We were together, right over there, then we weren't."

"Stop. Stop." He yanked her back, shook her. "Breathe."

"Sorry. I'm sorry." She shuddered, then scrubbed her hands over her face. "I was at work, but I wasn't. I couldn't have been. It was like being in a daze, going through the motions and not being able to pinpoint what was wrong. Then I heard Moe barking. I heard him barking, and I remembered. We were here. Then I was back, standing here in this—whatever the hell this is—and I couldn't find them."

She fought for calm. "The key. Malory said the key's here. I think she must be right."

"Go. Get outside. Wait for me in the car."

She breathed deep, shuddered again. "I'm freaked, but I'm not leaving them here. Or you either. Jesus, Flynn, your mouth's bleeding."

He swiped the back of his hand over it. "It's nothing. Okay, we stick together." He took her hand, linked fingers.

They heard it at the same time, the hammering of fists on wood. With Moe once again in the lead, they rushed through the room.

Zoe stood at the attic door, beating on it. "Over here!" She called out. "She's up there, I know she's up there, but I can't get through."

"Get back," Flynn ordered.

"You're all right?" Dana gripped her arm. "Are you hurt?"

"No. I was home, Dana. Puttering around the kitchen with the radio on. Wondering what to fix for dinner. My God, how long? How long were we separated? How long has she been up there alone?"

Chapter Twenty

She was afraid. It helped to admit it, accept it. To know that she was more afraid than she'd ever been in her life, and to realize she was determined not to give in.

The warmth was already being eaten away as the light took on that harsh blue hue. Fingers of mist crawled along the exposed beams on the ceiling, down the unfinished walls, along the dusty floor.

Through it, she could see the pale white vapor of her own breath.

Real, she reminded herself. That was real, a sign of life. Proof of her own humanity.

The attic was a long, wide room with two stingy windows at either end and the ceiling rising to a narrow pitch. But she recognized it. In her dream there had been skylights and generous windows. Her paintings had been stacked against walls done in soft cream. The floor had been clean of dust, and speckled with a cheerful rainbow of paint drops and splatters.

The air had carried a summer warmth and the scent of turpentine.

It was dank now, and cold. Rather than canvases, cardboard boxes were stacked against the walls. Old chairs and lamps and the debris of other lives were stored there. But she could see—oh, so clearly see— how it could have been.

As she imagined it, it began to form.

Warm, washed with light, alive with color. There, on her worktable with her brushes and palette knives, was the little white vase filled with the pink snapdragons she'd picked from her own garden that morning.

She remembered going out after Flynn had left for work, remembered picking those sweet and tender flowers to keep her company while she worked.

Worked in her studio, she thought dreamily, where the blank canvas waited. And she knew, oh, yes, she knew how to fill it.

She walked to the canvas waiting on an

easel, picked up her palette, and began to mix her paints.

Sun streamed through her windows. Several were open for the practical purpose of cross-ventilation, and for the simple pleasure of feeling the breeze. Music pumped passionately out of the stereo. What she intended to paint today required passion.

She could already see it in her mind, feel the power of it gathering in her like a storm.

She raised her brush, swirled it in color for the first stroke.

Her heart lifted. The magnitude of the joy was almost unbearable. She might burst from it if she didn't transfer it onto canvas.

The image was burned in her mind, like a scene etched on glass. With stroke after stroke, color blended on color, she began to bring it to life.

"You know this was always my deepest dream." She spoke conversationally as she worked. "For as long as I can remember I wanted to paint. To have the talent, the vision, the skill to be an important artist."

"Now you have it."

She switched brushes, glancing at Kane before she faced the canvas again. "Yes, I do."

"You were wise, making the right choice in the end. A shopkeeper?" He laughed, dismissed the idea with a wave of his hand. "Where is the power in that? Where is the glory in selling what others have created when you can create yourself? You can be and have whatever you choose here."

"Yes, I understand. You've shown me the way." She slid him a coy look. "What else can I have?"

"You want the man?" Kane shrugged elegantly. "He's bound to you here, a slave to love."

"And if I'd chosen otherwise?"

"Men are capricious creatures. How could you ever be sure of him? Now, you paint your world as you do that canvas. As you wish."

"Fame? Fortune?"

His lip curled. "So it is with mortals always. Love, they say, is what matters more than even life. But it's wealth and it's glory that they really crave. Take it all, then."

"And you, what will you take?"

"I have already taken it."

She nodded, switched brushes. "You'll have to excuse me. I need to concentrate."

She painted in the warm bath of sunlight while the music soared.

Flynn hit the door with his shoulder, then gripped the knob and prepared to ram it again. The knob turned smoothly in his hand.

Zoe gave him a jittery smile. "I must've loosened it for you."

"Stay down here."

"Save your breath," Dana advised and pushed up behind him.

The light seemed to pulse now, thicker and somehow animate. Moe's growling became wet snarls.

Flynn saw Malory, standing at the far end of the attic. Relief was like a hammer blow to his heart.

"Malory! Thank God." He leaped forward, and hit the solid wall of mist.

"It's some sort of barrier." He spoke frantically now as he pushed and slammed against it. "She's trapped in there."

"I think we're trapped out here." Zoe pressed her hands against the mist. "She doesn't hear us."

"We have to make her hear us." Dana

looked around for something to batter against the wall. "She must be somewhere else, in her head, the way we were. We have to make her hear us so she'll snap out of it."

Moe went wild, leaping up to tear and bite at the wall of mist. His barks echoed like gunshots, and still Malory stood like a statue, her back to them.

"There has to be another way." Zoe dropped to her knees, pressed her fingers along the mist. "It's freezing. You can see her trembling from the cold. We have to get her *out.*"

"Malory!" Helpless rage had Flynn pummeling the wall until his hands bled. "I'm not going to let this happen. You have to hear me. I love you. Damn it, Malory, I love you. You listen to me."

"Wait!" Dana gripped his shoulder. "She moved. I saw her move. Keep talking to her, Flynn. Just keep talking to her."

Struggling for calm, he pressed his forehead to the wall. "I love you, Malory. You've got to give us a chance to see where we can go with it. I need you with me, so either come out or let me in."

Malory pursed her lips at the image taking shape on canvas. "Did you hear something?" she asked absently.

"There's nothing." Kane smiled at the three mortals on the other side of the mist. "Nothing at all. What are you painting there?"

"Uh-uh-uh." She wagged a playful finger at him. "I'm temperamental. I don't like anyone looking at my work until it's done. My world," she reminded him and daubed on color. "My rules."

He gave a single, elegant shrug. "As you wish."

"Oh, don't pout. I'm nearly done." She worked quickly now, all but willing the image from her mind onto the canvas. It was, she thought, her masterpiece. Nothing she'd ever done would be so important.

"Art isn't just in the eye of the beholder," she said. "But in that, in the artist, in the subject, in the purpose, and in those who see."

Her pulse skipped and stumbled, but her hand remained steady and sure. For a timeless moment, she shut everything out of her mind but the colors, the textures, the shapes.

And when she stepped back, her eyes glittered with triumph.

"It's the finest thing I've ever done," she declared. "Perhaps the finest thing I will ever do. I wonder what you'll think of it."

She gestured in invitation.

"Light and shadow," she said as he stepped toward the easel. "In looking within, and without. From within me to without and onto the canvas. What my heart speaks. I call it *The Singing Goddess.*"

It was her face she'd painted. Her face and the first Daughter of Glass. She stood in a forest, full of sparkling gold light, softened with green shadows, with the river sliding over rock like tears.

Her sisters sat on the ground behind her, their hands clasped.

Venora, for she knew it was Venora, carried her harp, and with her face lifted toward the sky you could almost hear the song she sang.

"Did you think I would settle for cold illusion when I have a chance for the real thing? Did you think I'd trade my life, and her soul, for a dream? You underestimate mortals, Kane."

As he spun toward her, fury leaping off

him like flames, she prayed she hadn't overestimated herself, or Rowena.

"The first key is mine." As she spoke she reached toward the painting, reached into it. A stunning blast of heat shot up her arm as she closed her fingers around the key she'd painted at the feet of the goddess.

The key that gleamed in a beam of light that cut the shadows like a gilded sword.

She felt its shape, its substance, then with a cry of victory, she drew it free. "This is my choice. And you can go to hell."

The mists roiled as he cursed her. As he lifted his hand to strike, both Flynn and Moe burst through the wall. With a barrage of sharp, staccato barks, Moe leaped.

Kane faded like a shadow in the dark, and was gone.

As Flynn plucked Malory off her feet, sunlight shimmered in the tiny windows, and rain dripped musically from the eaves outside. The room was only an attic, filled with dust and clutter.

The painting she'd created out of love, knowledge, and courage was gone.

"I've got you." Flynn buried his face in her hair as Moe leaped on them. "You're all right. I've got you."

"I know. I know." She began to weep quietly as she looked down at the key still clutched in her fingers. "I painted it." She held it out to Dana and Zoe. "I have the key."

Because she insisted, Flynn drove her directly to Warrior's Peak, with Dana and Zoe following. He kept the heater on high, and had wrapped her in a blanket from his trunk that unfortunately smelled of Moe. And still she shivered.

"You need a hot bath or something. Tea. Soup." He dragged a hand that was still far from steady through his hair. "I don't know. Brandy."

"I'll take all of the above," she promised, "as soon as we get the key where it belongs. I won't be able to relax until it's out of my hand."

She clutched it in a fist held tight to her breast.

"I don't know how it can be in my hand."

"Neither do I. Maybe if you explain it to me, we'll both get it."

"He tried to confuse me, the way he separated us. To make me feel lost and alone and afraid. But he must have some limits. He couldn't keep all three of us, and you, in those illusions. Not all at once. We're connected, and we're stronger than he realized. At least that's what I think."

"I can go with that. To give him credit, he had Rhoda pretty much down pat."

"I made him mad, just mad enough, I guess. I knew the key was in the house." She pulled the blanket a little tighter, but couldn't find warmth. "I'm not telling this in good journalistic style."

"Don't worry about that. I'll edit it later. How did you know?"

"The attic's where I made the choice, when he showed me all the things I wanted so much. I realized that was the dream place once I went upstairs with Zoe and Dana. And the studio, the artist's studio, had been on the top floor. The attic. It had to be where I had that moment of decision—like in the paintings. At first I thought we would have to hunt through whatever was up there, and we'd find something that jibed with the clue. But it was more than that, and less."

She closed her eyes and sighed.

"You're tired. Just rest until we get there. We can talk later."

"No, I'm okay. It was so strange, Flynn. When I got up there and I realized it all. My place—in reality and in my dream. And how he brought the dream back, tried to slide me into it. I let him think he had. I thought about the clue and saw the painting in my head. I knew how to paint it, every stroke. The third painting of the set.

"The key wasn't in the world he created for me," she said as she turned to him. "But it was in what I created, if I had the courage to do it. If I could see the beauty of it, and make it real. He gave me the power to bring the key into the illusion."

To forge it, she thought, with love.

"I bet that burns his ass."

She laughed. "Yeah, that's a nice side benefit. I heard you."

"What?"

"I heard you calling to me. All of you, but especially you. I couldn't answer you. I'm sorry because I know you were afraid for me. But I couldn't let him know I heard."

He reached over to cover her hand with his. "I couldn't get to you. I didn't know what fear was until then, when I couldn't get to you."

"I was afraid at first that it was just another of his tricks. I was afraid that if I turned around and saw you, I'd break. Your poor hands." She lifted his hand, pressed her lips gently to the torn knuckles. "My hero. Heroes," she corrected, looking back at Moe.

She kept her hand in his as they drove through the gates at Warrior's Peak.

Rowena stepped out, her hands folded at the waist of a flame-red sweater. Malory could see the gleam of tears in her eyes as she walked across the portico to meet them.

"You're safe, and well?" She touched Malory's cheek, and the chill Malory had been unable to shake slid into blessed warmth.

"Yes, I'm fine. I have—"

"Not yet. Your hands." She laid her palms under Flynn's, lifted them. "This will scar," she said. "There, beneath the third knuckle of your left hand. A symbol, Flynn. Herald and warrior."

She opened the back door of the car herself so Moe could leap out and greet her with wags and licks. "Ah, there, the fierce and brave one." She hugged him, then leaned back on her heels, listening attentively as he barked and grumbled. "Yes, you had quite the adventure." She rose, resting a hand on Moe's head as she smiled at Dana and Zoe. "All of you did. Please come in."

Moe didn't need to be asked twice. He bounded across the stones and straight through the doorway where Pitte stood. Pitte raised an elegant eyebrow as the dog skidded over the foyer floor, then turned the look onto Rowena.

She only laughed and hooked an arm through Flynn's. "I have a gift for the loyal and courageous Moe, if you'll allow it."

"Sure. Look, we appreciate the hospitality, but Malory's pretty worn out, so—"

"I'm fine. Really."

"We won't keep you long." Pitte gestured them into what Malory thought of as the portrait room. "We're in your debt, more than can be paid. What you've done, whatever tomorrow brings, will never be forgotten." He tipped Malory's face up with one long finger and laid his lips on hers.

Zoe nudged Dana. "I think we're getting gypped in this one-for-all deal."

Pitte glanced over, and his sudden grin was alive with charm. "My woman is a jealous creature."

"No such thing," Rowena objected, then lifted a brightly woven collar from a table. "These symbols speak of valor, and a true heart. The colors are also symbolic. Red for courage, blue for friendship, black for protection."

She crouched to remove Moe's frayed and faded collar and replace it.

He sat through the business of it, Flynn thought, with the stalwart dignity of a soldier being awarded a medal.

"There. How handsome you are." Rowena kissed Moe's nose, then got to her feet. "Will you still bring him to see me, now and then?" she asked Flynn.

"Sure."

"Kane underestimated you. All of you—heart and spirit and spine."

"He's unlikely to do so again," Pitte pointed out, but Rowena shook her head.

"This is a time for joy. You are the first," she told Malory.

"I know. I wanted to get this to you right

away." She started to hold out the key, then stopped. "Wait. Do you mean I'm the *first*? The first to ever find a key?"

Saying nothing, Rowena turned to Pitte. He walked to a carved chest beneath the window, lifted the lid. The blue light that spilled out made Malory's stomach clutch. But this was different from the mist, she realized. This was deeper, brighter.

Then he lifted from the chest a glass box alive with that light, and her throat filled with tears. "The Box of Souls."

"You are the first," Pitte repeated as he set the box on a marble pedestal. "The first mortal to turn the first key."

He turned, stood beside the box. He was the soldier now, Malory thought, the warrior at guard. Rowena stepped to the other side so they flanked the glass and the swirling blue lights inside it.

"It's for you to do," Rowena said quietly. "It was always for you to do."

Malory clutched the key tighter in her fist. Her chest was so full it hurt and still seemed incapable of containing the galloping racing of her heart. She tried to draw a calming breath, but it came out short and sharp. As she stepped closer, those lights seemed to fill her vision, then the room. Then the world.

Her fingers wanted to tremble, but she bore down. She would not do this thing with a shaking hand.

She slid the key into the first of the three locks worked into the glass. She saw the light spread up the metal and onto her fingers, bright as hope. And she turned the key in the lock.

There was a sound—she thought there was a sound. But it was no more than a quiet sigh. Even as it faded, the key dissolved in her fingers.

The first lock vanished, and there were two.

"It's gone. Just gone."

"A symbol again, for us," Rowena said and laid a hand gently on the box. "For them. Two are left."

"Do we . . ." They were weeping inside that glass, Dana thought. She could almost hear them, and it ripped at her heart. "Do we pick now, which one of us goes next?"

"Not today. You should rest your minds and hearts." Rowena turned to Pitte. "There should be champagne in the parlor. Would you see to our guests? I'd like a private word with Malory before we join you."

She lifted the glass box herself, carefully placed it back in the chest. When she was alone with Malory she turned. "Pitte said we owe you a debt we can never pay. That's true."

"I agreed to look for the key, and I was paid," Malory corrected. She looked at the chest, imagined the box within. "It seems wrong now to have taken the money."

"The money is nothing to us, I promise you. Others have taken it and done nothing. Others have tried and failed. And you've done something brave and interesting with the money."

She crossed over, took Malory's hands in hers. "That pleases me. But it isn't dollars and cents I speak of when I speak of debt. If not for me, there would be no Box of Souls, no keys, no locks. You wouldn't have had to face what you faced today."

"You love them." Malory gestured toward the chest.

"As sisters. Young, sweet sisters. Well . . ." She walked over to look at the portrait. "I have hope to see them like this again. I can give you a gift, Malory. It's my right to do so. You refused what Kane offered you."

"It wasn't real."

"It can be." She turned back. "I can make it real. What you felt, what you knew, what you had inside you. I can give you the power you had in his illusion."

Dizzy, Malory groped for the arm of a chair, then slowly lowered herself into it. "You can give me painting."

"I understand the need—and the joys and pain of having that beauty inside you, feeling it leap out." She laughed. "Or fighting to get it out, which is every bit as brilliant. You can have it. My gift to you."

For a moment, the idea of it swarmed through Malory, intoxicating as wine, seductive as love. And she saw Rowena watching her, so calm, so steady, with a soft smile on her lips.

"You'd give me yours," Malory realized. "That's what you mean. You would give me your talent, your skill, your vision."

"It would be yours."

"No, it would never be mine. And I would always know it. I . . . painted them because I could see them. Just as I could see them in that first dream. As if I were there, in the painting. And I painted the key. I forged the key, was able to because I loved enough to give it up. I chose the light instead of the shadow. Isn't that right?"

"Yes."

"Having made that choice, knowing it was the right one, I can't take what's yours. But thank you," she said as she rose. "It's nice to know I can be happy doing what I do. I'm going to make a beautiful shop, and a successful business. And a damn good life," she added.

"I have no doubt. Will you take this, then?" Rowena gestured, smiling when Malory let out a shocked gasp.

"The Singing Goddess." She rushed to the framed canvas that rested on a table. "The painting I did when Kane . . ."

"You painted it." Rowena joined her, laid a hand on her shoulder. "Whatever his trick, this was your vision, and your heart that found the answer. But if having this, if seeing it is painful, I can put it away."

"No, it's not painful. It's a wonderful gift. Rowena, this was an illusion. You brought it into my reality. It's solid. It exists." Bracing herself, she stepped back, kept her eyes level with Rowena's. "Can you—have you done the same with emotions?"

"You question if your feelings for Flynn are real?"

"No. I know they are." She pressed a hand to her heart. "This is no illusion. But his for me—if that's some kind of reward . . . it's not fair to him, and I can't accept it."

"You would give him up."

"No." Her expression went combative. "Hell, no. I'd just deal with it, and him, until he fell in love with me. If I can find some mystical key, I can sure as hell make Michael Flynn Hennessy realize I'm the best thing that's ever happened to him. Which I am," she added. "Which I absolutely am."

"I like you, very much," Rowena said with a grin. "And I'll promise you this. When Flynn walks into this room again, whatever he feels or doesn't feel will be a true reflection of his heart. The rest is up to you. Wait here, I'll send him in."

"Rowena? When will we begin the second round?"

"Soon," Rowena called out as she left the room. "Very soon."

Which one of them would be next? Mallory wondered as she studied the portrait.

And what would the second one risk? What would she win or lose in the search?

She'd lost one love, she thought, lifting her painting. One love, so briefly tasted. And now, with Flynn, she had to risk another. The most vital love of her life.

"I brought you some of this very jazzy champagne," Flynn said, walking in with two brimming flutes. "You're missing the party. Pitte actually laughed. It was a moment."

"I just needed a couple of minutes first." She set the painting down and reached for a glass.

"What's this? One of Rowena's?" He hooked an arm companionably around Malory's shoulder, and she felt his body stiffen when he understood. "It's yours? This is what you did? The painting you did in the attic, with the key. It's here."

He brushed his fingers over the gold key, only painted now, at the feet of the goddess. "It's amazing."

"Even more when you're the one who reached into a painting and pulled out a magic key."

"No. I mean, yeah, that's out there. But I meant the whole thing. It's beautiful, Malory.

Hell, it's stupendous. You gave this up." He spoke softly, then looked over at her. "You're the one who's amazing."

"I'll have this. Rowena clicked her heels together, twitched her nose, whatever she does, and brought it here for me. It means a lot to have it. Flynn . . ."

She had to take a drink, had to put some distance between them. Whatever she'd said to Rowena, she understood now that she was about to do something much more wrenching than giving up a talent with paint and brush.

"This has been a strange month, for all of us."

"And then some," he agreed.

"Most of what's happened, it's beyond the scope of anything we could have imagined, anything we might have believed a few weeks ago. And what's happened, it's changed me. In a good way," she added, turning toward him. "I like to think it's a good way."

"If you're going to tell me you turned the key in that lock, and now you don't love me anymore, that's too damn bad for you. Because you're stuck."

"No, I'm . . . Stuck?" she repeated. "What do you mean *stuck*?"

"With me, my ugly couch and my sloppy dog. You're not wiggling your way out of it, Malory."

"Don't take that tone with me." She set the flute down. "And don't think for one minute you can stand there and tell me I'm stuck with you, because *you're* stuck with *me*."

He set his flute beside hers. "Is that right?"

"That's exactly right. I've just outwitted an evil Celtic god. You're child's play for me."

"You want to fight?"

"Maybe."

They both grabbed for each other. With his mouth on hers, she let out a strangled sigh. And held on for her life. She drew back, but kept her arms linked around his neck.

"I'm exactly right for you, Flynn."

"Then it's really handy that I'm in love with you. You're my key, Mal. The one key to all the locks."

"You know what I want right now? I want a hot bath, some soup, and a nap on an ugly couch."

"Today's your lucky day. I can arrange that for you." Taking her hand, he led her from the room.

Later, Rowena leaned her head against Pitte's shoulder as they watched the cars drive away.

"It's a good day," she told him. "I know it's not over, but today is a good day."

"We have a little time before we begin the next."

"A few days, then the four weeks. Kane will watch them more carefully now."

"So will we."

"Beauty prevailed. Now knowledge and courage will be tested. There's so little, really, that we can do to help. But these mortals are strong and clever."

"Odd creatures," Pitte commented.

"Yes." She smiled up at him. "Odd, and endlessly fascinating."

They stepped back into the house, closed the door. At the end of the drive, the iron gates quietly swung shut. The warriors that flanked them would stand vigil through the next phase of the moon.